THREE LIFETIMES—
LESS ONE . . .

The iron of his sword met the iron haft of my axe. The blow rang in the night; the wolf in me raged, and his sword slipped. I can still see his face, wiped clean of triumph, naked in the moment before stunned surprise caught him. I raised my axe—light and swift as wind it seemed to me then—and brought it down for the killing blow.

Ghost Foot shouted warning. It came too late. The bear—its growl more than a beast's noise, filled with the shrill curses of an enraged witch—caught me hard with a broad and clawed paw, sent me crashing to the ground, weaponless, helpless . . .

SHADOW OF THE SEVENTH MOON

NANCY VARIAN BERBERICK

ACE BOOKS, NEW YORK

This book is an Ace original edition,
and has never been previously published.

SHADOW OF THE SEVENTH MOON

An Ace Book / published by arrangement with
the author

PRINTING HISTORY
Ace edition / March 1991

ISBN: 0-441-76055-4

Ace Books are published by The Berkley Publishing Group,
200 Madison Avenue, New York, New York 10016.
The name "ACE" and the "A" logo
are trademarks belonging to Charter Communications, Inc.

PRINTED IN THE UNITED STATES OF AMERICA

10 9 8 7 6 5 4 3 2 1

To my mother, Rose Lydia Varian;
to my father, Harry Lewis Varian.
Your example taught me
the love of reading.

Acknowledgments

Always first to be thanked in this and all my endeavors is Bruce, my husband and my best friend. Moving in tandem, he the architect discovered the poetry of design on the same day that I the writer discovered the design of poetry. There is nothing better than having someone with whom to share that kind of joy.

To Christine Redding: From all of us, thanks for the midnight hours.

It is again my pleasure to thank my good friend Douglas W. Clark. It was Doug's excellent suggestion to set this fantasy in real time, and his participation did not end with the suggestion. He was my constant companion on a trip through the Dark Ages as well as on the side trips to the mysterious realms of Norse mythology and Anglo-Saxon poetry. Along the way he read the first tentative notes for the story, the later and lengthy "Garroc Files," and the manuscript. His encouragement and faith, as well as his comments and suggestions, have been treasures.

Too, I thank my agent, Maria Carvainis, who did not doubt that Garroc's tale would see the light of publication, and whose support cannot be calculated by the percentage.

To Kathryn Ptacek and Charles L. Grant, these grateful thanks: Kathy, thanks for the many hours of sisterly chats, and for letting me plunder your wonderful library. Charlie, thanks for the best advice one writer can give another: Stop being nervous and get on with telling the story.

To Tom Fennell, Wayfarer Tomm: Thanks for helping me to figure out the electronics, and for sharing ideas about storytelling and storytellers.

Last, I must thank someone whose name, sadly, is known to none who lives today, who is only known to us by the name of his masterful work. My humble thanks to the *Beowulf* poet. Monk or scholar, court poet or simple soldier at the battle's edge, your *wundorcraeft* has taught me to love the old language and to hear the rhythms in my own heart.

Author's Note

Shadow of the Seventh Moon is a fantasy that takes place in Britain during the Dark Ages, a time when the Saxons warred with Welshmen and among themselves, and Christian contended with non-Christian. In this fantasy, as in the real world, the gods or god, the magic or miracles, that a person believes in are real, and these wonders are everywhere to be seen. Garroc tells his tale to Ellisif in the year A.D. 690; a story from his youth which takes place during the years A.D. 630–31. It is a tale woven of history and myth and religion.

Of the players in Garroc's tale, Penda King of Mercia, his Welsh ally Cadwalla, and Eadwine King of Northumbria will be found in the histories of Bede, Geoffrey of Monmouth, and in *The Anglo-Saxon Chronicle.* There they fight very much the same battles they fight here. However, as the various histories from which I drew my material are colorfully shaded according to the individual historian's religious, ethical, and political beliefs, I have not scrupled to color Garroc's view of this time, with his own personal beliefs, for he is as entitled to them as Bede is to his.

Christian or worshiper of Wotan, the Northmen who lived in 7th century Britain spoke the language we call Old English. It was not old in those days; it was young, and as vibrant and adventurous as the modern version we speak today, welcoming new words wherever a speaker found them. Many of the Old English words used here, such as *wulf, heall, helle, cynn, freond, faeder, is,* and *niht* have survived the ages and live in our modern language under slightly different spellings (wolf, hall, hell, kin, friend, father, ice, and night). Others, though spelled somewhat more confusingly, are also still with us. *Cyning* (used here to mean lord, in order to differentiate between an over-king such as Penda or Eadwine, and lesser kings such as Erich) means simply 'king.' If one pronounces the C in *Ceastir* as CH, one will hear the name of that town as it exists today: Chester. Imaginary *Rafenscylf,* with the SC pronounced SH is 'Raven Shelf.' *Mearc*—again the C is CH—becomes 'March,' a borderland; and *sceadu* is 'shadow.'

One Old English word that does not appear in Garroc's tale is *scop,* which means 'bard' or 'minstrel.' Garroc, only one generation (though a long one) removed from the European continent, uses the word his father knew: skald. It is a word the Englishman's northern cousins still use today, as is *dvergr* (dwarf).

As for the gods and witches, the giants and dwarfs, these are drawn from what little is known about the religious beliefs of the non-Christian Anglo-Saxons and the way they viewed the world and the beings who inhabit it. Most historians agree that the non-Christian Anglo-Saxon beliefs were probably not much different from those of their European kin, the people who lived in the places we now know as Germany and the Scandinavian nations. I have relied upon those Northern myths, those echoes of an old religion, to guide me both in the retelling of familiar myths—often faithful to the common interpretations of the myths, once or twice faithful to nothing but my story's needs—and in the creation of new tales such as the Winter War between the Aesir and the giants, and the Dwarf-king's gamble for Idun's golden apples.

SHADOW OF THE SEVENTH MOON

SIF

ELLISIF filled herself with the scent of newly risen grass, with the hush and lap of the Rill whispering past fog-cloaked banks. From behind, from within the cottage, came an infant's whimper, a cry like a gull's distant mewing. Hand on the door latch, Ellisif paused, but she didn't turn back. She knew that her little daughter would settle before these sleepy protests waked her husband or disturbed her sons. When all was silent again, she slipped across the dooryard, past the garden and into the unmoving night.

Dark and squat, apple trees huddled in the garth, shrouded in the fog at the water's edge. At night, or so it was said by old women and children, the trees are a gathering place for evil things, and devils lurk in the shadows. But Ellisif didn't fear the shadows pooled beneath the trees' arms. The thing she feared most was nightwind. And so, as she wrapped herself in her thick woolen cloak, made herself warm against the chill, she was glad that the wind didn't roam.

Yet, were the sky wild with stormwind, Ellisif would not have kept within the cottage tonight, for today she'd watched geese winging north, listened to their wild joyful songs as she fed the chickens and milked the goats. And at noon, when she'd nursed her daughter and the thin warmth of the spring sun blessed them both, she began to believe that tonight would be the one she'd waited for all winter.

So it was, and only a little time ago, she'd waked just as the slender new moon reached his highest point in the dark sky, and knew that Garroc was somewhere near.

1

Her Eldfather had never come home un-met, and so Ellisif
would have braved even the ghostly nightwind to go greet him.

All her life she'd called Garroc Eldfather; her sons named him
that now. He wasn't her grandfather. She was Ellisif, the daughter
of Hinthan and Anna, Man-kindred. Garroc was *dvergr*, a Dwarf,
and no kin to her at all. Unless spirit-kin.

Ellisif followed the path through the apple garth to the water's
edge. There was no fording place now, would not be one until the
river finished reshaping the low banks. Any who wanted to cross
the Rill in this season would do it soaked to the knees. But Ellisif
had no mind to cross the river; at night it was best to stay on this
side of the Rill. She leaned against an apple tree's gnarled bole,
watched fog drift like water-dreams over the river, and waited for
Garroc.

If she had crossed, taken the path on the other side, she'd find,
like dark sketches in the earth, the weed-choked foundations of
the old timber-built *cynings-heall*. Fire had gutted the hall in the
same year Ellisif had been born, and afterwards Erich War Hawk
had removed the seat of his power to another place and built his
new hall of stone. Now the War Hawk's son ruled there, proud
in his father's stone-built hall.

And, if she'd crossed the river, stopped just a small distance before the foundations of the old hall, she'd find a barrow, tall and
wide. She'd find the place where her own father was buried. Garroc had made the barrow from the hearth-stones of the old
cynings-heall, and when he'd made the earth-hall for the man he
called his old friend and young son, Garroc said that there was
no other fitting place. Hinthan's heart beat to the rhythm of the
Rill's song all his life. And he'd been the sworn man of lords and
kings—what better barrow stones than those which had once
guarded a *cyning's* fire?

Though the night was quiet, Ellisif clutched her cloak tighter.
In all the years since Hinthan's death she'd always taken great care
not to go near his barrow after darkfall, for sometimes, late at
night, when the wind blew from across the river, Ellisif heard her
father's voice. She'd loved that voice in life, but Hinthan was five
years dead. She didn't love the sound of a ghost's voice.

A shadow moved against the fog.

Heart racing, Ellisif caught her breath, then let it go on a soft
sigh. This was no ghost drifting. She knew whose shadow this was,
and all at once the cold went out of the night. Ellisif turned away
from the river.

"Ah, Sif," Garroc said, "I smell the welcome-fire."

"Just made, Eldfather, and ready for you. I knew you were coming tonight. I knew it all day."

Garroc's smile was one Ellisif had known all her life, a smile like a secret about to be told. Meant to be hidden in his beard, somehow that smile was never well hidden at all. His eyes always betrayed it. As they did now.

This never changes, Ellisif thought.

Though he was very old, nothing ever seemed to change about Garroc. His hair and beard, as always, recalled the color of autumn wheat. His face, a Northman's high-planed face, never showed the passage of years. He stood a head shorter than she, broad-shouldered with strong, strong arms.

He has a warrior's arms, Hinthan used to say.

And he'd said rightly, for Garroc had been a soldier for seven years before Hinthan was born, in the time when people of the Isle knew their country as Britain and the White Christ was only a rumor from the south. He was a soldier still.

But Ellisif's father had known Garroc almost all the years of his life and so he knew the other thing about him: The Dwarf's was a storyteller's heart; a skald's heart. That was not something Ellisif needed to be told. She and the Dwarf were spirit-kin.

And now, as the thinning fog drifted between them, as the night-wind stirred, the ghost-wind roused, Ellisif remembered something else her father had said, something Garroc had told him of a thing that is true only for *dvergr*: Who is close to the end of his years, who is near to dying, sees the stars as suns.

Ellisif wondered how bright the stars seemed to Garroc tonight. And because the wondering frightened her, she ran to him as she used to when she was a little girl.

Laughing, but only gently, he kissed her, swept her fast into his arms. Then it was as though magic had been done, for Ellisif's fears fell away and Garroc was again ageless, she again a girl giving the greeting she'd offered every spring.

"Welcome home, Eldfather. Oh, welcome home!"

Ellisif her mother named her, and so her parents called her. She knew that her mother had named her for one of the White Christ's legion of saints, but Garroc called her Sif for the Spring Goddess. And he told her that Sif's husband was Thunor, God of Storm and Harvest. He told her that Thunor's mighty war-hammer fired the lightning and was the voice of the thunder, and that Thunor helped to harvest the brave souls of the war-killed.

Garroc had told Ellisif all the fabulous and wicked tales of his ancient gods. He'd told her stories of his own making. These tales had the names of the old Saxon kings for gold; for the heart-stopping flash of silver, the deeds of mad Welshmen drunk with glory, wild Saxons dying for their *cynings* and for Wotan, the doomed god. These were the treasures in the small coffer of Ellisif's childhood.

Yet Ellisif knew that there was one tale Garroc never told, and in the years since Hinthan's death she felt the untold story breathing soft in the shadows, whispering behind the god-myths and the songs of kings. Still, though she wondered often what this tale could be, she never asked for it. A gift must be freely given.

Ellisif settled onto the rush-strewn floor at Garroc's feet. None had heard them come into the cottage. Swift-growing sons, her husband who was heart-tied to the land, even her little daughter, had not heard her return. In the morning the cottage would be filled with the boys' rowdy joy, her husband's welcome. For now, Ellisif was grateful that they slept. She knew that the night of a homecoming was for peace and the welcome-fire's warmth, for a tale maybe, or for silence.

Tonight Garroc seemed to have chosen silence, and it was a silence Ellisif knew, one filled with peace, as though he listened to both the sounds of the place around him and to some inner voice that spoke for him alone.

Outside the cottage the wind stirred. Ellisif thought of her father's deep-chested sigh, and despite the fire's warmth, she shivered. For comfort, she watched as Garroc, his large hands silvered with war's scars, traced the shapes of the hearth-stones.

Many years ago, in a time before she had been born, he and Hinthan had built the hearth. Ellisif knew the story of that building. And she knew, because Garroc had told her, that each piece of the earth has its own name and guards that name carefully. She knew that if a stone-built thing stands strong against the years, it's because the crafter learned the names and so bound the stones with something more than mortar. Even for rock and stone, names are true power-words. Any can use them who knows them.

In these times few knew them. Men built with timber and didn't understand stone, the heart of the world, as *dvergr* had.

And so, as the Man and the Dwarf took the stones from the fields and the Rill's bed for the hearth-making, Garroc had listened to the hard songs of farewell the earth keened, and told the names he heard to Hinthan. True it was that the hearth yet stood whole and strong, though the cottage had twice burned and been rebuilt around it.

Cold fingers of wind reached beneath the door to touch Ellisif like loneliness. She moved closer to the fire, closer to Garroc.

"It's the wind, my Sif, only the wind."

"It feels like ghosts," she whispered.

Garroc listened, head cocked. "So it does. Are you afraid?"

Ellisif said nothing. How to say—even to Garroc who knew all her secrets—that she heard a dead man's voice in the wind?

Garroc asked no other question, only stroked her hair gently, offering the same kind of comfort he'd given when she was a child and frightened by the Storm-god's roaring.

Flames like blue-edged fingers curled round the logs in the hearth. Bright bits of light, sparks flew up the chimney. Garroc watched the play of shadows and firelight across the rough faces of the hearth-stones. He seemed to have forgotten about ghosts, and after a time he said:

"I remember the names of these hearth-stones, ancient names. And I remember the names of the stones which make your father's barrow. Ay, barrow-stones are Earth Fast, High-Standing, Tree's Bane. If I could touch them now, they would remind me of the great debt I have owed your father these years since his death."

He went to crouch before the fire. With the iron poker he spread the glowing coals beneath red-hearted logs, loosed the heat. When he spoke again, it was as though he spoke to the flames.

"Sif, your *Cristen* priests have no good to say of my kindred. They say we have no souls. At best they name us children of legend, at worst devils."

"Eldfather, the priests are wrong."

"Yes, they're wrong. But I think it's hard for them to tolerate a kindred their god has left to its own path. And so they ignore what they should know, and there aren't too many of us left to teach them the right of it: Who feels joy has a heart; pain, grief, triumph, wondering—who feels those has a soul. And yet, how can I blame the new god's priests for believing what we *dvergr* tried to believe about ourselves? So many of us tried to deny heart and soul. We were afraid to feel our pain and so we didn't know how to feel our joy."

Ellisif went to sit beside him, but she kept silent. Something stirred behind his words, and she thought she heard again whispered hints of the untold tale.

"Sif, many of us chose the cold way, the winter way. And for a long time that was my choice, too. But came a time when I learned to feel the pain. And the wonder, the joy. Your father would not let me do otherwise. Hinthan is the difference between what I was and what I am."

Flames leaped high in the hearth and Garroc smiled as suddenly. He brushed Ellisif's tumbled dark hair away from her face, then closed his hands gently around hers, held them as though they were fragile things.

"You don't understand, do you, my Sif? Ah, but you're young yet. I know how that is. I was young for a long, long time."

In the hearth the fire leaped high, spun shadows across the walls and ceiling. As though called by the fire's glow, a light shone in Garroc's eyes, one that had burned steadily, brightly, for many years. He made a slow fist, blunt war-scarred fingers curling almost gently into his calloused palm.

"Hand and arm, mine are strong. But a skald's memory is stronger than these. And now I am a skald who owes a large debt."

"What debt, Eldfather? I don't understand."

"Sif, I owe your father his song, and I've been too long waiting to pay that debt. For a long time I believed that Hinthan's story was separate from my own, and try as I did, I could not make this separate tale. Now, in these years since his death I've learned otherwise. This tale of ours didn't start on the day I first saw him, my Sif, and it does not end because he is dead."

The fire sighed like ghosts stirring. Outside the wind spoke with a voice too much like dead Hinthan's. Ellisif wrapped her arms tight around herself, tried not to shiver.

"I am old, Sif, and maybe I will live for a long time yet. It's how things are with *dvergr*. If war doesn't kill me, if sickness or ill-luck doesn't take me, I will live to see your sons—his grandsons, ay?—become old men.

"And so for as long as my life may be, I am part of Hinthan's tale; that long will your father be part of mine. I understood this too late to start the telling of Hinthan's song when I should have, while I was making the barrow. A poor and silent making that was. But now—if you will hear it—I've come to pay the debt, to tell you a small part of the story that is owed."

Clear now, more certainly than she'd ever heard them before, the words of the untold tale whispered in the fire's hissing, breathed in the shadows. Ellisif didn't have to wonder whether she wanted to hear it. Gently, she said:

"Tell me, Eldfather."

But Garroc didn't settle and make ready to give his tale. Instead, he looked at her closely, in the way that he had, and Ellisif knew that he understood what frightening thing she heard in the nightwind.

"I warn you, my Sif: This tale has to do with ghosts."

She shivered, but she raised her eyes to his, and her trembling eased. She didn't have to think what to say. As she had when she was a child, she asked:

"Is the tale about kings?"

Garroc smiled and picked up the pattern of a story's beginning, a pattern familiar to both of them because they'd made it together. "Ay, and more."

"Are there gods in it?"

"Yes, and wonders."

"And will I believe in them?"

Garroc's voice dropped low, as it always did when he started to tell a tale. As though, Ellisif thought, he is coaxing some shy thing to his hand.

"That, my Sif, you'll have to tell me."

She settled, warm by the fire, warm with his voice sounding like far thunder around the rim of the valley. His words moved in her heart like dreams, like the magic light of the gloaming thrown on the men and events of a time not far distant, but still a time that seemed dark because few understood it now.

In her heart Ellisif saw war-grounds; she heard the rage of a battle, felt sunlight leaping along a sword's bright blade. In her soul she tasted the smoky sorrow of a world caught in change. And though a shiver of fear touched her, as a ghost might, she went with Garroc into the dark and the shadows, trusting that he would bring her safe again to the light.

SCIN-MONA
(Ghost Moon)

I

I stood on the hill's crest with the Hunter, with Halfdan the dying *cyning*. Faint and far, I heard the cries of wild geese heralding their return to the Isle from warmer winter quarters. A dark phantom arrow, the geese cut across the early risen moon. Flushed with sunset's light, nearly full, that moon. In two nights it would be free of its shadow.

Mann-cynn has a name for this spring moon, my Sif, and that name is Seed. *Dvergr* name it Ghost.

Halfdan shifted his weight, leaned heavily on his grounded spear, seeking balance and support. He could have reached for me, for my strong arm. It had always been his to use. But he would not, and I didn't offer what would have hurt his pride to accept.

The scent of quickening meadows danced behind us; the reek of battle's aftermath crawled up from the valley before us. Vengeance-seeker, Halfdan had taken bloody payment this day for the farmers killed in Welsh Vorgund's latest raid. He'd broken the back of the Welshman's army, given stead-holders safety, given Penda, our King, a peaceful western border for a time. And Halfdan, *mearc-weard*, border-ward, had taken mortal wounds in the day's fighting.

A raven screamed. Halfdan lifted his head, his pale eyes bright as though he heard a thing in the raven's voice that I didn't.

"He's close, Garroc, I hear him."

I shivered, and battle-sweat dried cold on me. I didn't have to ask who'd come close. When a soldier hears a raven on war-grounds, he thinks of Wotan. I looked out over the valley, knew that the Raven-god had good reason to come close today.

Narrow and deep, the valley's mouth opened to the west. It was a nameless place, and none of the old Roman *straets* ran through or even came close. Those southern Men might have known about the valley, but they had not built here, seemed to have had no interest naming this place. No one did, not even Vorgund the Welshman who had been lured here to fight.

At Halfdan's order, my scouts and I had been the wolf-bait. We'd ridden hard, wailing in high, eerie laughter, shouting with the voices of demons as our horses tore wind-sped into the mouth of the vale. We led the Welshmen howling for our blood into the Hunter's reach, split and cut behind them, blocking escape.

Halfdan and his army, seventy strong, *dvergr* and *mann-cynn*, fell upon them. Long and hard we fought, and the fragile spring warmth had become like a forgeman's fire, when Vorgund—his right arm useless from a sword cut, his foaming horse staggering under him—found himself with only a quarter of his soldiers and no choice but to scream the call to retreat. We *Mearc-Seaxe*, we Border-Saxons, had laughed to see them run.

The raven, wings black and glinting blue, plucked at the throat of a red-bearded Dwarf from Vorgund's army. Halfdan lifted his eyes to the slanting sunset light and drew a breath, wind rattling in dead bracken. He asked the thing he'd called me here to know.

"How many are dead, Garroc?"

"Eleven Men," I said. "And five *dvergr*."

I knew the names of them all.

My Sif, you have always known me for a skald, a teller of tales, a history-keeper. In the times I am telling you of, in those days when the Norns were only starting to weave together two fates, your father's and mine, I'd abandoned the art and the craft to which I'd been trained. I had no courage for keeping the history of a race who would have no future. And so I closed my heart to the *skald leygr*, the light which graces the dreams of skalds.

Like my father before me, like the Dwarfs in Halfdan's army and Welsh Vorgund's, I had chosen the soldier's path. Hard that life, but easier than making histories for a dying race.

Dying, yes; of pride and magic and the Raven-god's curse.

For in a far time, when Men were only beginning to think that your young White Christ might well be a god, proud Dwarf-kings and reckless witches tried to take for themselves the Aesir-gods' most precious treasure. They wanted Idun's golden apples for their own, wanted the long life those precious apples would give. Others had tried to get this treasure and failed. Still, the Dwarf-kings and witches thought they could do what others could not, and so they gambled on pride and *wundorcraeft.*

Ah, but it's not wise to gamble with gods. Those witches and kings learned that. They didn't capture the goddess's golden apples, and Wotan, jealous All-Father, wove their punishment from their desires. He cursed them to have what they wanted: For five generations *dvergr* would have the long life of the gods. After the fifth generation would come those who would be known as *Laestan*, the Last. After *Laestan*, none.

I am *Laestan.* I watched my father die and I know that I will get no son to follow me. None to love, none to hear my skald's songs, none to sing them when I am dead.

Yet I didn't leave all the skills of skald-craft behind me, for Halfdan didn't use me only as a warrior, though he was happy enough to have my good war-axe when he needed it. The *cyning* knew that a skald must see all sides of a thing, and seeing, tell it truly. What skills I learned for one craft, Halfdan had me turn to another. And so, brave soldier, cowardly skald, I captained his scouts and I gathered the names of his dead. This day I'd gathered eleven names. But though I always had before, I didn't give Halfdan the names of the dead now. And though he always had before, he didn't ask for them.

"Eleven dead." The Hunter sighed. "And five of them Dwarfs. I mourn with you, Garroc."

The sun dropped behind the tall peaks of the mountains, Vorgund's forested haunts. Witches lived in those mountains; I have seen them. Some of those witches worked their dark and terrible magic for the Welshmen, but none had today; today we'd used a lot of our luck.

"Halfdan *cyning,* they'll have set up a camp in the meadow. Erich will be looking for you."

Halfdan smiled to hear his son's name. He loved the young war hawk almost as much as he loved his holdings.

"Ay, Erich," he whispered. "There are things . . . things I have to tell him."

He got a better grip on his spear's shaft, walked straight-backed and tall from the hill. I stayed close, ready to help should he ask, knowing that, for the sake of his fierce pride, he would not. He had said it of others and I know he believed it then: Pain is nothing to one who knows he will soon take his mead in the hall of Wotan All-Father.

And tonight Halfdan would do that. Tonight the Raven-god

would have our best and leave us to find another *cyning* if we could.

I have a true telling from Grimwulf Aesc's son, Fierce Wolf, who was my father. One hundred years before the time of Halfdan, before the time of Penda the *god-cynn* King, Grimwulf fought beside brave men and a bright lord, against the Pendragon's son Arthur. Five times they met the Bear King's grim-handed war band. Most often victories went to Arthur, and for a time the Pendragon's son held the Isle and the hearts of his people. But only for a time. In the end, civil war and a treacherous kinsman killed him, and Welsh unity with him. Grimwulf told it that people thought glory-mad Arthur's death would settle all claims, that the Isle would know peace under Saxon rule.

My father, who lived his life to find his soul's peace in war, should have known that it doesn't ever go that way. Too many Welshmen had died on Saxon swords, and they didn't need a king to tell them that the war-killed cannot go unavenged. So they took their grief up to the dark mountains, honed it to gleaming blade-hate and passed the feud on to their sons with their swords and clan names.

Welshmen have true soldier's iron in their souls. In those days, as now, the Men among them were *Cristens*. And in those days, as now, their worship of this peace-loving young god didn't do anything to dent the soul's iron. Each spring the *Wealas* brought war down to our golden farmlands, crying to their White Christ and their dead king Arthur for victory. And though they never worshiped the White Christ, held close to their own British gods, Dwarfs of the Welsh kin remembered the Bear King and fought alongside their countrymen.

In that time, more than a hundred years after the Bear King's death, Wotan was happy, and his Storm-god son, Thunor, was busy gathering the shining souls of dead warriors for the All-Father's own war, for the Terrible Winter and Ragnarok to come.

It seldom takes much more than a war to make the Raven-god happy.

I walked the watch on the hill under the light of the Ghost moon, listening to the un-living singing in the valley, watching the silent camp in the meadow on the hill's other side. At the meadow's far edge a beck wandered and night mist rose above, a dragon born of air and water. Above the mist-dragon hung a grey draping of smoke. This was not the pall of *mann-cynn's* funeral pyres; it was the smoke of the army's campfires. The light of the pyres would not flare until well after sunrise.

For now, the dead, our own companions and our enemies, still lay in the valley. At night neither Dwarfs nor Men liked to go out to battle-grounds where ghosts roamed singing and Valkyries worked. After dawn, parties of soldiers would claim the bodies of our slain. Then trees would be cut for the pyre, and the ring and clatter of stone-gathering would echo against the hillside. Not for Dwarfs the pyre's flames; for *dvergr* the tall barrow, the cool earth-hall.

Moonlight and shadows spun across the hillside. Ghost-voices mingled with the wind's song—the thin voices of eleven dead Men, five dead Dwarfs. Raven-shadows, they would all be gone long before dawn's first glimmer. Ay, the ghosts would be gone—their voices, though, would stay to echo in my heart. As would their names, caught by me and waiting for a *cyning* to ask for them.

Not everyone can hear the dead sing, Sif, and I had not always heard them. It was not until I left skald-craft and went to be a soldier that I began to hear the un-living. Frightening those voices; they spoke words almost-heard, said things almost-understood. I didn't love those half-heard voices, for it seemed to me that only the mad could hear them. And in those days I knew madmen, *baresarks*, Dwarfs and Men whose souls had been caught by the *sceadu-wulf*.

I feared that shadow-wolf more than death, and so I dreaded the ghost-voices only a little less.

Wind moaned low, plucked at my hair and beard with cold fingers. Silver-edged clouds sailed before the moon. Along the side of the hill a stone rattled, went spinning downslope. Axe ready, I searched the night, then laid the weapon by when I saw a friend walking up the hill from the camp. It was not quiet-stepping Dyfed who had displaced the stone, not he who had made it rattle. We called him Ghost Foot for good reason. The noisy one was his dog.

Werrehund, Dyfed called him, war-hound; and the beast was well-named. He was loyal and fierce, for his were shepherd kin and hunting kin; a good combining in a soldier's dog. Now he was head-up, his tail a red banner waved in greeting. When I whistled low he arrowed for me, and behind came Dyfed, cloaked against the cold, my own mantle slung over his shoulder.

Werrehund rumbled deep in his chest, pushed his head up under my hand, a friend's greeting. I dropped to my heels, warmed my hands in the dog's rough red coat.

Dyfed tossed me the mantle. "I've been thinking you'd want this, Garroc."

"What I want is a fire."

He twisted a wry smile, his one eye gleaming. He had no left eye, only a webbing of scars to whisper of battle-wounds, to hint at how it had been lost. But only to hint. Long as I'd known him, I'd never heard the tale of that loss. I didn't know of anyone who had.

"No," he said, loosing a fat wineskin from his belt. "Fires have to be tended. What you want is this."

Mantle to blunt the wind's bite, thick sweet wine to fire the inside of me, and with luck, to muffle the voices of the un-living—ay, Dyfed was a good friend.

He was a strange-looking fellow, my friend. Beardless when most men were bearded, lean and tall, long-faced, one-eyed. And white-haired. His was not an old man's hair, white though it was. He claimed it had been colorless since the day he'd been born. At most that was twenty-five years ago. Now he plowed his fingers through that white hair, squinted up at the moon with his one eye.

"The Hunter is dying, Garroc. He won't live the night."

I knew it because I'd stood with the *cyning* on the hill's crest, stood with him while he made ready for his journey to Wotan's hall. Dyfed knew it because, while he was a soldier and one of my scouts, he was also a healer and sometimes he could make the sick well, mend the injured. He'd been with the *cyning* before he'd come up to keep watch with me.

"And Erich?"

Dyfed shrugged. "He waits. He'll let no man call him *cyning* before his father's dead."

It was then, Sif, as it is now: no over-king such as Penda could rule long without the loyalty of his *cynings*, battle-brave war leaders. For that loyalty, a wise King gave gold and praise and large tracts of land. And few *cynings* ever ruled their own wide holdings without the support of *thegns*, men of good family who in their turn had lands of their *cynings*, worked the farmlands in peace and provided strong armies at need.

And so, this both Dyfed and I knew: Were Halfdan dead this moment and riding the flames, Erich would not yet be *cyning*. That title he would have to earn. He was young, had not seen a score of years. He'd lead Halfdan's army only if he held the loyalty of Halfdan's *thegns* and warriors. Many of us, it is true, had seen the raising of Erich. Some of the *thegns* had taught Halfdan's son his war craft, had fought for life and home at the War Hawk's side.

Still, it is a bad thing when a *cyning* dies. He is the one his people trust, and while we are learning to trust another, even a bold son, we are limping, easy prey. If some in the Hunter's army wanted to call for a choice, it was their right. More, it was their duty.

Our borderlands, our Marches, have always tempted Vorgund's *Wealas* in the west. In the south the River Saefern lay between the Marches and Osric's valley holdings. That border would not hold Osric peaceful once he learned of Halfdan's death. In the east Cynewulf would quickly ally himself with Osric; he'd done it before. Too many hungry *cynings* there were in those days. None but a strong man could rule Halfdan's holdings, keep them in trust for Penda, our King. If Erich War Hawk was not that man, his warriors needed to know it.

The wind rose, and with it the singing of the dead. Dyfed looked at me sideways. I gave him the wineskin, watched him drink deeply. I don't think he ever heard the ghosts, but I knew that he didn't like the sound of nightwind moaning over a war-ground.

Nor did I like it, but the singing drew me again to look out over the valley. Werrehund went with me, his head close under my hand. They were only a few there now, waiting for Valkyries to find them.

I turned away from the vale. The rain I'd been scenting all night spat fitfully now, the wind breathed cold. The mist-dragon fell back to earth. Slowly, drifting singly and in pairs, the soldiers gathered, black shadows before Halfdan's tent. A shout rose high on the wind, sharp as a dagger's edge.

Halfdan was dead.

I'd made no song in all the time since I fled the *skald leygr* for the flames of battle, but one thing I never forgot of skald-lore, a thing Halfdan knew: We must always remember those who have gone before us.

If I'd never heard the *cyning* say it, never had even the least piece of skald-lore, I would have remembered Halfdan. Then I had seen fifty and nine years. My *dvergr* kin would have called me a youth. But for sixteen years I had been the Hunter's man, and sixteen years can seem like a lifetime. No one can forget the *cyning* he'd loved and served for a lifetime.

Dyfed laid a hand on my shoulder, the warmest thing in that cold night. "I have the watch, my friend."

Rain, spitting only a moment ago, swept like a black and silver curtain between the crest and the meadow below. In the valley all the dead were silent now but one. In my heart all the voices echoed but Halfdan's, the *cyning* who waited for a Valkyrie to find him.

II

TIMES there are when the foot-and-mouth disease strikes a farm-stead. One night a farmer goes to his bed listening to the lowing of his cattle. In the morning he is digging burning-trenches, and never fast enough for the spade's ring to drown the sound of cattle dying. By moon's rise he slaughters what stock still lives, and burns and buries all parts of the carcasses but the heads. By dawn-light he and his kin have plunged posts deep into the earth at the boundaries of his stead. Upon each of these posts they impale a horned and bleakly staring head. They have erected the skull-warnings and no man will go to retrieve any beast of his that wanders past the dread borders of a diseased stead.

As I entered the smoky, silent camp I saw great sorrow in the eyes of many of dead Halfdan's warriors. They must have seen the same in me. But in the cold eyes of the *baresarks* I saw the look of skull warnings.

None embrace pain as berserkers do, they are not as other men. They have been caught by the shadow-wolf, and it is true that god-Loki's son, hungry Wolf-Fenris, rules their hearts. In battle they fight wild and alone. They carry no shield, no weapon but mad-ness, and in the aftermath they pack like wolves, nursing their wounds and sleeping in shadows.

Six of the berserkers I saw that night were Dwarfs, three were Men. Among us these nine were known as the Hunter's pack, and I know it for true that those mad warriors loved Halfdan, though it is not often they love anyone. Now they stood apart from the others, stark-eyed and waiting, taking count of their sorrow as a miser does his gold, a warrior his weapons.

One of the *baresarks*, the Dwarf Blodrafen, watched me as I passed, his grey eyes tracking like an old and canny wolf's. One hundred winters and fifty the Blood Raven had counted; his dark hair was silvered with those years, his back just starting to bend with their weight. Once there were kings among *dvergr*, pale-eyed, night-haired; like Blodrafen. But *dvergr* have no kings now, only the lost sons of kings and many of them are not sane.

I felt the *baresark's* eyes follow me along the length of the silent camp as I looked for my scouts.

First of all of them, I saw bright-haired Aelfgar, tall *mann-cynn*, standing among the Dwarfs and Men gathered in the rain before the *cyning's* tent. He'd grown a man's beard, had a war-scarred face and thick broad shoulders, but he was child-minded, and his eyes, gentle and blue, were an innocent's. Twenty-seven winters Aelfgar had seen, and his smile, his heart, his mind, were a youngling's. When I saw him killing, watched him in the aftermath cleaning blood from his hands and arms with a child's fastidiousness, my heart sickened. I liked better to see him tracking through the woods, boy-wild.

He stood now, silent and wondering in the muttering crowd, looking like a boy lost. When he saw me, Aelfgar wiped rain, or tears, from his face, closed his eyes and nodded as though he'd been waiting for me. I found the rest of my scouts with him: Gadd, his dark-haired, black-eyed brother; Eadric, and the Dwarf Swithgar.

"Tell me," I said.

Eadric answered, his eyes narrowed in the way that I knew. He had news to report that he didn't like. "*Thegn* Dunnere's already made challenge."

A gust of wind sent the rain slanting against the tent with the sound of far-off drumming. I pulled my mantle tighter around me. Today I'd seen the *thegn* fighting while tears made scars in the blood and dirt on his face. His son Ceola's was one of the names I'd gathered today.

Cold in me, a wondering stirred: What must that be like, the losing of a son?

"Who supports Dunnere, Eadric?"

Eadric snorted. "All will if he wins. He's a good man, Garroc, though most would rather have the Hunter's son for *cyning*."

"What does Erich say?"

"Only what he's had to: that he'll accept the challenge." Eadric's eyes looked like slits now in his wind-roughed face. His big hands moved absently along the hilt of his short-sword. "It will go to blood."

"Who asked for that?"

Aelfgar answered. "Erich did, Garroc. He said . . ." Aelfgar closed his eyes, making certain to repeat the words exactly as he'd heard them. It is the first thing I teach a scout: Tell me true what is seen, what is heard. "He said, 'Best done now and the choice made with blood.' And he meant he didn't want to fight this fight again."

Some said that because Aelfgar's was a child's mind, he could not think. It was not so. He could think as well as anyone. The difference was that, like a child, it came easier to him to listen to his heart than his mind.

Gadd shifted restlessly, one foot to another, jerked his thumb at the tent. "Erich wants you, Garroc."

I thought of the Blood Raven's stare; cold wind driving a storm. "Dyfed's on the hill. Go up and keep watch with him."

Gadd loped off into the rain. When his brother made to follow, I caught him back. "Stay here, boy. He'll be back."

Aelfgar made no complaint. He trusted me as he trusted Gadd. I glanced again at Blodrafen, saw his back to me now, and entered the tent.

Erich War Hawk stood over Halfdan's body where it lay on a cold bed of folded blankets and mantles. The ruddy light of a camp brazier filled the tent. Smoke hung heavy on the air, overlaying the thick scents of wet wool, of blood and old sweat. Suddenly the wind cut under the tent walls and the bright flames leaped high, leaving all but Erich's face in shadow. It seemed to me, as I watched, that Erich became his father's ghost.

I almost spoke, almost called the son by the father's name. Halfdan he was, eyes glittering bright and wild.

And then he turned and was again Erich. Halfdan was dead.

"Garroc. Challenge has been made."

"I know it, *cyning*."

Erich's shoulders stiffened at the title. Did he hate the reminder of his father's death? Or was he bracing to take up the burden the address represented? I did not know. In the dim light I saw only hard blue eyes in a mask of shadows. I went to stand near the body at Erich's feet.

Halfdan had hair as red as a sunset. It lay combed on his shoulders, and his beard and face had been cleaned of battle grime and blood. His right hand closed stiffly around the gold-woven hilt of his dagger, and the ashwood spear I'd last seen used as a staff lay at his feet. Someone had made a start at grooming him for the pyre.

Cold, and caught by a sudden loneliness, I saw that the flesh had begun to sink around Halfdan's cheeks, become pinched around his mouth.

Erich's voice, battle-rough, rasped when he spoke. "You served my father for a long time, Garroc. For his sake, there is a thing I'd ask." He stepped into the light. "If I can't, I want you to see that my father has a *cyning's* sending."

"You know I'll do it."

He turned away, and though I knew myself dismissed, I stayed to ask my own questions.

"Erich, when do you meet Dunnere?"

"Now. Before the *baresarks* flare."

The tent walls shivered under an assault of wind-driven rain and I thought again of the Blood Raven, tight-strung and waiting, maybe wondering how Halfdan's death would affect him. The Hunter had ruled the berserkers like a wolf-king rules his pack. He knew them for dangerous and tolerated that danger because they served him well and because he'd thought them darkly beautiful in their madness and strength. And it is true that they, his pack, had loved him, but Erich did not consider berserkers beautiful, and I did not know if he would tolerate them, though I thought it likely that he would. They were more weapons than men.

Erich's eyes warmed suddenly, and I knew that he hadn't been thinking of *baresarks*. What choice was to be made about them, he'd made. He had another thing to think of now.

"Dunnere's challenge is honest, Garroc. Still, I will kill him. We've won a battle, but there'll be others. And no man," he said coldly, "will lead my father's army while I live." He ran long fingers through his close-trimmed beard; the gesture was one I'd always known to mean he wanted to ask for something. "Garroc, tomorrow the King will be here, come to meet my father. Halfdan told me this, but—he didn't have time to tell me why. He told you things, my father did, just as though you were his skald and had a right to know. Did he tell you about this?"

Penda King! I'd seen him once, from a distance, and I'd heard, as all had, that he claimed Wotan himself had fathered the royal line in long days gone. Maybe it's true. Big and bright, he looked like *god-cynn*. But I hadn't heard that he was here in the Marches. I'd believed the King to be fighting in the north.

In memory, I heard Halfdan's whispered voice as I'd last heard it at sunset.

"Your father said nothing to me, Erich, but that he had things to tell you."

"Ay, well, I'll know soon enough then."

So like his father! He put the matter of the King aside, did not waste time wondering about what he did not know. He loosed his dagger and watched the golden brazier light glinting along the iron's fine-honed edge. His mind was again turned to Dunnere's challenge, and by the look of him, I saw that he was certain that he would not die in the rain and the mud tonight.

But if he was certain, I was not. *Thegn* Dunnere had taught him dagger-craft.

"Come and watch the fight, Garroc. If you won't make a song, at least be among the witnesses, ay?"

I'd have answered *ay*, but, eager War Hawk, he did not wait for it.

Alone in the tent, I listened to the wind moan, the rain weep. Almost I turned to leave, but the firelight sliding along the blade of Halfdan's dagger, gold breathing on iron, caught my eye. I saw the *cyning*, alone and dead; and so I knelt beside him where he lay in the shadows and still as though he had never lived. I whispered him good-speeding as once, long ago, I had done for my own father. Halfdan had been my *cyning*, and for a soldier, the ties are the same. But I had no song for him. As I'd had none for my father.

In my heart I heard the voice of dead Halfdan's ghost. Firelight and shadow wavered on the tent walls, and from outside came the long moaning howl of a *baresark* sorrowing, a madman grieving. I turned away from the dead *cyning's* voice while I still could, rose and followed Erich into the night.

III

I know that the clouds are the wild, wind-tossed manes of Valkyries' steeds, the Night Maidens' horses. I know that the giant Hraesvelgr, the Corpse-swallower, has arms that are eagle's wings, and that he gathers the wind, sends it running through the world. That night I saw the Valkyries' steeds circling high above the earth, heard the wind in Corpse-swallower's wings as I went to watch a *cyning* made.

Beyond the beck where the mist-dragon had briefly lived, the ground lay in a wide level sward, already greening. Vagrant-willed, the rain stopped its mourning, and all of us who did not keep watch followed Erich and Dunnere to this place. Some had torches and held them high. Oily smoke and blue-edged flames staggered into the darkness as we fanned out to encircle the sward.

Dunnere and Erich stood silent in the circle. As we watched, they stripped themselves of mantles and byrnies, leg-guards and all weapons but their daggers.

Often in years past I had seen them practicing dagger-craft in the stable yards behind Halfdan's hall. Dunnere a deep-chested bull; Erich a newly fledged hawk. Now memory called faintly with Dunnere's voice, said, *Easy, boy. Don't tense and don't move until you know you have to.* And old soldiers would smile seeing Erich, saying they felt his eagerness like a storm in the sky. Now Erich stood so still that I thought he'd pulled every part of himself into the far center of his soul. He held his dagger easily, as Dunnere had taught him to do.

And Dunnere, weapons-master, nodded approval as he'd done in times gone.

Fear twisted in me suddenly. I saw confusion in Dunnere's eyes, the look of a man who knows where he is but doesn't know how he got there. I remembered tears, silver on battle-grime, knew suddenly that something moved Dunnere and it was not the need to be called *cyning*. Dark stormwinds howled in him. His eyes glinted balefully in the torchlight. Grief-ridden berserkers' eyes look like that.

Wind sobbed low around the hills. Dunnere, black-maned bull, shifted from foot to foot, watching. Erich held himself still, no overeager lad this night. He was man-grown, and Halfdan's iron ran true in his son, sharp-cutting. He knew that he needed to do one thing: kill Dunnere.

So quiet were we that I heard the snap and sigh of the torches, the chatter of the beck as it ran over stones. Orange torchlight gilded the faces of the gathered warriors, throwing high light and low shadows across their fear, their curiosity, their eagerness. Like hungry wolves, the *baresarks* circled slowly around us.

Restless, I thought. It couldn't be a good thing for anyone.

Blodrafen came to stand behind Aelfgar across the field of challenge. In the flaring light the berserker's eyes were hard and flat as slate. Eadric, at my shoulder, nudged me and jerked his chin at the Blood Raven.

"Garroc, I'm thinking there might be a better place for us with Aelfgar, ay?"

Neither of us held torches and so we made our way, dark and silent, around the outer edge of the circle. Tall Eadric shouldered into the crowd and I let him do the path-clearing for me. Aelfgar whispered a greeting. I hushed him with a gesture.

Blodrafen grinned wide and hungry when he saw Eadric and me. Breathing like a wolf panting, the berserker moved back through the crowd, fading into the darkness and the night. Though he was gone, I fingered the hilt of my own dagger. The tension in those close-standing warriors felt dangerous, like the tightness in the air moments before a storm.

And like a storm, the tension broke an instant before I expected it.

Erich War Hawk lunged at Dunnere, his dagger a streak of silver in the night. Voices thundered, light flashed on iron blades. The making of the *cyning* had begun.

Their daggers talon and horn, the two men fought with single-minded savagery. Dunnere feinted, drew Erich's eyes and then leaped, dagger plunging. I smelled the blood from Dunnere's strike before I saw it gleaming red along the length of Erich's left arm. One-winged hawk, Erich fell back, eyes narrowed as he sought an opening to charge again. Dunnere gave him no time but rushed him, blade low for an upward thrust into Erich's belly.

The thrust would have gone true had Dunnere not slipped on the rain-soaked grass and mud. He fell hard to one knee, and Erich's blade dove through the darkness, all the strength of desperation driving it deep into the meaty place between Dunnere's neck and shoulder.

Men roared then. Behind me I heard a *baresark's* wild howl. I thought it signaled the end of the fight.

I didn't reckon on the strength of what moved Dunnere. He flung himself aside, bleeding and cursing, and rolled to his feet, weaponless. Like a bull, he gathered himself and rushed Erich again. Dunnere's dagger arm hung useless at his side, the blade lay in the mud at his feet, but he had another strong hand. He grabbed Erich's wounded arm and raked iron fingers along the gouge.

Eyes wide with the pain, Erich jerked back. The same treacherous mud which had caught Dunnere betrayed the War Hawk now. He fell hard, the breath blasted out of him.

Worse, his dagger spun away into the night.

The crowd of warriors hushed.

Dunnere scrambled for his own weapon, found it and went left-handed for his unweaponed opponent. Erich pushed himself to his feet, never looking for his blade, knowing it was out of reach. He would not run, the War Hawk would never fly. He rushed Dunnere, head low and seemingly blind.

He hit Dunnere hard, and it must have been like hitting a wall. The bull never moved, but hooked a leg behind Erich's and tumbled him again. Snarling, Erich grabbed his wrist and, overbalanced, Dunnere fell with him. They fought for Dunnere's dagger, sliding in the mud, both grunting from the pain of their wounds.

A berserker howled again. I looked around, saw Blodrafen standing at the edge of the circle of warriors. Erich's dagger, the iron fouled with mud and Dunnere's blood, was clenched in his fist. His pale eyes followed Erich, never losing him in the fray. Then, faster than the lightning's strike, loosing his high, wild war-cry, Blodrafen leaped into the circle, Erich's iron flashing.

And the rain, never far, ripped out of the grey cloud-bellies, fell in cold, stinging sheets. Around me the crowd groaned with one voice. The two Men and the Dwarf *baresark* vanished, invisible behind an icy silver curtain.

Someone screamed high, the sound a man makes when he knows himself dying. Standing beneath the bitter lash of the rain, I knew that a *cyning* had been made.

I heard a bull roaring.

"Ceola!" Dunnere cried, "Ceola!"

I thought that the *cyning's* name was Dunnere.

I couldn't see much for the rain. What I did see chilled me to the heart. Dunnere rose from the battle-ground, back arching, head thrown back. He bellowed, the long roar of triumph I had often heard from him on war-fields. But he cried that triumph around Erich's dagger, blade-stuck through his throat. Dunnere fell slowly, first to his knees, then, wavering, finally to sprawl his length in the rain and the mud.

No one moved, not Dwarf, not Man. Though there were *thegns* among them, none stepped out of the crowd to see who lived, to call out the name of who was dead. Aelfgar pushed through to stand beside me, his eyes wide.

"Do it, Garroc," he whispered. "You have to do it. Garroc, go see, go look."

As a true skald would, a faith-bound history keeper. I was neither. I felt the warriors waiting, saw their faces, their eyes turned to me. They needed to know who to mourn—Erich, Dunnere, or both of them. But they had a sense of place; they knew what was right. I knew, too. If I did not consider myself a skald, still I had spoken the dead-call for Halfdan. Who should see the dead before the Keeper of the Names?

The rain stopped, men went to find flame to light wet torches. But I heard nothing but the sound of my boots sucking mud as I walked. Who was dead here had not begun to sing. I passed Dunnere, moveless as clay. An arm's length from him Erich lay, face up to the sky, rain streaming down the sharp planes of his cheeks, catching in his close-trimmed beard. Blodrafen stood over Half-dan's son as though warding.

I felt the *baresark's* eyes on me, wolf's eyes. He snatched a torch from someone on the edge of the crowd, brought it low. Light poured over Erich's face, turning rain into sliding gold.

I dropped to my knees in the mud. The long shallow cut scoring his left arm from shoulder to elbow had already stopped bleeding. I slid my hand behind his head and found the reason for his stillness. The back of his head was sticky with blood. Yet, though he bled, his skull was not broken. In Dunnere's clenched fist I found a jagged stone, held tight in death-grip.

Blodrafen brought the torch lower. I sought Erich's heartbeat and found it. Like the warmth of sweet wine, relief moved in me. I looked up, seeking the Blood Raven's eyes. "Who killed Dunnere?"

The berserker shook his silvered head, and rose. "Halfdan's son had the knife. Halfdan's son killed him. It's as it should be."

And so I knew what purpose had moved the Blood Raven this night. I had never known a *baresark* to care who led him into battle, only that someone did. But Blodrafen had loved his wolf-king. He was ready to love the wolf-king's son.

Suddenly Blodrafen laughed, a high, voice-split cackle. "Erich *cyning*!" he crowed. "Erich *cyning*!"

And all the warriors, so still and silent till now, took up the cry, sending it up to the cloud-hung sky.

I took Erich by the shoulders, sat him up, and with Blodrafen's help hauled him to his feet. I felt the *cyning* coming back to himself, felt it in the stiffening of his shoulders and the sudden lessening of the drag of dead weight on my arms. I saw it in his eyes, hot and blue as fire-edges when he heard his folk calling his name.

Erich *cyning*!

The men surged forward, lifting him, carrying him from the field of challenge.

I did not go with them. I heard another cry, faint and low, beneath their cheering. I heard the ghost, Dunnere Godric's son, and I turned back to the empty mud-churned sward, went back to the corpse which had once been Dunnere and carefully pulled Erich's dagger from his throat. I reached to close his dark, staring eyes, and stopped.

A dagger through the throat is a fearsome death. No echo of the pain Dunnere must have felt showed in the light just then fading from eyes I had known. His face should have been twisted into lines of agony. Instead his lips seemed to smile in the depths of a dark, rain-soaked beard.

I understood then why Dunnere had challenged Erich. Win or lose, it was all the same. He'd come here to burn away the pain of deaths, his son's, his *cyning's*, in battle-fire. Grief is a killer and it had killed Dunnere.

I straightened his limbs, rough-combed his mud-fouled hair, his blood-soaked beard. Then I covered him with my mantle and rose to go back through the cold night to find a horse to carry the body to the camp.

Erich had said it: He was not a criminal, Dunnere Godric's son. And so it was unfitting that he should lie in the mud like a thief caught and killed for stealing.

IV

WORDS are built, small pieces fitting together, so that all men may hear the heart-voice that speaks, separate, within each. And so, when the heart speaks of a friend, a generous protector, a faith-fast lord, the word we say is *cyning*, of the kin. Because a true *cyning* is all these things; a good man will die for him, will mourn him as he would his father. In that way did his warriors mourn Halfdan the Hunter, Skuli's son, Penda's sworn man. A pyre we made for him and the twelve Men who would ride with him. Dunnere would have a place in that burning. We piled the wood high, built the fire-ship wide at the mouth of the valley where these warriors had died. Those of us who felled trees and put our proud horses to hauling, worked in rhythm with the hard, final chants of stone falling on stone, the song of barrow-building.

All day we did that sad making, we Halfdan's men, Erich his son. When the pyre stood, dark and tall against the purple twilight, we hung it with the shattered weapons, hacked shields and blood-stained byrnies of Halfdan's enemies. The wooden shields nestled into the bones of the pyre as though they knew kindred things. The ring-woven byrnies gleamed silver in fading light.

All-Father, fierce Wotan, would know he was a good *cyning* who had led these strong warriors. Erich War Hawk laid the last shield in place just as the sun fell behind the black peaks of the witch-haunted western mountains.

He'd worked beside us since dawn. In the night Dyfed had cleaned his hurts of blood and mud, and the *cyning* was mending fast with the strength of youth. No sign had we seen that day of Penda, no trace or track did my scouts find. If Erich wondered, he said nothing, but went at the task of making his father's funeral pyre with the single-mindedness of a man who has only this to do.

Now he took the leather water flask Swithgar offered, drank his fill, and passed it on to me.

"Garroc," he said, "I'm going to get some food. Do the same, then come to see me before the burning. I've work for your scouts in the morning."

Swithgar watched him leave, said quietly, "He sweats and shivers both, Garroc. So does a man with a fever."

And he looked like a man fevered, strange-eyed and restless. So it is with some when they spend time with the dead. And yet, I wondered if something more left him looking fever-racked.

Dwarfs and Men had cheered Erich loudly last night, but this morning Gadd told me he'd heard it whispered that the making of the *cyning* was no true making, that he won his place with a berserker's help and trickery. Some who whispered were Dunnere's friends. Some were not.

Swithgar spat. "How can he go and eat? This place will be stinking of charred flesh soon."

I told him that men must eat—even before a funeral. "As for the burning—it's their way."

"Scattering themselves to the skies? What sense in that, Garroc?"

"Sense enough, to their thinking." I got to my feet and slapped Swithgar's shoulder. "And so we don't have to make sense of it at all, *dvergr*. We just have to pass them the fire-brands as they hand us the barrow-stones, ay?"

"And *mann-cynn* makes torches for Wotan to find *dvergr* homes." Swithgar laughed grimly. "Fate spins a tight web, Garroc."

I told him I thought he was right.

Penda rode into the valley with four warriors just before darkfall.

Mindful of my promise to meet Erich, I'd left Swithgar and returned to camp. I hadn't my friend's distaste for eating, and when Dyfed offered me meat and water I took them. Werrehund watched me carefully as he gnawed the bones of Dyfed's leavings; I watched the red thief just as closely as he did me, for the man who looked away when that dog was near soon lost his food. I'd just tossed the dog a grouse's carcass when I heard the cry of the watch, the voices of the warriors rising in question and wondering.

Dyfed and I went to watch as the King and his escort came riding on the sound of thunder.

The horses were soaked with frothy sweat, their nostrils flared and trembling, and the King's companions had fared little better. Dust-covered and hard-driven, Penda's escort; we could hardly see the fine plumage they flaunted.

"Ah, but give them some time," Dyfed muttered, "and a rag to polish themselves with, and those gems on the mantle-clasps will glitter again, ay?"

I supposed this was true, for these were land-holding *thegns* who accompanied the King, wealthy men. Yet when they'd restored the gleam to their jewels and byrnies, they wouldn't outshine Penda.

Mann-cynn, and big for it, the King moved with thoughtless grace. He dressed in soldier's gear, supple leather and unyielding mail. And no jewel's shine could do more to make him look like a king, for Penda wore kingship as naturally as the panther he'd been named for wore its own golden hide. He'd been bred to war and most men didn't have trouble believing that Wotan was kin of his, for he had the Raven-god's love of battle.

Dyfed caught Werrehund by the scruff as the dog made a lunge at the horses and the King turned, saw us, then looked beyond us to the skeletal pyre.

"You," he said to me, his eyes still on the pyre, "how many are dead?"

"Eighteen, King."

He swung down from his quivering grey, looked as though he might say more, but in that moment Erich came to greet him. The King and his *thegns* went within and left Dyfed and me to take the weary horses to the beck for water.

I thought a lot about Penda in the time before moonrise and the lighting of the pyre. I knew that Halfdan's last word of him had been that the King was in the north, across the Humber, leading his army through Eadwine's Northumbria as though it were his own kingdom, torching Eadwine's *Cristen* monasteries as though they were blights upon his own lands. He'd no love for Eadwine and his White Christ god, did Penda.

It was he who'd named Eadwine 'Faith-Breaker,' and Penda scorned him for abandoning the gods of his northern fathers. "He is a miserable wretch," the King once said, "who abandons the gods he has all his life believed in. He is a faith-breaker who runs to a new god for the glitter of priests' gold and the promise of power."

They say that Penda feared no Man, no witch, not the maddest Dwarf *baresark*. But I knew him, as much as any can know a king, and I think with him it was less a matter of scorn for Eadwine Faith-Breaker than fear of the White Christ. I believe that he hated the young god as the god of his enemies, and feared him for the changes the power-hungry priests would bring.

Today Penda is called the Enemy of the White Christ. He was that. And he is named King-Slayer. It is not a wrong-naming; before his life's end more than one king died on his blade, and not all of them were Welshmen.

The Enemy of the White Christ. King-Slayer. These were his names, but few now living remember Penda's best name.

We who served him, we who held faith with the old gods, called him Wotan's Blade.

All of this was true of Penda King, but another truth is this: He had a great lust for land-taking, and the power to keep what he took. When the maps changed in Penda's favor, his borders embraced timber-rich forests and generous farmlands. As I watched the moon rise and warmed cold hands at the camping fire, I wondered why, with the war season so young, Penda had returned south to the Marches. As I waited for the lighting of the pyre, I wondered why Wotan's Blade had come to meet with Halfdan on the edge of battle, and whether it would matter to his plans—whatever they might be—that the Hunter was gone, leaving a young war hawk in his place.

But after a time I stopped thinking about it, for Dwarfs and Men took brands and torches and went down to the pyre.

Penda King, his gold-proud *thegns*, and Erich Halfdan's son, carried the Hunter to the burning. We who waited by the pyre had shown the dead to their places before Halfdan was brought. Now five Dwarfs lay sleeping in the barrow, waiting for their stone covering. Thirteen Men lay on the pyre, waiting to ride the flames.

Penda spoke rich words, gilded and fair, at the foot of the barrow. He spoke of brave warriors, strong *dvergr* hearts, iron-bright souls. In the cold wash of moonlight he looked like iron himself, gleaming mail, light-chased helm, eyes the color of distant storms. *God-cynn*.

Swithgar and I were among the five Dwarfs who would cover the barrow after the pyre was kindled, and when the King stepped

away from the stone and took a snapping brand from a Man on
the edge of the crowd, my belly clenched. When I looked at Swithgar in the leaping shadows, I saw that it was the same for him.
Penda handed the flame to Erich, and Swithgar shuddered deep.

Erich, bright in the firelight, spoke no word but one, and that
in the language every creature knows. He threw back his head and
screamed a thing that meant pain and rage, reaving and abandonment. Then he thrust his torch into the kindling piled around the
pyre. Fire gasped, flames leaped.

The berserkers loosed their wolf howls. Deep, and sounding like
the earth breaking, Halfdan's warriors, *dvergr* and *mann-cynn*, answered Erich's grief with their own.

All but Swithgar and me. I stood silent and watched the fire-
brands arc through the night, dive back to the wood and the dead,
snapping and hungry. Swithgar dropped to his knees, pressed his
forehead to barrow-stones. I thought he was weeping, until I saw
how shallow was his sobbing. He was trying not to gag.

As Halfdan and his brave twelve became fire, flew to the night
and the stars, I sat on a barrow-stone and held Swithgar as we
used to do for each other outside the *cyning's* hall, drunk after
feasting, retching in the snow. And drunk I felt, numb in hand
and heart, cold as though winter winds blew through me.

Tall Men blocked my sight of the pyre. Their mourning voices
drowned the snap and rush of the fire. But I saw the flame-steeds
galloping through stinking smoke to the clean, cold sky.

Halfdan *cyning*! Dead and unsung, gone.

Men don't watch a pyre long. In winter-peace, they go to feasting, singing the deeds of the dead, weaving memories like bandaging for their hurts. Soldiers in the field go to their watch or sleep.
They weave, too.

Penda left first; most of the warriors followed him. Swithgar
pushed himself to his feet, lurched away from the barrow and the
pyre. He went into the dark and I didn't call him back. After a
time Eldgrim, young bear-chested Dwarf, moved the first barrow-
stone into place, and I helped Haestan make a long flat rock the
footstone.

One more helped to lay the roof of that earth-hall, but Blodrafen
worked alone, whimpering deep in his throat like a mad wolf
crooning.

When the building was done, the berserker walked away from
flame and stone. Eldgrim and Haestan followed. I stayed, empty
and shivering, but not alone. Erich sat on his heels a cold distance
from the pyre, staring at nothing, from a mask woven of shadow

and light. I went to sit beside him and we were quiet for a long time.

When he spoke at last, his voice scraped harshly over his words. "He died too soon."

I told him I thought they'd all died too soon.

Erich ran his hands over his face, tugged almost gently at his golden beard. "So will we all, ay?"

"So will we all, *cyning*."

"*Cyning*," he said, trying out the word. He jerked his head at the flames. "That word has always meant him. And now Penda uses it and he means me. 'Erich,' he says, 'you are their *cyning*.' "

I was very tired. I bowed my head over my knees, closed my eyes. In the empty darkness I thought of Dunnere smiling and dead of grief in the mud. The nightwind murmured, the fire spat and hissed. Even now, men whispered about the making of the *cyning*, about treachery, and suddenly, hardly understood for what it was, anger roused in me.

"You've won the naming," I said. "It's what you killed Dunnere for, Erich. If kill him you did."

Ah, he was his father's son! He rose, cold as an iron frost. Back-lighted by the pyre's flame, he seemed faceless to me then.

"I killed him, Garroc. It was me put the blade in him. Did you think it was the Blood Raven's deed? You're wrong." He moved then, half turned to the fire. His hands clenched into fists, fell open again. In the light I saw the shadow-mask slip. "But he used me. Dunnere used me, Garroc. He wanted to die."

"Yes," I said, "he did use you. Maybe that hurts, ay? But you used him, too. You've won the naming, the title you wanted. You've won the place your father wanted for you."

For a long time he was silent; shadows filled his eyes, closed around his face again. Wind keened high now; the night dreamed of winter. At last he nodded once, sharply. "I've won it. And now you're thinking that I have to earn it."

I said nothing.

Erich grunted. "But you won't say that, will you? Close with your counsel, that's what my father said about you, Garroc. Tell me this: I've won the naming and the title I wanted; do you doubt I can hold the place my father wanted for me?"

Shadow and light danced around us, me still sitting, him standing and looking like a hawk ready to leap for the sky. I answered him, but not with a yes or a no.

"Erich," I whispered. My voice sounded as though I hadn't

used it for days, rough and unsure. "*Cyning*, I haven't given you the names of the dead."

"You're no skald. I've heard you say it. I would think you'd consider yourself released from that duty now that my father is dead."

"A *cyning* needs to know who has died for him. Your father understood that."

"Yes, he did." Erich dropped to a crouch before me. His hands were not fists now, but open as though to receive something. "Tell me."

In the shadows crawling across the barrow, the smoke sliding on the wind, I heard the murmur of ghosts.

"*Mann-cynn* have died," I said to the *cyning*. "Godwine Anlaf's son and Ceola . . . Dunnere's son and Odda Skala's son. Aelfric Thorstan's son is dead, and Swerting Bardar's son and Beow Sigurd's son. Ecglaf Harald's son has died, and Eofar Thorfinn's son and Sigurd Tostig's son. Wulfmaer Hengest's son is dead, and Waltheof Thorkel's son and Dunnere Godric's son."

I listened to frost etching fragile runes into the barrow-stones. I heard the stones sigh.

"*Dvergr* have left us. Thorhall, Ivar, Aki, Hrolf the Mad, and Ulf, called by some Weyland. These didn't take father's names because they could have no sons to give their own to.

"Their *cyning* is with them. Halfdan Skuli's son, Penda's sworn man, keeper of the Marcher holdings. These are the battle-slain."

I looked up at him then, my eyes so hot, so dry of tears that they ached. "Close with my counsel? Ay, maybe, Erich. But I'll tell you what your father told me: Keep these names and keep their memories. And if you are wise, you won't let them become ghosts to haunt you."

Erich stared at his empty hands. "And you, Garroc? Are you wise?"

I shook my head. "No, *cyning*, I'm not."

That night, Sif, I didn't dream of ghosts. In truth, I didn't dream at all—though a dream moved in me. A dream where the sky was black as a moon-reft night and stars wore the colors that light borrows when it dances through a rough-cut amethyst. The wind in this dream, warm as welcoming, clean as hope, breathed no song I'd ever heard wind sing. Most like doves it sounded, like wood doves sighing.

Each knows the world in his own way. This dream was no reflection of how I knew it. Another had known these jeweled stars, heard the wind as a dove's song. She remembered them now as she slept, reached beyond the borders of her sleep, and mine, to give me the dream.

Ay, she. For as well as I knew this dream was not mine—that well did I know whose it was. This was the dream of a Dwarf witch, this was a woman's gift.

Something else she gave me, along with her vision of amethyst stars, her memory of the wind's song; she gave me the image of myself as she knew me.

I've seen my reflection in still pools, and so I know that my face is just a face—not handsome, not ugly. None would know me for any but a Northern son, blue-eyed, gold-bearded; all would know me for a soldier, my nose twice broken, my face battle-marked. Always when I'd catch sight of my face, my eyes, in the water, I would find the wary look of a man afraid to see that the *sceadu-wulf*, the berserker madness, had finally caught him. But this night the witch showed me another face.

In her dream she showed me how I look when she's surprised laughter from me, showed me how fire leaps in my eyes when love kindles. I saw myself as she knows me on winter nights by ruddy firelight, bright and hungry sometimes, filled with need; other times softer and somehow stronger for it.

But the dream didn't last long, and when I woke, my sight was my own, my eyes full of nothing but the Ghost Moon. Covered with silver he was, preening and proud. Tomorrow night he would begin the wane.

So long since I'd felt the witch dreaming! Hunter's Moon had fled his shadow, been caught by it. The *Wyrm's* Moon, the Wolf's moon cold as Grief Hound's heart, Ice Moon and Snow Moon and the Seer's bright candle had run from their shadows, been finally whelmed by them. In all that time the witch had left me to my own dreams.

I lay awake long, heart-shaken, roused and aching with a wanting that was both hers and mine. I breathed the moonlight, thought of amethyst stars and a Dwarf witch who lived in Vorgund's wild mountains. This night she'd dreamed of me.

V

ERICH called me to him as the mist-dragon slithered into the beck, its foggy hide stinking of pyre smoke and men's grief. The sky, innocent of the night's blue stars, empty of witch-dreams, stretched wide over the vale and the hill. The pyre still smoldered, embers breathing softly where once flames roared. I closed my eyes against the sight of fire-twisted iron blades, blackened shield bosses half-buried in the ashes; against frost-runes glittering on barrow-stones. My Sif, I could not look at that funeral place long.

I crossed the camp, listening to the horses snorting and stamping in the picket lines where Penda's *thegns* readied their mounts. All around the camp, Dwarfs and Men snatched hasty morning meals as they collected gear and weapons. Silent amidst the talk of men, the bright chiming of ringed mail, the hiss of swords and daggers going home to sheathes, the berserkers crouched by their fires, war-wolves waiting.

The air in Erich's tent smelled thick and close, of leather and smoke. The rich crimson heart of the brazier's coals spoke of an all-night fire. In the place where, two nights before, Halfdan's body had rested, Penda sat rough on the ground, his back against a tent stave, a thin-scraped hide map across his knee.

Erich looked around when I entered, gestured toward the map. "Garroc, is this still a true telling?"

Smoke and heat-dancing air rippled across the map, clouds on scraped hide. I knew the map; Dyfed had made it in the fall. He'd labored long over its making, squinting one-eyed before night fires, carefully crafting a true picture of the land here in the northern part of the Marches and the borderlands of the *Wealas* as we knew them from scouting.

In the far northeast corner of the Marches lay Ceastir, the only place worth calling a town in that quarter of Erich's holding. Cair Legion, the Welsh and old Romans used to call it. Dyfed had drawn the crumbling Roman buildings to mark the town, grim forts and the houses which are huddled there still. A bold line of black on the map—across the earth broken cobbles with grasses growing up through the stone's wounds—the old Roman *straet* still runs through Ceastir, still marches south and west through Welsh borders.

People say that the road runs straight to the sea. A time was,

or so I've heard men tell it, that a king of Rome held every part
of the Isle, took tribute from the whole world. I don't know if he
did or didn't, but that king did cause his people to make fine roads.

The land is low around Ceastir town, treacherous fenland, and
the cobbled road bridges across two rivers where it begins to rise,
climbing to the gleaming mountains all men call the Cambrians.
Between fen and mountain lay Vorgund's dark and dangerous
wildwood.

Witches live in those woods and the night before one, dark-
haired Dwarf woman, slender as reeds, gently wove her dreams
with my sleeping.

Between Ceastir and the mountains lie deep woodland valleys
where small villages and cleared farmlands settle, Vorgund's favorite targets for raiding. Two of the farmsteads Dyfed marked
last summer were burned rubble now; one of the villages closest
to the mountains no longer existed. For these Halfdan had ex-
tracted vengeance. For these the Hunter had died in this nameless
valley.

"Ay, *cyning*," I said. "The map's true enough."

Penda rose from his hard sitting, stretched high and long. Firelight flashed along his tight-ringed byrnie, spun down his arms as
though, like a god, he'd called it to him. "I hear it said that you're
a good scout, Garroc."

"Halfdan didn't complain of me. And I trust the man who made
the map."

The King laughed, a thundering noise to fill the tent, send the
brazier's flames leaping. "No, he never did complain of you. And
so I'll trust the map, too, *dvergr*. Show me the fastest way to Ceastir."

I traced a path wide of the marshes, a way to take him around
the mire. He shook his head.

"Not fast enough." His eyes narrowed to catch and steady the
firelight, his finger hovered over swamp-ways. "Can an army get
through here?"

Grim that fenland, greening now in spring to look like fine, level
ground, hiding shivering wet-sands and sucking mud. And always
the swamps moan by day, the wind keens by night.

"It would be a hard going, King, no night-marching or you'd
lose half your men and most of your horses in the mire. If you
traveled by day, you could bring an army through. If you had men
who know the place to guide you."

Erich spoke then. "Who mapped this with you?"

"Dyfed and Gadd."

Penda took Dyfed's map from me. "I want one of them with us, Erich. I'll get us where we need to go after that."

And because kings and *god-cynn* have no obligation to explain themselves to scouts, Penda slapped Erich's shoulder as a comrade does, said that he and his escort were ready to leave, and left the tent.

Halfdan's son twisted a wry smile. "Some of the brightness goes out of a place when he leaves it."

"Some of it," I said. "*Cyning*, you've work for me?"

"I do." He dropped to his heels where the King had been sitting and gestured me to join him. Smoothing the dirt, he said, "Make the map again."

I did with my finger and the earth what Dyfed had done with gum, soot, and hide, and when the map lay before him again, Erich grunted.

"Where did Vorgund go, Garroc?"

I pointed to the mist-dragon's beck where it ran into wildwood. "He likely followed the beck."

"He owes me a debt of vengeance." He got to his feet, blue eyes like brittle ice. "Yes, I know it, Garroc, no need to say it: Vorgund won't be easy to find now. He's gone to ground. And if you found him tomorrow, I wouldn't be able to do anything about it. The King has asked for my help, and what he needs will take me north."

What he said surprised me. I'd been thinking he would take the army south or east, to strengthen borders that would surely weaken when word of Halfdan's death reached there. I was no *thegn* with the right to ask, no skald either, to be told for courtesy. Still, I asked. It's the only way to know. "What did he want?"

Erich looked at me long. He'd heard me ask that kind of question easily of his father, heard Halfdan answer me more times than not. I'd put my songs aside, buried my tales and histories when I'd barrowed my father, but one thing of skald-craft I'd never been able to put from me: my curiosity. He'd indulged my skald's curiosity, did Halfdan.

But this *cyning* was not the Hunter. This was his War Hawk son. Here Erich's decisions began: Who should he trust? He did his thinking fast, blue eyes narrow, head cocked. When he answered me, he didn't do it because Halfdan would have. He answered me because he wanted to.

"What Penda wants is a bigger army than he has now. He's riding north again. He tells me there's a treaty to be made there that will be the crushing of Eadwine, and he says a wise man goes to a treaty-making with the same men he takes to war."

Ay, and likely calls them honor-guard or escort, I thought. Penda was a bold king, but not a fool. They didn't love him north of his own borders. I wondered who so close to Eadwine's *Cristen* lands would craft a treaty with Wotan's Blade. But I didn't ask. I didn't think Halfdan would have told me; I knew Halfdan's son wouldn't.

Erich dropped to his heels opposite me again, traced the beck to the wildwood, then made a line north along the forest's edge. All stone glens and high ridges was that place, the wildwood border.

"Garroc, take a patrol to this border. Vorgund's hurt, his war band cut to pieces. He'll be no threat to us for a while. But he has countrymen who'd be happy to pass the time between planting and harvest in raiding. They're small, scattered clans. No one of them has the strength to organize the rest. It's my thinking that they'll keep to the forest and leave our farmers alone if they scent watch-dogs."

I would find no ease for my curiosity then, no chance to see what kind of peace Penda would weave so that he could wage a stronger war against Eadwine Faith-Breaker. Instead I'd play guard dog at the edge of the wildwood where witches worked magic, where one heard the wind as the sighing of wood doves. Trembling went through me, but it was not cold fear-quaking, my Sif. It was a warm rippling like sunlight on water, a small echo of the night's rousing. It would not be too hard to let my curiosity about kings and treaties go unfulfilled for a chance at seeing the witch again.

I answered Erich steadily. "Give me a dozen men, *cyning*, two of them my scouts, and we'll keep the Welsh in the wildwood."

Of witches, a soft-eyed *dvergr* woman of the *Wealas*, I said nothing. I had no better reason to speak of her to Erich than I'd had to speak of her to his father. Never had Halfdan been hurt by my silence; never would his son be.

Erich scuffed the map away. "The King thinks this treaty-making won't last long. I'll return south after that."

I thought of hungry *cynings* in the south and east. "What about Osric and Cynewulf?"

He laughed—a short, sharp bark. So his father used to laugh. "They're already with Penda's army. It's what he's been doing this month past: collecting a bigger army than he has. All our borders but this western one will be safe enough for now."

I told him this one would be, too, and told him that I would

choose my patrol and be ready to leave at once. When I turned
to leave he stopped me with a hand on my shoulder.

"Take good men, Garroc, the best you know. And take a good
rider with a fast horse. A safe border is what I need from you.
But if you find Vorgund, I want to know."

The grief I'd smelled in this place two nights ago, smoky and
thick, had turned to hard bright fire. But a fire the *cyning* had well
under control. Erich didn't warm himself with battle-rages. Young
he was, still part boy, but he was Halfdan's son and had early
learned this from his father: Who would rule men must first rule
himself.

Erich's eyes hardened, turned cold. "He killed my father, Garroc. I want his head."

I understood that, knew it was right. A kinsman killed must
be avenged. "Ay, *cyning*, if I find where Vorgund's hiding his head,
you'll know."

I left him then, and after I'd been a time in the brightening day,
I saw that the winds had taken the smell of the pyre out of the
valley.

I chose my scouts quickly. One was Aelfgar, simple soul and
dogged tracker. He was a fine and skilled hunter; his bow and
shafts would feed us well. It was time Aelfgar knew the borderlands better. The other was Dyfed, who had been on the border
often, knew the forests, knew the glens. The soldiers who would
make the border-guard I chose as carefully I would choose weapons.

Ecgwulf who was true-named, red-haired Sword Wolf. The
brothers Waerstan and Wulfsunu, war-hungry youths whose father Hnaef was one of Erich's *thegns*. Grimmbeald, the fast rider.
Fearless Cynnere; the Dwarfs Aescwine and Godwig. These two
were father and son and Aescwine had seen one hundred winters
the year before I was born. Ceowulf, eyes grey as storms. And Haestan who had made the barrow's footstone with me.

One I didn't choose; one, Fate chose for me.

I knelt by the edge of the beck with Aelfgar. The sun stood,
bright gold, halfway to noon height. Most of the men who would
ride with me were readying mounts and war-gear in camp, but one
horse hadn't left the picket. Aelfgar and I filled waterskins and
listened to Dyfed as he strained the always-thin peace with his bay
mare.

The bay had no use for riding gear this morning and danced

away from Dyfed each time he reached for her, head tossing, black
tail arched. I sat back on my heels to watch. Beside me, Aelfgar
kept his eyes on the water and the skins, but I knew him, and knew
he laughed silently.

The meadow behind us rang with soldiers' calls, the trumpeting
of horses. I heard Erich shout, heard a voice like thunder laughing
and knew that Penda King was amused by something. Here, by
the sun-glistening beck, the sounds were smaller parts of the same
song.

Dyfed brandished a fist, flung a curse at his red dog weaving
dangerous games beneath the mare's hoofs. The bay danced res-
tively under his hands, her hoofs clattering against stone.

"Damn you, useless beast!"

Likely Dyfed cursed both horse and dog, but it was Werrehund,
jaws stretched wide and laughing, who splashed across the beck
and loped off into the meadow. The mare looked like she wanted
to follow.

Aelfgar rose, taming his own laughter. With patience born of
long familiarity, he waved Dyfed away from the mare and approached her, whistling softly between his teeth. The bay cocked
her ears, nodded greeting to a friend. Aelfgar took the mare's reins
and gentled her with secret whispers, soft-stroking her neck.

Sun splashed warm through the trees, edging new buds with
gold, spilling silver into the water, on to the rocks in the beck. So
must the witch be seeing tree and leaf, water and stone, this morning. Thoughts of the witch were warmer than the touch of spring's
sun, but that warmth fled when I heard the sound of an approach
from behind, heard the creak of leather, breath hissing like rain
in the grass. I tensed and turned.

Blodrafen gave no greeting, only walked carefully around me,
as though he no more trusted me than I did him. He stood with
his back to the water. His black shadow pooled on the stones at
the water's edge.

Aelfgar stepped out from behind the mare. Curiosity drew him,
but Dyfed's hand on his arm kept him back. Blodrafen's pale eyes
flicked over them both. I saw it in his face that he dismissed Aelfgar at once. Not so, Dyfed. The berserker held Ghost Foot's eye
long, then nodded once. That nod was not greeting, it was understanding. Dyfed didn't like madmen and the *baresark* knew it.

Most like a winter storm was Blodrafen. Cold and hard as ice-
winds. His eyes were not blue and they were not grey. They were
the color of blizzards. When he turned away from Dyfed, looked
to me, I heard Wolf-Fenris howling and my hands felt empty,

wanted an axe or a knife. I rose slowly, carefully swept the water-skins away from my feet. I don't trust berserkers. I never know what they will do—what word spoken, what word left unsaid, will drive them to rage.

The Blood Raven loosed his dagger, held it gripped in both his hands. Big hands he had and he didn't have all his fingers. Two from his left hand, one from his right, Blodrafen lost these in chances at Wotan's Valholl. Still, his grip was strong, his hands weapons.

When he spoke his voice was rough, his words came as though he were not certain of their use. "Garroc. I will come with you to the borders."

"No," I said. "I'll take no *baresark*."

"Why?"

I answered bluntly. "I don't trust you."

Sun glinted along the length of his dagger's iron, silver running. The light died in our shadows as Blodrafen crouched to put the weapon on the ground between us. "You can trust me," he said.

He rose, met my eyes steadily. I could see that it felt strange to him to do it. Often it seems that those not touched by Wolf-Fenris are no more than shadows to berserkers. Perhaps we are the ghosts in their world. And if that was true, Blodrafen was as haunted by the living as I was by the unsung dead.

I wondered if he thought Erich sent me to the border to find vengeance and the Welshman who had killed his wolf-king. "We're not going after Vorgund."

He laughed, a scornful sound. "I know that."

"Then why do you want to go west?"

Scorn, and scorn's arrogance, faded from Blodrafen's hard face, leaving only the look of a storm-lost man. "Because I don't want to go north."

A *baresark* is not born mad, he becomes that way. One time, in the *cyning's* hall, in quiet darkness after Halfdan retired, I heard it whispered that in the land beyond the Humber, in Eadwine's land, *dvergr* Blodrafen had killed his own son. I had not heard why he'd done it; only that he had done it, and that is enough, if it were true, to drive a man mad.

In the beck, water played with stone. Dyfed's bay mare shifted uneasily, pawed rich earth-scent from the ground with a hard hoof. Dyfed rumbled a curse, a grim warning sound. I didn't look away from the berserker, though I knew Dyfed's warning was meant for me.

"And if I tell you no, Blodrafen?"

He swallowed once as a man does who hears an expected doom. Old eyes, winter eyes, passed over the iron at my feet, then met mine again. "Then I ride with Halfdan's son."

He could have made no better answer. And he'd laid iron at my feet. A dagger is the only blade a berserker carries, and that, simply to cut his meat at mealtime. Blodrafen had given his to me because he needed a symbol, a cipher to show his intent.

He would be a fierce fighter. I thought Erich was right: We'd be doing no more than patrol the border, loping along the wildwood's edge like watch-dogs. Dyfed had no love for *baresarks*, but others didn't mind them so much. And it is true that a berserker's strength increases the ranks by more than one. A time might come when we'd be happy for that.

"I will tell you this, Blodrafen. If you come, you obey me as you would Halfdan's son."

He nodded once.

"Say it."

Old eyes, cold eyes. The *baresark's* baleful light flared in them. "As I would Halfdan's son."

I picked up his knife with one hand, the waterskins with the other, and gave him both. "Finish filling the skins."

Dyfed ploughed fingers through his white hair, spat and turned away. But if Dyfed thought me a fool, Aelfgar didn't seem to. He took the skins from Blodrafen and returned to filling them. After a moment the berserker crouched beside him, wary, unsure.

I waited until I saw Blodrafen plunge a skin into the water, then left them there and went back to the camp, wondering if I was the fool Dyfed considered me.

My horse's name was Dark. Long-legged, broad-chested, black as midnight, Dark had wide-set eyes and always looked at me as though he knew some secret about me. In later times, my Sif, I've heard it said that *dvergr* have no love for horses, horses no liking for us. The thing is no more true of Dwarfs than it is of Men. I have always liked the power of a tall horse between my knees, the trust that we make between us. And I like the speed. For his part, I believe Dark appreciated my light weight, for he carried me easily with no tack or gear except bit and rein.

The horse stood bridled and waiting for me when I returned to the camp. Gadd waited with him, lifted a hand in silent greeting when he saw me.

"Where's Eadric and Swithgar?"

Gadd jerked a thumb over his shoulder. "With Erich and the

King, working over the maps." His eyes narrowed. "What did the *baresark* want?"

"He wanted to ride with me."

"Ay? Will he?"

I nodded.

Gadd said nothing for a moment. Then, "Three scouts for Erich, three for the border?"

"A good, fair split, ay?"

He shrugged. "I suppose." But he didn't look as though he agreed.

"Gadd, tell me."

He squinted up at the hard blue sky, veered away from the question of scouts. "Garroc, I've seen others like Aelfgar, but not many." He ran thick, blunt fingers through his shaggy black hair. "Most don't consider folk like Aelfgar men. Not true men. They're considered mindless wights, feared and cursed and driven off to live wild or to die. But my brother's not mindless."

Dark nudged me, nibbled at my shoulder. I rubbed the horse's long face, stilling him. "I know it, Gadd. If I didn't, he'd be no scout of mine."

"And you trust him?"

"He's coming with me. I trust him."

He gnawed his bottom lip, thinking, then nodded once as though he'd convinced himself of something. "Garroc, I've taught Aelfgar as best I could. I taught him the things he needs to survive. He can find food when he needs it; can defend himself when he has to. I didn't set out to make a soldier of him. But he took to it. And you"—Gadd smiled and shook his head—"you're making a scout of him." The smile vanished as quickly as it had come. "One thing I've never been able to teach him: He doesn't know that he's different."

Though I said nothing, I didn't agree. Aelfgar knew he was different. But he was no deep thinker, and so he simply accepted that he was not like others and went on with the business of living. I wondered how it was that his brother didn't know this.

"What then, Gadd?"

"Always I've kept him with me."

His dark eyes filled with asking, with wanting me to change my decision, take Eadric or Swithgar and leave Aelfgar with him.

Dark raised his head, whinnied greeting, and I looked over my shoulder to see Dyfed leading his bay mare up from the beck. Aelfgar followed, Blodrafen sullen and quiet at his side.

"Don't worry about your brother, Gadd."

As I trusted my scouts, so did they trust me. Gadd wanted, needed, nothing more than my assurance. He nodded and went to have a word with his brother before I took him off to the wild border. As Gadd approached, Blodrafen dropped back, drifted off to find his own mount, and Dyfed lengthened his stride, raised a hand in greeting to Gadd.

But Dyfed said nothing to me as he passed, only reached out to pat Dark's black flank, then went to join Ecgwulf and the others.

VI

THIS world of ours is a middle-ground, Sif, a borderland where gods and giants sometimes come to fight. They don't war here often, and have not lately, but there was a time when they did. That war changed the earth.

In the time before Men, the world didn't look like it does now. Then it was smooth, had not yet grown mountain and fell. There were seas in those times, but no lakes or ponds, no becks or rivers. The Aesir were content to let the world grow as it would, but the growing didn't happen fast enough for giants.

Bergelmir Giant-Father took matters into his own hands. He left Jotunheim, strode hard-footed over the soft skin of the middle-world. Mountains surged up where he walked. Hraesvelgr, eagle-winged giant, laughed loud to see his kinsman's work. He beat his terrible wings, sent ice-winds howling across the earth. When Wotan saw this, he was angry. He sent his son Thunor to punish the world-spoilers, and Thunor went eagerly, for he does not love giants. He rode to Jotunheim in his golden wain, rode on the flames of the sun.

Thunor is mighty, Sif; none is stronger. But the gods do not go to him for deep-thinking. Through wit-craft and wiles the giants tricked Thunor away from his golden wain. In a dark place they prisoned the Thunderer, and stole away the sun.

Then they played hard on the earth, did those giants. Bergelmir bound the world in mountains, left no place for soil to gather, for forests to grow. Hraesvelgr taunted loud. His voice, heard in the winds, filled the skies with mocking. Stone giants reveled on the mountain tops. Frost giants ranged the earth, their breath ice, their touch snow. And these winter giants were the worst. The gods met them wherever they came, but could do nothing to stop the Frost giants' icy walk, for the sun was lost and Thunor gone. A long and bitter striving, that Winter War, and the ending of it was crafted by a god no one looked to for peace-making.

It is a thing we know about Loki, Wolf-Fenris' father: His heart is a Fire giant's, pitiless and devious. But he is Aesir and he found it hard, that fire-spirit, to see a world where the sun was not. Loki traveled far. When he must fly he was a bright-winged hawk; in the forest he was a high stepping elk. When danger threatened he carried a mountain cat's weapons of fang and claw. At last he found Thunor and the sun. Those two gods are not known as friends, but I have heard that Loki considered it worth the journey to see the Thunderer's face when he knew who it was freed him from cold giant prisons.

And so the Frost giants fled before Thunor's might; they could not stand against the Storm-god's rage and the sun's heat. Many giants died and their kin brought them back to Jotunheim, hauled the corpses across the face of the earth, dragged boulders in their wake. And the women of the giants wept; their tears filled the hollows, the gorges, the craters made by the corpse-dragging. Those weeping women made lakes and becks, ponds and rivers.

I know this is true. While the Winter War raged in the Outside, *dvergr* took life, heart, and soul in the wombs of the world. In deep caverns my most ancient fathers heard the war's ending in the grinding song of ice fleeing north before the Thunderer and the sun.

Memories of the ancient Winter War had strong life in the borderland between Penda's kingdom and the Welshmen's land. The mother-earth remembers it in glens and ridges, *dvergr* and *manncynn* recall it when they go there to fight.

Forty miles Erich's western border ran, along the forest's edge and into the foothills of the tall Welsh mountains. Soldiers from Penda's own army kept the southern twenty, a standing outpost the King would not weaken even for a treaty-making. Sheer rock face and what looked like half a fallen mountain kept the northern five. We, five Dwarfs and eight Men, would safeguard the rest.

No more than Erich did I have any thought that thirteen men would keep fifteen miles of border perfectly safe. But Vorgund was hurt, finished warring for a time. The only Welshmen we need concern ourselves with were the high-hearted farm lads who liked to cool hot blood on cattle raids, and if they wanted to risk their lives crossing the border, we'd take our rough pleasure teaching them that they'd fare better on their own side.

And pleasure it was; the reckless, iron-bright pleasure of men who liked to measure their courage against death's dark shadow.

All that day we followed the sun, climbed the foothills, rode the tall ridges to the best of marching songs: mail ringing, men trading jests and high boasts. No Roman *straets* ran here, just stony paths so narrow that only two could ride abreast. Always the forest lay, shadows and sun-glittering leaves, beside us on the left. Always the sky spread out over deep valleys on our right. There hawks glided easily along the roads of the cooling wind.

Dark went high-stepping along the stony trails. My own weight, the weight of the linden shield slung across my left shoulder, the iron-hafted war-axe strapped across my back, was as nothing to him. Dyfed rode beside me at the head of the line, dour and silent.

I understood what went unsaid between us: He was ever easy to read, my friend Dyfed. The stiffening of his spine, the clenching of his fists on the bay's reins each time he caught the sound of Aelf-gar's voice—low and gentle as he tried to coax a word, some slim conversation, from Blodrafen—told me all I needed to know.

Aelfgar's rewards were meager enough, I thought. A grunt, an impatient sigh, and once the flicker of a lean smile—half-seen in the depths of the *baresark's* dark beard, not seen in his eyes at all. These hardly seemed worth trying for.

"Tell me," Dyfed growled.

I guided Dark around a spill of rocks from some winter fall. "Tell you what?"

"Why you're bringing that madman along with us."

I thought about it for a moment, remembering the look in the Blood Raven's wintry eyes when he'd thought I would deny his stark plea to come to the borders with me. I didn't answer Dyfed true, didn't say that I wanted to bring the berserker with me, keep him close so that I would always remember what a madman's eyes look like. I didn't say that, seeing the *sceadu-wulf* in the berserker's eyes, I hoped I would recognize it if I someday saw the same baleful light in my own. I only said, as I'd said before, that the berserker might prove helpful one day.

"He's as good in war as any five men, Ghost Foot. You know it."

Dyfed looked at me long from that one eye of his, then shook his head. "I think you're wrong to bring him, Garroc. But you'll hear nothing about that, will you?"

When I gave him no answer, he slowed his mount, dropped back to ride with the others. I knew there would be no pleasing Dyfed that day, but I didn't care. I'd made my choice and I was neither able, nor inclined, to change it now.

And I had another matter to think about.

I like the borderlands, Sif, the mountains stretching tall past the clouds in the west, the highest peaks snow-gleaming even in summer, the wooded slopes dropping away in the east to river valleys and small farms. Most, though, I liked the ridges, rough and stony, the deep-carved glens that marked the place in between, sometimes Welsh land, sometimes Saxon.

I know this country well. With Dyfed and his red dog I'd ranged the stonelands and glens, the wildwood deep, spring through golden fall. When winter's iron skies hung low we'd come down from the mountains, back to Rilling and Halfdan's hall, back to *winterseld*.

Ay, winter-home and the vast wood-built *cynings-heall* where every warrior of Halfdan's had a place at table and high tales were told before bright fires, stories of battles won, of battles lost. There the hounds hunted the rush covered floors for their dinner and brave hawks cut the smoky air, sailing for meat flung high by their masters. It was a good place to be, and so I had always known it until a time when war caught me alone in the wildwood, winter caught me friendless on the border, and a Dwarf witch found me sword-bitten and dying with the year.

Some witches find their magic in darkness, in fouled wells of harm and pain. The witch Lydi's magic springs from light. Hope and healing are its sources. When she found me hurt to dying, she brought me to her valley, to Seintwar, and worked witch-spells for healing. The other magic, the love we made between us, tied her dreams to mine, my heart to hers.

Five years ago it was that I spent my first winter in Seintwar, and after that time, I left Rilling to Dyfed. I'd learned to love a witch, taught her to love me. Fine lessons those were, warmth found in cold seasons.

And so I came to know the stony borderlands as my *winter-seld*. If my companions wondered why I'd deserted the *cynings-heall* in winter, if Halfdan wondered, none ever asked and I never told. Young I was then, but old enough to know that sometimes men ask no questions because they want no answers.

Yet this winter past I'd not gone to the witch, had stayed in Rilling by my own choice.

So many are the differences between Lydi and me! She bright shining fire, I brooding storm; she *Wealas*, I of the *Seaxe* kin.

Like all Dwarfs, Lydi is no *Cristen*. She knows well enough that she is no child of the new-come god. Her gods, she says, are British gods, ancient as Wotan and his Aesir kin. They have strange names, these gods: Ludd of the Light and Annwn of the Underworld; the Sky-god Myrddin and the Sea-god Dylan and Rhiannon of the Birds. Yet, though we call our gods by different names, Lydi's Welsh kin tell the same kind of tale my Northern fathers tell of the ending of our race: a bitter story of a god made angry by Dwarf-kings too eager to trespass into the realms of immortality, witches too ready to use magic.

I need no more reason than this to mistrust magic and the ways of *wundorcraeft*. And yet, Lydi says that iron can make a plough blade or a murderer's dagger. Who can praise or blame iron for how it is used? Who can blame the magic, when it is a witch who uses it wrongly?

Ay, differences. Still, these things are as nothing to the matter which came, painful always, between us, and last winter there was no containing that pain. We could find no path away from her fire, no safety from my storm: Lydi would have had me unmake a decision made sixteen years before, said that I'd ill-served myself when I abandoned by skald-craft.

While the first snow of winter fell, her wildwood home hushed and holding its breath to hear the night's cold sigh, the witch had spoken of my abandoned skald-craft as though speaking of my heart or my soul. That nightwind keened high, mourning the warm days fled. And I, who once used words as a joiner does his tools, could not make my tools work for me then, for all words would have spoken of ghosts, the ghosts of *dvergr* hopes, the ghost of my own hope which had driven me to war and the thin wailing voices heard first on the battle's edge, heard ever after in my heart.

I could not speak of these things. I didn't want my Lydi to know that the shadow-wolf, the *baresark* madness, stalked me.

Yet, for all that we are different, Lydi and I share one thing in full measure. She is an obstinate creature, that lovely witch. And I would be lying, Sif, if I told it that I was not skilled enough at stubbornness to give lessons to old men. That winter night she stubbornly argued, and I stubbornly refused to hear her. It's not much of a wonder that we parted painfully.

And so, this day, in golden spring, I was happy to be climbing the western hills to the wildwood. I'd had years enough with the witch to know that last night's dream was a peace-offering, a gift. Strange and uncomfortable gift, yes, but one I accepted because Lydi's gifts are offered from love. I thought that it was past the time when I should make things well between my witch and me. This time I would find the words to make her understand that skald-craft or war-craft—any craft—is only a thing a man does, not what he is.

This time I was very near to believing that myself. Why shouldn't she?

"*Wealas*!"

Part warning, Dyfed's cry, and part warrior's joy. The red dog roared, hackles high, and an arrow hissed, tore the air so close to my face as to make me grateful for my beard.

I dropped low over my own mount's neck, got Dark's bulk between me and the forest. Gripping the horse with my knees, I freed my war-axe. The hissing of the first arrow became a harder song as others whistled in the cool air, hummed angrily, snared in shield-wood. Swords caught the late afternoon light as my men unsheathed their iron.

To my left I saw Aelfgar string his bow, nock a long shaft. He let fly, and a scream, high and filled with terror, rang loud from the forest. Werrehund plunged eagerly into the shadows. No sooner did the shadows swallow him than did we hear horses screaming. The red dog leaped among them, tearing at hock and flank, unseating riders, scattering the horses through the forest.

I dug my heels into Dark's flanks, heard the thunder of hoofs on my right as Godwig and Haestan, Aescwine and Blodrafen sped their own mounts forward. Halfdan, wily Hunter, had schooled us in war. He'd taught us that a Dwarf bent low over his mount's neck makes no target at all. We five became the van while tall Men, better targets, split four and four. Dyfed led one band, Ecgwulf the other. They broke wide for the woods, hoping to flank our attackers.

The blood rose in me, burning like a newly kindled fire. What I see then, I see sharp-edged, more clearly than I have ever seen. Then my sight is not honed by battle-lust. It is honed by fear to keep me thinking always, by anger to keep me fighting. I led my four into the darkly shadowed forest, straight into the teeth of the enemy. But we saw no teeth, no iron, only their backs as they fled afoot into the protecting shadows of the forest. I counted five *Wealas*: three archers, *mann-cynn*; and two *dvergr* swordsmen. One, dead with Aelfgar's first arrow in his throat, they left behind.

Off to my right I heard Werrehund snarling, heard the snarl become his terrible roar. He'd found prey. So then had Dyfed and his companions, for the red dog never fought far from his master.

Ahead we heard the shouts of embattled men, the high chime of
iron on tight-woven byrnies. Ecgwulf—Sword Wolf!—had gotten
behind the *Wealas* to greet them with iron and Aelfgar's biting
arrows. A simple hunt for Dwarfs then, driving our enemies into
the arms of Ecgwulf's men. I waved Aescwine off to join Dyfed,
kept Godwig, Haestan, and Blodrafen with me.

Trees grew only thinly here at the woods' edge; thick shafts of
late-afternoon sun lighted our way as we guided our mounts
around or over deadfalls. Dark gathered himself, long muscles
turning to iron. I shifted my weight forward to accommodate his
leap over a fallen oak.

"Garroc! Down!"

Behind me Haestan shouted warning. But warnings were coming just moments too late this day. At least one, maybe more, of
the Welshmen's archers had gotten past Dyfed's band. An arrow
tore skin along the inside of my arm from wrist to elbow, ploughed
a furrow of flesh before it struck mail and fell away, spent.

Searing pain splintered the clarity of my sight to bright red
shards. My axe fell from nerveless fingers. My mount scented
blood too close and forgot to touch ground before he swerved. He
staggered, lurched, and lost his footing. Cursing luck, cursing
Dark, I threw myself from his back. I hit the ground hard, but
kept enough breath and sense to scramble out of the way of my
floundering horse.

Behind me someone screamed. At once the scream died to a
sickening bubbling sound. Hoofs thundered, I heard Blodrafen's
wolfish howl as he and the others swerved to miss trampling me.
Late sun shone glittering on the berserker's bloody hands. When
I looked behind me, searching for the Welshman whose arrow had
caught me, I saw him lying flung against a thick-boled oak, his
throat torn, his neck broken.

The archer had been *mann-cynn*. Wide, terrified, his green eyes
stared at me from a dead face. I knew the marks of Blodrafen's
killing. The berserker, his mount never missing a stride, had
snatched the man up, dug and twisted, and tossed him down again,
dead. Hot, burning like the pain searing my arm, sickness flared
in my belly.

The Welshman's arrow had torn me, but not deeply. I bled, but
saw no muscle, no bone. Still, I bled strength as well as blood. My
axe was gone, my right arm useless now, but I am a two-handed
fighter when I have two weapons to use. Now I had only my dagger, useless against long-reaching arrows or swords. I looked back
again to Blodrafen's kill. The Welshman had been an archer, too

he had been a swordsman. I clenched my teeth, fought down welling sickness at the sight of the man's mauled throat, took the short sword he would no longer need.

Behind me, bracken snapped, a horse snorted. I spun, sword leveled.

"Hold! Garroc, it's me!" Haestan reached down, grasped my right hand. "I figured it might be worth coming back to see if or not you were dead. You want a hand up?"

I said I did, gave myself no time to think about whether or how much being dragged onto the horse's back would hurt. Some things are best not considered.

Wolf howls, *baresark* war cries, echoed through the forest. Haestan dug heels into his mount's flanks and we followed war cries, the sounds of iron clashing with iron. Trees grew close now, the ground rose. Haestan's hardy mount, following the trail of trampled brush and broken ground, climbed effortlessly to the top of a tall hill. Below us lay a small glade, greening with spring, ringing with the sounds of battle, iron clashing, horses screaming.

With no change to catch their mounts, the *Wealas* defended themselves on foot, bravely, defiantly. Ecgwulf and his men fought on the north side, ducking arrows, meeting Welsh blades with their own iron. Godwig and Blodrafen rode thundering to join the battle. From the east we heard horses crashing through brush, Werrehund snarling. Someone, it might have been Dyfed, laughed and urged friends onward.

Haestan held his eager horse back, turned and eyed me closely. "Garroc. Should I let you down or can you stay with me?"

My right hand was filled with my blood, my left with a Welsh sword. I held the blade out steady and strong before me. Fear and anger would keep me strong enough to fight. They rose in me now, fired my blood, sharpened pain-dulled sight. Haestan only had to look to be satisfied that I'd keep my seat behind him. He filled his lungs, loosed his own war-song, and sent the horse flying down the stony slope and into the glade.

They are courageous, those Welshmen who live on the borders. The two archers and two swordsmen had joined their fellows in the glade. I counted fast, saw four dead, seven standing. Ecgwulf and his men had been among them like harvesters with scythes.

Brave, ay, but seven unmounted; no matter how bright their courage, don't stand against eight mounted for very long. Aelfgar took the archers from behind with a hunter's cool aim: first one, then the other. The swordsmen, afoot and without the protection of their own bowmen, fought with steadfast hearts, but fell fast.

The last of them died just as the golden afternoon faded to purple dimming, a moment before Dyfed and his men stormed into the glade.

By that time I could not tell my own blood from Welshmen's. By that time, I'd again lost all the bright clarity of battle-sight. One thing I did see, though, as Haestan slid from our mount's back and ran to join our friends. And I saw it too clearly.

Blodrafen—hands, wrists, forearms crimson—crouched over a tall Welshman like a wolf over a kill. Beside him Aelfgar stood. As I watched, Aelfgar held out a hand to coax the berserker away from the dead man, to stop the mauling. But the Blood Raven would not be persuaded, turned a flashing snarl on Aelfgar, raised bloody fists.

So I have seen Werrehund snarl on the rush-blanketed floor of the *cynings-heall* when another dog comes too close to the bone Dyfed had tossed him.

Belly-sick again, cold with blood loss and what I'd seen, I didn't hear Dyfed approach until I felt Haestan's horse jerk and snort. Sweat-grimed, ay, and blood-spattered, still he was whole and unharmed. Good to see. He led Dark, had found my war-axe and carried it carelessly over his shoulder like a woodcutter's blade. He nodded toward Blodrafen.

"As good as any five wolves," he drawled.

"Not now, Ghost Foot," I warned. "Not now."

He looked away from the *baresark*, eyed me sharply. Ay, easy to read!

Not now, his expression said, but one day soon.

His one blue eye tracked the blood on me; his thin lips tightened. "Are you bleeding to death, Garroc?"

I marshaled a tired smile. "Not even close to it, my friend."

Dyfed laid down my axe, slapped Dark's shoulder, sent him trotting to join his fellows. "But you likely wouldn't mind some help down from there, would you?"

"I'd likely even be grateful for it."

Dyfed had a lean man's surprising strength. I was foot to ground before I could reach for his shoulder. He scooped my war-axe from the ground, carried it for me, took the horse's reins and walked in silence beside me, tamed his long stride to match my slow step.

This was not the brooding, angry silence of earlier; just tired, thoughtful quiet. Often we didn't agree on matters, Dyfed and I. Often our conversations could most rightly be named arguments.

In spite of this, and because of it, I have always known him to be a good friend.

I liked the glade, birms rising east and west like low ramparts, a small clear stream running through from the north. We found only the marks of one small fire. The *Wealas* hadn't been here long. The place would make a fine base camp for patrolling Erich's border, and it felt like a lucky place for us, for I'd lost no men, would have no names of friends to bring to Erich in a dead-call. And, though I had taken hurt in the fight as had Ceowulf and Wulfsunu, our wounds were small. Dyfed cleaned them quickly, bound them and left us in the hands of our fate. That night Fate's hands were as gentle as Dyfed's.

We loaded the corpses of the *Wealas* onto our horses, carried them out of the woods. Fourteen there were. Youngsters—farm folk and smith folk all by the look of their hands, for tougher hands a farmer or smith has than even a soldier. By moonlight, by starlight, we dug a long shallow grave for those farmers and smiths, buried Dwarfs and Men in the soft earth at the edge of the forest. Hard by the stony path we erected a cross to mark their cold bed.

We did this not to honor any *Cristen* custom, but as warning to any who would follow that Welshmen had died here. The grave made, we set our watches, and those who didn't watch slept.

That night no gentle witch-dream touched my sleep; my dreams were my own. I dreamed of my father, dead these sixteen years. In that dream I built his barrow again, and built it while a wolf, a beast made of shadows, howled.

WRAECCAS-MONA
(Wanderer's Moon)

I have ranged far, Sif. I have been to wonderful places. I've been
to the countries bound all in snow and mountains, the distant
Northlands our fathers came from, *dvergr* and *mann-cynn*. In
those places winter means night; summer lasts only long enough
to make memories. The Aesir live close to earth there, and I have
seen the god Heimdall's bridge shimmering like a rainbow, arching
across the sky to Valholl.

With Hinthan, then barely man-grown, I went even beyond broken Rome to the land where the *Cristen* god died. We went to see
that hard place where nothing grows that men do not coax from
the sand with pleas and promises and too little water. Those wide
hot lands have horizons a man can barely see, horizons he cannot
hope to touch. An unbounded wonder, your father called that de-
sert land. But it is not as strange as some places I've seen.

In the country of the *Wealas*, in Lydi's Seintwar, is a place they
name Gardd Seren. Warded and bounded by oaks that reach back
to become forest, the place is woodland and garden both. There
doves make nests in bush and thicket, fly high to see what can be
seen. More can be seen in that place than any would think.

I've stood in Gardd Seren—stood there at blue and blazing
noon—and looked up to see stars as clearly as any I've seen at
midnight. Caught between eternal sky and mortal earth, I've felt
the power of this place; when I let it take me, my soul is both singer
and song. Witches made that star-garden and it is a making to give
even gods pause.

I have gone far up the western coast to where the fierce Picts

live, where the rocks give only grudging space to the shore. There
I've listened to sea birds creaking their rusted-hinge song, watched
a selkie breast waves the color of winter as the ocean hisses at the
stony shore. Giving and taking, once the sea brought a selkie to
speak with me. There is magic in the selkie, my Sif, magic in the
twin-souled man-beast. I listened to him when he was a seal, spoke
with him when he was a man. And always, soft-eyed seal, hungry-
eyed man, he said the same thing:

Home! I want to go home. . . .

I saw his heart in his longing, felt his longing in my own wanderer's heart.

Land is not home to a seal; sea is not home to a man. And yet
he, wandering selkie, is both and he is neither. There is no borderland for him, no place where he can be both seal and man, no place
where he is whole. Remember the selkie, Sif, and you will know
one of the things I hoped to find in the borderland between Erich's
Marches and the Welsh mountains.

Ah, Sif. What a terror, what a joy, to be young for a hundred
years.

I

GHOST Moon, wearied of flight, fell before its shadow. Wanderer's
Moon rose, slim and swift, quickened and grew strong. By his pale
light the ridge fronting Erich's Marches became a place of white
and black, bled of color. Welshmen call that ridge Cefn Arth.
Those words mean "Bear Ridge' and we thought that, like Bedd
Arthur near the sea, like Moel Arthur near Ceastir, the ridge was
named for a dead king.

At night, when Wanderer walked the star fields, the farm valleys
we guarded lay black below us, deep lakes of darkness hiding the
patterned green of woods and fields, silver rivers, blue-glistening
ponds. Often when I rode the moon-drenched ridge, I would think
about Erich, young War Hawk, and wonder if some among his
army still whispered that he'd not fairly been made *cyning*.

I didn't wonder for my own sake; I'd given him my thin-hearted
dead-call as I'd done for his father. Erich was my *cyning*. And he
was Halfdan's son. I believed that he would silence the whispers
in the best way that he could, with courage and with strength. My
part was to keep the promise I'd given him, to hold his western
border safe.

With his pitiless curse, Wotan, mighty All-Father, has hollowed the children of the earth. He hollowed *dvergr* hearts, hollowed our souls, then filled the empty places with our bitter ending-fate. It seemed to me that Wotan left us no hope. But even he could not take our honor.

Pain and fate crowded me close, left no room for the histories the living needed or the songs the dead had earned, but I could still keep promises to those who lived. In those unquiet seasons, the last days of the Ghost Moon, the first of Wanderer's, I warded Erich's Marches as though they were my own. This I had promised to do.

Our gravemarker warned off some Welshmen, rose as stark challenge to others. Those who answered the challenge were cattle raiders who counted it the best part of the game that they must get past the border patrol going and coming. Bold they were, adventuring farm boys. Night was their favorite time to raid, and we thirteen—five *dvergr* and eight Men—soon moved to the wildwood's pattern, sleeping by day, ranging our territory by night.

Welsh raiders and Saxon watch-dogs, we played an old and deadly game while the earth greened and spring came to the forest. There was no peace on the border, would be none until summer when the Welshmen must train their wild hearts to suffer it for the sake of their crops and the fields they must tend.

And so there was no peace for me. Shivering with rain or warmed by the day's bright sun, I would wrap myself in my mantle and listen to the voices of the earth, the whispered stone-songs, seeking sleep and often finding Lydi's dreams. Then I walked with her in the secret places of the woods, sat quiet by small becks and sun-dappled ponds with her, loved her through all the long lifetimes of a star-filled night.

Those dreams didn't make sleeping easy. I woke from each, roused and hungry with want. If I could have done it, I'd have pulled summer up from the earth, down from the sky, for until the Welsh raiders remembered they were also farmers I could not go into the wildwood to find Lydi. I could do nothing but what I'd promised Erich I would do: prowl like a watch-dog along stony Cefn Arth.

In the hissing of your hearth-fire, Sif, I hear echoes of my men, my night-riding *mearc-threat*, Erich's border troop. I hear again the tales red-haired Ecgwulf told of the witch-haunted wildwood. He crafted stories of dread in a voice as hollow as an owl's. Some he learned from his father, some he spun from moonglow and strands of night. Some were true; through these Vorgund strode boldly.

Other voices I hear: Yellow-haired Aelfgar's, bright with the curiosity that always moved him. In the snap of the flames I hear Dyfed's wry drawl, hear him weaving riddles, laughing as he catches Aelfgar's attention, then lures him from Ecgwulf's dark tales.

> Hard things I suffer.
> The forest-shaker takes me
> As I stand under bitter rain,
> Blinded by sleet, stung by hail.
> Frost bites me, snow shrouds me.
> Firm I stand before all;
> I cannot fly the fate that binds me.
> Say, Aelfgar: What am I?

Always he tracked steadily, did Aelfgar, following the winding paths of the riddles as though tracing a deer's trail. He was a better stalker of deer than of a riddle's answer. In Dyfed's words he didn't see a weather-cock standing firm in wind and sleet and snow, but he seemed to find the game better amusement than Ecgwulf's witch-tales.

Storm-eyed Ceowulf had a voice like Thunor's hammer rolling across the sky. No squirrel could rival Wulfsunu's cackling laughter; his brother Waerstan's was dry as rainless summer wind. Haestan's words sang like a ring-woven byrnie chiming. The *baresark* Blodrafen whispered like wind across an ice-field. If we didn't hear his voice often, more than a few of us were grateful for that.

And the others, Grimmbeald, Cynnere, Godwig, and his father Aescwine—in the whispering of your hearth, Sif, I hear the voices of all of these.

"Rider!"

Aescwine's shout cut like honed iron through the crackle of the fire, stilled Waerstan's joking, Wulfsunu's laughter. The high whine of a whetstone on sword's edge stopped, faded to echoes as Ceowulf put the sharpening stone by. He didn't sheathe the sword.

The night breeze, warm from the south, heavy with the scents of greening forest and rich fertile earth, hissed through the oaks and rowans crowning the birm. The red dog, dozing beside me, raised head and hackles, sniffed the air. The breeze brought him no news. He growled far back in his throat.

Ceowulf moved restlessly. "Garroc—"

I waved him to silence, flattened my palms against the ground, reached for what earth felt. Stone passed news of a horse's beating hoofs. I looked for the rest of my men.

By the stream, soothing restless horses, Aelfgar cocked his head to listen to a forest gone suddenly still. I looked to the birm, where the glow of the newly risen moon silvered the broad leaves of an oak, made a featureless silhouette of Aescwine. I knew what the taut, sharp line of his back meant. Aescwine hoped he'd heard a friend riding and not some witch-summoned *helle-cynn*. Oldest among us, he'd fought witches before, knew what terrible creatures those men and women could become.

Godwig paused in his watch-walk on the eastern side of the birm. Unlike his father, he didn't fear witches. Godwig feared nothing. He braced, sword ready, barked fierce challenge: "Who rides?"

Stiff-legged with his own challenge, Werrehund rose growling again. I took up my axe. The haft, cold heavy iron, was damp with night mist. I rolled it along the side of my shirt, thinking of Dyfed and his patrol an hour gone to Cefn Arth. They were not due back until moonset.

Brush rustled on the south side of the glade, disturbed by more than the evening breeze. Waerstan reached for his sword as a smaller shadow separated from the darkness of the woods. The shadow became Haestan.

"*Freond*," he whispered. His grin flashed briefly as he stepped past Waerstan's leveled blade. "Waerstan, friend, eh? Put up the sword."

Waerstan lowered the sword and snarled. "You make enough noise for a troop, *dvergr*."

Again Haestan's grin, teeth white against his brown beard. "That's so you'll look before you start carving me for a Welshman." He dropped to one knee beside me, placed palm to ground, found the thunder of a horse hard-ridden. "Only one."

In the light of the common fire, hearth and home to us in our glade, Ceowulf's iron still gleamed red. Like Aescwine, he thought of witches. He raised an eyebrow. "Garroc, the horses?"

"Go," I whispered and he ran for the stream and Aelfgar. At my word our mounts would be ready to carry us into battle.

A horse whinnied high from the stream. Out of the eastern

woods another answered. A man cursed roughly, and I knew the
curse for Dyfed's. Werrehund, jaws wide in a grin, wagged his tail.

"Ghost Foot, *hael*!" Godwig cried.

Dyfed took no time to return greeting, sent his bay mare
plunging down the birm to the glade. Haestan leaped to catch the
bay's bridle, held her steady while the red dog reveled around the
mare's legs.

"Mount up, Garroc," Dyfed said, one eye gleaming, white hair
clinging to his neck with sweat. "*Wealas* coming down the north
ridge. Raiders—or I'm a farmer."

"You saw them?"

Dyfed grinned. "They're careless with their torches."

Wulfsunu leaped to his feet. He had the look of a fine swift horse
eager to run. I stilled him with a gesture.

"Ghost Foot. The others?"

"Waiting."

"How much time do we have?"

Dyfed took the waterskin I offered and gulped it dry. "Plenty,"
he said. He dragged the back of his hand across his mouth. "If
we hurry."

Dark shifted restlessly under me. I felt the eagerness in him as
I felt my own blood rise. Beside me Dyfed warned his bay mare
to silence with terrible threats whispered in the gentlest of tones.
I looked beyond him and saw Ceowulf and Aelfgar, looked right
and saw the gleam of Haestan's grin from the shadow of the forest.
Darker shapes behind him, Waerstan and Wulfsunu waited. We'd
left our watch, Aescwine and Godwig and noisy Werrehund, at
the glade.

Cefn Arth loomed dark against the jeweled sky, a stark place
of shadow and cold moonlight. A long rocky spine cut by some
dragged Frost giant a far time ago, the ridge fell away on its
eastern flank to the farming valley below. The west flank sloped
back to the forest, where we waited in the secret shadows. No sign
of Cynnere did I see, none of Grimmbeald, Blodrafen or Ecgwulf.

"Ghost Foot, where are the others?"

He pointed south to a place I knew, where a stony path breached
the ridge and ran down into the farms. It was one of the trails
raiders liked, wide enough to drive cattle back up into the
mountains. No path as good cut Cefn Arth north of here.

"Halfway down the trail." Dyfed cocked his head. "We can
catch them coming and going, ay?"

"Could be." I slid from Dark's back. "Show me where you saw the lights."

I followed him into the moonlight under the high-arched, star-shining sky. Soundlessly, Dyfed drifted off to the north, kept to the shadow of the ridge. He dropped to his belly, flattened against the stone. I dropped beside him as he squinted north, traced the winding line of Cefn Arth with his finger. Like a snake it curved, and its clearest trail followed those curves faithfully. I saw nothing but moon-washed stone.

Then lights sprang out of the darkness, began a bobbing and swaying progress south. Torches held in riders' hands. The flames leaped and danced and the wind changed. Warm from the south only moments before, it cut sharply now through the valley below and ran down from the north. We would hide quietly in the shadows and downwind. The raiders would not see us, their horses would not smell us.

"Only four torches," I said. "Fifteen or sixteen men, likely."

As I spoke, the line of light flowed west and vanished in the shadow of the hills. Only a moment later, the lights sprang out of the blackness again.

Dyfed nodded once. "Wager they'll damp those torches somewhere in the next bend of the path." He grinned. "Wager my horse they'll ride the west side of the slope and keep the ridge between them and the farms."

"Keep your wager, Ghost Foot. That's a bet I'd lose."

From where we'd spotted the torches to where we lay, Cefn Arth ran straight. Any farmer out tending a sick cow, any man tasting the warm spring night with his woman, could see the torches from below, pick out dark shapes against the stars and the moon. It was not something the raiders would risk. Better to sneak down in stealth, torches dark.

In the blackness of the forest behind us a horse snorted, someone whispered quieting words. Softly, softly, a sword sighed as it was pulled from its scabbard.

The sound found an echo in me. Sometimes I have to mix anger and fear as a brewer does his ale, carefully, exactly. Tonight I'd made the battle-drink without thinking. I looked south to the place where Dyfed's patrol lay hidden, saw clearly the trail down to the farmlands, silver-chased, moonlit.

Dyfed nudged me. "What do you think?"

"I think we can spring a neat trap. Get back to your men, keep quiet as you can. Between us we'll teach them this isn't the road to the market fair, ay?"

Dyfed's one eye glittered as we parted, he for the shadows on the path, I for the wildwood. He'd drunk deeply of his own war-brew.

We heard the Welshmen before we saw them. A hoarse question, a soft laugh and softer answer, the echo of a cough against the stone ridge-wall drifting back to the swallowing silence of the forest. Leather creaked as Aelfgar leaned forward, searched the moon-dappled spine of Cefn Arth. Even in darkness there are shadings, and a blacker thing than black can be seen if a man knows where to look. Aelfgar knew. He laid a hand on my arm, pointed toward the ridge.

Ten shadows, three more and then another. I smiled. Only fourteen. "Wait now," I whispered.

Aelfgar nodded and nudged Ceowulf beside him. He only mouthed my caution. Ceowulf passed it to Haestan and the warning moved like voiceless instinct down the line.

The *Wealas* passed us and never knew what the black shadows hid. They rode tough, shaggy mounts, the hardy, swift breed that seem more mountain goat than horse. All wore daggers at their belts, some carried swords older than Aescwine or Blodrafen. Two of them rode with strung bows, quivers at their hips bristling with arrows. For all that they carried soldiers' weapons, still they were farmers. If the wind brought them no tidings, it spoke clearly to me of cow byres and pig runs.

I saw no faces, only saw how they rode, tight-strung and hoping for a fight as much as they hoped for cattle, ready to make a place for themselves in a tale of cunning and courage. Brave dreamers, these *Wealas*, and they learn to dream young. I got the balance of my axe and made ready for battle. The dreams of Welshmen too often mean death for Saxon farmers.

The first of them found the path, the rest followed raven-dark and eager. Wulfsunu growled low in his throat. The sound died half-uttered behind Aelfgar's hard hand.

I lifted a hand, caressed the darkness as though gentling a restive horse. Aelfgar sent the gesture down the line.

Moonlight glinted on iron, a small star of light from the honed edge of a Welsh sword. The last of them, a lean lanky youth, paused at the head of the trail, leaned forward over his horse's neck. I heard his whispered word of encouragement. His mount had no liking for the dark path, danced skittishly in the cold moonlight. I looked away.

It's delicately mixed, this battle-brew of anger and fear that I

make, this thing which lets me plan a killing ambush. Easier for
me if I don't see a beardless boy whispering a calming word to
his frightened horse.

A good word it must have been, soothing and kind. The horse
took the path. For the space of five, maybe six, heartbeats the only
sounds we heard were the rattle of hoofs on stone and our own
breathing.

Then the song that ravens dream of shattered the night's silence.
Blodrafen's high, howling war cry echoed against Cefn Arth and
we six waiting hidden broke cover, raising echoes of our own.

A fast thing, a battle, and a slow thing. Caught between Dyfed's
band and mine, the *Wealas* had nowhere to run, nothing to do
but stand and fight. Aelfgar, at the crest of the ridge where he'd
do the most good, picked off their archers with two well-flown
shafts then sent his mount plunging down the rocky path, voice
raised in a chilling echo of Blodrafen's war song.

Those Welsh mountain ponies were not war-trained. Many
panicked and bolted, throwing their riders and scrambling
mindlessly, driven by terror up to the ridge or down the path and
into the valley. Ghost Foot's band fell upon the unhorsed raiders
like winter-starved wolves.

Moon-bright swords—Waerstan's, Ceowulf's, Wulfsunu's—
flashed and sang around me. Haestan's axe and mine howled, like
Hraesvelgr's stormwind. A black-bearded Welshman went down
under Dark's hoofs, cried a curse, and rolled, scrambled to his feet.
Listing, hunched over shattered ribs, he fumbled for a better grip
on the sword still clutched in his bloody fist. His left arm hung
useless. Moonlight picked out gleaming blades of bone tearing
through flesh. Teeth bared, snarling, he lunged at Haestan.

Ah, what a reaver, my axe's blade! The black-bearded
Welshman heard it, but he never saw it.

All around me other storms raged. Iron rang loud against iron.
Horses screamed, floundering on blood-slicked stone. Men cursed
mindlessly against pain and fear, a wild and ranting battle-chant.
Echoes tumbled into the valley, finally rolled away, leaving behind
only the moans of the dying, the silence of the dead, the bloody
aftermath so terrible to see.

Sweat and the blood of others grimed my face. Dark danced
nervously beneath me. I calmed him with one hand, dragged the
other across my eyes, smeared blade-edged sight to glittering
moon-dazzle. Spattered with blood and breathing like a winded

horse, Haestan stumbled toward me out of the night and the shadows. I reached down from Dark's back, took his arm.

"Are you hurt?"

He shook his head, but slowly. War-stunned, he only half understood who'd spoken. "Don't think so," he mumbled. His quick grin flashed. He knew me then. "Ay, you, Garroc! I owe you, *dvergr*."

"Likely not," I said. He'd been close as my shadow through all the battle. If I'd saved him once, surely I'd only repaid a debt. "Anyone else hurt?"

"Waerstan's bleeding like a slaughtered pig, but there's more blood than hurt. Grimmbeald took a dagger through the shoulder. Ghost Foot says that looks like the worst and it's not as bad as it could be."

Haestan thumped my leg with his fist, pointed downslope. I saw shadows and the dark forms of men gathered in the lee of the tumbled boulders which had hidden Dyfed's ambush. A long hungry moan wound through the night. Blodrafen.

"We've got a survivor," Haestan said. "Aelfgar snatched him out of the *baresark's* way at the end." His expression darkened. "Can't blame him. It's a bad way to die even for a Welshman. Cynnere's got him now."

I recognized the boy who'd stopped at the head of the path to soothe his skittish horse. He'd lost his horse, lost his sword. Now he flung a blade-broken dagger from him in disgust and faced Cynnere, head high and waiting for a clean finish. Moonlight splashed across a face wide-eyed with terror. Starlight ran on blood-wet iron.

I shouted "Hold!" and Cynnere held.

"Bring him here."

Curious, Haestan leaned against Dark's shoulder, watched as Cynnere dragged his prisoner forward.

The boy would not look at me. Cynnere took a handful of matted dirty hair, pulled the young Welshman's face up to the moonlight.

"Not much to him," Haestan muttered.

No, not much but rage and terror. He wasn't very old, that boy. Fourteen, maybe sixteen winters. Filthy with blood and sweat, he'd come through the battle looking like he'd been through a threshing, bruised and bleeding and battered. And frightened. He'd been saved from an ugly death at Blodrafen's hands.

He tried—with no luck—to spit. Like it was he'd never been drier than he was then.

I speak Welsh like a Welshman. I'd learned the words of that swift-flowing tongue on the borders, then learned from my Lydi how to make them sing. In the boy's own speech I asked his name.

He said nothing. Cynnere showed him the sword's edge.

"Easy, Cynnere." I nodded to the boy. "It won't hurt to tell me, *crwt.*"

It might be he didn't like being named a youngling, he who'd fought well and bravely beside men tonight. The boy set his jaw, glared up at me. Then the Blood Raven's howl wounded the night's silence, chilling me and helping the boy to a quick decision.

"Rhodri ap Iau," he snarled.

I thanked him, for that is courteous among Welshmen, then looked around the hill, slowly, carefully. As I knew he would, he looked where I did and saw the stony path littered with the bodies of his friends, the blood pooling in white moonlight. I gave him time to see it all, then said, "A night's work this was, Rhodri."

"And damned little glory," he whispered.

"Damned little for any of us. Do you farm?"

He nodded as best he could with Cynnere's hand full of his hair.

"Ay? Back over the mountains? In Vorgund's lands maybe?"

"*Na, na,*" he said, soft as a snake hissing. "You've killed the lord, haven't you? Sent him back dead to us. A dead lord's got no land but what he's buried in."

"What? Vorgund dead of that little scratch?" I shook my head, not even pretending to believe. "Come, boy, I've fought your lord long and often. He'd not permit himself to die of Saxon iron. Where is he, then?"

Rhodri held my look and gave me back some iron of his own. "Dead," he said fiercely. But there was no grief in him, no mourning flaring to vengeance. Vorgund was no more dead than I.

From the dark places in his grieving heart, Blodrafen sounded another howl. Rhodri quivered in Cynnere's hold, exhausted and waiting for the questions to be done, waiting for his death.

Praying, I thought, that I'd give him to Cynnere's sword and not to the wolf-voiced madman.

"No," I said, "I don't want to kill you, Rhodri. I want to make a messenger of you." I jerked a thumb at the dead, spoke roughly. "You have a friend here?"

He swallowed and nodded.

"Take his dagger and go on home now. It's finished. Tell your kin there's no cattle to be had here. And tell your lord there's no land for him in the Marches."

"Vorgund's dead," he said sullenly.

"Ah, yes. So you've told me. Then whisper it at his grave, *crwt*."

Haestan stood away from Dark, became fascinated by the glittering sweep of stars over Cefn Arth. Cynnere looked at me, raised an eyebrow. Neither Dwarf nor Man spoke Rhodri's language, and so they had no idea that I intended to let the boy live. Still, they sensed that the conversation was at an end. Cynnere was ready to kill the boy; Haestan was content to continue his study of the stars.

"Cynnere, let him go. I've given him leave to take a dagger and a message to bring home."

Reluctantly, Cynnere loosed the boy. He didn't love cold killing, but he didn't like sending an enemy home with a weapon either. Still, he was a soldier and knew an order when he heard one.

Freed, Rhodri darted past two of his countrymen to fall on his knees beside a third. The dagger he took was a fine one, its bone handle wrapped in silver wire. For a moment, a weapon again in his hand, Rhodri looked as though he'd like to kill. He shot a glance over his shoulder at Cefn Arth, looked again at me, at Cynnere and Haestan.

Ah, young Rhodri hated! I saw the fire of it in his eyes.

But he was no fool. He leaped to his feet and bolted up the hill as swiftly as one of Aelfgar's well-flown arrows. He gained the ridge and vanished below the crest.

Cynnere, eyes on the ridge-back, grunted. "A messenger?"

"Why not?

"You should have let me kill him."

"Maybe. And maybe the word he brings will keep his kin quietly tending crops for a while. Sometimes it works."

Cynnere turned war-red hands up to the moonlight, regarded them soberly. "I wouldn't mind if it did, Garroc. Killing plough-boys from ambush isn't the work I like best. I heard Vorgund's name. What did the boy say?"

"Said Vorgund was dead. Insisted."

Haestan, with no more need to watch the sky, snorted. "Dead? I wouldn't bet on that."

"Neither would I, *dvergr*."

He looked around. "What do we do with the bodies?"

I shrugged. "Take what weapons are good. The wolves will feed full tonight; ravens will finish the meal tomorrow."

It was a tired thing to think on. The *baresark* yowled again and

I couldn't stay there to listen. I strapped my axe to my back, turned Dark and rode for Cefn Arth.

When I reached the crest I saw no sign of Rhodri ap Iau. The night forest had swallowed him. Like it was he'd be halfway to home by moonset.

II

DYFED'S dagger hit the rotted tree stump with a dull thud. "Ay, Ghost Foot you call me. Eagle's Eye is what you *should* call me."

I said nothing, only watched him lope to the stump and recover his blade. He'd come to keep me company during my turn at noon watch and had been wounding the stump and trotting back and forth like a restless hound for most of the time. I wished he'd content himself with napping in the sun.

But for Dyfed's restlessness, all was quiet in the glade, for most of the border-guard slept now, tired from the skirmish with the *Wealas*. Ay, most slept, but not all. In a pocket of shade at the edge of the woods Aelfgar and Blodrafen crouched over the making of game-snares. As I watched, Blodrafen held up a thin leather plait for Aelfgar's approval.

Eagle's Eye, maybe. But Ghost Foot was a better name. The mother-earth never felt him walk when he wanted to be silent. I knew he was beside me again when I heard his gusty sigh. He sheathed his dagger and dropped to his heels. In the glade Aelfgar took the snare from Blodrafen and the two bent close to inspect it.

"Ah, now," Dyfed said, "thanks to Aelfgar I think we're sighting along a quiet summer."

I yawned, stretched high, and leaned back against the cool strength of an oak's trunk. "And what does Aelfgar have to do with it?"

He cocked his head, squinted at me. "Seems to me you wouldn't have had a messenger to send back to the Welshmen if Aelfgar hadn't snatched that boy out of the *baresark's* way." Dyfed grunted. "He sticks close to that madman, Aelfgar does. Why?"

"I don't know. Why don't you ask him?"

"I did. He says Blodrafen's his friend. Damn spooky friend, if you ask me."

"Ay, well . . . that's Aelfgar's business, don't you think?"

"No, I don't think."

I smiled into my beard. "I won't argue with you there, my friend. But if you did think, like it is you'd consider that we count on Aelfgar to fight well beside us, depend on him to get us our food. Likely we can let him make his own choice of friends, eh?"

"He's a boy, Garroc."

"No. He's man-grown—when people let him be. Leave him alone, Ghost Foot. Let Aelfgar make his own choices."

But as I spoke, I had the uneasy feeling that I wasn't thinking of Aelfgar but of Blodrafen. Grief-haunted berserker, he seemed easier in Aelfgar's company than any other's. Surely, I thought, this was not a bad thing.

From the forest behind me I heard the sudden clap of a wood dove's flight. I turned to watch as she glided on wings the color of a storm-sky, showed breast feathers soft and blue as smoke. A peaceful creature, this dove didn't care that men lived in the glade, that horses stamped and snorted by the stream. She came to rest in an oak and spoke as the wind does in Lydi's dreams.

Dyfed rested his chin on drawn-up knees, brooding eye on the snare-crafting in the glade. "Garroc, you should have brought Swithgar instead of me. He likes the peace times better than I do. Me, I'd rather be with Erich."

"You wouldn't find much to do at a treaty-making."

Dyfed chuckled. "I'd find plenty to do. They may be thieves, cowards and unholy Christ-worshipers, those Northumbrians, but they know how to wager and their women aren't hard to look at."

I swallowed a smile and stared up at a green dazzle of leaves and sunlight. The wood dove sighed over her song's ending. Dyfed looked where I did, then leaned back against the oak, made himself comfortable. After a time he said, "I've noticed that about you, Garroc."

"You've noticed what about me?"

He spread long arms wide as though to gather golden sun-pillars, glittering leaves, even the craggy-shouldered boulders thrusting up from the forest floor. "You like this place, even to the birds." He nodded sagely. "Wager you're not thinking you'd rather be with Erich just now."

A horse whinnied at the stream, another snorted. Werrehund, soft-stepping thief on the scent of someone's uneaten breakfast, padded among the sleeping soldiers. In the pool of shade at the forest's edge Aelfgar held up a snare, tugged the plaited leather noose tight around his wrist. Blodrafen bared his teeth in a grin.

I regarded Dyfed as though I'd not heard what he'd said. "I think you're right, Ghost Foot. It's going to be a quiet summer.

Likely the quiet starts now—no matter how Rhodri's message is greeted. Thirteen Welsh farmers aren't going back to tend the fields. That will be more for the rest to work." I scratched my beard, cocked my head in imitation of his own gesture. "Wager Aelfgar and I can safely spend the day hunting, ay?"

Dyfed shrugged, willing to let the matters of the dove and the borderlands rest. "Sounds like a good idea. Werrehund and I are getting tired of hares and squirrels. We'd be grateful if you could find us something different."

The dove resumed her song and Dyfed squinted up at her again, then slid his back lower down the tree's trunk, laced his fingers behind his head and closed his one eye. He seemed content now to match my silence with his own.

I sat beside my friend, watched sunlight creep across the glade, listened to the scurrying of dormice and voles in the brush behind me, the rowdy cries of jays and red squirrels flinging insults at each other in the high trees above.

Friends we were, Dyfed and I.

A long time ago, on a cold night, when the Wolf Moon hung high and cast light like purest silver over the black waters of the Rill, Dyfed had heard me sing the last song I'd ever made. I'd made it on the day Grimwulf Aesc's son died, made it as songs of good-speeding should be made, while the barrow is being built. But I didn't make it for my father; I made it for myself, and these are the words of it:

> Of our treasure we are reft,
> King and crofter alike.
> We are god-cursed.
> We are beggared.
>
> Vacant the halls of our hearts.
> Cold and cold our arms!
> They hold no fair child.
> Fading the light of our souls.
> Empty and empty our eyes!
> They see no youngling's smile.
>
> As prayers to heedless gods:
> Our proud histories are echoes,
> Tales told to no one,
> Songs sung to empty cradles.

And those words had made Dyfed, bright cool Ghost Foot, weep.

Ay, friends. Dyfed knew my last song, and he'd known Dagain, who was the daughter of Arn the stone-fitter; Dagain, who had inspired me to sing my sad song on that cold night.

They are lovely creatures, the women of my *dvergr* kin. Slender little wisps of women, Dyfed used to say. Dagain was like the sun among them, and she'd brought her warmth to me on cold winter nights. But after a time she needed more than a war-scarred soldier in winter, and so she wed a smith's son, a strong Dwarf iron-maker who would stay with her always, and I, drunk after the wedding feast, sang the saddest song I knew. If Dyfed wept to hear it, I didn't weep to sing it. Winter's bitter winds, sharp as iron, could sting tears from me; a battle wound's fiery pain could. But I didn't ever let sorrow close enough for weeping.

Ay, he knew Dagain, but Dyfed didn't know about Lydi. Of the Welsh witch from the borderlands, I spoke to no one, not even to Dyfed, for most Saxons don't like the *Wealas* and none like witches. Dyfed never asked about the winters I spent away from the Halfdan's hall, forbore even to guess, and I told him no more than that I stayed in a warm place.

And neither of us spoke of this winter past but to agree that it had been a cold one.

Down in the glade Aescwine roared curses at a foul thief. Werrehund dashed for the forest, a half-eaten hare's carcass in his jaws. Beside me Dyfed rolled onto his side, and I'd have thought him asleep if I hadn't seen his shoulders shaking with laughter caught tight.

I nudged him with my foot. "You never should have taught that dog to steal."

"Hunt," he mumbled, by way of correcting me. "Werrehund doesn't steal; he hunts."

"Looks like stealing to me. Ghost Foot, what would that dog do for food if he didn't have soldiers to steal from?"

He rolled onto his back, grinned up at me. "Eat squirrels raw and complain about it. No matter. You'll be bringing back a spring-fat deer tonight and Werrehund won't need to resort to hunting—"

"Theft."

"—hunting for his supper, ay?"

"Oh, ay, Ghost Foot. We'll do our best."

Dyfed yawned, turned onto his side again. "Wake me when you leave. I'll take the watch."

In the glade men woke, looked for water or food, checked the fit and repair of their byrnies and took whetstones to the edges of their weapons. Aelfgar and Blodrafen were gone from the shadows. High in the oak behind me the wood dove yet sang, a peaceful song drifting above the chime of ringed mail and the rough voices of soldiers. Dyfed's breathing slowed to soft snoring, and I sat alone and quiet beneath the oak's wide spreading boughs, thinking of Lydi, and of Ghost Foot, of my friend Dyfed.

There were things I hadn't told him then, and I knew that he held to some secrets of his own.

As Dyfed had asked, Aelfgar and I did our best hunting. I knew the forest well and Aelfgar found a boy's pleasure in learning its paths and streams, its thickets and sudden, surprising reaches of meadow. Twice he showed me places I'd never seen before then. Tall Aelfgar, man and boy, displayed them to me with pride; teaching him the ways of these borderlands had become as easy as letting him teach himself.

And he was a hungry learner. After the night patrols, when the rest of us returned to the glade tired and aching from the long ride, Aelfgar often slipped into the forest, bow in hand, to find and follow deer trails.

"If you know where the deer go when they're thirsty," he'd say, "then you know where to find them when you're hungry."

Now, tracking north into the wind with him, I saw that he knew as well as the deer where they went to sleep, where they went to eat, where they went to drink. Before day's end Aelfgar brought down two stags, horned forest lords caught unready in the hunter's aim. The sun hung low over the western mountains when we lashed the stags across our horses' backs. Aelfgar hung his bow and quiver from his grey mare's tack, grinned at me over her neck.

"Good hunt," he said.

I told him it was better than good, for now we'd not hear Ghost Foot's complaints of hare and squirrel.

Aelfgar shrugged. "Maybe. But we're going to have to do something with what Blodrafen catches in the snares."

I watched, quiet for a moment, as Aelfgar stroked his mare's broad flat cheek, spoke kindly to her. She didn't like the dead thing tied to her back.

"You sent him out snaring?"

Aelfgar nodded. "Yes. I didn't know if we'd have luck today— I hoped, but I didn't know. And we'd want to eat something

tonight—" He cocked his head and squinted one-eyed at me.
"Even squirrels and hares. Did I do right?"

I told him ay, he'd done well. But I was thinking about
Blodrafen.

Most often we didn't think of berserkers as people. Most often
we thought of them as madmen, or mighty weapons that could
walk by themselves to a battle. The cares and concerns of other
men were not theirs and I'd never known a *baresark* to do anything
to earn his keep but kill his lord's enemies; a well-struck deal for
berserker and lord alike when warring was a *cyning's* chief
business. And so even in winter-peace, when hunting was lean and
trenchers stood half-filled on the board, Halfdan's *baresarks* had
been fed and kept warm in the hall though they'd made no
contribution to what was set before them.

Yet now, a small but real wonder, I had among my men a
berserker who would hunt and snare and share his take with
others. And it seemed that Aelfgar was the one who'd taught him
new ways.

"Tell me, Aelfgar, will I be bringing Erich another hunter back
from the border?"

He considered it, brow deeply furrowed. "I don't think so," he
said slowly. "But he's good company when I'm braiding snares."
He smiled then, and I was struck by the child's sweetness of it.
"We'd best be going now, ay, Garroc? There's one more place I
want to show you. It's on the way back."

I let him lead, and as I walked behind I wondered what it must
be like to be both man and boy.

The light of day's ending lay like old, tarnished gold along the
rocky shoulders of the small waterfall, became a mist of blue and
green, red and gold, as it joined the water's race to the basin below.
The water had no great distance to fall, perhaps only a drop of
two times Aelfgar's height. Still, it was a lovely, gold-laced tumble.

Aelfgar's smile was woven of both pride and shyness as he
looked away from the water's race. "I found this place two days
gone, Garroc. Have you ever been here?"

I had. I'd seen the fall frozen, the water held still and silent in
winter's grip. I'd watched the moon rise over the tops of naked
trees, seen stars glitter like diamonds caught in the black webs of
ice-sheathed branches. The last time I stood there, I'd been with
Lydi, both wrapped in one mantle and clinging to each other for
the best warmth.

"Garroc?"

Reluctantly, I let the memory go. Lydi's Seintwar was a half-day's steady riding from here, north and west through the forest, straight to the foothills of the tall Cambrians. It seemed to me that Lydi herself was farther away than that.

"I've been here."

Aelfgar handed me his grey mare's reins and dropped to his heels on the slick stone. "There's no stream coming from the pool." He looked up at me. "Where does the water go?"

"Ah, this isn't like the woods of home, Aelfgar. Here the forest is floor and roof both."

He frowned, combed his fingers through his mist-damp beard. "Is that one of Dyfed's riddles, or an answer?"

There's this about innocent-eyed Aelfgar: His questions were like his arrows, fast-flown and direct.

"Only the start of one."

"Riddle or answer?"

I laughed. "Each, boy, each."

A jay shouted from the rowan behind me, another answered from across the fall. I showed Aelfgar the path we'd take down to the basin, the one we'd follow for two miles, maybe more, through the woods to the glade. "The ground here is riddled with caves, miles of them. Like it is this water feeds an underground stream."

"But you don't know?"

I didn't know. I'd never been here but in winter, and then was not the time for tracing currents. "Not for sure."

"How can we find out?"

I grinned. "Strip down to your skin and swim until the current gives you the answer. Want to do that?"

He did. I saw it in the sudden lighting of his blue eyes. If he hadn't been as tired of leading the stag-laden horses through the forest as I was, he'd have been out of his shirt and trews and into the water before I could ask again.

He shook his head. "Maybe tomorrow. Will you come with me if I do?"

He was eager for play and eager to share the joy of it. And this is true, Sif: I didn't often find it easy to follow my own advice. Though I'd told Dyfed only that morning that Aelfgar should be treated like a man grown, I was myself often confused in the matter of Aelfgar. And so, sometimes I found it easiest to answer him as though he were a child, for all that tall Aelfgar was older than Dyfed. Not always best, but easiest.

"We'll see what tomorrow gives us to do."

Dark snorted and stamped hard enough to make the stones groan. Aelfgar's grey caught the gelding's restlessness and tugged hard on her reins. Hardly seen beyond the thickly laced branches of the forest, the sky had faded from day's deep blue to the washed color of opals.

I gave Aelfgar his mare's reins. "Best be going if we want to get back before nightfall."

He fell into step behind me, quiet as we followed the downward sloping trail along the fall's edge. He was quiet as we gained the level floor of the forest again, quiet as we walked beneath the thickly woven branches of oaks ancient before my father was born. Day's light had become dimming when he spoke again.

"Garroc, I don't understand something."

"Ay? What then?"

"I don't understand why Vorgund would want people to think he's dead if he's not."

I hadn't expected that question. I'd discussed the matter last night with Dyfed, Cynnere, and the others. Aelfgar had been there. I looked at him now and remembered that though he'd been there, he'd said nothing, offered no thought, asked no question.

A wave of pity rose in me. He'd offered no thought because he knew that his best skill was not thinking. Like it was he'd asked no question because it would have shamed him to have carefully explained the things his friends already knew. Hard to be a child wearing a man's brawn.

"Have you thought about it, Aelfgar?"

"All night. And all day. But I still don't understand."

Off to the east a woodpecker hammered for its meal. Tired and impatient, Dark pulled back on the reins, shied at the sound. My axe, held by the lashing against the stag's back, had slipped and begun to rub against the gelding's withers. I put it right and eased him forward again with a word and a careful hand.

"Have you thought about not understanding, or have you thought about what you'd be doing now if you were Vorgund and your enemies believed you were dead?"

Aelfgar smiled sheepishly. "I've thought about not understanding."

"Ay, well. That's easy enough to do."

He stopped, surprised. "Is it?"

Ah, yes it is. And any god who knows anything about me, knows that I've spent a deal of time thinking about not understanding. But I said nothing of this to Aelfgar, only nodded my assurance.

He fell silent again, tugged at the grey's reins and followed me. The path narrowed to no more than a thin tracing of game trails. A small beck, sprung from no source that we could see, ran skipping and laughing beside us. We went carefully, guiding our horses through close-crowding trees. A fox barked, near by the sound, but hidden in the deepening shadows. Another yipped high in answer.

"Garroc, is it that . . . if we think Vorgund's dead, then we'll leave him alone?"

"Could be. But—"

An idea leaped like blue fire in his eyes, a fine thing to see. "—but Vorgund doesn't really want to be left alone, or he'd leave us alone, ay?"

"It's a good way to put it."

"But is it true?"

Some days Aelfgar seemed plagued by Wotan's own consuming curiosity. "I don't know. What do you think?"

He sighed deeply. "Sometimes thinking's hard for me."

"Ah. Who says that?"

"I do."

"And who else?"

Aelfgar shrugged. "No one, but—Well, my friends are—my friends. And so they're courteous, you see. They don't say thinking's hard for me. But they know it just the same." He glanced keenly at me. "You're my friend, Garroc, and you know it."

"No. I don't know it."

But I did. I knew and pitied. Yet pitying him seemed as wrong to me then as denying the thing I knew to be true about him.

Aelfgar let my denial pass with more grace than I'd had to offer it. "About Vorgund: I've thought now. If we believe he's dead, we won't think about him anymore except to say 'good, he's dead.'"

Slow he might be, but Aelfgar could hold tight to an idea until he'd found the right of it. "And then?"

"And then he can surprise Erich any time he wants to, because we'll tell Erich he's dead and Erich will believe us. But we won't tell Erich that, because we've thought about it. Good thing we did, ay?"

I nodded soberly.

"Garroc . . ."

I checked a tired sigh, hoped he wasn't about to loose a new flood of questions. He lifted his head, smiled and drew breath to

speak. All in one instant I saw fear tear the smile from him, heard
his bellowed cry of warning. He gave me no time to turn, to look
for the danger. He hit me like a tree falling, swept me hard to the
stony ground.

A long scream tore the night, and the cry was not Aelfgar's.
He made no sound but a shuddering sigh. A dagger's hilt, bone
wrapped in gleaming silver wire, stood quivering in Aelfgar's back
like a thick finger pointing to the laced branches above me. Again
the scream, a triumphant wail. Dark bolted, the stag and my war-
axe still lashed to his back. The grey mare's hoofs passed
dangerously close to my head as she thundered after him.

So long in the telling; these things I hardly noticed then, only
remembered later. Then I was fighting for the breath torn from
me, struggling with the weight of Aelfgar's heavy body pinning
me to the ground. I was not careful with him. Fear and anger,
the old battle-brew, would not allow it. Freed of his weight, I
snatched my own dagger from my belt even as I scrambled to my
feet.

No sooner had I gained my feet than did another flying weight
hit me, carry me hard to the ground. A knee drove into my ribs,
another into my belly. Lean strong hands tore at my beard, dug
for my throat.

I gagged on the stench of cow byres and pig runs, fear and old
sweat. I choked on the smell of Aelfgar's blood. My head filled
with a high thin whining as strong fingers found my throat. My
hands, my dagger, were pinned useless beneath my attacker. Sight
narrowed to a dark-edged tunnel, filled with a face so twisted by
rage that I barely recognized it. But I did recognize it, and knew
it by the hate I saw blazing.

Strong I am, but never a match for the full weight of a tall Man
with one knee on my ribs, the other planted squarely in my belly.
I'd have died there but for guile.

Ay, I am a skald. And so I know that the tale should never be
heavily gilded when a suggestion will do. I drew one shuddering
breath, then went limp, and my attacker, for triumph or for
pleasure, laughed. He loosed my throat, swung off me and knelt
beside me to check his kill. Freed of his weight, I wasted no time
breathing. I closed both hands round my dagger's hilt and lunged
for him. I struck once and struck true.

Like it is no man was ever more surprised to find himself dead
than Rhodri ap Iau.

III

QUIET the place where the Welshman died, purple with shadows, chill with dimming's breeze sighing through trees. Beside the path, water still played with stone. Both laughed together, but softly. Then, closer, came the buzzing of hungry black flies fighting for places on bleeding wounds.

I only needed a moment to assure that Rhodri was dead. Ay, he'd hated, Rhodri ap Iau; hated enough to lie spying and waiting for his enemies through all the night, all the long day. He'd brought no message back to his kin, none to Vorgund. In the path behind me Aelfgar lay hunched on his side, managing only shallow breaths. I went to him, my hands shaking with a sudden trembling. Only in that moment did I truly understand that I lived because Aelfgar had thrown me out of harm's way. I reached for the dagger, laid palm to his bleeding back and pulled the blade free. He didn't scream, hadn't the strength for it. But he'd have liked to.

Aelfgar looked at me, eyes filled with terror. His lips moved, tried to frame a word, stilled when he found no strength.

"You're not dying, boy." I said it before I believed it, and so said it roughly.

He dragged a hand through the dust to touch mine. Then he closed his eyes.

I spoke quickly, sharply. "Aelfgar!"

Crickets shrilled, an owl's long, wondering cry wound through the dimming. Aelfgar drew breath and closed his fingers around mine as though to assure me that he still lived.

A horse whinnied from far down the path. A black shadow, Dark stood between two tall oaks, the dead stag still lashed and stiffening on his back. Panic hadn't carried him far. When I whistled he trotted toward me, stopped a short distance away. I saw no sign of Aelfgar's mare, wasted no time looking for her. I hoped she'd fled straight along the path to the glade, for once Dyfed saw her, riderless and frightened, he'd be quick to send men out searching.

But if the mare didn't return to the glade?

I held Aelfgar's hand in a gentle grip, leaned over him to inspect the wound. It bled freely, but didn't gush as it would have if he'd been heart-struck. I bent close over him, heard him breathing cleanly. The iron hadn't found his lungs.

"Aelfgar . . ."

Again his fingers tightened around mine.

"I'm going to leave you for a moment—"

He spoke then, one dryly whispered word. "No."

"Ay, boy, I have to get—"

"Please."

Ah, the fear in him! I felt it in my own heart, but only a shadow of what haunted his eyes. My hand trembling still, I brushed his yellow hair back from his face, combed my fingers through his dusty beard. These poor gestures were all I could manage to ease his fear.

"Garroc—I hurt—"

Through much of my life I'd only known tenderness as a thing trapped inside me. So it was then, and I ached as though this feeling were not tenderness at all but some savage gnawing pain swelling painfully in my chest, clawing hard against my throat.

"Aelfgar, think, now. You know what Ghost Foot says about a knife wound, don't you?"

"Yes," he said, groaning as though I'd dragged the word from him.

"It must be cleaned and bound, ay?"

He nodded weakly.

"I'll be gone only a moment. For water."

Aelfgar closed his eyes, and as he did, his hand fell away from mine. I hoped he would not wake again until I'd finished tending his wound.

I am no healer such as the witch Lydi is. I have no magic, only a soldier's skills in cleaning and binding a wound, skills learned at the battle's edge, and these are far smaller than gentle-handed Dyfed's were. But I knew what must be done; it was done easier because Aelfgar never came to himself while I worked.

The bleeding stopped, the wound bound by cloth torn from Aelfgar's shirt, I gently turned him, face to the sky, and lifted his head to help him drink. He took none of the water, only lay still as though dead. An ill thought. I put it away from me and sat back on my heels.

Night gathered close under the eaves of the forest. Deep silence waited beyond the piping of tree frogs and the silver song of crickets. I went to where Dark stood nervous and snorting by the side of the path. I cut the stag free and heaved it into the brush, strapped my axe to my back again. We were no great distance from the glade, a mile, maybe less. When I looked into the crowding blackness I saw no torches, heard no searchers' cries. Wherever she'd come to rest, Aelfgar's grey mare had not made it to the glade.

Two choices I had, and neither of them good. I could leave Aelfgar and ride for help or I could sit here hoping help would find us.

Even if I were able to lift Aelfgar onto Dark's back, the ride to the glade would open his wound, set it to bleeding again. I was afraid that if this happened he'd be dead before I saw the watch striding the birm. I made the best choice I could.

It has always seemed to me that nothing is heavier, more unwieldy, than the dead weight of a Man who cannot move. If the gods had a reason for fashioning Men so large and long, I've never learned it. I got my hands under Aelfgar's arms and dragged him from the path. I got him through the brush, found him shelter in a small beech copse.

Of Rhodri ap Iau, the beardless boy whose life I'd spared in the night only to take in the day, there is only this to say: I left him in the path. I hoped that if there were wolves about they'd settle for an easy meal and not look farther to where Aelfgar lay, helpless and hurt.

Dark had felt my heels in his flanks before then, maybe never so hard-driven. I knew it: I'd be back with help quickly. Still, it was hard to leave Aelfgar, hard to think of him waking in the black night to find himself alone.

Dyfed was the first to see me. He shouted loud *hael!* and loped down from the birm, his red dog at his heels. "Ay, Garroc, I've been wondering where you've—" He stopped, looked past me. "Where's Aelfgar?"

I slid from Dark's back, quickly told Dyfed what had happened. "I need you, Dyfed, and another horse. I don't know where Aelfgar's has got to."

He wasted no time with questions, ran back to the glade for the things he would need. Werrehund dashed after him, barking high. Like water flowing into a breach, my men, dark shapes and curious voices, crowded me close, asking questions, some reaching for swords. Dark whinnied, danced skittishly. I had no soothing words for him, only wished, as he did, that the men would not press so close. Far back at the edge of the crowd I saw Blodrafen, head up, winter eyes gleaming.

Cynnere took Dark's reins from me. "*Wealas?*"

The men around me fell silent. In the quiet I heard the horses stamping in the picket line, heard the soft hiss of Blodrafen's breathing.

"There was only the one." My hands became fists, tight knots of bone and muscle. "The boy I should have let you kill."

Cynnere sighed through his teeth.

I was tired from the hunt, tired from fighting, heart-filled with fear for Aelfgar. I didn't stay to answer the questions rising around me, pushed through the crowd of warriors to the fire leaping and snapping in the center of the glade. Cynnere gave Dark to Godwig, told him to water the horse well, and followed me.

"Cynnere, who's on watch?"

He scooped up a waterskin from the ground, handed it to me. "Haestan, Ceowulf, and Aescwine."

Ay, it was good, that water, though it was warm from lying near the fire, though it tasted of leather. I drank the skin dry and tossed it to the ground. "Leave them here. Take the rest out to the ridge."

"Are you expecting trouble?"

"I don't know. I'm fair sure the boy was alone. Still, it wouldn't hurt to ride."

He agreed, left me and went among the men, snapping swift orders. Like a soldier's blade, those men were always ready. I watched them as they took up their weapons and chose their horses, watched them as they rode from the glade. Blodrafen was the last to leave, a small dark figure on an unsaddled horse. As though he felt me watching, he turned, looked back at me.

No way to see his face in the darkness beyond the fire's light, no way to see his eyes. Still, I did see him lift his head, hunch his shoulders as a man does who is striving to master some long-aching pain.

Dyfed came to stand beside me, leading Dark and two other horses. One was his dancy bay mare. A soft-tanned leather scrip hung from her saddle, stuffed with cloths for bandaging and the small stone pots of ointments and salves Dyfed was never without. He jerked a thumb at the *baresark*, now riding to catch up with the others.

"What's gnawing at him?"

He's hurting, I thought. And that is like saying 'He's breathing.' Wretched, grief-ridden wight. How could a man sort through the tangled strands of a berserker's pain to find and trace only one?

"I don't know. Who ever knows about him?"

"Damn spooky *baresark*." Dyfed spat into the fire. "You ready to show me where you left Aelfgar?"

Fat and fair, the Wanderer's moon lent his light to our ride.

Dyfed and I went in silence. My friend listened for *Wealas*, I for wolves. We heard neither, only the high shrilling of crickets, the piping of tree frogs, a fox's distant bark in the moment we sighted Rhodri's body. Moonlight caught and glinted from green eyes near the young Welshman's outflung hand; a water rat squealed and fled his dinner. The rat had been busy; finger-bones gleamed in the pale light.

Dyfed shuddered. "Where's Aelfgar?"

I pointed to the thickly shadowed forest to the left of the trail. "There, just into the woods."

I slid from Dark's back, Dyfed from his bay mare. I followed my own trail of beaten-down brush, broken ferns, the marks of Aelfgar's heels where they'd scored the earth. Dyfed came silently behind me, slipping through the beeches, passing over the snapping brush like a shadow.

I stopped at the edge of the copse, waved Dyfed forward. "In here."

He stepped past me into the clearing, then halted suddenly, looked back over his shoulder. "Garroc," he said, his voice thin as the moon's light, "you'd better come here."

My heart turned over hard in my chest, kicked against my ribs, but I didn't move. Tears I would never shed crowded in my throat. The unvoiced tenderness trapped within me began to die and rot all at once, began to change to dangerous grief.

Aelfgar is dead, I thought, and he'd died alone with no hand to hold at the end, no friend to whisper him good-speeding.

When I went to stand beside Dyfed, I saw that the copse was empty.

IV

WANDERER'S pale glow flooded the clearing, leached all color from the tall, glossy-leafed beeches, thickly clustered ferns. Dark patches on the moon-lighted ground, blood soaked the soft cover of old leaves and mosses. The cool touch of the rising wind breathed on the back of my neck.

Aelfgar was gone.

And yet, I knew that he hadn't crawled, hadn't crept away. He had no strength for that. Was it, then, that Rhodri ap Iau had not been alone in these woods?

As though he knew my thought, Dyfed laid a gentling hand on

my arm. "Aelfgar's here somewhere, Garroc. No *Wealas* has him—ay, think on it: What Welshman would carry off Aelfgar and leave his own friend to feed the rats? He's here. Somewhere."

And, ever a man to act upon his own thoughts, Dyfed began to search the clearing for signs. But I stood where I was, caught in moonlight. Because I was listening for it, I heard the subtle whisper of brush carefully moved aside, the dash and scurry of small night-creatures fleeing Dyfed as he made his way back to the path.

Loud in the night stillness, wings clapped and a wood dove came to perch in the tall beech beside me, dropped one sleepy note into the night.

And I thought, I should be searching, too. I should be quartering the forest looking for Aelfgar. But I didn't move, only stood in the moon-dappled clearing, still as though I were one of the deep-rooted beeches grown to guard this place. The shrilling of crickets, the distant shriek of a hawk-caught squirrel, had no more substance than memories.

Feathers whispered like wind over water. The dove spread her wings and preened.

The hair stirred on the back of my neck. Something moved in the night, a thing unseen. I tasted the night-breeze. Among the braided scents of the wildwood I found the dark, rich smell of earth, the lighter scent of crushed ferns, the deep musky odor a wildcat leaves when he marks his territory.

The wood dove sighed again, rustled her wings.

Sometimes it is true, Sif, that my heart knows a thing moments before my head begins to understand. So it was then. In the empty place between knowing and understanding, I looked up along a milky shaft of moonlight to where the dove rested. All in one moment I understood what I knew.

In the woods behind me I heard bridle iron chime, heard Dyfed speak to one of the horses. I knew he had found no sign of Aelfgar, and I knew why. Relief warmed away cold fear. I knew that Aelfgar was safe.

The breeze shifted a little, strengthened. The dove murmured deep in her breast, spread her wings, then settled again. The night-breeze spoke with a voice I knew.

Prydydd, the breeze said.

I felt my own smile warm me like sun's light. I knew the Welsh word. In our speech we say 'skald.'

Prydydd, the dove sang.

Eyes filled with Wanderer's silver, I lifted my hands, cupped as though begging a boon. Or accepting a gift. The night air warmed, tingled along my skin. Sudden fierce eagerness filled me as moonlight glinted on the dove's wings. That pure thin light glowed in her eyes, and I thought of stars the color of amethysts, stars I'd never seen but in Lydi's dreams. The dove caught the breeze under her wings, glided down to my hands. She rounded her breast, settled easily.

In me, eagerness became longing, and that, too, was a fierce thing, but I held her gently, all the while afraid that my hands, too used to grasping a war-axe, could never be gentle enough. With the tips of scarred fingers, I stroked breast feathers the color of silky fog. Light as mist she was, and her heart beat fast against my palms. She spread her wings, covered my wrists.

I felt Lydi in my arms, the dove in my hands, all at the same time.

Then there was only Lydi.

Slender as reeds, bones light and as delicate as the dove's, she stood only as tall as my chin, had to tip back her head to show me her blue eyes, alight like the stars she dreamed for me. Wanderer's pale glow shimmered in her dark hair, and that hair spilled like a mantle across my arms. She laid her head on my shoulder, covered my heart with her hand, and all the loneliness of the winter past drifted from me as easily as mist rises to the sun.

My longing was sweeter now, though not a tame thing.

Still closer she pressed, warm along the length of me. I didn't know whose was the trembling, hers or mine.

"Ah, my Lydi, how is it with you?"

"Better now," she whispered, her breath warm on my neck.

Then gently, reluctantly, she pushed away from me and Wanderer's light filled the place where she'd been. I reached through the thin silver glow, not ready to let her put even the small distance of a step between us. But she held up a hand, lifted her head to listen. Dyfed no longer tried for silence as he searched the woods for our missing friend.

"Garroc, you're not alone."

"No," I said, "Ghost Foot's with me."

Laughter sparkled in her eyes. I found it hard to breathe seeing that light.

"Do you really call that man Ghost Foot? The horses are quieter than he is."

"He's not trying to be quiet just now, my Lydi."

And he'll be here soon, I thought, for he'll find no sign of Aelfgar and come back to wonder and talk of armed searching parties.

The breeze dropped, the night grew cooler again.

"Lydi, the man who was here—"

"That long golden man. He's your friend?"

"Aelfgar. Where is he?"

"In Seintwar." She smiled again, and lifted her hands to the sky. Wanderer's light lay all around her like a shimmering mantle. Real she was, warm and smelling of her gardens and the forest; still it seemed that I could see through her. Or into her. Magic sighed in the air around us, warm as Lydi's breath on my skin. As a dream might, a shadowy dove took form within her, spread wings, leaped to greet the starred sky.

Fear crept like ice into my heart. Lydi began to tremble and I saw the stars through the dove's eyes. This time the stars were no small amethyst lights. This time they shone bright as suns. And ay, Sif, you know what is true for Dwarfs: Who sees the stars that way is closer to death than life. That much of her strength had my Lydi spent in her magic this night. And though she can snatch that strength back, heal herself as well as she heals others, still I always fear for her.

"I was flying." Lydi's voice softened with wonder, deepened with joy. She didn't speak to me now. She spoke as a child does who tells over her joys privately and to herself. The dove in the heart of her folded her wings tight, dropped past brilliant stars and dark trees, glided down to the earth again. "I saw your Aelfgar."

Then joy vanished. Sorrow, deep-running, filled Lydi's blue eyes with sudden tears. "And I saw the man by the stream."

The darkness trembled around me. I am a soldier and some dangerous things I love. Others I flee as a man flies from plague. Grief was one of those. Hard it was, a cold shame, to stand there feeling her sorrow and knowing in the heart of me that I wanted to turn away.

"I couldn't help the dead man, Garroc. And I couldn't leave your Aelfgar here to die."

No, she couldn't; it was not her way to turn away from any who needed her help. None knew that better than I. And it may be that there was some courage in me, even then. What there was, I spent. I crossed the moon-silvered distance between us, held her as gently as I'd held the dove.

"My Lydi," I said, "we're a half-day's ride from Seintwar." With my rough fingers I wiped the tears from her face. "Tell me. How is it Aelfgar's in Seintwar now?"

"I am not always a dove," she whispered.

A cool breeze caught the witch's hair, lifted it from her shoulders, sent it rippling around her. She stepped back from me, raised her arms, palms to the sky again, called visions. There was no shadowy dove within her now, but a sparrow hawk, a dark-winged kestrel, head high, eyes gleaming. Almost I heard the kestrel's proud cry winding through the night, out beyond the stars. Almost I felt the rush of wind under her wings. Held gently in the sparrow hawk's talons, something small stirred once, then stilled. Then the kestrel and its burden, the light tingling of magic along my arms and face, vanished. The night stilled and Lydi came into my arms again.

"Garroc, none of us, even your Aelfgar, are only what we seem."

I held her, felt her shaking as one does who has run too far. "Why did you come back here?"

"To bury the dead. I didn't know the boy, but I can see he's a countryman. Maybe he needs a friend to send prayers to his god for him." She lifted her eyes, blue as the stars she dreamed, to mine. "What will you tell your friend Ghost Foot?"

I didn't know what I would tell Dyfed. I needed everything I could summon from heart and soul just to think, and suddenly there was no time for it. Leaves rustled behind me, a twig snapped. I turned to see Dyfed standing in the shadows, head cocked, one eye on the witch in my arms.

"Ah, Garroc, I see you've found a friend." Moonlight and night-dark flowed across his face, hid his expression from me as he stepped into the clearing. "Though not the one we've come looking for."

A swift smile lighted Lydi's eyes and it seemed to me that I felt her heart beat fast with a joy unlooked for. Her hair flowed along my arms, trailing warmth behind as she turned. "Cyfaill!"

Dyfed stopped, cocked his head again and squinted into the moonlight. "You," he whispered. "Lydi?"

Lydi laughed, held out her hand to him. "Ay, me, Cyfaill. Now you call yourself Ghost Foot?"

He smiled. Not the familiar wry twist of his mouth I'd come to know. This was a different smile, bright and sprung from the heart of him. So he would have smiled when he was a boy, I thought, before the world lost its ability to surprise him.

"Garroc calls me that. I call myself Dyfed." He dropped to his heels beside her. "It's good to see you again, Lydi."

"And you, my friend." Fingers light, eyes soft with some memory I didn't share, Lydi brushed his white hair from his forehead, traced the thin scars, the faint trail which began at his temple and led to the place where his left eye used to be. "It's been a long time."

Dyfed's smile faded, replaced by the shadow of some old pain. He hid that pain beneath questions he likely already knew the answers for. "Aelfgar? Lydi, is he with you?"

"In Seintwar," she said gently. "A friend watchês over him and he's safe."

"Is he badly hurt?"

She brushed her dark hair from her cheek. I saw her hand tremble. "He was. But he's strong. And so am I."

She is. I'd seen and felt that strength before now. Yet she'd spent much of herself in magic this night. Lydi began to shake as though with sudden cold. If I'd known how to do it, I'd have given her all my own strength. All I could do was gather her close and hold her.

I looked at Dyfed—or Cyfaill—and saw that he thought much as I did. And so I understood that he not only knew Lydi, he knew her for a witch.

Dyfed and I hauled Rhodri's body from the path as Wanderer fled before quickening clouds, storm clouds riding an east wind. Were it a matter for Dyfed or me to decide, we'd have left the Welshman there to feed the wolves, but because Lydi asked it, we covered the body with what stones we could find, crafted a rough and shallow barrow. Neither of us asked questions of the other as we worked, though questions hung between us in the rain-smelling air. All the while we worked, Lydi sat by, still and silent. She didn't speak until we were finished. Then she thanked us for our labor.

One stag remained of Aelfgar's kills for Dyfed to bring back to the glade. I went to help him tie it to the brown gelding's back. As I worked I watched Lydi kneeling by Rhodri's barrow, heard her whisper words in a language I didn't know. Dyfed told me that the words were prayers to Rhodri ap Iau's White Christ.

V

I leaned my back against a boulder. Though the night was cool, the stone still held some of the day's warmth and lent it to me now as I sat by the stream, Lydi in my arms. Only a moment ago I'd felt her fall into sleep. Now, sighing once, Lydi nestled closer to me, shivering as the east wind quickened. I stroked her arms gently, reveling in the smoothness of her skin beneath my own calloused palms, breathed the tangy scent of herbs in her dark hair. I traced the line of her cheek, held her closer as the wind whispered through the wildwood. The fierce, sweet longing I'd felt only an hour ago was tamed to an ache of tenderness.

Dyfed came to sit beside me. Dyfed the healer, Ghost Foot my battle-friend and scout. Now Lydi called him Cyfaill. I'd known this Man as a friend for several years and yet suddenly it seemed that I knew very little about him, not even his name. He sat cross-legged, hunched a little. When he looked up, he smiled. And ay, it was the old wry smile I'd come to know well.

"Cyfaill." I tried the unfamiliar name and found that it suited him. "Lydi calls you Cyfaill?"

He shrugged. "It's a name, more or less."

It was a good name; in the Welsh tongue it means Friend.

"Will you tell me, Ghost Foot?"

Dyfed shrugged. "I was Cyfaill a long time ago, and—now I'm not."

Sad his words, spoken as though no one had called him Cyfaill since the Aesir-gods first made the world. And yet, young as he was, 'a long time ago' he could have been no more than a child. When I said this, he twisted a smile.

"A few things I've been, Garroc, but never a child." His expression grew thoughtful as he looked at Lydi sleeping in my arms. "But you, *dvergr*, you needn't waste words on any tale of your own. Wager I know now where you've been spending your winters." He scowled. "Or did till this one past."

Ah, Sif! In that moment I understood a thing that most men learn soon or late: It is one matter to go roistering with a friend, passing pleasant nights with what women are willing. It's well and truly another matter to sit with a woman—who is the friend of your friend—sleeping in your arms and try to speak of love. Your words will seem fair to you, but they will seem otherwise to your long-memoried friend, for he has heard them all before.

"Ghost Foot," I said, not comfortably balanced between amusement and the wish that he would attend to his own business. "You're too long and tall to be Lydi's kin, ay? It'll go better for all if you save your kinsman's frowns for when they're needed."

He laughed, a bright sharp sound. "Agreed. But can a friend ask this: Is it well with you two now?"

Perhaps Lydi heard his question; though she still slept, she reached for my hand.

"You think it hasn't been?"

"You hold your witch like you've found a lost treasure. Would you have been wintering with me in Rilling this year gone if you hadn't lost her for a time?"

When I didn't answer, Dyfed nodded slowly, thoughtful again. After a moment he squinted at the thickening clouds.

"The most part of the night's gone, Garroc. We"—he glanced at Lydi, then shrugged a little—"or one of us—should be getting back to camp."

And so the time had come to think again, to consider the ten men who waited for us at the glade, the one who waited in Seintwar. I gratefully took the chance to change the subject.

"Ghost Foot, you know Seintwar, ay?"

He nodded. Something in his expression told me that he knew it well; I understood without having to be told that he'd learned his healer-craft there.

"But Aelfgar doesn't know the place or the way back," he said. "Someone will have to fetch him." Suddenly he smiled. "I don't think you'd thank me for offering to do that."

"Probably not." I remembered Ecgwulf's owl-voiced tales of the witch-haunted wildwood, heard again the sharp fear in old Aescwine's voice when he'd challenged Dyfed the night before. "And I wouldn't thank you for telling the men that Aelfgar is mending with a Welsh witch."

Dyfed had considered that already. "I'll tell the others that he wasn't as badly hurt as you'd thought. I'll tell them we brought him to some farmer that we know from winters past. It wouldn't be too much of a lie. These woods aren't always Welsh lands and we do have some friends here—though they live a bit farther south, ay? I'll tell the others that you thought it best to stay with Aelfgar. When will you be back?"

"Two days. Three maybe."

It seemed to me that Dyfed's smile was made of mostly wistful-ness now. "Maybe three, ay? Well enough."

But one more thing I'd thought of, and spoke of it now. "The *baresark*—"

"What of him?"

"Peace between you two, ay?"

Dyfed scowled. "I don't like that madman; I don't trust him."

"It's not a matter of liking him or no, Ghost Foot. And he's proven himself trustworthy so far. I need you both. It's a matter of that."

He said nothing, but if there were some things I didn't know about Dyfed, others I did know. He'd do his best to keep peace between himself and Blodrafen, and he'd do it for my sake. Our decisions made, Dyfed went to get his bay mare, caught her with only a little difficulty. After he'd swung into the saddle, took the stag-laden gelding's reins, he listened to the forest, sniffed the wind, then squinted at me.

"Tell Lydi . . ." But then he abandoned his thought unspoken. "Ask her if she can spare me some linen for bandages and some of her ointments and salves."

"I will."

Cyfaill, Dyfed, Ghost Foot looked at me for a long time before he spoke. "*Dvergr*, come back to us, will you?"

Bridle iron rang like an echo of a war-song, Lydi stirred against me, closed her fingers round mine. Warm as welcoming she was, and I thought then that if I'd made no promise to Erich I would never leave the wildwood again.

I chose from among my friend's names and called him by the one I'd given him. "Ghost Foot, two days, maybe three. Depend on it."

Dyfed put his heels to the bay mare's flanks. She jerked her head against the pressure, danced and snorted, then settled into the smooth trot that made her a good horse for long riding. The brown gelding kept the easy pace.

For a time I listened to hoofs clattering on the path. When I no longer heard them, could not feel them through the earth, I listened to the rocks in the stream bed singing as the water hurried over them. Sometimes I thought about Dyfed, wondered what he'd been a long time ago if not a child, wondered how he'd come to learn healer-craft in Seintwar. Most often, though, I thought about nothing at all, only listened to the night, and it seemed to me that some of the aching in me, the tenderness I'd taught myself to keep

well and strongly caged, eased as I watched Lydi sleep, as I felt
her heart beating slowly, steadily against mine.

Lydi woke toward dawn, when rain started to fall softly. Glistening drops of water shimmered in her hair, sheened her cheeks.
She reached sleepily to catch back her hair with one hand, wipe
her face with the other.

Me, I thought it a much better idea to kiss away the rain.

The witch lifted her face to me and laughed. "You can't kiss
it all away."

"Do you think so?"

"I know it."

She leaned back against my arms, turned her eyes to mine. In
one swift and breathless moment her laughter, the warmth of her,
ignited all the longing I'd kept tamed till now.

"Ay, well. Like it is you're right." I kissed the hollow of her
throat where the pulse beat quickened, felt the life-dance against
my lips. "But I can make it so you don't care whether it rains or
how hard."

"Do you think so?"

I nodded soberly. Rain fell harder, coaxed a rich and sweet fragrance from the earth as I gathered her close.

"How?"

I kissed her, tasted the rain on her skin. "Magic, witch. Magic."

Around us the wildwood woke to the day. Squirrels traveled
the high roads of the trees; a russet jay darted down to the beck,
flipped his wings and followed the breeze upstream. Lydi watched
the jay, then turned back to me, a smile dancing in her eyes.

"You are not the one of us who plays with magic, Garroc."

I cupped her face gently in both my hands. "My Lydi, tell me:
Will Aelfgar be well without you for a time?"

"Yes," she whispered. "Someone is there to tend him."

Her lips trembled, a small sighing. In her amethyst eyes I saw
all the dreams she'd shared with me since the night the Ghost
Moon ran full through a field of stars. And true it may be that
the two of us sat wet and chilled in the rain, but I knew how to
make a fire to warm us.

Somewhere beyond the wildwood's green roof, in a far corner
of the sky, thunder rumbled. In distant places men warred and
Thunor struck his mighty war-hammer against the mountains of
the sky to summon his father's Valkyries.

I might have thought of Erich then, of Penda King, who had
taken my lord north to craft a treaty so that he could better wage

a war. But ever it is that the fire love kindles in me drives out all thought of anything else. I spared nothing for warring kings and gods then.

"My Lydi."

She laid a finger on my lips and I saw a look in her eyes that matched the hunger in me. Rain hissed through the trees, danced on the surface of the stream. I gathered my treasure close again and between us we made such a loving that we didn't care whether it rained or how hard.

And that is magic of a kind.

VI

THE rain stopped mid-morning; the thunder in the east rolled away to leave the sky again peaceful. As it does in late spring, the sun broke quickly through the dark wall of clouds, sent its light through the wildwood's dripping roof in long misty columns. I led Dark to the rain-racing beck, stood with him while he drank. As I listened to the water run I watched Lydi kneeling by the stream's edge.

The freshened breeze played with her hair, sunlight danced along her arms. She dipped her hands into the water to drink and I saw diamonds spill between her fingers. When she turned to smile at me, I saw that the blue-dyed tunic she wore would be a while at drying. I sighed to see the shadows of her breasts beneath the thin cotton as she sat back on the wet grass, held out her hand to me.

"Come sit by me," she said.

I needed no second invitation, needed only to feel Lydi warm against me again. I held her close and she rested her head on my shoulder, her hands on mine. When she asked me where Cyfaill, Dyfed, had gone, I told her that I'd sent him back to our friends.

Despite the warmth of the morning, Lydi shivered, looked suddenly lorn and lost. "You've come warring?"

I took her hands in mine, held them tight, for I feared suddenly that she would fly from me. My healer-witch does not thrill to the deeds of war, has little love for the lords and kings who fill barrows, make fuel for pyres. In those times, Vorgund was master of the land where Lydi lives and she well knew the enmity between her people and mine. But Lydi strives always to keep away from

the feuds lords make for themselves. She says that a healer's only
concern is to heal.

Always I thought this was a good thing, and so I told her easily
about the border patrol, told her about the Dwarfs and Men waiting for me at the glade. But I didn't speak of Halfdan's death, and
my silence had nothing to do with whether or not it was a good
thing to let a woman of the *Wealas* know that the Marcher *cyning*
was gone from his people.

We are heart-tied, Lydi and I. She needed only to listen to my
silence to know of the fettered grief in me.

"What have you lost, Garroc?"

A *cyning*, I thought, a friend who'd taught me war-craft and
who took no more than he needed of the ragged shadows of my
skald-craft.

"Halfdan is dead."

Lydi had never known my *cyning*. Still, I'd spoken of him often
and so she knew this was no small hurt. In her eyes I saw the great
tenderness she feels when she is wanting to heal.

"Garroc, will you come home with me?"

"Only for a time."

She nodded slowly, as though she'd expected my answer but
had hoped for more. She ran her slender fingers through my hair,
tugged a little at my beard, then laughed suddenly. "You need a
combing, man dear! And a shearing, I think."

I agreed that it was so, for I'd come from winter shaggy as an
untended mountain pony.

Nimble and light, Lydi's fingers stroked my arms, my hands,
as though touching memories. She found the long arrow trail along
the inside of my arm, touched the ridged scar gently, then turned
her eyes to mine. "This is new. Who tended it?"

"Dyfed." I bethought myself and added, "Cyfaill."

A small frown furrowed her brow, and to me it seemed the
frown of a teacher who comes upon an adept's work and wonders
if he has remembered all he'd been taught. She lifted my arm to
inspect the marks of Dyfed's healer-craft. I made a tight fist and
the scar writhed over the play of muscle.

"He did his work well, Lydi." I sat silent for a moment, thought
of riddling Dyfed who was himself a riddle. Then, like Aelfgar
reaching for the answers to one of Dyfed's word games, I seized
upon the shining pieces I could at once see, hoped they would cast
light on the shadowed parts. "Was it you who taught him?"

Dark as violets Lydi's eyes are when she is thinking. She broke
my embrace gently. "Cyfaill must tell his own story, for how can

I know the whole of another's tale?" Lightly she rested her hand on my shoulder. "And, however it is, I'm not the one who plays with storytelling, Garroc."

Cold, haunting like ghosts, memories of lonely winter came stalking, lay across my heart like a wolf's shadow on snow.

"Nor am I, my Lydi."

"*Prydydd Distaw*," Lydi whispered. Silent Skald.

Well, it was a good-naming, Sif, and one I'd set about earning. I'd have been a fool to think Lydi spoke it as a challenge. But in those days, though even bold Penda King knew me for a good scout and a brave soldier, I was not widely known for wisdom in matters of love.

And a shadow-wolf snapped hard at my heels.

I drew away, angry that this matter should rise so soon again between us. Coldly, I said, "Are we going to talk about my heart and my soul again, Lydi? Is that why you sent your dreams to find me?"

She didn't answer for a long time, and that was strange, for I'd expected her quick temper to rise flaring. When at last she spoke, her voice was a pale thing. The past winter had been no easier for her than it had been for me.

"Man dearest, I dreamed because I couldn't help it. I gave you the dreams because . . . I couldn't help it. I missed you, Garroc. I wanted you to know that, and I wanted you to find me, and I wanted—"

Lydi's eyes flashed, jewel-bright; her hands reached for mine, stopped, then fell away like broken-winged birds. As fast as it had flared, that quickly did my anger cool. I held her again, felt her heart beating fast with fear. Her heart's pace matched my own.

"My Lydi, I've found you. But I haven't changed." I faltered, my words trapped inside me by the fear that there was nothing now to speak of but the ghosts which haunted me. That I could not do. "I am only Garroc Silent Skald, and so I am no skald at all. Still, all there is of me loves you."

Lydi said nothing, only offered a hopeful smile and her silence for truce. Even then, I knew that truce is only the illusion of peace. But knowledge is not wisdom, and wisdom is hard-bought. I reached for the illusion eagerly.

"Take me home now, Lydi, and comb and shear me and show me what you've done with Aelfgar."

Violet-eyed, she agreed.

•   •   •

We traveled through the forest using paths we both knew, followed the sun, climbed stony tracks to the Cambrians' foothills. Sometimes Lydi spoke to me in the soft, sweet voice I'd known in dreams, told me how the folk fared in Seintwar, told me that her gardens grew strong in the mother-earth, what the doves said in Gardd Seren. And sometimes she was silent, resting easily against me. Then our hearts beat to the same rhythm and it was as though the empty winter past had not separated us. Then in unspoken accord we let the singing of birds, the gossip of squirrels, the sighing of the wind, fill the quiet. Our truce was not a hard thing to honor.

After one of these silences Lydi stirred in my arms, tipped her head back to see me.

"I have been wondering about your Aelfgar."

"Tell me," I said, though I knew what her wondering would be.

"He has the seeming of a man, but when I reached to touch his heart, to stand beside his soul, it was a boy I felt."

Lydi spoke of her enchanted healing easily, framed the wonder and the joy of it as though she knew nothing more natural than touching a man's heart, standing beside his soul. Trying not to feel uneasy about the magic, I held her closer as I guided Dark across a swift-running stream.

"None of us are only what we seem, my Lydi."

She laughed to have her words given back to her. "No, none of us are. Is he a soldier then, like you?"

"Yes, and a good one. But he's a better hunter. I think he'll make a good scout." I reached again for the riddle of Dyfed. "So does your friend Cyfaill."

Lydi's laughter carried the same delighted ring Dyfed's did when none could unknot his puzzles. "Does your healer choose your scouts for you, Garroc?"

"Dyfed *is* one of my scouts."

"Ah." She nodded, settled easily against me. "And a friend?"

"A good friend."

"Then I know Cyfaill is well."

She said no more about him, and as we rode I came to think that it would be a good idea not to press the matter. Lydi was right: Dyfed's tale must be his to tell. I could make no claim to it simply because he'd known my Lydi in his childhood, the long time ago when he was no child.

Just before noon we gained the high clear stonelands, the foothills of the tall shining Cambrians. Deep cool glens cut the world here, Dark's hoofs rang against rock more often than they whispered against soft earth. We threaded a maze of glens and gullies, heard water reveling in the heel-marks of ancient Frost giants.

Uneasy the feelings crowding close against each other in me. For, though I rode to Seintwar, to my winter-home, with a fair treasure in my arms, a witch who would readily warrant my safe passage through these stony hills, I didn't ever forget who was the lord of this place. Neither did I forget that Erich War Hawk had sworn an oath of vengeance against the Welshman Vorgund, an oath I'd promised to help him carry out.

My war-axe a cold weight of iron against my back, Lydi warm and light in my arms, I thought it strange to be riding home to Seintwar trying to balance a hunger for peace with a promise of vengeance.

The cool evening breeze brought the sound of cattle lowing from the valley below. I smelled thick peat-smoke from hearth-fires, and once, when the breeze shifted, the stinging scent of the manure the farmers plough into their fields. I slid from Dark's back, steadied him while Lydi found a comfortable seat without me. Dark stood still, content to swat flies with his tail and nod in the late sun as I leaned against his shoulder to watch sparrow hawks dance with the sky high above Seintwar.

Lydi tells me that in times past her little valley bore the name of a goddess, that Dwarfs and Men called it Glyn Rhiannon. And she tells me it was a good-naming, that Rhiannon has a great love for the birds, her own singers. Now the valley is called Seintwar, for the Men who live there have gone over to a new god, the young Christ, and the Dwarfs who live there worship their old gods quietly. For the sake of peace, the folk of the valley—Dwarfs and Men—call the place Seintwar, and the Christ's priests like the sound of it.

Seintwar, too is a good-naming. Welshmen say 'seintwar' when they mean sanctuary, and all who live in this high and stony part of the Welsh country know that no one who comes to Seintwar's witch for help and healing need ever fear that he will be given into the hands of his enemies.

Yet, though the valley is no longer named for the goddess, she must be near, for the music of Rhiannon's birds fills Seintwar. The drumming of the woodpecker, the wheatear's harsh *chak!*, the swift's chatter, are countered by the blackcap's sweet whistle, the wren's liquid notes. Flashing blue kingfishers dart over the river, rattling; jays and hooded crows sound rowdy songs in the fields.

I'd never seen the valley in spring, never seen it green and thriv-
ing. I'd been here only in winter, when snow covered the hills,
blanketed the fields, when ice laid a hard cold shield over the river.
Now I saw Lydi's valley with new eyes and I filled myself with
the sight, hoarded each sound and scent as though they were jewels.

The valley lay between softly rounded hills east and west. A narrow vein of silver, a slender river, cut through north to south. That
river watered marshes in the low southern end, rich dark-earth
farmlands mid-valley, and deep forests the high north end. I
searched the trees for a place I knew where doves flocked. Gardd
Seren, the witch's star-garden, lay in those woods and close by the
water, at the river's stony shore, stood Lydi's house.

A flight of doves, wings flashing in sunlight, wheeled high above
the trees, showed me what I searched for, the small stone cottage
I'd known as my *winter-seld*, my winter-home. Light as the breeze,
Lydi touched my shoulder. Blue eyes bright with silent laughter,
she asked me if we'd be standing here till night.

I thought it might be a good thing to watch the stars replace
the sparrow hawks in the sky. But I told her no, we wouldn't be
standing there that long. After a time I took Dark's reins and led
him down the gentle slope to the river, brought my Lydi home
to Seintwar.

VII

LYDI'S cottage lies in a broad clearing at the foot of a wooded hill.
It is shaded by oaks and straight slim beeches, hedged round on
all sides by gardens. And it lies under a sky that is not like the
sky anywhere else in the world. One who comes unaware into that
place thinks he has wandered into the land of dreams.

Ay, it rains and it shines from that sky; that sky is bright in
daylight, dark at night. But in all times, day as well as night, the
sky over Gardd Seren gleams with stars. In a far time the witch
who was my Lydi's grandmother wove *wundorcraeft*, made the
day sky a garden of stars. Lydi's own mother had the care of the
star-garden in the years when the king of the *Wealas* was called
Arthur, but this witch died young, didn't have a long time to stay
in her garden. Since then, Gardd Seren has been tended by my
Lydi, and she says it is one of her deepest joys to live in the garden
that her grandmother made, the one her mother tended.

And this is true, Sif: Though I am not fond of magic, I have always loved to be in Gardd Seren. Maybe this is because I've made some magic of my own there, or maybe it's because we are none of us constant—not Dwarfs, not Men—and the things we fear in one place are not dreadful in another.

My witch's cottage is built of stone, the strong bones of the world. In the deep night-darkness I have been lulled to sleep by their murmuring. I have heard them sighing at noon, old stones rejoicing in the sun's caress. Always, night and day, those stones love the small, playful light of the enchanted stars. In the earth-beds surrounding the cottage agrimony and angelica grow, mountain mint and dog rose, chamomile, larkspur and hart's-tongue. Some are for healing, some for magic. Some my Lydi nurtures for the simple joy of their beauty. Their mingling scents—golden-green songs of the mother-earth, drawn by sun and woven by wind—make the air a heady thing to breathe.

Earth-garden, star-garden, Gardd Seren holds the sights and scents of enchantment. Of these sights and scents are woven songs only the heart can hear, songs made by a witch who worships an ancient goddess, who has put her soul into the hands of gentle Rhiannon. My witch weaves the garden-songs as a promise of light and hope, and she loves and needs her magic, embraces it as joyfully as ever she embraced me.

That evening, as we rode into the garden, I felt Lydi turn toward her magic, felt her eagerness to be down from Dark and with the injured man in the cottage, and no sooner was she foot to ground than did she leave me alone beneath noon's stars, alone with the sun-quickened scents of her garden.

I slipped the bit from Dark's mouth, let him stand and cool for a time before taking him to food and water. It was a good thing to do for far-traveled Dark, but also a way to get hold of the uneasiness creeping round in my belly, the sudden coldness of wondering how Aelfgar had fared during the night while Lydi had been with me.

Soft as the wind's murmuring, Lydi's voice came to me where I stood in the dooryard. She asked questions of someone, received answers I didn't fully hear. I waited for a moment, eyes on the stars in day's blue sky, then knew that they must have been good answers, for no one came to call me to grieve. Easy again, I led Dark around the gardens into the shade of the wood's edge and the small byre waiting for him there.

•   •   •

I stepped sun-blind into the cottage. My war-axe hung heavy in the straps on my back, heavier here than in other places, as though the iron clung hard to me, friend to friend. Dim and cool the cottage, the air a tangle of hearth-scent and cooking smells, smoke-blackened wood and freshly thatched roof; rich with the mystical odor of drying herbs and the sweet or pungent scents of oils, salves and powders. Shelves lined the walls, filled with stone pots, twists of wicking, skeins of wool, candle-ends waiting to become whole candles again. Small carved boxes, each lid etched with symbols only Lydi could decipher, had places among cooking gear and drying flowers and herbs.

My Lydi lives with no borders between the homely tasks of cottage-living and the work of *wundorcraeft*.

Two south-facing windows admitted only a faint silvery glow. Lydi's bed lay beneath those windows, and often in winter I'd wakened there, my witch warm beside me, to watch a winter moon and listen to ice booming on the river. The high window in the west wall blazed with ruddy sun, and below it, on a pallet fat and newly stuffed with sweet rushes and straw, I found Aelfgar.

Lydi, kneeling beside him, turned quickly, motioned me to silence. Aelfgar slept deeply and well, had the settled look of having done so for a long time. Dust motes drifted along the shafts of light, made a shimmering mist, fell all around him to give him the seeming of a creature dreamed.

A shadow moved on the floor before me. I heard the hiss of an in-drawn breath, turned to see a honey-haired girl—*mann-cynn*, though not much taller than I. Brown eyes wide, she looked from me to the axe on my back, then slipped out the door, left behind only a faint whisk of skirts brushing the clean-swept floor, the memory of a quick swirl of bright-dyed wool the color of the sun.

I unstrapped my axe, set it to rest against the wall. "Your friends have grown shy, my Lydi."

She smiled. "This one, ay. Branwen, she's called. She comes to help me when I need her, but I don't think she's ever seen a *Sais* before last night." She held out her hand. "Come see how well she's cared for your Aelfgar."

Swift-footed Branwen had tended him well indeed. She'd cleaned him and combed him, and beside the pallet Aelfgar's shirt and trews lay newly washed and mended. He slept warm in the sun, covered by only a light blanket. I moved it aside, careful not to wake him. The flesh I'd last seen torn and spilling blood had healed to a purpling scar. This was Lydi's work. A month, maybe two, of Dyfed's care would have brought that scar. Lydi had made the healing in moments.

I touched the place where the wound had been, felt the faint, warm tingling of magic. Aelfgar was not wholly healed, not yet, but Lydi had taken him far from death's hand. She'd reached for his heart, stood beside his soul, come closer to him in that moment than anyone, his brother, his friends, ever had.

And close, bright as a hundred suns, she'd asked him: Aelfgar, will you leave the matter of bone and blood to me? Will you let me mend the torn flesh?

Like it was he'd been frightened, dazzled in the blaze of enchantment, wordless when the voice, soft as a dove's, asked him to trust. It is not a small matter to give the control of bone and blood and torn flesh to another, no little thing to suddenly yield the pain of a deep wounding.

How else but by gauging his pain will the dying man know he is still alive?

My hand shaking, I pulled the blanket high to Aelfgar's shoulders, covered the healing wound. But I could not cover the memory, crowding close, of how it felt to give the wound and the pain over to someone else.

Four years before, I'd been touched by Lydi's enchantment, and never have I forgotten the empty time when pain and sickness became Lydi's to master and not mine. Dark and cold the age it took to understand that I'd still lived when the agony of torn flesh, shattered bone, leaking blood, became only a deep, hungry need to sleep.

Lydi turned to me, sun-glints and faint starlight dancing in her dark hair.

"You slept for days," she whispered. "I had to wake you to eat, to drink. And you weren't happy to do either. 'Sleep,' you growled, stern and terrible-eyed. 'Woman, just let me sleep!' It was a week gone before I even knew your name."

And a winter gone before I went back to the Marches, back to Rilling, and Halfdan gathering his army for another season of war. By that time Lydi knew a good deal more about me than my name.

"Will Aelfgar sleep that deeply?"

Lydi leaned over him, touched his neck where the blood pulsed beneath sun-browned skin, brushed his gold hair away from his face. "He'll sleep that way tonight, likely most of tomorrow. Is he sweet-tempered, Garroc, or will I have another growling wolf to nurse?"

I stood, raised her to stand beside me. "Aelfgar has never

snapped at a soft hand. Like it is he has more sense than I do. Should we wake him soon?"

"Not yet. We've time."

"Ah," I said, gathering her close. "Time for what?"

Lydi tugged at my beard. Her smile caught my breath away. "Combing and shearing and a bath in the river."

It is a thing that I have always liked about my Lydi: She is full to brimming with good ideas.

Three times, maybe four, during the long purple dimming and into the night, I went to Aelfgar, coaxed him awake to drink some of the fine clear broth Lydi had made for him. I did this because I thought that he of the thousand questions would have a few about where he was and how he came to be there. But he had none, though he seemed pleased to see me. He was content to sip the broth or cool his throat with water. I wondered about this as I lay wrapped in Lydi's arms, covered by the mantle of her dark hair, wondered as I watched Wanderer stride across the black sky from the windows by her bed. Understanding came suddenly complete, settled upon me in the same moment that sleep did.

What question could Aelfgar ask that had not already been answered?

Lydi had touched his heart, stood near his soul. So close had she been to him in those moments of healing that each chance she had to know what others might think unknowable was also given to him, reflected like an image in a deep and still pool. In the moment of healing, Aelfgar, childlike and trusting, had asked his questions and my witch had gently answered.

True it is, Sif, that the wonder of day-shining stars is enough to give anyone reason to make a journey to Gardd Seren. Yet there is another thing that brings the folk of Seintwar up the long river road. There is a kind of peace that hangs in the air about Lydi's cottage, and the people of Seintwar come to taste it. I am not certain how they balance this with the commands of the Christ-priest who insists that they have no dealing with witches, but balance it they do.

Perhaps it is that the folk of Seintwar have long memories and know that there has always been a witch in Seintwar, tending Gardd Seren, tending the hurts and sicknesses of all who come to her. When the valley was called Glyn Rhiannon, the witch was Lydi's grandmother. After that, Lydi's mother saw the valley become Seintwar. The lives of those witches spanned six generations

of Men, and to the villagers and farmers that is so close to eternity
that no one bothers about the difference.

Once a young farmer told me this:

"After all the years t' witch who lives in your valley comes as
much part of t' place as wind and rain and t' sun. And if t' stars
shine there at noon, well, 'tis naught but t' way of things there,
yes? Soon you think there's always been t' witch and you stop trying to untangle tales of her doings from those of her mother—who
lived so long ago e'en your gran'da's uncle didn't remember her.
You forget that your witch had a grandmother. What matters is
that always a witch is there in the cottage at the river's head, part
of you. Like wind and rain and t' sun. And if priests tell you to
have no dealin' with wind and rain and t' sun, it'd be a hard thing
to do, too, wouldn't it?"

And so, the priest's wishes don't stop the folk of Seintwar from
coming to Lydi's cottage from time to time, to see the stars, to
feel the peace there, to beg a poultice for a wound, to ask for a
wash for a stinging and troubled eye, a drink to cool a fever or
to lure a sleepless child to rest. Each who comes brings some small
gift for the witch, a loaf of newly baked bread, a skein of wool,
new honey, a pot of freshly churned butter. The poorest of them
brings news and gossip. Lydi thinks this is the finest gift of all,
for after the valley-folk have gone, the news of their doings lingers
to help ward off the loneliness of long days and nights spent with
only wind, rain, and the sun as companions.

From the gift of one poor man I learned a thing about Vorgund
that would not otherwise have come to me were I riding the ridge
and chasing cattle-raiders.

I kept myself to myself when the folk of Seintwar came visiting.
Some knew me from winters past, some had only heard of me, but
even the most wide-minded of them knew it for a strange thing
when a Welshwoman takes to the company of a *Sais*. And if the
farmers and shepherds believed that their witch had a right to any
company she chose, still they didn't know how to greet the *corrach
Sais*, the Saxon Dwarf, with anything but unease.

I found enough to keep me busy. Though Aelfgar still slept the
healing sleep, at times I had to wake him to give him what food
and water he could take. This was not an unpleasant task, for each
time he wakened I felt him growing stronger, felt the hold of his
sleep-hunger lessen. Then I would sit with him in the spilling sunlight beneath the west window, watching the stars in the bright
blue sky, listening to him as he tried to find words to frame the

wonder of that. Sometimes we sat in silence, eating dry old winter apples and listening to voices as they came to us on breezes scented by the river and the garden, speaking the lilting Welsh language, the speech of enemies.

"*Wealas*," he said once. "Lydi's friends? Maybe Branwen's friends?"

"Lydi's certainly." I looked at him sidelong. "You remember Branwen?"

He nodded absently, had nothing to say about the honey-haired girl who'd bathed him and tended him. He was more interested in the state of my beard, close-trimmed and no longer winter-wild. This seemed to amuse him greatly, and a gleam of something part mischief, part wisdom, lighted his eyes.

"Ghost Foot told me that only two things will make a man wash and get himself trimmed and looking as fine as a king's glossiest horse."

"Ay? What are those two things, young Aelfgar?"

He smiled sheepishly and shrugged. "It's one of his riddles. It wouldn't be right to tell you the answer without telling you the riddle."

"Tell me the riddle, then."

But he couldn't, for he didn't remember the patterned words of it and only a little recalled the sense of it as something to do with things that get under a man's skin. And then, forgetting not to give me the riddle's answer, he told me that the cause of my newly tamed beard must be a woman, for he hadn't noticed that I'd been scratching too much lately.

"And she's very pretty, the *dvergr* lady who lives here. Don't you think so, Garroc?"

I told him I did think so and offered him another apple, but he didn't take it, said he was tired and would like to sleep again.

And so I left him to his sleeping and went out behind the cottage to work on a stonerow Lydi had only partly built before winter as a ward against the land-greedy wildwood. I enjoyed the work and it seemed to me, as I played at being something other than a soldier, that if all days could be as this one—blue and bright sky filled with stars, soft warm air filled with the garden's songs—ah, if it could always be like this, the truce Lydi and I had worked between us would grow to strong peace.

I hear the voices of stone in my bones, Sif, and their songs run through me like echoes; voices that are deep and hollow, or light as slipping scree, or dry and brittle as snapping shale.

Said one moss-cloaked rock as I lifted it:

> A river tumbled me,
> Rolled me along the backs of my kin.
> They smoothed me and soothed me
> And called out my name,
> Cried *welfar!* as I fled.

An old song, I said; I've heard it often. Tell me, friend, what is the name they cried after you?

The rock laughed, a deep sound, and repeated its song, then sang it yet a third time.

I smiled and patted its rough sides in the same way I have stroked Dark's broad shoulders. I told the rock that 'farewell' seemed a soft name for hard stone, but Welfar only said:

Dvergr, my son, how else should a rock be called who has been riding storm and flood since the time when old gods were young?

Seen in that light, Farewell seemed a good-naming.

I moved the old rock to its place in the stonerow, said: Welfar, will you ward my Lydi's garden?

Welfar didn't think that would be hard to do, sighed deeply as I found a place for it, sighed as though all the past winter had been spent waiting for just this place, just this task.

Like it is, I thought, the demands of impatient rivers are wearying.

I sat back on my heels to judge my work. This morning the row had not gone a quarter of the way along the cottage's back wall. Now it reached more than halfway.

Gauging the amount of work yet to do, I wiped sweat from my face, scratched my chin through my beard. In that moment while the stones sat quiet in the sun, I heard the reedy piping of an old man's greeting in the dooryard, the bright welcome Lydi gave him.

"I am Adda," he said. He hawked and spat. Though I could not see him, I thought it likely that the pause he made was for wiping his chin. It hadn't sounded like a well-aimed spitting. "I come to 'ee, *corrach*, to beg t' wrappin' for t' joint-ill."

Like it was ancient Adda was not only afflicted with joint-ill and poor aim; like it was he was more than a little deaf. I heard Lydi's answer clearly, smiled to hear her address him with an endearment to put him at ease. "Come sit and rest, Adda-*bach*. I'll fetch you water, cool from the river. You can tell me what you want and you needn't beg."

Adda groaned deeply. I imagined that he'd taken a seat on the smooth wooden bench outside the cottage door. At this hour, well past the sun's noon height, light and warmth was best there, made a good place to warm old bones. It was the best place to watch the enchanted stars dance.

"Ay, but *corrach*, beggin' now is what I do best. T' lord has driven me out. Ay, out, he has, and turned old Adda onto the road. A poor thing, a shabby thing for him to do for all that he needs a place to house himself and t' witches he gathers."

Cold I was then, and though they are always generous in lending their warmth, the sun-heated stones could not warm away the chill of fear that crept through me at old Adda's words.

Not all the Men of the *Wealas* embrace the whole of the White Christ's teaching. Some, men and women, still practice the old arts of druidism, some still go to dark places to find magic. We'd been glad to find none of those with Vorgund at the mist-dragon's vale, but we'd not been so shortsighted as to think we'd never see them again. Aescwine, old and canny Dwarf, knew that. He always rode the border-ridge between the Marches and the wildwood with one eye cocked for raiders, one for witches. If we smiled at his caution, we didn't laugh.

From the woods behind me a jay shouted. A butterfly came gliding, tapestried wings bright as Heimdall's bridge. It settled to rest on the stone I knew now as Welfar. As I listened, Adda sighed heavily, wheezed and spat again.

"But lords'll do 'at lords'll do and old Adda can say naught about it. Nor should I, for his father was m' own lord, the father before that m' father's lord. And that 'un, that father-lord, was *combrogi* and rode with the Bear King. A pity this lord can't recall what his gran'da knew."

Ah, *combrogi*! Legend gives them fame as gentle lords, the even-handed companions of the Bear King, the king no Welshman ever forgets. Lords call upon their names to win the favor of peasants; peasants call upon their names when they wish for more courteous lords. I've noticed that Arthur's name and the names of his war-band work as a fine talisman for the lords. I have not noticed that this talisman often works for peasants.

Adda wheezed again, rattled a bit in his throat, left the matter of lords and dead kings, steered straight for what he needed to know. "*Corrach*, they tell me in t' valley that you're a witch. An' my eyes're old, Lady—but I can see by yon sky that magic lives here. Be 'ee a white witch, Lady? For I've walked all this way in hopes that y'are; come to beg a poultice."

Sweetly, using a gentleness the old man could not often have known, my Lydi assured him that her magic didn't know darkness, bade him rest there in the sun while she went to make the poultice he needed.

I wondered where the old man had lived before Vorgund turned him out. I considered going round the side of the cottage and sitting with him in the sun, but after some thought, I turned back to my work. No matter how talkative the old man might be, he'd turn dumb as a door-post when faced with a *Sais*, and so I judged that there was no sense in adding the terror of a sudden meeting with a dire Saxon wolf to the rest of his woes.

Jays still laughed in the woods; the butterfly took wing and sailed to a thick cluster of dog rose, disturbed the golden bees foraging there. I worked steadily in the warm and fragrant garden, but I no longer listened to the stones talking, no longer tried to learn their names from the grinding songs. I didn't bind the stones, only piled them.

After a time, when old Adda had gone, I felt the air thicken, the sunlight grow heavy on my neck and shoulders. No wind stirred the air. When I walked to the river for a drink, I saw that the eastern sky, where no day-stars ever shone, had grown grey and hazy. I smelled a storm coming.

From the doorway of Lydi's cottage I watched Thunor come down the sky-roads above the river. Small trees at the edge of the water bent in the wind of his passing. Each time Wotan's son struck the tall clouds, the war-hammer giants called Crusher beat sparks from those sky-mountains, lightning shining like flung spears. In that god-light the dooryard, the gardens, the riverside, seemed like dreams of foreign places. As the god strode through Seintwar, my heart rose to the call of his wild wind, his terrible war song. Though it is not my truest calling, I have never hated being a soldier.

After a time, wrapped in blankets, barefoot and sleepy, Lydi came to stand beside me. She laid a hand on my arm in silent question and I told her that the old man Adda was much in my mind.

No longer sleepy, Lydi drew herself up, held still. "Not only Adda, I think, but Vorgund, too, yes?"

"Yes." I scratched my jaw through a shorter beard, asked what I'd wanted to ask all night. "Lydi, where did the old man come from?"

Stone walls echoed the clash of Thunor's hammer, lightning flared. Lydi's face shone white. The blue of her eyes deepened to

the color of violets at the shadowed edge of the wildwood as she
thought about my question.

It was never a matter of how she would answer me; Lydi's
richest coin is truth. It was a matter of whether she would answer
me at all, for she has very particular notions about her tradition
of sanctuary. The fact that Adda had not asked for it didn't mean
Lydi hadn't granted it. Had Vorgund himself come riding to her
with an army behind him, my Lydi would have told him nothing
about Adda if the lord meant him harm. In matters of sanctuary,
Vorgund and I might well have been one, and when she spoke at
last, Lydi's trust made me proud.

"By his speech I think he comes from the north, from the
highlands. I don't know more than that."

Outside the cottage Thunor raged, roared a message to me from
his father, called me back to the border and the glade where
warriors waited for me. Across the room, against the west wall,
Aelfgar slept as though no god's bellowing could ever disturb him.

"Can Aelfgar ride?"

Lydi nodded.

"Then we're leaving. Ghost Foot is riding patrol with two men
less than he should have, and old Adda made it plain that Vorgund
is waxing strong. Maybe he'd like to test his new strength on a
Saxon border patrol, maybe he wouldn't. My Lydi, I can't know
what Vorgund is thinking, but I know this: I have to go back."

Lydi looked at me long, and I knew she was thinking about the
slim and fragile truce we'd made between us. We'd taken good care
of that truce during the day and night past; we'd not strained it,
for it was yet a small thing, a young thing. But just for a moment,
in the flaring light, I saw pleading in Lydi. Then the light was gone
on a roll of thunder and the pleading was too.

Quietly, Lydi told me that if I would wait until after sunrise
she would have a horse for Aelfgar.

Outside Thunor still bellowed, and the only silence in the
cottage was the silence between us as I led Lydi back to bed.

In the hour before dawn, when the wildwood filled with the first
bird-song, when the scents of Lydi's gardens were things to be
tasted, Branwen came riding a dun mare and this mare she gave
willingly to Aelfgar. Though she seemed to have lost some of her
fear of me, still she didn't get too close and always her eyes were
more upon my war-axe than anything else. Gently, and with great
care, Branwen helped Aelfgar to mount, saw him settled. She
accepted his shy thanks silently, for she didn't speak our language

and could not answer him but with a smile. Saying nothing to me, she retreated to the cottage, safely away from dire wolves and weapons.

I was not thinking much about Branwen, and only a little about Aelfgar. Mostly I was thinking about Lydi, small and warm in my arms as I stood in the dooryard ready to leave.

"This is not winter," she said at last. "I know you can't stay, and I know you can't come and go as you wish. But, Garroc—"

She stopped then, her words caught in nets of conflicting feelings. One small hand she held clenched and fisted at her side, the other wide and open against my own heart. I reached for the tight hand, brought it up to my heart, stroked her fingers until there was no more fist.

Eyes bright, Lydi raised herself up on her toes to kiss me. "But I can make the distances between us smaller. Yes?"

Winged when she wished to be, Lydi could make distance vanish, could find her way to me along the sky-roads. I held her close, and so tightly that I felt her breath catch in her breast.

"Yes," I said.

I cannot say that with this promise given Lydi was content to let me go; I cannot say she let me go easily. But she said no more, only kissed me again, and went to speak a word of farewell to Aelfgar.

I turned to watch the newly risen sun spill gold into the river, saw last night's rain become soft grey mist. When I looked back to the cottage, Aelfgar was alone in the dooryard.

Pale and looking like he'd happily spend the next few days sleeping, he told me that though he didn't know just where we were in relation to the camp, he expected it would take us twice as long to get there than whatever time was usual, for he was tired and didn't think he would be doing his best riding today. "So it'd be good idea if we were going now, Garroc, ay?"

I said yes, it would be a good idea.

We rode for the river and I listened to our horses echo the thunder that last night had come to call me back to my men and my promise to Erich War Hawk.

Yet we didn't ride alone. As we went up the stony path to the heights where first I'd seen Seintwar two days before, Aelfgar pointed to the sky, showed me a kestrel, russet wings tipped with black. As we watched, the sparrow hawk wheeled and turned above the valley, sailing the sky east. Sunlight flashed along the kestrel's wings, her high *killy!* cry tumbled down the wind.

The witch had come to see that we made the journey back to our friends in peace.

Aelfgar was right in thinking that we'd be the whole day riding. We rested long at noon and more frequently as the day grew older. I tried not to grudge the time, for I knew I'd taken him too soon from Lydi's healing. Yet, though we often saw the kestrel riding the sky ahead of us, I was eager to be out of the deep woods before full dark. We passed the waterfall and Rhodri's barrow just after nightfall, and in a clearing, where the forest hangs back a little from the banks of the stream, the kestrel left us, flew deep into the forest.

Aelfgar watched until he could no longer see her, and when he looked at me I saw that he was tired, white-faced keeping his seat on the mare's back with more will than strength.

After a moment's thought, I said, "Aelfgar, about Lydi . . ."

His grin flashed in the gathering darkness. "You don't want me to say anything to the others, do you?"

"I'd be grateful if you remembered these three days as time spent with some farmers I know from winters past."

Aelfgar regarded me soberly for a time. Then his smile returned, bright and filled with mischief as he jerked a thumb at my newly trimmed beard. "Because maybe you wouldn't want such fine and handsome fellows as Haestan or Godwig to know about your Lydi, ay?"

I told him I hadn't thought about that, started to explain just why it wouldn't be a good idea to go back to our friends full of tales of a Welsh witch's doings. But he only laughed and turned Branwen's dun mare toward the glade. There was nothing for me to do but follow.

A thin veil of clouds covered the sky; Wanderer didn't shine brightly. Still, we didn't need moonlight to ride the last mile to the glade. We knew the way. Before long we heard the challenges of the night watch. We answered quickly, and Haestan and Godwig, those fine and handsome fellows, cried us glad *hael!* from the birms.

STACGA-MONA
(Stag Moon)

COME look at the moon, Sif. He runs high, and swiftly. The Wolf will not catch him tonight.

I have always been fond of the moon, always thought of him as one who understands some of the same things I do. True it is that we each believe we know how to keep one pace ahead of the Wolf's shadow.

He has many names, does the moon. Gods call him Mild Light and giants call him Speeder. The dead who have gone to live with Hel, with Loki's dark daughter, call the moon Wheel, for that is how they see him, spinning high through the night. *Dvergr* call him Splendor and we love him for the light he lends to darkness. These are not the moon's only names. Dwarfs and Men, we give the moon a new name each time he slips through the black jaws of the shadow-wolf.

In winter we call him *Wulf*, and *Is*, and *Sna*, for winter is a time for wolves and ice and snow. Then he is *Forewitol*, the Far-seer, and he is called so to honor Thunor's wife, who is Sif the Seer.

Men call the next moon *Saed*, the Seed Moon. Dwarfs call him *Scin*, the Ghost. All agree that the moon which follows is *Wraecca*.

In the seasons of summer, first the moon is *Stacga*, the Stag's moon; then as war and battle roll loud across the land, he is Thunor's, and then *Wicce*, the Witch's moon.

In the wealthy seasons of gold and brightest red the moon watches the harvest and the hunting, and so he is *Haerfest* and then *Hunticge*. Comes the time between fall and winter and he is *Wyrm*, the Dragon, lonely and old as the year.

107

I know the names of many things. I know all the names for gold and for gods; I know that giants call fire Greedy and they call the wind Roarer; I know that gods call the sky High-Arched, that *dvergr* call the night Weaver of Dreams. These things I was taught by a Man, and he was called Stane Saewulf's son.

Do you think it is strange, my Sif, that I didn't learn skald-craft from a Dwarf? Ah, but there were no *dvergr* skalds among the hungry fighters who came to the Isle in the time of the Pendragon and his son. And so my teacher was *mann-cynn*.

So old was Stane that his father rode the longships, fought in wars beside my own father, and Saewulf the longship-rider was a good skald, had taught his son Stane well. Because neither my father nor Stane believed that a god's curse should be the cause for Men to forget that once Dwarfs lived among them, Grimwulf Aesc's son gave me to his friend Stane for teaching when I was a boy.

It was not a hard thing to learn the old craft from Stane. The twinned histories, the ancient tales of Dwarfs and Men, lived in him. Stane had been taught these in the old way, knew each word of every tale as they had been passed to him by his father.

When he had proven his teaching and I my own skill, Stane showed me how to see clearly in the shadowless *skald leygr*, the wonderful storyteller's light. He taught me the way to find a new tale, how to bind it tight with poet's silver, words made from a mating of heart and soul, words born in the *skald leygr*. In that light, Stane told me, the memories of those who have died become torches of hope for those living. He told me that I must never think of the *skald leygr* as anything else but Hope's birthplace.

I never did think it was anything else. But for a long time I didn't understand that I, *Laestan*, had the right to traffic in the things of hope. Stane knew my feeling and he believed that I was wrong.

But, Sif, when do the young ever truly do more than nod politely to the beliefs of their elders?

Still, even in those unlighted times when I'd shut my eyes tightly to the *skald leygr*, I remembered the teachings of my old friend, of Stane Saewulf's son. One of the things he taught me was this:

"Men and Dwarfs, we are all riddles," he said. "We are puzzles to our friends, puzzles to ourselves. Who finds joy in riddling, pleasure in the patient stalking of the hidden truth, that man knows how to live."

But what do you think happens, my Sif, when truth becomes the hunter, man becomes the hunted?

To me, it seems that the man stalked by a truth he does not like to face becomes a brother to the wolf-haunted moon.

I

As he'd promised on the night we built the barrow for Rhodri ap Iau, Dyfed went back to the glade with a tale to make our friends believe that the young Welshman had not hurt Aelfgar as badly as I'd first thought. "A hard wound," he'd told them, giving enough of the truth to make his story worth believing. "But nothing like a deadly one. Wager Garroc lost the truth of the matter when he saw all the blood."

When Cynnere asked why it was that Aelfgar had been sent to strangers, borderland farmers, Dyfed told him that the borderland farmers were friends of his and mine. Then he asked Cynnere if he thought it would be better to let the wounded man lie out on the hard ground, cold in the night air and wet in the morning mist. Cynnere didn't think long before he agreed that likely Aelfgar would do better sleeping warm and dry for a few days.

And so, on the night Aelfgar and I returned to the glade, all saw what Dyfed had prepared them to see: Aelfgar, weary from riding, weak still, but safe now and mending well. Any number of willing hands lifted to help Aelfgar from Branwen's mare, but it was Blodrafen who offered his shoulder and strength for the prop Aelfgar needed, Blodrafen who helped him to a sleeping place by the fire.

I caught only one swift glimpse of the *baresark's* expression as tall Aelfgar limped beside him, but I was not fast in forgetting what I'd seen. His lean face, deeply lined and ravaged by the claws of some old grief, smoothed just a little; his ice eyes warmed to the soft grey color of the sky just before dawn. It was a strange thing to see.

The dun mare took her place among the rest of our mounts, but in the morning she was gone. Most thought she'd broken her tether in the night, gone back through the woods to friends and a manger filled with the sweet fodder farm-horses know as their due. So she had, for in the darkest part of the night, while Dyfed and I sat late before the fire and talked of Vorgund Witch-

Gatherer, we heard a kestrel's wild cry and knew that Lydi had come to show Branwen's mare the way home.

When the kestrel's cry faded, vanished into the night, Dyfed poked at the fire, urged it to bright life. I watched the shadow-dance of light and darkness play across his face, sat quiet while he worked among his thoughts and feelings. When he spoke at last, his voice low, his eyes on the flames, it was as though he addressed the fire and not me. "Is Lydi well?"

I told him she was.

He grunted thoughtfully, then cast a sideways look at me. "You, too?"

"Me, too," I said.

As he looked over the linen and small pots of oils and powders Lydi had sent, I wondered whether he'd answer some questions of mine. Before I could muster them, however, Dyfed turned the talk back to Vorgund.

About the Witch-Gatherer we held similar opinions: We didn't doubt Lydi's belief that old Adda had come from the high north-ern part of the Welsh country. We took it for given that Vorgund must be hiding himself in the northern mountains.

Dyfed spat into the fire. "But that's like saying he's somewhere on the Isle. We already knew that. More or less. Didn't know about the witches though, did we? That's not good. If he'd had *helle-cynn* with him in the spring, we wouldn't be sitting here now. Vorgund would have run through Halfdan's army like a plow through sweet earth, ay?"

He would have. And fire would have rained from the sky and the gods of dread would have done hard work. All witches were kin to my Lydi in magic. Not all of them were kin to her in spirit.

"Garroc, will you send a message to Erich?"

I told him that I would, and I didn't doubt that Erich would want to know that somewhere in the high places of the Welsh lands Vorgund was gathering witches.

Fire snapped, smoke curled away from the flames' tips then stretched high, drifted into the darkness. On the other side of the fire Aelfgar slept. As I watched him he twitched a little, started to curl tight, maybe to hold some dream close. But the pain of the yet unhealed wound caught him, and though he didn't wake, Aelfgar shuddered.

Dyfed started to reach for him, then stopped suddenly, drew his hand back carefully as though he'd encountered an adder. Be-fore I could question, another hand reached out of the darkness

behind Aelfgar, three-fingered, silvered with scars. The Blood
Raven stroked Aelfgar's shoulder, swept gold hair back from his
forehead. I couldn't see the berserker's face, only made out the
shape of him because I knew he was there.

Dyfed came slowly to his feet. Cool nightwind ruffled his white
hair, firelight gilded the edges of it where it lay along his neck.
His fingers twitched close by the sheathed dagger at his belt and
he cocked his head, gave his good eye full view as he did when
wanting to take careful aim at something.

I closed my fingers hard around his wrist. Cold his skin was,
as with fear, and so I didn't loose my grip, I tightened it.

Someone whistled to Werrehund and the dog yipped high in
answer. On the eastern birm Haestan called to Godwig, a joking
question. Flames played with the wind, danced high. In that moment Blodrafen withdrew his hand. For a brief space, firelight gave
bright glinting to the Blood Raven's cold eyes, then I heard a rustling as he walked away into the night.

Dyfed spat into the fire again. The burning wood hissed. "He's
like a dead thing, Garroc. He walks past me and I feel the cold
coming out of him like the air crawling out of an underground
place."

Then, as though he'd said too much, Dyfed gave me one sharp
look and twitched a smile. He slapped my shoulder in his old
friendly way and went off to find a place to sleep.

Alone with the fire and the night, I thought about the Blood
Raven and the light I'd seen glinting in his eyes. That was the second time I'd seen, not the baleful berserker's glare, but the kindling
of true affection.

The long days after Aelfgar and I returned, the last nights of
Wanderer's Moon, the first of Stag's Moon, were the fairest of
summer. Soft breezes carried sweet, deep forest-scent when they
came to us from the west. If the wind was an eastern traveler, he
brought us cooling rain. Once, when I stood at the edge of Cefn
Arth, near the stony path littered now with the clean-picked bones
of Rhodri ap Iau's companions, north wind and east wind met and
gave me echoes of the hard flat bleating of sheep from far down
in the valley. In the Marches, farmers hurried to shear the rich
wool from their sheep, rolled and sacked it before the highest hottest part of summer.

Like it was the Welshmen were shearing, too, hauling wary
sheep to the knife, piling the thick wool high. But soon the wool
sacks would be full and the *Wealas* would look for other amuse-

ments. Old songs would sound stale, old tales of courage seem brittle. I knew it would not be long before they would remember the feud between their folk and the *blaidd Sais*, the dire Saxon wolf.

I didn't forget that feud either. I remembered how I'd watched Thunor stride through Seintwar, making war with the sky giants. That night the thunder had echoed in me, sounded like battle-songs. And I had risen for those songs, taken up my axe, left the peaceful place I'd longed for all winter.

During those long sweet days I watched often for my Lydi, checked the sky for the dark-winged kestrel, listened to the wildwood's mingled songs for the wood dove. Though kestrels sailed over the Marches, none knew me. The doves in the forest sang no song I understood. And when I slept in the sun-dappled glade, I dreamed my own dreams, in sleep visited places my Lydi had never known, saw folk she'd never seen.

Grimwulf Aesc's son was one of these folk. I saw him often, the Fierce Wolf, my long-dead father. In my dreams I heard his voice, and it was not the heavy deep voice I knew. He spoke in the thin urgent way of ghosts.

Ghosts and the threat of battle, before them memories of the short time spent in Gardd Seren faded fast.

By the time Stag Moon's gleaming new horns hung bright in the night sky, Grimmbeald had been gone three days. He'd not thought his ride to Erich, his return to me, would take more than ten days and I hoped that he was right, for he would be missed. Though Aelfgar grew stronger with each day, Dyfed didn't think he would be able to ride patrol with us until the Stag was old. Two men always remained at the glade as watch, and so we were only nine patrolling the ridge now. We didn't ride in shifts as we once had; we were too few for that. Each night we set out at day's end and we didn't return to the glade until dawn. Always we rode untroubled by raiders. While my high-hearted warriors sometimes chafed at the long peaceful rides, I was glad of the quiet and I marked the time till Grimmbeald's return by carving a notch on a long smooth stick for each day that passed.

Just after dawn, on the day I would carve the fifth notch on my counting-stick, came a dove winging, smoke-breasted, amethyst-eyed, singing soft songs to draw me into the wildwood.

Of those gathered near the pale morning fire, three saw the dove alight, three saw the new sun shining on her wings, the bright gleam of her amethyst eyes. One was Dyfed, one was Aelfgar. The other, heart racing, was me.

We three, and Aescwine and Wulfsunu, sat waking before the fading fire. The rest had found places to sleep while restless Werrehund prowled the glade and Cynnere and Haestan walked watch on the birms. As though the dove softly sighing in the oak above him were merely a cousin to the countless birds who lived in the wildwood—no friend of his, no friend of mine—Dyfed yawned and stretched out on the damp ground. One eye bright with mischief, he said:

"Who's for a small wager? I'll stand the watch of any man who can guess my riddle. Any man who can't, stands mine."

Wulfsunu nudged me and grinned. Most often, Wulf guessed the word puzzles before any of us, and he had drawn the noon watch, hottest and longest of the day. Though he didn't lean forward as eagerly as Aelfgar and Aescwine did, still he gave Dyfed all of his attention. Wulf didn't like noon watch, would not have been unhappy to give it up to Dyfed.

Me, I had the dove in my sight, watched her settle beneath the shady oak boughs. With bronze beak and a delicately clawed foot, she began to groom grey breast feathers, and I wished my hands didn't feel so empty, didn't remember so clearly what it felt like to be filled with the dove, with Lydi.

Maker of riddles and wagers, Dyfed chose his word puzzle, cast his net. "Hangs by my thigh a wonderful thing," he drawled. "Below my belt, 'neath my clothes it swings. This thing of mine is stiff, long and stout—"

Wulfsunu snorted. "So you say, Dyfed. Might be I've heard another account."

Dyfed didn't deign to reply, but Aescwine's bellowed laughter sent the dove winging. I cursed old Aescwine silently.

Hands working at the knots and tangles of the fouled gamesnares, Aelfgar sat silent for a moment, watching the dove circle the glade. From the corner of his eye he studied her, then smiled secretly into his beard. He put the snares aside, leaned forward eagerly and said:

"Go on, Dyfed."

"Yes?" Dyfed feigned doubt.

"Yes," Aelfgar said firmly, glaring at Aescwine, who had not yet tamed his laughter.

The dove settled again, closer now to me. Head cocked, amethyst eyes bright, she looked as though she, too, wanted to hear the rest of Dyfed's riddle.

"This thing of mine is stiff," Dyfed said again. "And long and stout. I know a hole this thing will fill best when it's at full length."

He leered knowingly, nodded to Aelfgar, now his most attentive listener. "And this hole I've filled before, likely I'll fill it again—"

"Ay, Ghost Foot," Aescwine muttered, "I've never met a man more full of hopes than you."

Dyfed smiled good-naturedly, said softly, "Nor I a Dwarf more surely bound for two turns at watch than you, Aescwine." He sat up, leaned forward. "Can you say what it is, Aelfgar?"

Aelfgar didn't have the answer, only the illusion magicked by Ghost Foot's words. He looked down at his lap, then up at the sky, tangled his fingers in the disorder of game-snares. "Maybe I can say, Dyfed. But should I?"

"Of course you should. Why not?"

Before Aelfgar could draw breath to reply, Wulfsunu answered around a grin. "Because if this thing of yours is not what you lead us to think it is, you'll have to unmask the illusion so we can find the answer." He tried for a sober expression and mostly succeeded. "Want to do that, Ghost Foot?"

Dyfed scratched his belly, low, and yawned. "Want me to, Wulf?"

Eyes bright, the dove flew high, left in a whir of winged laughter only barely heard above Wulfsunu's protest and Aescwine's lusty roar. Someone among the sleeping roused, cursed the noise. Werrehund loped across the glade, head high and eager to join in the play.

While the red dog curled comfortably against Dyfed's side, I got to my feet, took up Aelfgar's snares.

"Ay, Garroc," Aescwine said. "Don't you want to know the answer?"

I checked the slide of my dagger from its sheath, strapped my axe to my back and smiled. "I know the answer."

Aescwine looked doubtful, but Dyfed nodded solemnly. "Garroc's the one who taught me the riddle."

That was true, and with it I'd won, with no dispute, one of the few wagers Dyfed had ever lost. Shortly after, my friend had discovered a deep interest in riddles.

Dyfed cocked a thumb at the snares. "Let Garroc go catch us some supper and let me hear your answers—and they'd best all be good ones or I won't be standing my next few turns at watch."

Some grumbling there was at that, and then a sudden burst of laughter as Aelfgar offered his solution to the riddle. It wasn't the right answer, but it was the usual guess and good-natured Aelfgar laughed along with the rest. I thought he and Dyfed seemed pleased with themselves.

• • •

I'd marked the direction of the wood dove's flight, north and
west. We'd known the forest there to yield us good trapping, and
as I walked, my hands were busy untangling the snares. The work-
manship was good, knots tight where they should be, nooses ready.
Blodrafen and Aelfgar had made these, and I knew by their condition that Blodrafen had used them last. Though he'd become a
good net-maker, a fine snare-crafter, the Blood Raven always left
the tangles for Aelfgar to smooth.

Though sunlight had begun to gather up the mist in the glade,
here beneath the wildwood's whispering roof the air still felt like
damp fingers, shadows yet seemed like night. I set the traps in hidden places near beck and pool. The last of them I placed in a thick
stand of high sedge near the stream where Rhodri's barrow stood,
then walked on toward the falls. Better to wait for my Lydi by the
water's silver tumble than in a barrow's shadow.

I took the rising path, damp earth and slick rock, to the top
of the falls, listening to liquid notes of water and stone. There is
a harp the *Wealas* play, small and tightly strung. Some of the notes
called from that harp cannot be heard, only felt in the deep places
of your heart. This morning the music of the falls sounded like
that, and I liked to hear it.

Lydi didn't keep me waiting long. When the ground mist began
to fade, as the last shadows of night crept back beneath oak and
rowan, I heard the dove's wings whisper, the fey wings of magic.
Like a cold-footed spider, dread's chill crept along the back of my
neck, for this was not Gardd Seren where *wundorcraeft* seems
comfortable and familiar, nor the birch copse where surprise had
overridden my mislike of magic. Hard it was not to close my eyes
as I held up my hands for the dove. Hard to keep still and steady
as the dove became a drift and tumble of heatless blue light and
the witch came into my arms.

I held her close, held her tightly. I held her so as a form of silent
apology, a wish that fear was not my first reaction to her magic.
It was a long time before the warmth of her, the sweet garden-scent
of her hair, the way her loose linen tunic, green as newest grass,
slid so easily between my hands and her soft skin, became the reason for not letting her go.

Lydi didn't go far once I loosed my hold, no farther than a step
back so she might see me. Her keen blue glance lingered on me,
and I wondered whether she'd sensed my fear. If she did, she said
nothing about it, only gathered up my hands, held them tightly.

"Have you been well, Garroc?"

"Well enough," I said. "And surely better now that you're here."

"Ah, *prydydd*," she said, then shifted course abruptly. "How is Aelfgar?" Her eyes darkened. "I wish he could have stayed longer. I wish I could have sent him back wholly healed. He's not in pain, is he?"

"No, no. He's still weary, but more of the game of pretending to mend than of any pain. Ghost Foot takes good care of him."

Because I could not help it, I freed my hands, let them wander through the dark river of her hair as I spoke. I was not thinking too much about Aelfgar just then.

Lydi looked up at me, laughing. "You must tell me something."

I told her I would, if I could.

Her eyes sparkled and the new sun on the water was not more brilliant. She stretched up on her toes, wrapped her arms again around my neck. Her breath warm and sweet on my cheek, she said:

"What is the answer to Cyfaill's riddle?"

"What do you think it is?"

"I'll gladly tell you what first comes to mind, man dear. But I suspect that what first comes to mind *isn't* the answer to Cyfaill's riddle. I've a feeling I'd be closer to the answer if I guessed dagger and sheath."

I shook my head. "Key and keyhole. And I would be happy to show you how like they are to what first comes to mind."

If sunlight were voiced, it would sound like my witch's laughter. "Maybe you should."

Then, as though she were no more substantial than the mist, she slipped through my arms, took me by the hand, drew me into the forest.

I stood no watch until the late part of the day; no one would miss me until then. I followed the witch willingly and we didn't go far. We liked the song of the waterfall and only needed a softer place than stone.

II

You have seen the circles on the land, Sif, circles of tall standing stones, or of high-reaching oaks, set to guard deep and shadowed hollows, enchanted meadows, holy glades. These are the marks of the people who used to live here, the holy places of the *Wealas*.

These circles, living stone or silent wood, mark the places where their magic was done, where they prayed to their gods to make the land fruitful or to bring terror to their enemies. Witches made those circles; they made the stone giants dance, set the trees to ward the sacred hollows. Such a place is magic Gardd Seren.

Such a place was the soft place Lydi found for us, the magic place, the bluebell wood. Day sky was only day sky there, the same my friends in the glade might see were they not sleeping. Blue and filled with golden sunlight, no enchantment showed me stars there; the bluebells had another kind of magic.

Ay, bluebells. Witch-bells we call them, Sif. Some think no lie can be told in a bluebell wood. Might be that's true. One thing I know is surely true: You have to try very hard to ignore truth when the bluebells are ringing.

A woodlark flew singing. High up in the circled oaks red jays bickered. Noon sun spilled gold through the wildwood's roof, dappled the hollow, coaxed scents from the earth to echo the enchantments in Gardd Seren. We had not gone far from the falls. I still heard water tickling stone, still smelled the wet rocks, deeper scents running beneath the bluebells' fragrance. Eyes half-closed, sleepy now, I watched my Lydi where she knelt in a sunny patch of witch-bells. She whispered a word, then another. A small breeze sighed to life, caressed the blue flowers. Dancing lightly, the flowers made a song that bells in dreams might sing.

Again magic!

This place was like Gardd Seren, but it was not Gardd Seren. I didn't feel as comfortable here. Tight-coiled and dark, fear gathered itself in me, poised to leap, ready to turn the soft notes of Lydi's magic into cold clanging. I closed my eyes, tried hard to keep the fear down in the deep dark places in me. A shadow passed between me and the sun, and the sun warmed me again. Hands gentle, Lydi touched my face, kissed me. Fear vanished, warmed away by her voice.

"Day's light is the most beautiful gold I have ever seen," she said.

My eyes on the swaying flowers, I agreed that day's light was beautiful, but I told her it wasn't gold.

"What is it, then?"

Still watching the witch-bells, I said, "It's memory, bright so we don't forget why god-Freyr fell in love."

Lydi's soft sigh sounded like the wind's. "I don't know this Freyr."

"There is a lot to be told about Freyr, my Lydi. He is Njorth's son, the bravest and most beautiful of all the gods."

"And when he fell in love . . .?"

I breathed in the sweet fragrance of her hair, my heart as warm as though sunlight touched it. "When he fell in love he forgot all else."

I sat up, took her in my arms, glad when she rested her cheek against my shoulder. The delicate song of witch-bells rose around us, and something long stilled moved in me, memories of a song built upon a tale learned from Stane Saewulf's son.

> Quiet went Njorth's son
> To Wotan's throne,
> Soft, on the last day
> He owned his heart.
> Boldly he sat
> In the Raven God's place.

Ay, memories, and I shied from them, for even in this magic place they sounded like the voices of ghosts. Still, a tale begun must have its end, else it haunts the teller. Stane taught me that, and so, caught between the ghost of my old song, the ghost of my teacher, I reached for Stane's words. Like a loved voice in a peaceful dream, I heard them in my heart:

Maest deorcful in niht, Stane had said, *com gan god-Freyr to Wotan-setl . . .*

I spoke slowly, searching for words in the Welsh language to match the ones Stane had given me in our own tongue. Word cannot be matched to word in these two languages and I wanted to be careful of my teacher's tale.

"One time, in deepest night," I said, "god-Freyr went to Wotan's throne, the highest place in all the nine worlds. He looked out, and though all that he saw was lovely, nothing seemed more fair than a very great hall in the most northern part of Jotunheim, the giants' world. Walking toward that hall, as Freyr watched, was a beautiful woman, and she was Gerth, a daughter of cliff-giants. Now, Freyr thought this was a fine thing to be watching. And, as gods are much like Dwarfs and Men in these matters, he didn't turn away from the sight but settled back on Wotan's throne and made himself comfortable."

Lydi curled closer to me, her hand warm on my heart. The tale came easier then, and each of Stane's words found good match in the Welsh language:

"Freyr watched Gerth as she walked, graceful as mist rising, and filled his eyes with her loveliness. Through dark woods and mountain passes went Gerth, and when she came to the wonderful hall, she raised her arms to bid the doors open. Ah, then Freyr saw a thing to make his heart tremble, heard a song to rouse his soul. As Gerth lifted her arms, smooth and white, they shone so brightly that night became day. The seas girding the world sparkled as though diamonds had been cast upon the waves."

Lydi sighed. "Magic," she whispered. I heard delight in her voice.

"Even so. My Lydi, there has never been friendship between the gods and the giant-kin, but this didn't matter to Freyr. He was heart-stricken, filled with a deep love for the beautiful daughter of the cliff-giants. Sick with longing for her, he sent his servant Skirnir to bring her to his hall. As reward, Freyr gifted his servant with his own sword, which was a good one, made for him by Dwarfs and enspelled by witches so that it could fight by itself. Skirnir was happy to have it."

Lydi stirred. "And Gerth? Did she want to go live with this Freyr-god?"

"She considered it for a time, and in the end Skirnir convinced her that there would be harder things to live with than a god who so deeply loved her."

Eyes darkly thoughtful, Lydi removed her hand from my heart. After a moment, she said, "Did this Freyr-god think his love was worth his wonderful sword?"

I told her that I'd heard people say that things didn't turn out well for Freyr, heard some say it will not be a good thing for him to be caught without his famous sword at the end of the world when the wolves come harrying from Hel.

But Lydi said, "I don't think it's all that bad, Garroc. He has his Gerth and she loves him. And your Freyr-god still has time to find a Dwarf with enough heart and skill to make another good sword."

Ay, still some time, I thought grimly, but not much. Like it is the world's life will stretch on for more years than Dwarfs or Men can imagine. Maybe the Terrible Winter is not a thing for any to concern himself with now. But the time is coming when Njorth's son will look about him and find no Dwarf to replace that good sword of his.

"*Prydydd*," the witch said. "Skald, you are not so silent today." She placed her hand on my heart again, tilted her head a little as though listening for something. "Garroc, how many wonderful tales do you keep locked up in here?"

"A few," I said, carefully. "One or two."

The warm breeze quickened, witch-bells sang and their voices carried a deeper tone, a more urgent note. Lydi drew a soft quiet breath. "Does it warm you to tell them?"

Almost I shied from the question, almost. But I could not shy too far. I sat with a witch in a bluebell wood.

"Yes," I said, and it was hard to say even that.

"Man dearest, I watched your face while you told Freyr-god's story. I saw the peace in your eyes, felt your heart warm as you made your tale. It was a peace of a kind I don't often see in you." Great sadness came like a shadow across her face, darkened her eyes. "Garroc, will you never make another tale, never craft another song? Will you live cold in winter always and not reach for the warmth in your heart?"

Bleak and cold as the winter she spoke of came the old questions: Why did it always come to this? Why could the peace between us be no more than illusion?

"My Lydi," I said, simply and clearly as I could. "I don't want to talk about this."

Sharp bright anger flared in her eyes. Maybe I should have expected it, for Lydi is patient only so long. But that anger took me by surprise, left me gaping at her like a witless boy as she leaped to her feet, hands fisted, eyes blazing.

"Ah, you never do, Garroc Silent Skald! Tell me then: What is it you want?"

Her naming stung me. Yet, hoping to hold back what must be, I tried for a smile. "Only you."

Even as I spoke, Lydi sighed, shook her head. "No, you don't."

Ah, Sif! How quickly we are spun from one feeling to another. Anger rose in me then, dark and resentful. And then the breeze stilled, the witch-bells fell silent so that I heard, quick behind my anger, the voices of ghosts, a shadow-wolf growling. And angry, suddenly frightened as Lydi walked away from me, I leaped after her, grabbed her arm and jerked her around to face me.

"Then what *do* I want, Lydi? Tell me, if you know and I don't."

Maybe I looked dangerous to her then, storm-eyed and hard-handed. If I did, the danger didn't stop her from firmly removing my hand from her arm. My fingers had left marks, red prints on her soft skin, which would soon turn to dark bruises. Lydi didn't look at her arm; she was thinking of the greater hurt we shared.

Eyes soft and sad, she placed her hands gently over her belly, flat as a girl's and never reshaped by the weight of a wombed child. Her lips formed silent words, words that could tear our truce beyond healing.

You want what you can't have.

I did, yes, I did.

Dying, nearly dead, we *dvergr* are. But all the wants and all the needs that move every creature who lives still move us. Strong for us, as for all, is the need to make a claim on the future, to make a child, the next part of the song we sing.

I looked at Lydi, and the sun had no power to warm me. Seeing her, I knew what a son of ours would look like. Dark-haired he'd be, as she is; light his eyes, Northern-blue as mine are. Hurting deep inside, I recalled the sound of the wind-ringing witch-bells. That song was the voice of the daughter Wotan denied us.

I wanted that strong son badly, wanted that fair daughter always. But those wants, too, were ghost-voices, urgent and thin as my father's dream-voice, as the voices of all those who haunted my heart. Those are the grieving voices berserkers hear, waking and sleeping.

Lydi touched my face. "Garroc," she whispered, "what is it you're afraid of?"

Madness, I thought, unwarmed by her touch. The shadow-wolf, I thought, eyes on her bruised arm. The berserker-madness.

Strong in me rose the need to walk away from the bluebell wood, from cold sorrow. And, ay, the path away was one I knew very well. The wind along that way whispered coldly, told me that I would have no child to teach my histories to, none to make the next part of my song. Laughing, that wind said that a voice is no voice at all if there is none to hear it, a song not a song if there is no one to pass it to. Dark the path, unlighted, and it had led me from skald-craft to war-craft.

I held myself still, dared not leave for fear that I would not again find the way back to my Lydi.

"Garroc, I know only one way to love you. Your lips, your arms, the whole strong body of you: I love these." She placed her hand again over my heart. Tentatively, as though she were afraid of what her next words would waken in me, Lydi said, "But this I love best, for here is your true fire. Maybe it will be that I can't always keep still when I feel your heart aching. This I know—only you can heal the hurt. But, too, I know how that can be done. Garroc, won't you let me teach you?"

She was a healer, and one who could soothe more than torn flesh and broken bones. Maybe it was that she could show me how to heal my own hurts. Stranger things have happened. But I could not talk about grief, didn't have the courage to navigate those cold winter seas.

Her words came soft into my silence. "I know—I know how you feel about my magic, Garroc. Now, though, I am not speaking of magic. Please, won't you trust me?"

Ah, there was a blow! Hard and breath-taking it was, and one to make me dodge sharply and scramble out of its way.

"My Lydi," I said quickly, urgently, "I've trusted you with my life, with my friend Aelfgar's life. How can you think that I don't trust you?"

Ay, foolish, I was in those days, Sif. Maybe blind. But I wasn't witless. I knew well how she could think I didn't trust her, knew that if I'd trusted her fully, I'd not have wasted my breath proclaiming my trust.

She knew it too. I saw it in her eyes. Before I could see anything else—anger, or worse, terrible pity—I cupped Lydi's face in my hands. Though I feared that she would remember the bruises on her arm and pull away from me, she didn't shy from my touch. Grateful, I drew her gently closer, kissed her. Her lips trembled beneath mine, her breath caught in her throat. My witch seemed helpless then, as helpless as the small birds who suddenly find themselves caught in hunting-snares.

And so she was, for I'd snared her with a truce, one I knew she wanted to keep as much as I did.

For a long time I sat in the silent bluebell wood, my arms filled with Lydi. Sometimes we were still, sometimes I rocked her gently to the quieting rhythm of our two hearts. When shadows grew long on the ground, darkened the witch-bells, Lydi told me that she must leave, and I knew that I should return to the glade. She raised her hands, stroked the sides of my face gently.

"Do you know," she asked, "that I love you?"

I told her that I knew it.

Tears glistened in her eyes, made dark crescents of her lashes. "And do you know that I am afraid for you?"

"I know it," I whispered. "But—"

She shook her head sadly. "No. Please don't tell me that there is nothing to fear. There must always be truth between us, Garroc. Maybe then . . ." She stopped, caught her breath as though afraid to go on. But she is brave, my Lydi, and so she finished her thought. "Maybe then there can be trust between us."

And then I didn't feel fingers against my face, but wing-feathers, soft as blessing. Striving for at least the semblance of the trust she deserved, I held still, didn't flinch from magic's touch. When my arms were empty I kept the dove in my sight until she flew beyond the warding oaks of the bluebell wood.

The day had grown old; I smelled sunset in the listless, aged breeze. When I checked the snares I'd earlier set by Rhodri's barrow, I found that they were gone, and farther on toward the camp, near a quiet shady pool, I came upon Blodrafen harvesting the traps. I wanted no company, most especially not a *baresark's*, so I only lifted my hand in wordless greeting and went on.

But once, I looked back, and I saw him watching me. He skinned his teeth in a mirthless smile, then went eagerly back to his work, wringing the necks of rabbits and small trapped birds.

III

ON the day I scored the ninth notch in my counting-stick, a great hunger for deer meat took hold of my friend Dyfed. He borrowed Aelfgar's longbow, stuffed the quiver full of arrows. He said he would rather lose a day's sleep hunting if he could gain a rich roast for supper. Me, I was glad to wish him good luck in his hunting. I'd lost my taste for the rabbits and small birds Blodrafen killed so joyfully. When I watched Dyfed leave at dawn, I didn't expect that he would come back until night-fall, but this was not the case.

Day-sleeper, dreaming haunted dreams in the sun-dappled glade, I woke at noon, driven from sleep by Haestan's cry of alarm. I wake quickly for a cry like that. Axe in hand, I ran for the birm.

Haestan pointed west, and I squinted into the shadows of the wildwood, saw Dyfed coming toward us. He walked hunched, slowly, and I thought he was staggering with pain. Cold fear washed through me when I saw the blood streaking his bare chest, matting the white hair on his arms. I thought that blood was his, until Haestan slapped my shoulder, pointed, and I saw the limp shirt-wrapped bundle in Dyfed's arms. I didn't know that it was Werrehund he carried until I ran down to meet him.

Dark eyes hot with pain, the dog shuddered in Dyfed's arms, shook in a way that made me fear for him. I put up my axe, gently took the dog from my friend. Dyfed ran ahead to the fire, shouted to Aelfgar, sent him running for water. Close and curious, men crowded round me, harried me with questions I could not answer.

In the picket, horses stamped and snorted, scenting blood, sensing trouble. I sent most of the men to calm them, sent the rest to watch on the birms. In my arms Werrehund trembled and moaned deeply. I knew he was badly hurt, but I didn't have my first clear look at him until I laid him down carefully near the fire.

He was in a bad way, Dyfed's red dog. Something clawed had raked him from shoulder to hip, torn fur and skin, scraped ribs. His belly was whole though, and I thought this might be the saving of him.

Dyfed dropped to his heels next to the dog. Sweat mingled with Werrehund's blood on him and he breathed hard.

"Dyfed, tell me."

He did, and it didn't take him long. "I tracked a doe for most of the morning, Garroc, followed her to a leah and then lost her." He ran a shaking hand over Werrehund's head. "I found the dog in that clearing, all—cut the way you see him."

"What did this to him, Ghost Foot?"

He shook his head, looked up at me, white-faced. "I don't know."

"Did you see track or sign?"

"Ay, I did. But I swear to you, Garroc, I've never seen tracks like these before." He held up his hand, fingers wide-spread. "This big, they were. Long as my hand and as wide. The thing was clawed—" He stroked his red dog's head again, whispered comfort when Werrehund whimpered. "Ay, it was clawed. And long from the stride-marks. But for the claws, I'd say it looked most like the mark of a man's bare foot." He shook his head, then tapped the inner side of his own foot, near where the large toe is. "No, not exactly like. If it was a man's foot, the biggest toe would be on the inside. On this print the biggest toe was outside. I don't know what it was, Garroc. But it was big."

As he described the tracks, I looked at the dog. I'd seen wildcats slash in the way that Werrehund had been slashed. But I'd never seen a wildcat bigger than the red dog. Whatever had done this was clearly bigger. And it had coarse dark fur. Tufts of it still clung to Werrehund's jaws, stuck there with blood and thick dried saliva.

Again the red dog whimpered. Dyfed bent close over him, spoke softly, soothed him with gentle words. A small movement, a barely seen twitch, Werrehund tried to wag his tail.

"Ah, dog," my friend whispered. "Dog, dog . . ."

I saw a thin mark of sweat, maybe tears, on his face, and so I turned away in case he might be weeping. In the picket the horses calmed as the men went among them, patting glossy necks, stroking soft muzzles. Wind whispered high in the trees, cooling now as the day aged. After a time, I said:

"Ghost Foot, did you see the beast?"

He shook his head wearily, drew breath for a better answer. Before he could speak, a shadow cut the sunlight on the ground between us, and wet from their filling, two fat skins of water dropped with heavy thuds at our feet.

Blodrafen wiped dripping hands down the front of his shirt, then jerked a thumb over his shoulder, showed us Aelfgar coming slowly back from the stream. The berserker fixed Dyfed with a cool, scornful look.

"The boy's not fast enough for your errand-running, yet," he said. "Or haven't you noticed that, healer?"

His voice curled like a snake around the word 'healer,' made it sound like a curse. But Dyfed said nothing. Maybe he thought the *baresark* wasn't far wrong; maybe he regretted sending Aelfgar running to the stream. One hand on his red dog's head, he turned to watch Aelfgar as he walked toward us.

"Aelfgar!" he called. "Are you all right?"

Aelfgar waved good-natured assurance and came to join us. He dropped to one knee, sighed in pity. "Poor Werrehund," he said. "Dyfed, is he going to get better?"

Dyfed said he didn't know, said he'd try to help the dog.

At that, Blodrafen snorted, a sound of mingled disgust and heartless amusement. He toed the waterskins and then the scrip filled with Dyfed's powders and salves. "Your dog's going to be a long time dying. But I guess you know that, healer." Winter-eyes glinting with an eerie light, he moved his hands quickly, jerked his wrists sharply. "I'll help him to an easy death if you—"

Hands fisted, Dyfed made to rise. I held him back, kept him where he was with a heavy hand on his shoulder. Before I could speak, Blodrafen laughed.

"Dyfed," he said in his wind-hissing voice. "You're not really looking for a fight with me, are you? I'd have as good a time twisting your neck, healer, as I would the dog's."

Knuckles white, jaw clenched, Dyfed leaped to his feet, broke away from me. But when he lunged, Aelfgar came between them, grabbed Dyfed's arms and held him. "No, Dyfed," he said, his voice low and urgent. "Don't do it."

Blodrafen jerked his chin at Aelfgar. "You don't credit him with much skill at thinking, do you, healer? You think he's best for making your riddles seem like clever things. Ay well, clever Ghost

Foot," he said bitterly, "maybe you're right. But I'll tell you this:
He's thinking good now. Best you listened to him, healer."

Aelfgar flushed, then paled. At the sight of the sudden shock
of pain in his eyes, anger rose in me. I held tight to sense, though,
held tight to the knowledge that, unweaponed, I was no match
for the berserker. Still, he'd sworn to obey my orders as though
they were Erich's. I used that now, said coldly:

"Go back to the horses, Blodrafen."

His stormy eyes never flinched, but his hands twitched as
though he exerted great effort to keep them by his side. "The dog
would be better off dead. You know it, Garroc."

I did. But Dyfed didn't, and the dog was his. I didn't take my
eyes from the Blood Raven's, but I knew just where my axe was
and how long it would take me to reach it.

"Get out of here, *baresark*. Now."

With no further word, he went off, passed like a winter wind
through the lengthening shadows. Much later I wondered if the
baresark had meant to hurt the only friend he had among us.

That afternoon I went with Aescwine and four others into the
wildwood to find the tracks Dyfed had described and to search
for other sign. I didn't know what this thing was that had done
so much harm to Werrehund, but I wanted to be certain that it
didn't prowl near our picket or our camp. Though we were gone
long, we saw no other sign, no tracks but the ones Dyfed had seen.
These were just as he described them, and no one of us knew what
kind of beast would make those tracks, though old Aescwine grew
silent and thoughtful when he saw them, and remained so for the
rest of the day and much of the night.

None of us expected that Werrehund would live till night, but
Dyfed, at least, hoped. He nursed his red dog as tenderly as he
would have nursed one of us, and he had Aelfgar to help him.
What the dog needed most was a gentle hand; Aelfgar had that.

Though Blodrafen sneered at Dyfed's chances to bring the dog
alive through the night, the rest of us didn't laugh at Dyfed. Nor
did we think it strange that he would spend all his time with Werrehund, cleaning the wound and urging him to drink from his
cupped hands, praising the dog when he did. A friend does not
have to walk on two legs to be a friend.

All of us, though, puzzled over the dog's injuries, wondered
what had done the fierce fighter Dyfed rightly named War Hound
such terrible hurt. And we puzzled over the tracks in the leah.

That night I didn't go out to Cefn Arth with the others. I stood watch on the west birm. I wanted to look into the forest from the highest place in our camp.

My watch-mate that night was Aescwine, and though he, too, kept an eye on the woods, he had a closer interest in something he was drawing with a stick on a patch of smoothed ground. When I wasn't watching the wildwood, I was watching him where he crouched on his heels in a shaft of milky moonlight.

Beast-tracks, I thought.

He'd been drawing and erasing them, thinking about them and studying them, all night. Now he looked up, saw me watching. With a gesture he called me to him and I went, for all his drawing and thinking had roused my curiosity.

Old he was, our Aescwine. If Grimwulf Aesc's son were yet living, Aescwine would be older than he. And, ay, he was a pirate, a longship-rider. He'd fought the Pendragon's son a hundred years before. Tonight, in the soft moonlight and forgiving shadows, his face, scar-seamed, age-marked, didn't appear so old. He was remembering far times, distant places, and the days when he was young. He spoke to me from those times, from those places.

"See, youngster," he said, gesturing to his drawing. "I've been thinking about these." He pointed with the sharp end of the stick to the track he'd drawn.

It was wider than my own hand, half again as long. The toes were in the wrong places to be those of a barefoot Man's, though if I didn't look at the marks of claws Aescwine had drawn, a Man's print is what this most resembled.

He laughed, and I looked up at him, saw great amusement in his eyes. "Aescwine," I said, "do you know what kind of beast would make this mark?"

Moonlight glittered in Aescwine's beard, shone brightly in his eyes. When he saw my puzzlement, he shook his head reprovingly. "Skald, reach back for the oldest tales you know."

"There are a lot of old tales," I said, and northwind was not colder than my voice.

Aescwine, undaunted, only chuckled. He didn't think a man could stop being a skald simply because he wished to; he'd told me that before now. No doubt he'd have thought it strange that he and one of the witches he feared would so closely agree on this matter.

"Ay, there are a lot," he said softly. "And I think you know most of them, youngster. Think on the ones from Daneland, the ones from Seaxeland. Do you remember the tales that tell us of bears?" He jerked his thumb at the sketched prints. "These are the marks of a bear."

When I started to scoff, he nodded soberly. "Yes, they are. I know it, young skald, because I've seen bears in the old land, in Daneland."

Cefn Arth. The Bear's Ridge. It seemed to me that the night-wind, the west wind, blew cooler. It seemed that the shadows flowed darker across the glade, darker than night.

"Aescwine, have you ever heard of anyone who's seen a bear on the Isle?"

He admitted that he hadn't. "But I did hear, once and a long time ago, that the Roman Men liked bear-baiting. I have been to Lundenwic, Garroc. They say ghosts haunt Lundenwic, ghosts of *Wealas* and of the Roman Men."

He looked into the forest, thoughtful for a while. Then he said:

"Me, I'm always worrying about witches, ay. That's because I know about witches, know what they can do." He shuddered. "I know. I've seen the sky turn to fire at a witch's word. But ghosts—ghosts don't bother me. Can't see 'em, can't hear 'em." He regarded me closely. "Though I've heard that some can."

I didn't answer the question I heard in his voice. Not even with wise Aescwine would I talk about the ghosts I heard at the battle's edge, the ones who mourned close around me when I slept.

Aescwine got slowly to his feet, groaning. Age was stiffening his joints.

"Ay, well. Ghosts . . . I was not afraid to walk in the ruins of broken Lundenwic, young skald," he said. "In one part of the city, I saw a stone pit, ay, a wide and deep one and it was filled with the rubble of past times—cut stone and shaped stone. Those old stones, lonely and sad, they liked to have a Dwarf to talk to. They told me how the Roman Men brought bears there for baiting.

"In other places men told me that once and long ago folk got rich bringing bears to the Isle for Romans. So there were bears here once, yes?" He shrugged. "Seems to me a bear would have to have a lot of courage to face a baiting, to go to a fight it was never meant to win.

"Cefn Arth. Could be the *Wealas* didn't name this ridge to honor their old and famous king. Maybe the *Wealas* named the ridge to honor the bears—and only later the Pendragon thought Arthur—the Bear—was a good name for his boy."

We stood silent for a moment, then Aescwine smiled slyly. "And maybe all the bears didn't die in the baitings, ay? Maybe

now you know someone who's seen a bear in these lands. Werrehund."

What Aescwine thought made some sense. What made no sense
was the cold feeling of dread that touched deep places in me.

Ay, Sif, I am a strong believer in omens. And the return to the
borderland of the creature for whom a legendary enemy-king had
been named didn't feel like a good one. I looked again at the tracks
Aescwine had drawn, then scuffed them away. Not so easy,
though, to erase the feeling of the wildwood grown closer, the
darkness more dangerous.

IV

THE day after the red dog met the bear, Thunor came down from
the north, flinging his silver spears, beating his war-hammer hard
against the sky. His rain, sharp as arrows, kept us close to our
camp. Only Dyfed was glad of the storm, for now he could spend
the days and nights with his red dog, coaxing him back to health.
His faithful helper was Aelfgar, and between them they kept the
dog's wound clean, his bandages dry. Both rejoiced when, weak-
legged but determined, the red dog staggered to his feet, lurched
a few paces closer to the fire, settled nearer the warmth with a
deep, satisfied groan.

Close and quiet in the shadows was one who didn't rejoice at
Werrehund's recovery; he was Blodrafen, lorn and sorrowful.
Aelfgar was his only friend among us, a friend he'd wounded with
harsh words, and now Aelfgar spent the most of his time with
Dyfed.

For the rest, they counted the dog's returning health a good
thing, then turned again to marveling at Aescwine's stories of bear-
hunting. They talked of digging bear-pits and the best way to make
good hunting spears, and they watched the wildwood eagerly for
signs of Werrehund's enemy.

Quiet and close in the shadows was one who didn't share in the
wonder of Aescwine's tales; that one was me. I thought the talk
of bears ill-omened, but I said nothing. In this way my men
amused themselves and held onto their patience while they waited
for Thunor's rages to end and bring us good war-sport again.

And so it happened. After a handful of days, the Thunderer put
an end to the time of shearing, sent the farmers of the Marches
to warm themselves by their fires and worry about their crops.

Wotan's son borrowed some magic from his father and made the farmers in the Welshlands war-seekers again.

No magic was needed to make a battle-seeker of me: Ghosts haunted my sleep and the watch for the dove had been a lonely one. I didn't know where Lydi was, but I guessed that she was in Seintwar. Often and often I told myself that the witch's concerns would keep her busy there; her gardens needed her care, the folk of the valley would need her care. But I took little comfort from this reasoning, didn't much believe it. Easier to believe that my Lydi kept far from me because she didn't like feeling mistrusted and trapped by an ill-made truce, one that neither of us had been able to honor long.

What else to do then, but what I'd been doing so well for so long? What else to do but wish for the war-work I did so well?

Bright the ruddy sunset light glinting from byrnie and iron, sharp its gleam on rain-wet stone. We'd not seen sun's light in four days, not seen moonlight or the cool sheen of stars for five nights. We saw them all, my *mearc-threat* and I, as we left the shadowed wildwood, saw setting sun, slender wolf-haunted Stag, and the first eager stars.

Cynnere's roan horse snorted, jerked hard against the reins. Dancy as Dyfed's bay tonight, the roan shied from the last of the sunlight lancing from the jeweled brooch pinned to Ecgwulf's shirt.

"Ecgwulf," Cynnere growled. "All these nights riding beside you and I don't know what hurts more, my backside from this horse or my eyes from the shine of your gold."

Ecgwulf grinned, moved his mount easily away from Cynnere's roan. With a studied, careful gesture, he buffed the brooch, told Cynnere he was sorry for his pain on both counts, told him he could do nothing for either his backside or his eyes.

"Your horse's back is hard, *freond min*, and gold—well, gold will shine, ay?"

Ah, the Sword Wolf was proud of that brooch, the gift of a woman who loved him. Two dragons sported across its golden face. Their sinewy bodies were crafted of brilliant blue enamel; blood-hued garnets these dragons had for eyes. Who looked closely could see the gold shining in the spaces between the dragon's twining lengths as shapes much like the patterned links of a mail-shirt. Ecgwulf called his brooch Wyrms Mail, and he wore it always.

Ecgwulf kneed his mount, urged it to a sharp trot. With hands

and heels, he turned the grey neatly, guided it dancing and curvet-
ing in tight circles around Cynnere. With each pass, sunlight
gleamed from Wyrms Mail. Laughing, he said:

"I'm thinking Wyrms Mail might look even better holding tight
a bearskin mantle comes the winter."

Cynnere agreed, but he didn't think that red Ecgwulf would be
the one to claim the bear's pelt. "More like, the bear's pelt will
be mine. Garroc! When are you going to give us time for a hunt?"

I held Dark firmly while he tried to decide whether the antics
of Ecgwulf's roan were a challenge to race, told Cynnere that he'd
hunt bear when he could tell me the *Wealas* were tired of stealing
Saxon-grown cattle.

Cynnere snorted. "Bear'll be old and dead by then. We're letting
a good hunt go, Garroc. Tell me: When have you ever seen a bear
before now?"

"Never." I eased my grip on Dark's reins. "And I haven't seen
one yet. We're hunting raiders tonight, Cynnere. Take your band
north." I cast a look at the sky, deeply blue as Ecgwulf's dragons,
clean-washed after the day's rain. I pointed to the failing Stag
where it rose, sharp thin silver riding the last mists. "Highest over-
head—meet me back here."

He knew the nightly pattern, and he knew the work he must
do, though he'd rather have been hunting. He called his men to
him, set Godwig and Ceowulf riding ahead, bade Ecgwulf follow.
Blodrafen he sent next.

Aescwine watched them ride off, studied Cynnere thoughtfully.
"I think he likes to keep the *baresark* in his sight."

"Maybe," I said. "Or maybe he likes to keep all his men in his
sight so he knows where his weapons are when he needs them."

Haestan chuckled, nudged Aescwine's ribs. "Ay, weapon, let's
get our places in the line so Garroc knows where to find us."

Weapons. Strong, sharp, bright as newly polished iron, made
for war. Dangerous, we were, Dwarfs and Men. But we were not
the most dangerous things haunting Cefn Arth that night.

We four rode south through the dimming, drifted in and out
of purple shadows while aged Stag rose and stars jeweled the darkening sky. In the wildwood, cricket-song rose and fell, the pulse
of the night. While we rode, Haestan asked for another tale of
Daneland bear-hunting and Aescwine gave it to him gladly. From
my place at the end of our line, I heard snatches of his story, and
if they sounded like good-telling to Haestan and Dyfed, to me they
sounded like the ragged ends of bad dreams. I'd no liking for this

talk of bears and hunting, none for the cold feeling it called up, the feeling of bad luck stalking.

For a time Dyfed listened to Aescwine's story with the same careful attention as Haestan. Then he dropped back, brought his bay mare beside Dark. After a moment's thoughtful silence, he asked me why I didn't think Werrehund had met a bear in the woods.

The night-pulse, the cricket-song, quickened. Shadows darkened. I thought Dyfed's was a strange question.

"I do think he met a bear."

He grunted. "But you don't ever sound like you believe it when the talk turns to hunting, Garroc."

"I believe it. I just don't like this talk of bear-hunting. There are too few of us now. I don't want to lose anyone for a chance at a bear's pelt."

"Ay, well," Dyfed said, suddenly dark. "I'd risk a lot for a chance at that pelt." He raised a hard fist, one eye gleaming coldly. "The bear owes me something."

"Forget about the bear, Ghost Foot. We have other work to do."

Dyfed shook his head, hard-eyed still. "I'm not going to forget about it, Garroc. Know it."

I started to tell him that his idea of collecting a debt for a dog—from a bear—was foolish. I didn't speak the first word of my advice before Dyfed kicked up the mare and left me.

I listened to hoofs clatter on stone, listened to Haestan's eager question, Dyfed's growled answer. In the deepening twilight Aescwine's voice sounded distant as he counseled patience. I left the line, rode out to the edge of Cefn Arth, watched the sky darken over the Marches. Night had come to the valleys below, and now, in high summer, I could not see the faint gleams of farmers' hearth-fires for the leafed trees. All was dark but for the whispered glimmer of moonlight on the river. Somewhere in that deep darkness Grimmbeald might have lit a fire, might be sleeping even now. Or not.

Grimmbeald had been gone for four more than his ten days. I wondered whether he had reached the *cyning* with my message. I wondered if he'd reached Erich, then met with ill-luck on his return. Maybe he would not come back to Cefn Arth at all.

I didn't like the thought. A soldier checking to see that his weapons were close to hand, I looked for my men. Black shadows they were—vengeful Dyfed, tale-weaving Aescwine and sharp-eyed Haestan. When I looked to the north, I could not see Cynnere's band. I held myself still, tried to ignore the constant feeling that bad luck roamed abroad this night.

I slid from Dark's back, placed my hand over his nose and mouth, held him silent. Through the earth, through my own bones, I heard the speech of stone. The ridge spoke in deep echoes, rumbling murmurs. Softly it told of Cynnere's band riding.

Then, like a long cold cry echoing in me, the earth shouted suddenly of many horses running.

"Ghost Foot!"

He turned, head up in silent question. Aescwine halted; I saw moonlight run along the blade of Haestan's axe, Wotan's fire.

Many things happened then, Sif, but these three I remember clearly:

From the north came wild wolfen wailing.

Aescwine cried out sharply. "*Wealas!*"

And from the wildwood directly opposite me, ten mounted raiders broke cover. Their iron gleamed cold as ice under the Stag's light.

Blood smells like iron; iron flashes and screams like Thunor's storm. So it was that night under the Stag's waning light. While Cynnere and his four were still too far away to help, the Welshmen smashed us like battering waves, scattered us along the ridge. Haestan, my battle-shadow, was first to fall—and he fell cursing, sword-cut, bleeding under deadly hoofs.

Dyfed bellowed "Roll!" and Haestan did, curled tight and choking with pain; tried to protect himself. I lost sight of him then, lost sight of Dyfed and Aescwine.

Hemmed on all sides by enemies, crowded too tightly for axe-play or sword-work, I used the only weapon left to me: I used Dark. With heels and knees I guided him, caused him to rear high. When he came down, I heard terrible cries of agony from a tall Welshman. He'd lost the side of his face to Dark's slashing hoofs. Raging, Dark kicked out behind us, shattered the foreleg of a Welsh pony. When that pony went down, so did his rider. The grey-eyed Dwarf screamed as Dark trampled him, but he didn't die cheaply. With his last strength, the Dwarf thrust up hard with his short-sword, tore open Dark's belly.

My brave Dark foundered, crashed to his knees, shrieking. I flung myself from his back, landed hard and rolled, scrambling. I didn't roll far enough, didn't scramble fast enough. Sharp as lightning, hard as thunder, the blows of deadly hoofs; pain like fire raced through my left leg. Then, strong hands hauled me up and out of danger. I clung hard to my rescuer and thanked the warrior-god, praised hard Wotan, as Cynnere's band, riding like a cold northwind, broke the ranks of the Welshmen, sent them scattering.

Wolf howls, the Blood Raven's war-song, rang in the night, ran like mad keening over the cries of the hurt and dying. Eddying, swirling, the battle surged around and beyond me, left me alone with the friend who'd snatched me from sure and terrible death.

And ay, it didn't surprise me that the friend was Dyfed. Panting, stinking of his own sweat, blood and the bay's rank froth, he heeled the mare sharply, didn't stop till we'd reached the edge of Cefn Arth. Even here, I heard the Blood Raven.

"You hurt, Garroc?"

I heard Dyfed's question only dimly, as though he'd shouted from a great distance. What I heard best and most clearly were the *baresark's* howls, a sound like cold hands reaching to drag me back to battle.

Struggling to hold his mare still, to hold me steady, Dyfed shouted, "Garroc! You hurt?"

I thought I was. I remembered feeling the thunder, the lightning. But now I felt only a deep and urgent need to answer the *baresark's* war-song. Maybe I answered Dyfed, maybe I didn't. I don't remember now.

I do remember that a horse, wild-eyed, sweating, left the war-grounds, came to stand trembling beside us. I knew it for Ecgwulf's grey. I grabbed the reins, cut the saddle loose with two dagger slashes and leaped from Dyfed's bay to the grey's back. Empty as an old, old memory, some of the pain Dyfed seemed so worried about stirred, tugged at my leg. But the berserker howled again, and I loosed a like cry, a roaring blood-song.

In me, like a deadly shadow rising, came the memory of the terror in Haestan's cursing as he fell, the knowledge that I rode Ecgwulf's grey and that, unhorsed, the Sword Wolf was likely dead. Swept hard into the tide of killing, I didn't care about pain, cared about nothing but vengeance; for it I would have counted life fair payment.

We didn't come easily away from that battle, Sif. We didn't find ourselves whole and hale, bright with victory. When the last of our enemies fell, we stopped where we stood, too tired, too hurt to move.

Ten Welshmen lay on hard stone beneath the cold moon, some dead, some dying. Nightwind prowled Cefn Arth, and though it was a warm south wind, still I shivered. All the blood in me felt cold as snow-melt. And cold, I still didn't feel the pain of my wounds, though I saw blood on me and knew some of it was mine. Nearby, close behind me, someone groaned, a curse or prayer in Welsh. I couldn't tell which and I didn't try to learn. Reaching deep for the cold still in me, I gave hard orders to the *baresark*. I'd not repeat the mistake of leaving any enemy alive, and red-handed, eyes like winter, Blodrafen went to kill helpless men, went to do my bidding.

Three horses needed mercy. One of them was Dark. The sounds of their pain, hard animal-squealing, filled Cefn Arth. I told Cynnere to free them. Still cold and holding tight to it, I called Dyfed.

My friend came limping. Sweat and shadows, blood and moon-light, changed his face to one I didn't know.

"Garroc, Ecgwulf is dead."

Ecgwulf, red Sword Wolf. His father's name was Icel.

Uneasy, Dyfed looked away from me, looked over his shoulder. "And I think Godwig is dead."

Dyfed moved then, half-turned to the glittering sky, and I saw that Aescwine sat weeping a little way away from his son, close by the ridge's edge, near the deep drop into the Marches. Shivering now, I knew that he was learning what it is to be the last of a kindred.

Godwig. He took no father's name because he could give his to no child.

"Who else?" I asked. My voice sounded distant, like the eagle-winged giant's northern wind-song, not like my own.

Dyfed shook his head, looked around the ridge. "No one else."

Anger, sudden as fire's leap, flared high in me. I grabbed his arm, spun him back to face me. "Who's hurt?"

Dyfed ignited his own anger from mine. "Ceowulf," he snarled. "And Haestan. And Cynnere and Aescwine. Even the *baresark*. Even you, Garroc; even you, ay?"

Even the berserker—even me.

Suddenly I felt what I'd been too cold to feel before. Torn flesh, aching bones, a leg too hurt to keep me standing for much longer. I let Dyfed help me to sit, let him do the work he did after the war-work was done. These were the things Dyfed could heal, this was the pain I could afford to let him see.

What I needed to hide, keep close and never speak of, was the other pain, the memory of the heart-numbing coldness that had carried me through this battle, cold with a voice like a madman's war-song, a *sceadu-wulf's* howling.

The ridge became quieter and I tried not to count the last deaths, men and mounts.

"Wager you'll be wearing the prints of that horse's hoofs for a while, Garroc. But your bones are whole and that's no small piece of luck."

He looked toward the wildwood, the dark place. In the shadows and thin moonlight I saw his expression change, harden suddenly. "The glade," he said, his voice a whisper. "Wouldn't the raiders have passed through the glade to come out of the forest where they did?"

I thought: Maybe. Yes, maybe.

I looked around the ridge. Aescwine still wept over the hacked body of his son. All the horses in need of mercy had received it. Blodrafen knelt, dark and bloody-handed, to kill the last of our enemies. In the sudden quiet, I heard my own breathing, thought it sounded ragged, like the harsh sob of an ale-ruined drunk.

"Come back with me, Ghost Foot. Get horses and come back with me."

He ran for our mounts, and while I waited, the wind dropped suddenly. But Cefn Arth was not silent. Like an echo, the voices of ghosts mimicked the wind's song.

V

DYFED and I didn't cover half the distance to the glade before we knew that the *Wealas* had come this way. No scout-craft was needed to know that: We saw Waerstan's body sprawled in the path, sword-hacked. Dyfed would have stopped; he would have stayed to see if our friend yet lived. Me, I knew Waerstan was dead. I heard the ghost. And so, when Dyfed slowed his mare I reached out, lashed her hard with the grey's reins. Dyfed followed me; he had no choice.

We drove our horses hard through the forest, heeled them recklessly up the east birm. Dyfed, having more sense than I, played my own trick, lunged across his mount's neck, yanked my horse to a hard stop at the crest.

"Wait," he whispered, his voice hard, harsh. "Garroc, wait! Use your head, will you? We don't know what's down there."

He slid from his bay. When I hesitated, he hauled me to the ground, didn't waste much care on the wounds he'd tended only a little while before. Or maybe he was thinking about preventing new ones. Dyfed dropped to his belly and dragged me down with him.

Heart hammering, trying to catch back my frozen wits, I listened hard to the night, hoped for a challenge from the camp, for a glad *hael!*—I heard only crickets singing the night's heartbeat. I crept closer to the edge of the birm, searched the darkness for something to show me that Aelfgar and Wulfsunu still lived. All I saw was the fire, our hearth-fire, our home-fire, scattered to frail dying embers.

Dyfed's breath hissed between his teeth. "Garroc, they're—"

I held up my hand, stopped him from naming our friends dead. Looking for shapes darker than the dark, I saw a shadow moving in the glade. I listened again for what I'd been afraid to hear. Light flared suddenly, someone gave life to a torch. Red light and black shadow wove a weightless cloak for a tall golden-haired figure.

Dyfed said heavily, "That's Aelfgar. I don't see Wulf."

Neither did I. But I heard him. Thin the sound, fragile the voice raised to join the ghost-songs I'd heard on Cefn Arth, the one I'd heard in the forest. Dyfed held my mount still, gave me a leg up and pulled himself onto his bay's back. Slowly, too tired now for speed, we rode down into the glade.

Aelfgar wept. Tears like thin silver ran down his face, caught in his beard. Shudder-voiced, he said:

"It doesn't feel right."

Darker than night, slow-moving, limping stiffly, Werrehund, another battle-survivor, crept from the shadows. He groaned deeply, sank to the ground at Aelfgar's side. As though nothing could surprise him, not even that the red dog, helpless to defend himself, had lived through still another fight, Aelfgar reached absently to stroke Werrehund's ears, spoke to Dyfed again.

"It doesn't feel right, Ghost Foot."

Shaking, tired and hurt, I gathered the little bit of kindling and wood I could find and called our broken fire back to life. I left Aelfgar and his grieving to Dyfed. But I listened to them, watched them as a man watches something that is darkly fascinating.

Dyfed dropped to his heels beside Aelfgar and the dog. "What doesn't feel right?"

"That Wulf is dead and Waerstan is dead. And . . ." He fell silent, unable to give words to the thing battle-survivors always feel.

But Dyfed knew what went unsaid: How is it that I am alive and my friends are dead?

"You fought hard, Aelfgar, ay?"

He nodded. "But Wulf did, too. They were too many."

"How many?"

"I don't know. Fifteen, maybe more. I killed some, Wulf did and Waerstan did. But then Wulf fell. He didn't die right away. And I tried to help him when Waerstan rode to warn you. He didn't get to you, though, did he?"

"No, he didn't."

"And now he's dead. And Wulf. And . . ."

Dyfed spoke gently, told Aelfgar that our friends had died bravely, that we who still lived had fought bravely. Only Fate, he said, made the difference—and we have nothing to say about that.

Good words he spoke, and I think they were meant as much for me as for Aelfgar. Maybe Aelfgar heard him, maybe those words comforted him. They did nothing to ease me where I shivered by the rising fire.

After a time, Aelfgar wept again. Dyfed held him as he would a child, and he didn't try to take his mourning away from him. They grieved for friends—for Waerstan and Godwig and red Ecgwulf. They mourned Wulfsunu, *thegn's* son, riddle-solver, hater of noon-watch, Waerstan's younger brother.

Me, I grieved for no one, though I would miss them all.

What was left of my *mearc-threat*, my brave border-patrol, came back from the ridge slowly. Grim-eyed, each passed fallen Wulf, grieving Aelfgar, and none spoke. I counted them as they came: Ceowulf and Haestan, Cynnere, and far behind him Blodrafen. The berserker's twitching hands were terrible to see.

Worse, though, to see a new kind of recognition in his old grey eyes when he looked at me.

"Ay, Garroc," he said, his voice a hissing. "Wolves fight hardest in cold winter, yes?"

I said nothing, dared not respond.

Dyfed looked at me, looked at the berserker. I could not read my friend's expression, could not tell what he was thinking. He watched the Blood Raven walk away, then he left Aelfgar, came to sit close beside me as though offering warmth.

"Aescwine didn't come back, Garroc. Wager he's still sitting with Godwig, eh?"

I nodded, looked away to the east, toward Cefn Arth.

"Maybe someone should go get him."

He wasn't offering to do that, and if he had offered, I'd have told him to stay and take care of the injured.

I didn't want to go back to the ridge. Neither did I like to leave
Aescwine sitting with the ghosts of his son and his friend. I listened
to crickets shrilling for a little while. When I couldn't think of anything else to do, I took dead Ecgwulf's grey horse, mounted stiffly.

Dyfed drew a short breath, tight with sorrow. He said it would
be good if I looked for Ecgwulf's Wyrms Mail. He knew the
woman who'd gifted the Sword Wolf with the brooch. He thought
that, though she couldn't have her red Ecgwulf, her gift to him
should not lie lonely on a battle-ground.

The Stag, his horns frail and old, hung low over the dark edge
of the wildwood, gave little light. Warm wind sighed across Cefn
Arth. Louder now, as though they knew one was near who could
hear their song, ghost-voices greeted me. I led the grey horse
across the ridge, didn't look at the dark, stiffening bodies of men
and mounts, friends and foes, and I limped out to where Aescwine
sat. Tired, I sat beside him, glad to rest.

He didn't look around, stayed just as he was, hunched over
drawn-up knees, rocking a little, watching the stars gleam in the
dark hall of night. After a time he sighed.

"I saw the bear a little while ago."

I turned sharply, surveyed the ridge north to south. Almost
gently, Aescwine touched my arm, pointed north to a place not
far from where we sat, where Ecgwulf lay and the shadow-dark
wildwood flowed out to meet the stone of Cefn Arth.

"I saw it there," he said. "Just for a bit. Old bear came out for
a look, then went back to finding supper."

I held myself still, listened hard to the night, thought that perhaps, dark omen of bad luck, the bear had come to see what kind
of ending had been made for us.

Aescwine regarded me for a long moment, then spoke of other
things. "Young skald, I see it in you: They haven't fared well in
the camp, have they?"

Wind mourned, ghosts sobbed. I forced words past a sudden,
dangerous tightness in my throat. "Waerstan is dead. And Wulf."

He didn't seem surprised. He'd had a while to sit here and think;
he'd pieced the thing together. "That'll make things a little hard
for us now. We didn't feel like too many tonight when the raiders
hit us." He quirked a grim smile. "Don't suppose we're going to
feel like a crowd if more decide to come at us, will we?"

"No," I said. "I don't suppose we will."

Neither did I suppose that we, four Dwarfs and four Men,
wounded and weary, would survive another attack.

He looked at me closely. "Do you ever weep, youngster?"

Ah, Sif. I strangled on it sometimes, but I didn't ever weep. I lacked the courage needed for that.

When I didn't answer, Aescwine went back to his own thoughts. After a while he looked over his shoulder, looked at his son, dead and singing a thin song only I could hear.

"There's a riddle," Aescwine said softly. "One Ghost Foot is polite enough not to tell when Dwarfs are around. I've been re-membering it tonight. Can't get the sound of it out of my mind."

I knew the riddle. Stane had not taught it to me. Maybe he never knew it, or maybe Stane, too, had been polite enough not to tell it when Dwarfs were around. I'd learned it in an ale-house where men aren't always courteous.

"Son of the mother-earth," old Aescwine whispered. "Limned by Wotan's light." He raised a gnarled fist, placed it with strange gentleness on his heart. "I am the wolf-feeder, easer of the raven's thirst."

Aescwine fell silent, but the riddle once started must have its end. I heard some of it in the wind's voice, thought I heard the rest of it echoing just under frail ghost-songs:

> When battle-storm rages
> No voice sings sweeter than mine.
> For this men love me,
> Name me faith-fast friend.
> For this kings clothe me in jewels.
>
> Your fathers knew me,
> The sons of your foes will fear me.
> But when battle breaks me,
> When I am war-shattered,
> No daughter will mourn me,
> No son avenge me.
>
> Hard the fate of my kind,
> None may change it:
> Though often I thrust,
> No child do I make,
> And my name among women
> Is sorrow's shadow.

Aescwine closed his eyes, leaned a little forward. I thought he was too close to the edge of the stone, too close to the long drop into the valley. I laid a hand on his arm. When he moved back, looked at me, I saw that he had the courage necessary for weeping.

"Do you know the answer to that one, young skald?"

"Sword," I said. "The answer is sword."

He put a hand on my shoulder, pushed himself to his feet. "No, youngster, not 'sword.' The answer is *dvergr*. Everyone knows that."

The wind cooled a little, dropped and then picked up pace, running from the north now. Aescwine walked over to where Godwig lay, went down on one knee. After a moment he looked up, searched the ridge until he saw Ecgwulf.

. "They've come, haven't they, Garroc?"

"Who's come?"

"*Waelcyriges*," he whispered. "The Valkyries."

Cricket-song, the silver beat of the night, pulsed in the wildwood. Here on Cefn Arth the wind sighed and I heard Aescwine's rough breathing. But I heard no ghost-songs in the wind, heard those thin wandering wails only in my heart now.

"Ay, Aescwine, they've come."

Aescwine touched his son's bruised and bloodied face, stroked it tenderly as though caressing the face of a sleeping child.

"Son of the mother-earth," he said, "limned by Wotan's light. You were the wolf-feeder. You were the easer of raven's thirst."

We were quiet for a while, then Aescwine got to his feet. "Young skald, Garroc my friend, I'm tired. Let's go back to the glade, ay?"

I told him we would, but asked him to come with me first to see if we could find Wyrms Mail.

Between us we combed the ridge looking for Ecgwulf's blue dragon brooch, but we didn't find it. No Welshman had left Cefn Arth alive and so none could have stolen the dragons from Ecgwulf's corpse. Likely, I thought as we rode back through the night, likely the brooch had come loose and fallen. Likely some horse's hoof had sent it skittering down into the valley. I didn't think about it much, thought more about the bear, bad luck, and keeping the weary grey horse headed in the right direction.

I didn't think about Wyrms Mail again until a long time after that night.

THUNORS-MONA
(Thunor's Moon)

I have been thinking about thunder, Sif, thinking about the sound of Thunor's hammer, Giant Mauler, mighty Crusher. Thunder is the echo of war-songs sung, and it is the long, tearing birth-cry of new ones. Terrible the sound, a rolling deadly growl of warning, a promise of danger. In the song of Thunor's hammer lies the cold fear a man feels when his back is to the cliff's edge, his enemies too many, his hope for life changing to a hope for the All-Father's welcome.

And the lightning, bright across a night sky—flung spears, unwarm light—I have been thinking about that, my Sif. That light makes strange all it shows, makes unfamiliar the landmarks we know. In its glare the faces of friends seem like the faces of strangers. Unmasked fears stand naked in their eyes.

Ay, but something else there is in Thunor's rages, something powerful, livening. You can feel it skittering along your skin, hear it crackling in the air. There are some who love Thunor's storm, who go out to high places, taste the risk, revel in the dance of lightning and Thunor's hard war-songs. We storm-watchers, we lovers of the heights learn this: Once tasted, the storm does not let go, calls us always to that high place, that dangerous place, and we drink the danger eagerly, the way a drunkard sucks at a wineskin.

But some there are who hear the storm and hardly know that the Thunderer is raging.

Have you ever stood close to the edge of the woods, Sif, when the first storm-darkness shadows the land, smelled the sharp air, looked out to the horizon to see Thunor's gleaming spears? Have

you heard, in that deep pause between the time when there is not
thunder and the next long roll, the wood dove singing quietly?
She's prudent, ay, no fool. She's found good shelter, a safe and
dry place. But she does not still her song, does not sit mute and
terrified before Wotan's son. Her song, sweet comforting notes,
continues, will not be stilled by any god.

It takes a sharp eye to see the dove sheltering from the storm,
a quick ear to hear her soft song. Only a brave heart can follow
her gentle counsel of hope.

In those days, Sif, days of war and gold-bright battle-kings, I
found it easier to listen to the Storm-god, easier to follow his voice
to the high and dangerous places.

Ay, well. I was still young in those days when the Norns were
weaving the threads of your father's fate and mine, still learning
about courage.

I

I no longer listened for the wood dove, no longer watched for my
Lydi. Now I was glad that she didn't come to me, for I dreaded
the thought that were she to touch me she'd feel in me the grey
cold echoes of the *baresark's* howling, the ice-wind song of the
shadow-wolf that mad Blodrafen had recognized. Surely those
bleak echoes would terrify my Lydi, and like a merciless wolf,
chase down love and devour it, leaving only the stark bones of pity
exposed.

But I watched for the bear, Sif—for the old forest-roamer. Him
I saw once, dark-shouldered, broad-armed, dagger-clawed. He
rooted round the piled stones of Rhodri ap Iau's barrow, and when
he paused in his foraging, snout smeared with dirt from his grub-
bing, when he looked at me, sounded his low moaning cry, I heard
hard fates stirring. That day we walked away from each other, old
bear and me. Some men would have counted it good luck to have
come safely away. I didn't. I'd learned that good luck never followed in that bear's tracks.

On the night when there was no moon, when Stag had fallen
to the shadow-wolf and Thunor's red moon was yet unborn, my
men and I left the glade, went to make our camp on hard Cefn
Arth. A fine camp that glade had been when we were thirteen
strong. Now it was indefensible, for we were only eight—four
Dwarfs and four Men; and of us, Haestan and Ceowulf had no

strength for fighting. The bear-ravaged red dog was in better health than they.

We didn't ride the ridge anymore, kept our horses picketed close at the wildwood's dark edge. We only watched, day and night, and waited for our fate, kind or cruel, to find us. Still, none—not my battle-brave men, not I—talked of leaving the borderlands. We didn't think it better to flee, snatching at reasons along the way to excuse abandoning Erich's borders. The War Hawk was our _cyning_. We'd had food and keep in his father's hall; we had Erich's trust and friendship now. Good men know that cowardice is shameful payment for these things.

Yet, for all our talk of obeying the _cyning's_ orders even to death, it might be the War Hawk himself would have had a hard time coaxing us away from that ridge. _Dvergr_ and _mann-cynn_, we were the good friends of men killed in battle. We were vengeance-minded.

Dyfed sat counting skulls in the bright dawnlight. Perched high on the watch-stone, the tall boulder where he could see north and south along Cefn Arth, he didn't watch the ridge now, but studied the good path that led down into the Marches. There we'd tumbled the bones of the _Wealas_ who'd attacked us on the night Godwig and Ecgwulf were killed, the night Wulf and Waerstan died. In no mood to dig a grave, we'd burned our enemies' bodies with the dead horses, sent their fire-black bones to join the clean-picked ones of Rhodri's friends.

Because we'd burned the corpses of the _Wealas_ and the horses, we lighted no pyre for Ecgwulf and Wulf and Waerstan, didn't mingle their ashes with the smoke of carrion. They shared Godwig's barrow, and maybe they didn't mind. Those four had been friends.

Dyfed picked out the skulls one by one—soot-darkened or sun-gleaming—folded down first the fingers of his left hand and then the ones of his right. Holding up his two fists, he grinned coldly.

"I've run out of hands, but not skulls. Seems to me, Garroc, that half a village is lying there. Wager the other half will be coming to look for their friends one of these nights."

"Ghost Foot," I said, leaning against the night-damp boulder, taking my weight from a leg still sore, still hoof-marked, "you keep offering wagers I'd be a fool to accept."

I looked north along the ridge, then south, avoided the sight of the barrow as carefully as I would avoid the company of a plague-struck beggar. From here I could not see the camping fire, could not see *dvergr* and *mann-cynn* sleeping just below Cefn Arth's humped spine. Along the high part of the ridge nothing moved but shadows running back to the forest, retreating before day's light.

Dyfed grunted thoughtfully, looked out over the Marches again. "Garroc, do you think we're going to die here?"

"Maybe," I said. "Maybe not."

I didn't worry too much about Vorgund Witch-Gatherer. If it had been in his mind to fling us all into the arms of the *Wael-cyriges*, he'd have done it before now. I did worry about the raiders, though, and with them the thing could go one of two ways: Either they'd lost enough men to count stolen cattle not worth the risk of more lives, or they would take it into their heads to avenge kin and friends. We wouldn't know what they'd do until they did it.

Eye on the Marches, the tapestried pattern of greens, Dyfed said that he supposed dying on the doorstep of home was better than dying in foreign lands.

And it was strange, Sif, the feeling I had then. I could find no reason for it, but it seemed to me that Dyfed was not looking to home when he looked at the Marches. But I asked no question, for in those days that was not the way of things between Dyfed and me.

Werrehund came to meet me as I walked back to the camp. Now that he was up and walking, he had no patience for bandages, and Dyfed bowed to his red dog's wishes. Long wounds were healing now, skin closing around cuts. He was not good to look at; much of him was scab-skinned and hairless. His gait was strange, no longer a high-stepping dance, only a limping shuffle, but his tail still worked well and he waved it in greeting, slid his head under my hand for petting.

Sunlight lay warm on Cefn Arth, calling deep sighs from the stone. A lazy breeze, cool from the forest, told of horses moving restlessly, brought the sound of Cynnere's and Aescwine's soothing words as they went among the mounts, ready to take them into the wildwood for water. Huddled and dark, the Blood Raven slept in the sharp-edged shadow of the ridge, well away from the light. He twitched a little as the red dog and I passed, moaned as though dreaming wild war-songs. Werrehund and I didn't disturb him as we went to sit by the morning-pale fire.

Ceowulf slept there, and Haestan did. Between the two, watchful friend, sat Aelfgar. I laid my hand against Ceowulf's throat, felt the strong rhythm of blood beating. The deep-scored lines of pain I'd seen in his face last night had eased. The bandages wrapping his sword-bitten leg and dagger-gnawed shoulder were new and clean. I glanced at Aelfgar.

"Did you do this?"

He nodded, shyly pleased when I praised his work, told him that he'd learned some things from Dyfed that Ceowulf would be grateful for. But when I asked him how Haestan did, all gladness went out of his blue eyes. He answered carefully, as though giving a scout's report.

"I got him to eat, Garroc, but not much. It hurts him to swallow. He said there's an anvil's weight on his chest. And he said he's getting tired of trying to lift it every time he wants to breathe."

Sword-cut, his ribs and left arm shattered by trampling hoofs, Haestan slept, but only fitfully; breathed, but only barely. It was hard to look at him, hard to hear him struggle for breath. Sweat sheened his grey, old-seeming face and, unbidden, came the memory of the last time I saw Halfdan alive. Then his face was grey, like Haestan's was now; then the Hunter had seemed far older than his years, as Haestan did now.

Aelfgar sat quiet for a time and I watched him closely. In the days past, a change had come upon him and it seemed to me that I could no longer think of him as Aelfgar of the thousand questions. Since the night Dyfed and I had found him weeping for Wulf's death, Aelfgar had become quieter, more thoughtful.

Ah, Aelfgar, I thought, maybe you are finally becoming more man than boy.

I thought that sadly, for it is hard to lose childhood—even at the age of twenty-seven winters—to the understanding that, this way or that, death will find your friends. From there it is only a short way to knowing that, this way or that, death will one day find you.

And maybe it seems strange to you, Sif, that a man who'd spent most of his years a soldier would not understand about the nearness of death. But this is Aelfgar I am speaking of. Some things he understood well, and some things—even things you'd think obvious—he was a long time understanding.

But not all of his questions were gone from young Aelfgar. After a time he looked at me, and his eyes shone brightly with the light of a new idea. "Garroc, do you think maybe we should go find your Lydi?"

Breeze whispered across the ridge. In the shadow of Cefn Arth the Blood Raven moaned over his dreams of war and killing. I shuddered. Most often these days, when I didn't dream of ghosts, I dreamed of war and killing, too.

I'd thought before now that were I to send for the witch's help, she'd grant it. Haestan could not ride. He'd die before we got him onto a horse's back. If Dyfed had occasion to make a joke of my inability to recognize that once before, he had none now. Every man of us could see it. Lydi would have to come to him. She'd do it. I knew that too. And some way could be arranged for her to be alone with Haestan. Horses needed to be run . . . hunting needed to be done. . . .

But I hadn't seen the dove since I'd told her god-Freyr's tale in the bluebell woods, had not seen her since we'd spoken painfully of trust and fear. And maybe I would not have been the one to ride to Gardd Seren to fetch her, but I could not send Aelfgar or Dyfed either. We needed more men here on Cefn Arth, not fewer. My battle-shadow, my friend Haestan, would have to take his chances with his wounds, would have to get well with Dyfed's help and Aelfgar's. Or he would have to greet the All-Father when the god came calling for him.

I said nothing of this to Aelfgar. I told myself that he wouldn't understand, but the truth of it is that I didn't want to talk about Lydi. Instead, I told him that he'd have to make Haestan as comfortable as he could, for there was nothing else we could do.

"Nothing, Garroc?"

"Nothing."

Trusting, not trying to understand the reasons for my answer, simply accepting it, Aelfgar nodded slowly, solemnly. "Then I'll take care of him, Garroc, just as I have been. I promise it."

Ah, words, Sif, words!

Sometimes we understand what is meant when we hear them, sometimes we don't. That morning Aelfgar didn't understand the meaning of my words, and I didn't comprehend the meaning of his.

At day's end, when the sun had gone to rest behind the tall peaks of the Cambrians, leaving only the last slanting red light behind, Aescwine and I sat with Cynnere, who kept watch at the edge of Cefn Arth. For the most part there was only silence among us while we waited to learn that Haestan was dead. Tall on the watch-stone, the last sunlight giving gold to his long hair, his raggedly trimmed beard, Cynnere looked out over the valley, all along the ridge. When he looked behind him in the direction of our camp, his eyes grew still and thoughtful. He had the look of a man preparing for sorrow.

"Ay," he said, as though answering a question. "I am going to miss him."

I chose not to understand his meaning, but Aescwine nodded. "A good one, that Haestan," he whispered.

Cynnere leaned down from the stone, nudged Aescwine's shoulder. "Do you remember, *dvergr*, what you always used to say about him?"

Aescwine nodded, a grim smile tugging at his lips. "Oh, yes. 'Worst when he's drunk, best when he's sober.' "

Cynnere snorted. "That's what he used to say about you, old'un. You used to say that you were often glad that Haestan fought beside you and not against you."

"So I did. So I did." He looked at me sideways, silently invited me to call up my own memory of Haestan.

I said nothing. Haestan was not yet dead and I was not eased to hear these two talk about him as though he were two years in his barrow. Almost I walked away from them, but I didn't like the idea of going back to camp just yet. I didn't want to watch my friend wane with the day.

Aescwine combed blunt, war-scarred fingers through his beard, gently stroking. His eyes still on me, he said:

"Cynnere, I'm thinking I wouldn't mind taking your watch for a time, and maybe you'd like to sit for a while with our Haestan, yes?"

Cynnere slid down from the watch-stone, made the ridge grumble a little for his weight. Eyes strangely bright, as a man's are just before he weeps, he said, "Maybe I would, old'un."

When he looked to me, asked silent permission to leave his watch, I waved him on, still said nothing. In truth, Sif, it would have been very hard for me to speak then.

Aescwine knew that and kept his own silence until Cynnere was gone. Then, pushing away from the watch-stone and its cool shadow, he said, "Tell me, young skald, do you know about the Geat king, the one who died fighting a dragon?"

He wanted an answer. I could see it by the sharp look of him. Glad for the moment to turn away from impending grief and the dangerous shadow it had lately been able to call up in me, I told him that the Geats have had a good measure of kings over the years; and some dragons, too.

"Well, both things are true. But maybe they've never had a king before this one who died because he was too strong." .

Almost I smiled and for a moment the tightness lessened in my throat, for that moment I spoke easily. "That's a strange thing to die of, too much strength."

"It is, young skald, but that's what killed him. You see, this one's strength was a wonder. In his youth, before he was a famous king, he killed sea-drakes with his bare hands. And fought giants. One time he tore the arm off a terrible monster, ripped it right from the shoulder socket. He was strong! But he was too strong. No sword that he wielded could withstand the strength of his arm. Each blade, no matter how well made, shattered after one strike."

"And so," I said, "he could not bring a sword against the dragon, yes?"

"Yes."

"Yet, if he was as strong as you say, he could have ripped the dragon's head off."

Aescwine shook his head sadly. "Ever see a dragon, youngster?"

I admitted that I hadn't, though once I'd heard that something long and big, perhaps dragon-like, lived in the icy lakes in the lands of the Picts.

"Well, if you'd ever gone to see the thing that lives in the Pictish lakes, you'd have seen a sea-drake, and you'd know why the Geat king didn't just rip off his dragon's head. A dragon's head is half the size of a hall, legs're like young trees. No, a sword was what this king needed, and only a sword would do. With it he could have darted in swiftly, put out the *wyrm's* eyes, hacked its throat, and killed it at his leisure. But he didn't have a sword, you see. Shattered the thing the first blow he struck." Aescwine sighed deeply. "Poor brave fool died because he was too strong."

The sky above the ridge grew pearly, washed with the first of dimming's light while we stood in silence. After a time, Aescwine reached across the distance between us, tapped his old fingers against my heart.

"Sometimes, young skald," he said gently, "it's a good thing to have the strength not to weep. Sometimes it's not a good thing at all. Take care, Garroc my friend, that your strength doesn't kill you, ay?"

So saying, he left me.

Alone in the shadow of the watch-stone, I thought there was a thing I knew that Aescwine didn't: I fought no dragon, as the Geat king did. I fought a shadow-wolf. Grey-cold and deadly, it lived within me and its name was Grief, though sometimes it answered to Despair. And it knew magic, this dread *sceadu-wulf*, it

knew how to transform the unwatchful from a sane man to a berserker.

Maybe the Geat king thought it was a good idea to try to kill
his dragon. Me, I judged it better not to go waving swords under
the snout of Fenris' kin, thought it best to use all my strength to
keep the *sceadu-wulf* chained, as the gods kept terrible Wolf-
Fenris chained, so that I'd never have to fight it.

Ecgwulf Icel's son was dead on Cefn Arth; and Waerstan
Hnaef's son, and his brother Wulfsunu. And Godwig was dead,
who was a Dwarf and *Laestan*; he took no father's name.

And Haestan. I never knew the name of Haestan's father, never
knew a thing about him. Had he been, like his son, a soldier? Had
he been a smith, a stoneman, a hunter? Or was he simply one of
many who died unsung, unremembered? I never knew, and Haestan—my battle-shadow, my friend—had never spoken of him. So
it is with *Laestan*. We hold our sorrow tight to ourselves, don't
let others see it, don't look long at it ourselves.

We sat waking through the night, my men and I, for while the
night held the faint echo of Haestan's ghostly voice, a voice only
I heard, the wind brought distant growling, far rumbling, filled
the northeast sky with the sound of Thunor moving. Wind piled
clouds high, then smoothed them over the earth, hid stars and the
Storm-god's thin new moon. The heavy air crackled, spoke of danger.

"Ay, battle-signs," Cynnere said, his voice low and eager. He
reached for his sword, and Ceowulf handed him a whetstone.
Aescwine thought so too; he took his axe out to the edge of Cefn
Arth, went to stand watch and to look at Wotan's son riding the
night.

Of us all, only Aelfgar showed no interest in the god's progress,
none in the thought of battle. Silent, tight and hard-eyed, he kept
himself apart, would not let Dyfed offer the comfort he'd offered
once before. From time to time he watched as Blodrafen, head up
like a dog scenting something good, prowled restlessly at the dark
edge of the wildwood. Dyfed was troubled to see Aelfgar's lonely
grief.

"He's seen men die before now, Garroc. Why does he take it
so hard?"

I told him that I didn't know, told him that Aelfgar, being Aelfgar, would likely come to himself soon, as he had after Wulf's
death.

Ay, Sif, I didn't know, neither did I take the time to learn. I was caught between trying not to hear the echoes of Haestan's ghosty voice and trying to keep hold of my strength so that I would not weep.

And this is the thing that we didn't know, Dyfed and I, the thing we didn't understand:

Dyfed had been glad to have gentle-handed Aelfgar to help him with his healer-work, and glad to share the credit for his successes. But he'd shared that credit too generously, much as a father will who tries to teach his young son a skill, and hoping to encourage, too strongly praises the childish work of his little boy's hands. And it's true that I'd done the same. We didn't think, never considered, that Haestan's death would feel like failure to Aelfgar, or seem like his fault and not the fault of the Welsh raider who'd hurt him—or of Wotan, who, in godly greed, didn't resist calling another soldier to Valholl.

We didn't think; we didn't consider.

II

AT night's-end I left the camp, went out to the watch-stone to keep Aescwine company. I walked carefully past the barrow that held Godwig's bones and Wulf's and Waerstan's and Ecgwulf's, kept well out of its broad dark shadow, stepped quickly around the small sharp shadow of the new barrow. Last night, in the long summer dimming, we'd made that barrow, placed it close beside the taller one, gave Haestan back to the mother-earth.

Aescwine turned away from the Marches when he heard me coming, grounded his axe. Pale dawnlight ran along the iron horn of the weapon, glittered on its broad scarred beak. Eerie, that light; it seeped from behind dark-bellied clouds like ghostly silver.

Yawning, Aescwine said, "He's taking his time, ay."

I looked out over the sky, listened to Thunor prowling his storm-hall. "He'll be here today."

"It's what I figured. And he's bringing a big army with him."

Eyes still on the deep clouds, I said I'd not heard that the Storm-god preferred to travel with an army, had always heard that he liked to do his giant-fighting alone.

"Oh, yes, young skald. I've heard the same thing." Aescwine

pointed north and east, into the valley. "But I was talking about the *cyning*."

I shaded my eyes against the pale eastern light. Dark, darker than the night still lingering in the Marches, shadows moved, wove through the valley like a dragon winding. No *wyrm* this, but a long line of mounted men riding. Erich War Hawk rode down from the northlands, returned to his Marches, came to see how well his fierce pack of watch-dogs had guarded his holdings.

Bright as a king's hoard, mail and golden hair shining against Thunor's dark and angry sky, flanked by swift-riding Grimmbeald and another man, Erich rode up from the Marches. His horse was the long-legged, surging grey I'd last seen Penda King riding. I wondered about this only briefly, for the grey's sharp hoofs called echoes from the hard stone of Cefn Arth, and Aescwine—even Blodrafen—cheered to hear the *cyning* riding. Dyfed and Ceowulf and Cynnere cried out gladly to see Halfdan's son, but their cries were soft whispers beside the sudden shout that rang out from behind me. Ay, another man rode with Grimmbeald and the *cyning*. Aelfgar knew who it was before any of us.

"Gadd," he cried, wildly, joyously. "Ay, Gadd!"

And none could keep Aelfgar from his horse, none could keep him from galloping his mount, headlong and reckless, down the stone paths to join his brother. As we watched from the sharp edge of Cefn Arth, the War Hawk left swift-riding Grimmbeald and Aelfgar and Gadd behind, urged his mount to greater speed.

"Ah, Garroc," Dyfed said, grinning wide. "There's a sight I've been wanting to see for a while."

I nodded, quiet now because I heard, whispering in me, the new words to my old song, the five new names I must add to the dead-call.

Blue eyes dark as new iron, Halfdan's son leaned against the watch-stone, looked at the cross-marked grave of the *Wealas* who died defending the glade when the moon was called Ghost, at the barrows that housed the bodies of his own good soldiers. Then he looked at the Dwarfs and Men gathered near the fire. Like palest gold, the flames shone bravely against the storm-threatening sky. So shone the tales of Dyfed and son-reft Aescwine, Cynnere and wounded Ceowulf. They told Grimmbeald and Gadd stories of the bear and the battles on Cefn Arth, tales of courage bright against sorrow, victory shining against loss.

Only two didn't contribute to the story-making, and they were

Aelfgar and Blodrafen. The one sat close to his brother, grim and thoughtful. Aelfgar no longer had a great store of joy and what he had was quickly spent. The other, the *baresark*, kept to the shadows, storm-eyed and brooding. The Blood Raven did not like to share his friend.

Erich listened, deep in silence, then looked at me. He tugged at his close-trimmed golden beard, forced himself to speak the hard words. "Who is dead, Garroc?"

I heard the echo of funeral flames in the damp wind.

"*Mann-cynn* have died," I said softly. "Ecgwulf Icel's son and Waerstan Hnaef's son and Wulfsunu Hnaef's son." In the stamping of horses, the sound of men's footfalls, I heard the echo of barrow-building. "*Dvergr* have left us, Godwig and Haestan."

Erich pushed away from the watch-stone, his face like wood, hard, immobile. So much like his father in form and feature, yet so unlike! I'd never needed to guess what the Hunter was thinking, almost always knew what he was feeling. Not so Erich; not so the cool and distant War Hawk.

Eyes on the brooding sky, he slid his sword halfway from its sheath, rammed it home again with a hard and final snap, gestured sharply for me to follow him. Together we walked south along the edge of Cefn Arth, Thunor's cool wind at our backs. Erich stopped at the head of the good path down into his farmlands, looked at the white bones of Rhodri ap Iau's companions and the blackened bones of dead horses and the last Welshmen who'd tried to raid here.

"How many were there, Garroc?"

"Fourteen and then ten, maybe twelve. There were others; they kept us busy. Some got away, some are dead in the forest."

He looked north, eyes half-shut as though gauging the speed of the Storm-god's approach. "What about Vorgund?"

"We haven't seen him, *cyning*."

Erich turned, eyes sharp as cold blades. "Grimmbeald said he was hiding in the north. Do you think he's still there?"

"Could be. Me, I'm glad to have him keep to his mountains if that's where he wants to stay. We aren't too many here now, *cyning*."

"How many men will you need to hold this border for a while longer?"

I answered quickly. "More than twelve."

He looked around the ridge again, at the grave and the barrows. Most often the War Hawk's eyes were cold, most often they were not easily read. So it was then. I didn't see his regret for the deaths of his men, but I thought I heard it in his voice.

"I wish I'd had three times twelve to give you in the spring, Garroc. Will you take them now?"

Three dozen men, Sif! He offered me riches. With thirty-six hard soldiers—more when I counted what men I already had—I could garrison the ridge north and south.

From the wildwood's edge where the horses were picketed came a wild trumpeting, the call of a restless stallion. The horse Erich had ridden, Penda's grey, might make such a song. I thought about that horse, and I thought about how my *cyning* was better dressed than when I'd last seen him. He'd changed his old and battle-stained shirt and trews for new, clean ones, had given up his sword-dinted byrnie for a stronger one. These were Penda's gifts. I wondered whether Wotan's Blade, open-handed King, had been as generous with men as he had been with war-gear and mounts.

As though he'd guessed my thought, Erich's blue eyes glinted proudly. "Ay, Garroc. The King has given me more men, the pick of his best. He says I've done him good service. Now I can afford to be no less generous than he."

My old curiosity rose, made me ask whether the King's treaty-making had gone well.

"Well enough. Penda is still in the north. He gave me these men to hold the Marches." He turned, dropped a hard hand on my shoulder. "Garroc, come down with me now, make your pick of them. *Faeders-freond*, it's been hard for you here. I can see it. Can you hold this border, keep it safe a while longer?"

Father's friend. He needn't have named me that. Tired I was of the borderlands, but Erich was my *cyning* and I'd have done what he wanted if he'd asked me in his own name.

I looked north, looked south. I didn't look to the mountains where Gardd Seren lay nestled in its little valley, for there my Lydi kept close to her magic garden, didn't come to me, didn't send her dreams. And I was both afraid to see her and afraid that I'd driven her from me. I didn't look east to the Marches, to Rilling where too many of my friends would no longer sit with me in our *cyning's* hall. All that remained to me then was this borderland, ill-omened Cefn Arth.

My Sif, we stand where Fate puts us. When we move, it is only in the patterns the Norns weave. Me, I would always do what my *cyning* bade me do, for love of him, for deep-sworn oaths, and for pride. Around this design my own small fate is woven.

"Erich," I said. "With two garrisons I could hold this ridge till winter."

He laughed, young war hawk, and that sound was bright and bold against Thunor's growling. "Ah, Garroc, you won't have to hold it that long. I'll be wanting you and your men in Rilling before winter."

And then he told me that Penda King was not the only one who came away from the northern kingdom with an alliance. Cynewulf, who had been hungrily eying Halfdan's Marches these many years, had seen the Hunter's son riding to Northumbria at the King's side, brave and strong at the head of an army, and quickly decided that it might be best to tie this war hawk to him, bind this king's friend with gentle bonds.

The woman's name was Gled and men called her Gled Golden-Hair. Though her father had never been a friend to Halfdan, Erich said he didn't mind, for Cynewulf promised to dower his youngest daughter well, and she was said to be very beautiful. Maybe Erich would have to teach Cynewulf's daughter friendly ways, for her father had never been over-generous in his love for Halfdan's kin and likely would not have taught his daughter differently. But he thought the dower and the beauty were good compensation for this. Too, he thought that Cynewulf would make a better ally than enemy.

"She'll be at Rilling in midwinter," Erich said. "And then we'll be wed." He nodded, deeply satisfied. "A warm way to pass cold months, ay Garroc?"

Ay, warm, I thought. But she was Cynewulf's daughter, and so maybe Golden-Hair would not give off the kind of warmth young Erich was thinking of. But I said nothing of this to Erich, only went with him to get our horses, eager now to ride down to the valley and choose my garrisons.

As soon as Erich left the stony path down from the Bear's Ridge, the strong scents of a war-camp—fish and meat roasting over afternoon fires, bitter iron, sweat and the thick smell of horses—came to greet us. We smiled, each secretly into his beard. These were the smells of home. These were the comfortable smells he'd grown up with, smells I'd known all the sixteen years since I'd left Stane Saewulf's son for the places of war. Erich put his heels to his mount, sent him galloping. Blood singing warm songs in me, I kicked up Ecgwulf's grey, rode with the *cyning* toward the shining sea of soldiers, bright under Thunor's iron sky.

The army filled the valley which my *mearc-threat* had warded

all the nights since spring. The camp spread from the foot of the
ridge to a small band of woodland beyond the edge of the glittering
river I'd watched so often from Cefn Arth. Wotan's Blade had
dealt generously indeed with his faithful Erich. For every man I
knew, I saw two who were strangers. All of them, friend and
stranger alike, bore the stamp of Penda's generosity. Their mail
shone brave and bright; they carried strong weapons, wore handsome harnesses over newly made shirts and trews. As we rode,
Erich watched me trying to count them.

"Two hundreds," he said proudly. "My father never led such
a force."

"No," I said, and it was hard to speak evenly. Erich's proud
words stung me, made me want to rise in his father's behalf. "Halfdan never had an army so large. But he led what men he had well."

Erich looked at me sideways, said stiffly, "I'll lead these well,
too, Garroc. Just as he taught me to."

Then I smiled, for it was hard not to with such a bright eagle
beside me. "I know it, *cyning*."

Head high, blue eyes gleaming, he swept past the guards' watch-
fire at the edge of the camp. I kicked up Ecgwulf's grey and kept
pace.

III

As I walked through the wide camp, looking for the Dwarfs and
Men I wanted, I saw berserkers wherever I went. Gathered in
packs of five or six, they kept to themselves, welcomed no intrusion
from others. I knew by sight the *baresarks* we'd always called the
Hunter's pack. Blodrafen had been one of these until I took him
away to Cefn Arth. I counted twenty and nine berserkers who
were strangers to me, and the sight of them made me uneasy.

I wanted to keep Gadd with me, and I'd chosen the others,
Dwarfs and Men who knew me and who were not unhappy to take
their chances on the wildwood's border, when Eadric found me.
He greeted me gladly, asked news of Aelfgar and Dyfed, told me
that he and Swithgar were well, then walked beside me, quiet company as I went to the river to fill my lungs with the freshening
breeze of the oncoming storm. Though he kept his silence, his narrowed eyes told me something I didn't need words to know: My
scout Eadric had something to say and he didn't consider it good
news.

After a time he looked up at the sky, winced as the first fat drops of rain fell. Ploughing a thick-fingered hand through his beard, he said, "Garroc, the *cyning* is looking for you."

"I figured he would be soon or late. I'm going there now."

Eadric caught my shoulder, stopped me. "But wait a bit, will you? I want to talk to you."

Wind hissed through the reeds, tossed the plumes of the sedges at river's banks; rain pocked the river's surface. High in the sky, thunder growled.

"I figured that, too, Eadric. Tell me."

He stopped, looked at the sky again, then at the Dwarfs and Men around us. He drew a deep breath, the kind a man sucks in when he's about to plunge into cold waters, and jerked his chin toward a group of Dwarfs and Men, five dark shadows moving to get their gear and kindling under cover. "Those are *baresarks*," he said.

I told him I could see that; I told him I'd seen a lot of berserkers in the camp.

"Ay, Garroc. That's the thing—there's a lot of them. Some came with the men the King gave to Erich. Some we picked up in the north. You know how they are."

I did. It is never the same with *baresarks* as with others; *dvergr* or *mann-cynn*, most often they serve what *cyning* provides the best chance for fighting, rewards them best for killing. Borders mean nothing to them; they don't know what a homeland is. This is why many thought the long and deep loyalty of the Hunter's pack a true wonder.

Rain fell heavily now. Thunor's bright spears danced wildly. Around us men either cursed the rain or cried greeting to Wotan's son, depending upon the state of their cover. I pushed Eadric toward the shelter of the woods, urged him to talk as we ran. But he said nothing more until we'd found good shelter beneath thickly woven branches in a small grove of oaks.

Wiping streaming rain from his face, he said, "I don't think Erich likes those crazy-headed berserkers, Garroc. But he suffers them because they're strong, they fight forever. They make a difference."

"Ay, but . . . ?"

"Some of them don't like him."

Cold touched me, and it might have been caused by the rain, but I didn't think so. "Eadric, does the *cyning* know this?"

He laughed humorlessly. "I wouldn't try to guess what he knows and doesn't know. I'm not you, Garroc; he doesn't tell me much."

Erich didn't tell me much either. *Faeders-freond*, he called me. That is not the same as saying *freond min*.

"Why is there trouble, Eadric?"

"It's not the northern berserkers, or Penda's either. Not yet, anyway. The trouble comes from the Hunter's pack. They think it's a shameful thing to have a *cyning* who takes no vengeance for his father's killing."

I looked at Eadric closely. In the flash of Thunor's cold silver I saw that he didn't think the *baresarks* were far wrong. The berserkers were not the only ones who had loved the Hunter. Yet as I'd felt the need to defend Halfdan to his son, so now did my heart urge me to defend Erich to my scout.

"Eadric, the *cyning* is caught between what he knows he should do and what he knows he must do."

"So he is, and I said it to Swithgar this morning: I count myself a lucky man that I'm not in Erich's place. He has two duties—one to avenge his father, one to safeguard the Marches. He can't honor one without failing the other. I know it, Garroc, there's no way for him to please everyone. But I keep remembering how the War Hawk made himself *cyning*. It was a *baresark* helped him to that. I'm hoping it's not a *baresark* who takes it from him."

I looked out from our shelter to the driving rain, told Eadric to find Swithgar and then keep close to the *cyning's* tent, to wait until Erich was finished his business with me. I thought I'd like to talk to my two scouts again before I returned to Cefn Arth.

In early spring, in the mist-dragon's vale on the day after Halfdan died, Erich and I had sat alone in his tent and I'd drawn a map on damp ground. It was not so this summer's day. This day he had Dyfed's scraped-hide map of the northwestern corner of the Marches spread out on a makeshift table, the broad flat stump of a recently felled oak. This day, too, we were not alone. The *thegn* Hnaef stood the darkest corner of Erich's tent.

Sometimes Hnaef was solid-seeming, as when brazier light caught the hard facets of his brightly enameled shoulder clasp, gleamed from his broad belt buckle of twined gold and silver. Sometimes he seemed to have no more substance than a shadow in the uncertain, wavering smoke. A rich man was Hnaef, a holder of many farms in the fertile Saefern valley. But he was also a poor man, for he was the father of Waerstan and Wulf, and his dear sons were dead.

The *thegn* turned as I entered the tent, came fully into the light of the three-legged brazier. Though the sons had been tall, the father was not. He stood high as Erich's shoulder, not a head taller than I. Firelight gilded his grey hair, gleamed in his thick red beard. I looked at Erich, and when the *cyning* raised his eyes from his map and nodded curtly, I spoke with stiff and clumsy formality.

"*Thegn*, I am sorry for the death of your sons."

Rain drummed on the tent walls. Lightning flashed, and our shadows, tall as the ghosts of giants, leaped along the thin hide walls. Hnaef drew a tight breath, let it go hissing through his teeth, a sound like a wince.

"Did they die well, Garroc?"

Though the question had always seemed strange to me, I always used to know how to answer it. But now the words I needed didn't come readily, were held back, halted by the words I wanted to speak.

How well, I wanted to say, is any death, *thegn*? How well was Halfdan's death? How well Ecgwulf's or Godwig's or Haestan's? How much better is it to take your meat and mead with gods in great and golden Valholl than with men in this world?

But these were not questions Hnaef wanted to hear; these were not questions any who lived knew the answers for, and so I tried hard to recall what Dyfed had told Aelfgar about the deaths of our friends, reached for my friend's words of comfort. I'd found no ease from pain hearing those words, but maybe Hnaef would.

"Hnaef, your sons died well, as soldiers should. And they were brave while they lived. We had no better friends."

The lines of pain eased from his face. I saw it happen by the brazier's ruddy light. Hard fingers restive, he played with the bright clasp at his shoulder, traced the twisting patterns of the enameled design. "Where was their pyre?"

"There was none, *thegn*. They are housed in a barrow with Godwig and Haestan."

Outside, where rain fell like dark arrows, Thunor roared. When the god was silent again, Hnaef spoke with the gentleness I'd not been able to find. "*Dvergr*, I'm sorry for the deaths of your kindred. We cannot afford such deaths."

Erich looked up from his map again, his face unreadable, wooden. "We can't afford any deaths," he said abruptly. Then, as though he'd suddenly heard the sharpness of his own voice, he spoke more softly. "Hnaef, is there anything else you need from my scout?"

The *thegn* had all he wanted from me, simple word that his children had died bravely, were honored by friends. He took up his mantle, used his beautiful clasp to fasten it tight around his shoulders, and left us to the smoky darkness and the sound of rain on the tent walls.

Erich didn't watch him leave, moved on at once to what concerned him most: the Marches. He waved me to the tree stump, moved the brazier closer for better light. Shadows of smoke poured across the scraped hide, ran like swift dark currents across the map. Someone had added to Dyfed's picture of the Marches, for now it showed all of Erich's holding.

With a rough finger, the one broken in some long-ago battle and only crookedly mended, the *cyning* traced his eastern border from the west arm of the River Tren to Caestir in the north. He shared that border in common with Cynewulf who was the father of Gled Golden-Hair, the woman who would be his wife come the winter.

Erich smiled grimly. "These eastern lands are fair safe for now."

"Do you know how long Cynewulf can tolerate peace?"

His blue eyes glinted with amusement as he pulled thoughtfully at his short beard. "Do they ever call you Garroc the Distrustful?"

"Could be, *cyning*, but if they do, they don't say it where I can hear them. Sometimes your father called me a careful-goer, though."

Erich grunted as though to say he thought his naming a better one than Halfdan's.

"Cynewulf will tolerate peace for as long as it takes to get his Gled safely wed to me. Maybe for as long as it takes his daughter to get a good hold on her marriage share by giving me a child. That never takes much less than three-fourths of a year, ay? At the least, we can count on peace from him until after next harvest."

He turned back to the map, traced around past the Cambrians' foothills and down again to the broad point below the River Saefern where Osric's northern border was his southern one.

"This one, Garroc, this Osric, is another matter. He has no daughters, only hungry sons. And too many of those." He stroked the parchment gently, caressed his southern border. "Osric hasn't got enough land to keep his young brands happy. He needs more. I think he'd like to have mine."

Thunder rolled, a long lazy growl, as the Storm-god moved south. I thought that Osric would surely be a fool if he didn't covet Erich's Marches. Osric's lands were mostly dense and dark forestlands, hard to clear and hard to keep. I'd known the *Wealas* to enjoy raiding in Osric's lands nearly as much as they liked troubling the Marches. They found it easy to steal Osric's farmers naked, take women and children for slaves, and lose the vengeance-seekers in the deep woods. Those few parts of Osric's lands that were free of forest and raiders were made up of stony downs or shallow wet marshlands. Useless to farmers, those lands, for Saxons—*mann-cynn* if not *dvergr*—are farmers when they aren't soldiers.

"I'm thinking, *cyning*, that you'll go south soon."

"At dawn tomorrow," he said. "Osric needs to understand something about borders. I think I can teach him well."

I didn't doubt it. Erich had not been *cyning* of his Marches for more than four months, and already he'd earned Penda's regard, led an army twice the size of the one Halfdan had left him. Halfdan had trained his War Hawk well, taught him battle-craft and how to lead men. If Erich remembered that teaching, Osric would have no cause to boast of lands won this year.

I moved the brazier closer to the map, traced the northern border and the western one. "What of these?"

Erich ran his hand along the side of his face, dragged his fingers through his beard. He looked tired now. "Don't worry about the northern one. The King will see to it for me."

He stabbed the crooked finger at the western border, at the Cambrians, and pale lightning shivered the darkness, the flames in the brazier leaped high. A chill crept along my spine. The *cyning's* rough battle-scarred finger lay close to the place where Lydi's Seintwar is.

"Worry about this border, Garroc. You're the one who has to defend it now. And if what you tell me about Vorgund is true, maybe you'll have to worry about witches, as well."

Almost I laughed. I'd been worrying about witches long before now. I didn't think I'd stop worrying about them any time soon.

To Erich I said, "You've given me enough men to do what I have to do. As for witches . . ." I shook my head. "Maybe a hundred men wouldn't do against them, ay? And maybe Vorgund won't bring them against me just now. He hasn't yet."

"Why do you think that is, Garroc?"

He asked his question quietly, but it was a sharp-eyed kind of quiet, the kind that hides fear. I watched him carefully for a long moment and, because I did, I saw the reason.

Young War Hawk, Halfdan's proud son! I think the only thing he truly feared about Vorgund at that time was that the Witch-Gatherer considered him less than worth the effort of a quick assault. I wondered if he knew what the Hunter's pack said of him, wondered if he thought that his decision not to take fast vengeance upon Vorgund gave him a shameful coward's seeming in the Witch-Gatherer's eyes.

"Erich," I said, at last, speaking as gently as I dared. "*Cyning*, I don't know much about Vorgund, only what I've learned in battle. He's a wild-hearted fighter, but he's no fool. Your father beat him badly in the spring, shattered his army, scattered his warriors halfway to the western sea. I said it in the spring and I still believe it: Vorgund won't fight until he's certain that he can win. If that means letting his countrymen harry the farms, play deadly games with the border-patrol, I'd wager that he'll gladly do that and count each one of us who's dead as one less to come against him when he's ready to leave his mountains again."

Erich leveled a long, considering look at me, then smiled grimly. "Your gamble is a large one, Garroc: the lives of the men still up on that ridge and the lives of the thirty-six you've chosen."

"I know it."

I did know it, but though Vorgund's witches and soldiers might well overwhelm my two garrisons, still forty and four men were half an army. Witch-Gatherer would pay dearly for our deaths, and I didn't think he had the price of that yet.

I thought about the Hunter's pack again, then said to Erich the thing I'd have said to his father. "*Cyning*, I'm wagering, ay, but I don't think I'm the only one gambling. The Hunter's pack is not happy. Do you know it?"

Lightning flared, one last spear of the god's light. Shadows darkened Erich's face. "I know it," he said. "And I know why. But I don't choose my war-fields on the whim of berserkers, and my father's ghost doesn't haunt my sleep.

"My father loved his Marches, Garroc, and most breaths he took were taken while he fought to keep his people safe. And ay, I'd like to hang Vorgund's head from the highest rafter in the hall, but I won't do it at the expense of my father's Marches."

"Your Marches now, Erich."

He laughed bitterly. "*Faeders-freond*, if you're thinking that I earned these lands on the night I killed Dunnere, you're wrong. That night I only earned the right to try to hold them. Now I'm trying. The King has given me men enough to make the southern border safe. He is holding the northern border, Gled Golden-Hair's hand will keep the eastern one peaceful. And you will watch the west.

"As for the *baresarks*, I've never known one yet who would rather think than fight. Soon they'll have enough work to make them forget their unhappiness, ay?"

Maybe, I thought. Maybe not.

To Erich, though, I said only that I would hold his western border. I didn't speak again about my doubts for the berserkers' happiness, for I knew that to speak further of my misgiving would be no more than wasting breath on unheard words.

But two thought as I did, and they were my scouts. From Swithgar, from Eadric, I took a deep-sworn oath, one they gave willingly because they loved their War Hawk *cyning*. And so when I rode back to Cefn Arth with my two garrisons, I knew something even Erich didn't know. The *cyning* had among his men two scouts, Dwarf and Man, who were sworn to be shield and weapon and guardian-friends to the War Hawk. Each would cast his own life into the balance if it meant the saving of Erich's.

IV

DURING the long wet dimming, with Dyfed's help, I made plans to safeguard the *cyning's* western border. I'd send half the men north, half south. With miles between the two garrisons, I didn't like to ride with one and not know how the other fared, and so my scouts and I made up a third band to ride sometimes with the northern garrison, sometimes with the southern. The next day, when the rain stopped and the sun gleamed on wet ridge-stone, most of us gathered at the edge of Cefn Arth to see the *cyning's* army ride away from the borderland. When the army had gone, I sent Dyfed and Cynnere far north. Dyfed knew what I needed: a clear map of the border, as far as the place where the rubble of a long-ago landslide narrowed the ridge to an impassable, broken ledge.

I told Cynnere to look for a good camping place for the nineteen men I would give him. Solemnly, Cynnere said that he would, and when he rode away with Dyfed, tall and straight-backed, he wore the sober dignity he thought fitting to a garrison leader, wore it proudly the way a man would wear a fine new mantle. That mantle slipped a bit after they'd ridden out of sight. Cynnere's wild whoop, his bright joyous shout to celebrate his new position as a leader of men, sailed back to us, clearly heard.

Aescwine leaned against the watch-stone, pulled at his white beard thoughtfully as he listened to that wind-borne laughter. "Boy's a bit young for it, Garroc."

The 'boy' had seen thirty-four winters, but I didn't argue. Aescwine was very old; everyone seemed young to him.

"If you like age in a leader, Aescwine, then I'll try to please you."

I looked for Gadd, saw him sitting in the sun with his brother. He seemed to be trying hard—and with no luck—to have some conversation with Aelfgar. I called them both to me, told them to get ready to ride south, gave them the same orders as I'd given Dyfed. "And take Aescwine with you, ay? Help him find a comfortable camp for his nineteen."

Gadd, tired of inaction, maybe tired of his brother's brooding silence, ran for the horses. Aelfgar followed more slowly. Aescwine watched the brothers for a long moment, then looked away, searching the dark at the wildwood's edge.

Though I looked where he did, I saw nothing but shadows moving on wet leaves.

"Garroc," he said, "I've been talking to some of the men you brought back with you." He jerked a thumb at a small group of Dwarfs standing close to the edge of the ridge. "Those fellows. They've brought some tales back from the north, and one of them was about Blodrafen.

"Did you ever hear the rumor that he'd killed his son?"

Eyes on the shadows again, knowing now who Aescwine had been looking for a moment ago, I said I'd heard the rumor.

"Ay, well. That rumor is the end of the story. I'm thinking you need to hear the beginning, Garroc."

Me, I was thinking that I didn't want to hear any part of it.

Maybe Aescwine knew that, for he laid a hand on my arm, said quietly, "This is no tale of dragons and foolhardy Geat kings, young skald. This is a true telling, and I give it for Aelfgar's sake."

For Aelfgar's sake I listened, and knew again—for Aescwine's tale showed it—that berserkers are not born, they are made.

Blodrafen had been a soldier all his life, but he'd taken enough time from fighting to get himself a son, and he loved that boy very much. Not for Blodrafen the grief and despair of knowing that he'd fathered a child who was *Laestan*. It was enough for him that he had a son to love, one he could teach the honorable skills of war-craft. Aescwine heard it that Ingild Blodrafen's son was a good and fierce fighter.

But even the best soldier cannot defend himself against arrows shot from behind. In a long battle, one waged at the edge of winter, when men should not have been fighting far from home, Ingild fell, three arrows in his back.

"And it was a bad thing," Aescwine said. "Because that boy should have died of any one of those bolts. But you know how it goes with battle-wounds, Garroc. Sometimes a man dies of a wound no one thinks is serious; sometimes he lives when everyone knows he will die. Ingild didn't die, though he should have. A healer got to him before Wotan did.

"Now, some healers are sensible, but others are fools who like to wrestle with the All-Father, like to keep the god's prize from him as long as they can. This healer had the desire to wrestle, but not enough skill and not enough strength to win. Ingild lived for a time, and in terrible pain. At the last, on a cold night, when the snow was falling, the Blood Raven could no longer bear to see his son racked and ruined, dying but not dead. For love, he chose mercy. Blodrafen killed his son." Aescwine looked at his hands, big hands scarred by war, fingers twisted a little by age. "Do you know how he did it, Garroc?"

Sick in my belly, I nodded. Blodrafen twisted Ingild's neck, snapped it hard and sent Ingild to the Raven-god. It was there for all to see each time the berserker killed in battle.

Aescwine looked to the barrow, the dark stone shadow on Cefn Arth where his own son slept. "I don't judge him for what he did to his son. I don't. How could I know what I'd have done in his place? But he doesn't remember the mercy now; he only remembers that he killed his Ingild. And so all his killing is ugly and makes a man sick to see it.

"He's not sane, Garroc. He's a *baresark*. And one of those fellows I was talking to last night said a frightening thing about him. He said that most people in the north who knew the Blood Raven before he came to join Halfdan's army know this about him: That *baresark* killed what he loved; now he loves what he kills."

I heard what Aescwine said, but only dimly. I was remembering the night I'd sent the *baresark* to kill wounded raiders, remembering my bitter determination to leave no one of them alive. I'd ordered the Blood Raven to do my killing for me, ordered him to kill his enemies as he'd once killed his son. No mercy for the *Wealas*, maybe none for the berserker.

Aescwine tugged at his beard as though tugging his last thought into shape. "Anyone can see that the *baresark* is fond of Aelfgar. Maybe it is that he hasn't had a kind feeling toward anyone since he helped Ingild to his death. But he doesn't think right . . . when he thinks at all. Maybe it is that his regard is a dangerous thing.

"Our Aelfgar has a man's brawn and a child's mind, Garroc. He follows his friends, does as they do. I'm thinking that lately his closest friend has been the *baresark*. And I'm thinking that there are ways to kill a man without shedding his blood, ay? Maybe without even knowing that you're doing it."

"I hear you, *freond min*. I hear you." I thought for a moment, then asked him if he would take the Blood Raven with him when he led his garrison south. "Dyfed and Aelfgar and Gadd and I will make our own band. Scouts and runners for both garrisons. You know about the *baresark* now. Can you use him wisely?"

Aescwine snorted. "And why am I the choice? Why not Cynnere?"

I smiled then, though without much humor. "I'm thinking maybe an older, wiser head is needed."

Caught, he gave in, though he did it grumbling.

Three days after my talk with Aescwine, both he and Cynnere had found good places for their garrison camps. My scouts and I would ride first with Cynnere, would go to join Aescwine and his men later. In the dark hours before dawn my half an army made ready to leave the Bear's Ridge.

A noisy crowd, those newcomers to Cefn Arth. Among them, we seven who had held this ridge alone were silent as shadows. All of us had lost friends, one had barrowed a son, and before Erich's coming it had been hard for us to camp within sight of the barrows. Now it was hard to leave them behind. Even I, who didn't much like the sight of those earth-halls, felt that.

Saddest to leave, though, was Blodrafen. I don't think he cared about the barrows or the Dwarfs and Men who lay beneath the stones, but he cared about Aelfgar. I heard him almost say that when Aelfgar went to wish him well.

"Fight well," the berserker said. His wintry eyes grew dark; he made a fist of his three-fingered hand, laid that fist against Aelfgar's heart. "Listen to what this tells you."

The fist or the heart? I was wondering which, when Gadd came to stand beside me.

"He's made a strange friend, Garroc."

I nodded, eyes still on the *baresark*.

"Aelfgar used to be full of talk, but he doesn't talk much these days. When he does, his talk is full of Blodrafen."

I looked at Gadd then, saw the shadows of trouble in his eyes. "What does he say?"

"That he taught the madman how to make game-snares and how to use them, that the madman is his friend."

"Does he name him 'the madman,' Gadd?"

Gadd shook his head in disgust. "No. He names him 'my good friend Blodrafen.' He's no deep thinker, my brother Aelfgar."

No, I thought, he was not. But he was open-hearted.

Aelfgar laid a hand on the Blood Raven's shoulder, said something to earn himself one of the berserker's rare thin smiles, then went to make another farewell. The red dog was not yet strong enough for the long run north, and so he would go the shorter distance south with Aescwine.

His farewells given, Aelfgar went to join Cynnere. Soon after, Gadd followed, but I stayed to watch the *baresark* ride away. It wasn't a good thing to see. Lorn, he looked, strangely frightened, and in the bright hot light of the young day, as I watched him ride away, my heart became confused.

Maybe what Aescwine feared was true, maybe Blodrafen was not a good friend for child-minded Aelfgar. But maybe it was also true that gentle-hearted Aelfgar, who didn't hold Blodrafen's madness against him, was more real to the *baresark* than all the rest of us. If that was so, I'd arranged matters so that the Blood Raven was living among unreal creatures, men who haunted his days in the same shadowy way that thinly wailing ghosts haunted my nights.

That was not an easy thing to think about, and so I didn't think about it. I urged Ecgwulf's grey horse to speed, caught up with the rest of the men.

In the northern part of Erich's border the wildwood is scored by glens and gorges—the deep marks of the dead giants, defeated Winter-Warriors hauled back to Jotunheim by their grieving kin. Some of those deep places are choked with boulders, treacherous scree, sun-whitened corpses of trees fallen long ago. Others are wide, tall-walled glens with clear-running streams cutting through sun-warmed stone on either side of the waters.

Such was the place Cynnere had chosen for his garrison's camp. Narrow at both ends, the glen was easy to ward, for no man could take a horse down the pathless, steep stone walls and none could approach the mouths of the glen without alerting the watch.

At day's end, while the westering sun filled the glen with red light and deep purple shadows, I stood with Cynnere high on the eastern wall. Proud as a *thegn* who shows off his fine new *heall*, was Cynnere. But after a time, his eyes on the glen and his men working there, he said:

"Will you be riding back tonight, Garroc?"

There was eagerness in his tone, a yearning to have his garrison all to himself. I didn't blame him, for I knew that while I was here men wouldn't hear an order from Cynnere without looking to me first for confirmation.

I looked for Gadd and Aelfgar, found one gathering wood, the other helping to set up a picket for horses. I had to look harder for Dyfed, finally found him sleeping comfortably in the midst of the noisy camp. I thought about the long hours of the dimming still left to us. We could ride back tonight, reach the barrows and our old camp by midnight. Then, leaving at dawn, we could reach Aescwine's southern camp before noon. I wanted to see that camp, wanted to let Aescwine know just where Cynnere and his men were.

And so I said, yes, we'd be leaving soon. I didn't think too much about raiders, for we were not a noisy, mail-rattling troop of soldiers. We were four scouts who knew well how to look and sound like shadows.

We left Cynnere and his men a short time later, when the first stars shone faintly against the softly darkening sky. Dyfed said that the stars seemed weak and hesitant, flickered in the sky over the Marches as though they had cause to fear the night. I didn't give too much credence to his idea, told him that the stars always looked that way in summer when twilights are long.

"Dimming has no fit sky for stars, Ghost Foot. Maybe they know it."

Dyfed shrugged, fell silent and thoughtful, his one good eye more often on the stars than on the stony ridge before him. I didn't think my words had changed his opinion at all.

I slept in the shadow of the wildwood, within sight of the barrows, the large one and the small one, and a dream came to me which was not my own. The air in that dream smelled of rain-washed gardens, warming and drying now under summer sun. The breeze in that dream sounded like doves calling, and in that dream the stars shone as gleaming amethysts.

Ah, Sif, it is always strange to feel the witch's dream in me, to see what she sees, to know what she thinks and feels as surely and intimately as though these were my own thoughts and feelings. Of all the gifts my Lydi gives, gifts of love and healing, these offerings are the most beautiful, the most haunting.

And the most frightening. When Lydi gives her dreams to me I am always at risk of seeing myself as she sees me, knowing myself as she knows me. When Lydi dreams of me I watch myself from without as though I were not myself at all, but some person who looks like me, a person whose heart and mind are closed to me. That is frightening.

That night, as the witch-dream came upon me, fear chilled me, and the fabric of the dream wavered like a wind-caught tapestry, then steadied. The witch wanted me to have this dream, wanted that more than she wanted me not to fear. Maybe I trust easier when I am asleep than when I am awake, for very soon I felt no fear at all.

The stranger who was me watched the stars in the clear noon-day sky as he walked through the gardens with the witch, sat with her, his back to the sun-warmed stone of the low wall he'd started to make when he'd come to Gardd Seren in the spring. He didn't speak, kept silent.

Ah, the witch thought, most times it is so hard to get him to talk! When he is thoughtful, he keeps his thoughts to himself. When he is sad, he keeps his sorrow buried deep within him. If joy should rise in him, he does not often speak of it, keeps it safely hidden away in his heart as though he is afraid that joy will flee the sound of his voice.

Sad it was, but the witch had learned to watch his face, learned early that his expression would sometimes show his heart to her.

The wind's song changed tenor, dropped low as though tired doves, doves who'd flown far and fast, sighed over their weariness. The witch looked at him and thought that lately his expression, his eyes, his face, were a better guard of his feelings than they had once been. A thread of loneliness wandered through the witch's dream as she wondered how soon the day would come when she would look into his eyes and not find him, would watch his face and see a stranger.

But he was not insensible, this man she loved. The tall, strong walls he was building to hide his heart were not yet completed. He turned to her, silently as ever, and took her in his arms.

The fear of loneliness haunting the witch faded like frost fleeing the sun's warmth. She rested her head on his shoulder, breathed deeply and smiled over the familiar smell of him, a scent made of the wind and horses, the stony earth that was most often his bed, sweat and smoky campfires. A knot of sorrow, unnoticed until now, loosened, eased as tears welled in her eyes, spilled warm onto his neck.

Ah, he spoke then! Quickly, urgently, wanting to know what saddened her.

But she, knowing that she could not explain, only shook her head, said that she was not sad at all, said that she was happy.

He wondered over that; she could see it in his eyes, and so the witch looked away, gave him time alone with his wondering.

She turned her own eyes to the sky, watched her beloved stars, tracked them in their wheeling, thought that they looked like diamonds in that noon sky. Deep in her, pride stirred and flowered. These stars, bright by day as they were by night, were the work of her grandmother's hands, treasured by her mother. The enchantment which kept them visible always was one she had learned early. She had as much joy from caring for the star-garden as she did from caring for her earthy plantings.

Ah, beautiful stars, my Lydi thought. Beautiful . . .

But I didn't learn what else she thought. A shout of mingled wonder and terror rang through the dark night, and that cold cry sent the witch-dream fleeing, banished it as northwinds banish summer. I woke hard, woke fast, as a soldier does.

I snatched up my war-axe, scrambled to my feet. The shrilling of crickets filled the hot night, then fell suddenly still. In the silence Aelfgar whispered a hoarse question. I saw Gadd silence him with a sharp gesture. I looked for Dyfed. I didn't see him, but in memory I heard again the cry that had wakened me, and knew that it had been his.

"Gadd," I whispered. "You two stay here, be ready."

Low to the ground, keeping to the safe darkness of the shadows, I went silently as I could out to the wildwood's edge, ran along the sharp shadow of Cefn Arth's crest until I saw Dyfed, back rigid, dark as a raven, standing at the edge of the ridge.

My first thought was that silver rain fell all around him, wondrous showers. Then, cold and shaking suddenly, I saw that no rain fell at all. Only stars, bright streaks of light arrowing from the sky, stars raining down like night's tears, stars falling as though some giant's hand had shaken them loose from the sky.

V

DAWNLIGHT, red as blood, seeped across the eastern sky, made shadows sharp as my scouts and I watched the last stars fall. A hot wind blew from the south, fitful and gusty. Small clouds of dust and grit hovered around the edge of Cefn Arth. I listened for thunder, heard nothing but the prowling south wind.

Aelfgar, his eyes wide, watched the last of the silver rain in deep silence. When his brother, voice hushed to a whisper, said that he'd never seen a star-fall last so long, Aelfgar's eyes grew dark with dread.

"Gadd, Blodrafen told me that each star you see falling counts a death."

Gadd paled, answered sharply and with the same kind of instinctive haste a man uses when he makes a sign against bad luck. "That's madman's talk! Stars fall all the time. It means nothing."

Dyfed, still white-faced, still shaken, looked thoughtfully at me. "They say in Welsh lands that sky-signs announce the rise and fall of kings. What do you think it means when a thousand stars fall weeping?"

I listened to the threats in the south wind, thought of the *baresark's* saying, thought of Vorgund Witch-Gatherer. Dread crept along the back of my neck, chilled the sweat on me. Like the return of a bear to Cefn Arth, something deep in me knew this for bad luck.

"Maybe it means nothing." I said it firmly, tried to believe it. "Maybe it only means that stars are falling. Gadd is right. They've fallen before, and usually it has no meaning until someone looks back later and gives it one."

Dyfed's expression was one of mingled astonishment and curiosity. In another place, another time, it would have been comical. "Do you believe that?"

Clearly, he didn't.

"Ghost Foot," I said, "I believe this: We surely weren't the only ones who saw the stars fall. You think it means something. I agree. Maybe it is some god's sign, but more likely someone will take it as such and think today is a good day for fighting. I'm thinking we'd best split up here. You ride north with Aelfgar. Tell Cynnere to send you to me if he needs help. If Aescwine needs help, I'll send Gadd to let Cynnere know."

Gadd didn't wait to hold further discussion, told Aelfgar that he'd like some help with the horses. Aelfgar followed his brother slowly, his eyes still darkened by fear.

But Dyfed didn't follow at all, only waited until they were out of hearing before he spoke, and then he didn't say much, only wished me luck. Yet there was a look in his eye—a grim, troubled look—that made me wonder if he'd been remembering the last time we'd fought together. Then I'd fought half-mad, and that had frightened him.

I looked at the sky again, watched the red line of dawn grow broader. So deep was that red that I thought it looked like a storm of blood hanging over the Marches.

"Ghost Foot," I said, "save your good wishes for yourself. Could be you'll need luck more than I will."

Of a sudden I recalled Lydi's dream, remembered how she'd looked at the stranger who was me and thought that it was very hard to know him. There was something of that look on Dyfed's face now. But he said nothing, only gripped my shoulder hard, as though he wanted me to remember always that a friend's hand could warm.

Aescwine had gone into the wildwood for his garrison camp, holding that he liked the cover of the forest better than the naked ridge. He'd chosen a broad *denn,* one of the wide reaches of woodland pasture that is often found even in the deepest forest. The day before, I'd thought to reach Aescwine's camp by noon. Now, demanding all the strength and speed our mounts possessed, Gadd and I reached the *denn* before the sun had climbed high enough to rise above the wildwood.

A tall, hard-eyed Man on watch challenged us, sword shining in the morning sun. We approached him carefully, to let him get a good look at us. When he was satisfied that we were friends, he shouted for Aescwine and passed us through. All around us men had the look of sleeplessness, and Gadd grinned sourly as he led our horses to the picket. I knew what he was thinking. We were not the only ones who'd watched sky-signs last night.

Ceowulf and Aescwine sat near the largest campfire, the red dog stretched comfortably between them. Werrehund rose stiffly and came to greet me. Ceowulf, seeming stronger now, recovering well from his wounds, offered me food and water, asked how his friends fared in the north, asked if I'd seen the star-fall in the night. I told him that I had, and told him that Gadd would give him the news of his friends.

Ceowulf glanced from Aescwine to me, then left us, and Aescwine didn't wait until I'd eaten before he said:

"You came in good time, *dvergr*. I was ready to send for you. Yesterday I had hunters out at dusk. They didn't find much game, but they saw something very interesting. The marks of heavy-laden horses heading north. My men followed the trail for a while, then lost it when dark came. By then it had turned west toward the mountains."

When I asked Aescwine if he'd sent someone out to look at that trail in daylight, he said that he had, said he went himself to see it.

His eyes darkened, he reached absently for his war-axe. He never had it far from him, but something about the way he reached for it now made me think that he'd been holding tight to it all morning.

"I found something better than a trail. I found a camp. A whole nest of *Wealas,* and these weren't farm boys and cattle-raiders, Garroc. I saw one of them close up. Dark-haired fellow, lean and tall, dressed in linen and rich hunting leathers. Me, I don't understand that singing *Wealas* tongue, but the way men spoke to him made me think they'd be calling him *cyning* if they knew the word.

"He was very careful about his right arm, this one, and when he snagged his fine shirt on a branch, I saw why. Someone had dealt him a nasty sword-blow. Not recently, mind you. The wound was healing cleanly, starting to scar." He grinned, a soldier's deadly, battle-hungry smile. "Garroc, I think that was the mark of the Hunter's sword. I think it was Vorgund himself that I saw."

Aescwine's words might have been the rumble of distant thunder. The hair rose prickling along my neck and arms, as it does when lightning crackles in the air. In me, a *sceadu-wulf* roused.

Always-hungry Werrehund, eyes on my uneaten food, came to sit close beside me. I gave him what he wanted, sat still, eyes tightly closed, as I tried hard to tame the shadow-wolf waking in me.

Might be I'd have done it, might be I'd have kept that wolf still, but in the darkness rose the memory of Halfdan's death. Close behind came the memory of my words to Eadric when he'd told me that the Hunter's pack of *baresarks* thought it a shameful thing that Erich had not avenged his father's death.

Then I'd said that the *cyning* was caught between what he knew he should do and what he knew he must do. Now I thought that this would no longer be true if I could ride back to Erich with word that Vorgund was dead.

"How many men does Vorgund have, Aescwine?"

And, ay, the shadow-wolf liked that question, grinned wide as it waited for Aescwine's reply, licked its lips greedily when Aescwine answered quickly, eagerly.

"Too many for me to want to fight with, Garroc, but not enough to stand against Cynnere's men and mine together." He raised his hand, ground thumb and forefinger together as though killing a louse. "They're right in the middle, between us both, and I'm thinking that they don't know we're here or they'd not be taking their rest so comfortably—they'd have fallen on one or the other of us by now."

I could have it all my own way. In one stroke I'd gain vengeance for Halfdan's death and peace among the Hunter's pack for Erich.

"Aescwine, did he have witches with him?"

Old Aescwine looked about uneasily. My friend was not fond of witches.

"I don't know," he said. "It's hard to tell, but I don't think so. They all looked like soldiers, some Dwarfs, some Men. That doesn't mean some of 'em aren't witches. But witches are canny ones, ay? I'm thinking they'd have known we were about when even the soldiers didn't."

I thought so, too. I took the map of these southern woods, the one Gadd and Aelfgar had made only a few days ago, then took Dyfed's map of the north and laid them side by side. I did this for Aescwine's sake, so that I could explain my plan easily.

Me, I already knew what I was going to do. I needed no map to help me see it. I was going to crush Vorgund.

After I explained my battle plans to Aescwine, I sent Gadd to Cynnere, told him to lead the northern garrison west into the forest, bring them south again only when they were well behind Vorgund's camp. It would not be easy going through those close-growing trees; Cynnere wouldn't have his men in position before the day was old. Eager as I was for fighting, I knew how to wait until the time was best for bringing down my prey. Aescwine and I spent the rest of the long hot afternoon acquainting the men with our plans.

We would not ride to the battle. We would go afoot, close in on Vorgund's camp like silent winter-wolves and await Cynnere's arrival. Five men, among them Gadd, would find places near Vorgund's picket. When the fighting began, their first act would be to scatter the Witch-Gatherer's mounts into the wildwood. Signals between Cynnere and me would pass swiftly. When I heard his

approach, we would fall upon Vorgund's camp from the east;
when Cynnere heard the din of our war-cries, he would charge
our enemies from the west.

It was a simple plan, Sif, one uncluttered with needless details.
I'd learned war-craft from the Hunter, and Halfdan had been
heard to say that the fewer details a man had to worry about, the
fewer he'd forget in the rage of battle when thinking isn't easy.

Vorgund had picked a cool leah, a shady glade, for his camp,
sensibly picketed his horses near a swift-running stream. As the
day waned and shadows grew long, just as we approached the leah,
the south wind dropped, gave way to a breeze from the north. I
wordlessly praised Thunor's northwind, for now the five waiting
to scatter Vorgund's horses would be downwind from the beasts.

Eager as an arrow nocked for flight, I had difficulty holding still,
often pressed my palms to the ground, seeking the deep earth-song
that would herald Cynnere's approach. I was hungry for war.
Close beside me, Aescwine held himself motionless as a deep-
rooted tree. Head cocked, he didn't listen to the earth. He listened
to the Dwarfs and Men in the leah. He didn't waste time trying
to understand words, he listened to the tones of their voices, smiled
in satisfaction when he heard only the lazy sound of men convers-
ing at ease. Of the two of us, Aescwine was wisest.

One hand still to the ground, the other gripping my axe's helve,
I tried to untangle one Welsh voice from another. It was only the
work of a moment before I separated Vorgund's from the others.
Hard his voice, low and deep. He spoke as one used to having his
every word attended, and spoke now impatiently.

"A witch," he said, and the earth told me that he'd slammed
a fist to ground. "If I had one with me, Iwan!"

Ay, I'd have this all my own way . . . . He had no witches with
him, none to fling fire at us, none to confuse our senses with images
of what was not, none to make up the difference between our forty-
four and his thirty. Cold joy filled me.

Vorgund growled again. "Ay, then we'd know, Iwan—then
we'd know how our army fared against Cadwalla and his pet
blaidd Sais, wouldn't we? They are the devil's twins, those two.
They've had luck through the summer, but this time things will
be different. And after that we'll see how Halfdan's whelp is faring,
ay? Though Christ's truth, boy, I hate having to wait for that."

"Ah, but there is no better way to bind an ally," Iwan said,
"than to fight his war for him and so oblige him to fight for you
when the time for that is right."

Vorgund grunted something, a word I didn't hear, and the two fell silent. I tried to think in that silence, tried to figure who this Cadwalla might be and how he'd come to tame a Saxon wolf. It was a Welshman's name, Cadwalla, and it seemed he'd been plaguing some ally of Vorgund's, a friend the Witch-Gatherer now had to defend.

That explained why Vorgund hadn't troubled us through the late spring and summer. And, if there were indeed some significance to last night's rain of stars, maybe this Welshman Cadwalla and his Saxon ally had come to understand it.

I wondered idly who Cadwalla's Saxon ally could be, decided that some enterprising *cyning* of Eadwine's had seized the chance to expand his own borders westward, maybe even southward, while Penda harried the Northumbrian king. What pact this canny Saxon wolf had made with Cadwalla might well have been sealed with an agreement to divide the lands they hoped to win from Vorgund or his ally.

I thought this would be a good thing to remember, a thing Erich might like to know about. Cadwalla and his Saxon friend seemed to be about the business of rearranging borders which were very close to Erich's northern one, and if Vorgund's campaign against them had succeeded, we must watch for the Witch-Gatherer not only from the west, but from the north, too.

Well, that was one way to figure the thing, Sif. Only later did I learn that it was not the only way.

Vorgund snarled over his impatience again, and Iwan said—wearily and as though he'd told him this often before—that the horses were spent, would not carry them fast or far without a day to rest.

I didn't hear the rest of what Iwan counseled, for deep in the earth, so deep that only Dwarfs could feel it, I felt rumble of horses galloping hard from the north.

From Vorgund's camp I heard the conversation between Iwan and his lord fall still, heard someone mutter a question, then another voice repeat it. He had Dwarfs with him, did the Witch-Gatherer, and it was their voices I heard, their questions.

I gestured to Aescwine, signaled him to be ready. Cynnere was close now. In another moment, just a little before Vorgund's Dwarfs raised the alarm, he'd be close enough for me to signal the attack. I looked around me, saw that the men were ready. Last, I looked at Blodrafen, and in me, grey and cold, the shadow-wolf growled.

Wintry eyes glinting, the *baresark* nodded in a friendly way, and

wolf spoke to wolf in a language the Blood Raven had known for
many years, one I was learning only now. Powerful, that silent
speech; terrible as the words of a deadly enchantment, horrible
as the words of a god's curse.

The ground-thunder of Cynnere's approach sounded like storm-
called waves battering at the shore. I was caught by the berserker's
icy smile, and the rhythm of that pounding matched the thundering of my own heart. How easy to let the memory of the mind-
numbing battle-rage which had once before swept me into war
overwhelm me now. I'd tasted the rage on Cefn Arth, would happily have tasted it again.

Aescwine grabbed my shoulder, gripped me hard, and I remembered how Dyfed had done the same only this morning; saw again
the memory of fear lurking in my friend's eye. I used all my
strength to look away from the *baresark*.

Though it was hard to do that, hard to quiet the wolf howling
in me, with my own voice, and not the *sceadu-wulf's* cold howl,
I raised the wild battle-song. At that signal, the five who waited
near Vorgund's picket cut his horses loose, scattered them quickly
through the forest. Vorgund and his men scrambled for weapons,
cried out in alarm or anger, and the thunder of Cynnere's charge
roared in my bones.

Vorgund and I, we crafted war-treasures that day, *wael-gimum*,
slaughter-gems. We filled the leah with blood bright as garnets,
the silver light of swords, the gold-glint of mail-shirts. That is not
a beautiful hoard; every piece of it represents death and hurt and
loss.

Many men died that day, and fifteen of them were mine.

As the day ended, as darkness fell, I looked around the war-
ground and counted the men left to me, counted Vorgund's dead.
Torches sprang up in the darkness, red light and black shadows
ran around the leah. Wounded men cried out in pain.

Dyfed rose up from where he knelt by one, walked wearily to
another. His work didn't end when the fighting was done. When
Halfdan was alive, his soldiers called me Keeper of the Names.
They thought that I was first to know who was dead, but they were
wrong. Dyfed was first to know.

War-tired, arms aching from the weight of my axe, heart trembling from the effort it took even now to keep the shadow-wolf
chained and silent, I went among the living, praised them for their
good work. I searched always among the dead for one long, lean,

dark-haired Welshman. Among the enemy dead I counted six Dwarfs and twenty-two Men. None of those Men was Vorgund.

When he saw me searching among the dead, Aescwine came to me, told me that he'd seen the Witch-Gatherer flee the battle with one other man. "Ay, but not till the last of his men was down, Garroc, not till he knew the last of 'em was dead. I'll give him that. They ran afoot, and they ran fast for all that one of 'em was hurt."

I heard his words and my victory tasted like ashes, dry and choking.

After a time, long after full darkness had fallen, Dyfed came to me, bearing the names of the injured. Those given, he gave me the names of the dead.

Of those who had held Cefn Arth all through the spring and into the hot summer, Ceowulf was dead. Though he'd yet to recover from wounds gotten in our last fight with cattle-raiders, he'd refused to stay in the camp. He'd said it would be a cold shame to stay behind when his friends needed him.

Ceowulf Sicga's son.

Of the men Erich had given me only a handful of days ago, thirteen were dead, and of these, twelve were *mann-cynn*. I didn't know the names of their fathers, but I would learn them. The thirteenth was the Dwarf Hunberht. He looked to have been a young man—*Laestan*, as I was. After the custom of *Laestan,* he'd not have taken his father's name and so it was not likely that I would ever learn it.

"And one other," Dyfed said. He ran his hand through his white hair, ran it slowly down the side of his face, smearing blood and dirt and sweat.

As he drew breath to give me the last name, a wild wail—grieving, abandoned, wretched—tore through the darkness. Cold, that sound. I knew that howling voice for Aelfgar's, knew that Gadd was dead.

Gadd Ulfhere's son.

In a web of shadow and red torchlight, I saw Aelfgar kneeling over his brother's body. Aescwine stood with him, spoke softly, told him that it would be best to leave Gadd now and have his own wounds tended. Aelfgar shook his head, spoke his refusal in a ragged, grief-torn voice. When Aescwine reached to take his arm, tried to help him to his feet, white-faced, cold-eyed, Aelfgar jerked away, snarled a curse. Soon after Aescwine left him, let him mourn his brother in peace.

But Aelfgar didn't mourn his brother by himself. Blodrafen

came to stand close beside him, and Aelfgar didn't drive him off. The *baresark* placed one hand on the young man's shoulder; with the other he gently stroked Aelfgar's bent head.

'My good friend Blodrafen,' Aelfgar had called him.

Maybe I was of a mind that day to have sympathy for madmen, for I thought that perhaps Aelfgar was right after all in naming Blodrafen a friend. Perhaps Aescwine and I were wrong.

Dyfed didn't think so, I saw it in his look of disgust, in the way he shuddered as though he'd seen some dread shadow fall upon Aelfgar. Voice low, his one good eye on the Blood Raven, he said:

"Have you heard what some have said about him?"

"I've heard."

"He kills what he loves. . . ."

Blodrafen went down on his heels beside Aelfgar. He spoke in a low and urgent voice, but I didn't try to hear what was said. I was tired of war, tired of trying to keep the shadow-wolf quiet, tired of thinking about *baresarks.*

"Ghost Foot, Aelfgar's brother is dead. Let him have the comfort of a friend, ay?"

I expected an argument, but I got none. Maybe Dyfed was becoming weary of arguing with me to no advantage. True it is that he only shook his head and walked away from me.

Alone, I looked up to the sky. There was not much to see—thick branches of oak and rowan and ash hid it well. Still, I squinted hard. Bright across the sky, I saw the silver trail of a star falling. Late-come, he was, and searching for his fallen brothers.

I smiled a little, but coldly.

Vorgund had fled, but he could not have gone far. Most of his men were dead; he was not well-attended. If he'd found himself a horse, that horse was tired and not fit to run fast or far. If he fled afoot with a wounded man or was himself wounded, he'd be easy to track come sunrise, easy to bring down.

I was no longer thinking of killing the Witch-Gatherer. Now I was thinking that it would be a good thing to bring him back to Erich, a fine thing to let the *cyning* give out his own justice. In Welsh lands they say that sky-signs herald the rise and fall of kings. That night I determined to make the saying a truth that all men could swear by.

Dyfed and I rode west shortly after dawn. I gave Cynnere and Aescwine orders to wait for us in the leah, told them to occupy themselves by hauling carrion into the wildwood, building a barrow for our fallen friends, and caring for the wounded. I would hear none of their protests against Dyfed and me riding away alone.

I'd had time to think in the night. That morning I knew where Vorgund was headed just as well as though he'd told me. I took only Dyfed with me because two are better escort for a prisoner than one—and because I would not have to waste time explaining to him how it was that I knew the way to the place all Welshmen called Sanctuary.

VI

As I rode west through the wildwood and the stonelands, the maze of glens and gorges that score the foothills of the tall Cambrians, I thought I'd made a mistake when I decided to take Dyfed with me to Seintwar. I thought that I should have taken Aelfgar instead. I didn't consider this for Aelfgar's sake, though maybe I should have. I considered it for mine. Aelfgar had been known to drive a man to short-tempered impatience with his many questions, but his constant wondering would have been a welcome trade for the one simple question Dyfed asked.

"Garroc," he said, "if we find Vorgund in Gardd Seren, you know Lydi won't let you take him. What are you going to do then?"

I had no answer for Dyfed, none for myself. I had only a great need to find the Witch-Gatherer, and I believed that the thing I'd been taught to value most, my honor, drove me forward. I'd been Halfdan's man while he lived; I was Erich War Hawk's now. For the sake of his Marches, Erich could not take vengeance for his father's death, but I could bring the object of his vengeance to him. I believed I'd find no honor in letting Vorgund escape me.

Ay, Sif, that's what I believed, but it would be closer to truth to say that I didn't go to Seintwar honor-driven. I went ghost-ridden. For though Erich was not haunted by his father's ghost, I was. And Halfdan's was not the only ghost haunting me.

Noon's light spilled gold into the river, glittered on the leaves of the beeches and oaks surrounding Lydi's cottage. In the dooryard the low humming of bees, the sweet voices of birds, mingled with the heady sun-drawn scents of Lydi's garden. These wove a song of peace and enchantment for all the senses. I filled myself

with that enchanted song, breathed it hungrily. I didn't think I'd
soon have the chance to do that again.

No one came to greet us, none to wonder who'd ridden so fast
and hard to Gardd Seren. We heard no sound from the cottage.
No motion did we see at the window. Dyfed nudged me, pointed
to the bench near the open door. A split-oak bucket, recently filled
and emptied, sat in a glistening puddle on the bench. On the
ground lay a crumpled bloodstained shirt.

"You did some good thinking last night, Garroc."

He didn't say this with any satisfaction.

When I looked at that bloody shirt, I heard the faint whisper
of the pattern Fate was weaving for me, heard the hard clack of
shuttles as the Norns worked at their relentless loom.

I shivered to hear those things, shivered as though I'd heard
the first cold hiss of the northwind, the sharp and bitter crack of
river-ice. Skalds know that *wintra-gegang* is another way to say
Fate; it is no mistake that these words mean winter-going.

I slid from my grey horse's back, and Dyfed, tense and silent,
dismounted and stood beside me. He tilted his head far back, one
good eye on the stars gleaming in the noon-bright sky. He held
himself still, didn't move but to breathe. This was not how a man
looked when he saw those wonderful stars for the first time; it was
how one looked when seeing them at last after a very long time.

The hot summer breeze quickened, then dropped. In the garden
the bees became still, the birds stopped singing. It was as though
all Gardd Seren held its breath, waiting. In the stillness I realized
that Dyfed and I stood watching the open door carefully, closely
as men who approached an enemy's lair. I felt suddenly ashamed,
as though I'd come to a good friend's house with unfriendly intent.

Ah, but that was so, wasn't it, Sif?

A moment remained to me for changing my mind, for riding
away and leaving whoever lay within to Lydi's care. I didn't take
it, chose instead to stand where Fate put me, to move as Fate di-
rected. Even gods, even mighty Wotan, must follow the patterns
the Norns weave. I didn't consider that Dwarfs or Men had
strength to do what the All-Father could not.

I gave the grey's reins to Dyfed, unstrapped my axe, then
quickly thought better of approaching Lydi's door with a weapon
in my hands. That, too, I gave to Dyfed. Any who watched me
walk to the cottage would have thought, Ah, here is one who walks
certain of his welcome.

Any who thought that would have been wrong. None knew better than I that if Lydi were within, she would not welcome one

come to violate her sanctuary. And none understood better than
I that she would know I'd come to do that in the very moment
she saw me.

The sun hung too high to throw its full light through the south-
facing windows by Lydi's bed, not high enough to reach the west
window. I stood still in the doorway, waiting for my eyes to adjust
to the darkness within the cottage. An amethyst light flared with
the suddenness of a startled gasp. Bright, it flung tangled shadows
across the floor, up the walls. Then, like a fading star, it flickered
and died, left the cottage dark again, left my eyes dazzled. Soft
in the darkness, someone stirred, someone sighed.

I knew that ragged sigh for Lydi's. I had seen the bloodstained
shirt outside the door. I knew in what cause my healer-witch had
spent her strength, and at once I forgot why I'd come here, could
not think of anything then but that weary sigh. I went to kneel
beside her in the darkness, took her gently into my arms. I might
well have gathered up shadows, so light did she feel, so weightless
and without substance. White my Lydi's face; her eyes were filled
with fearful wonder. My heart beat hard to see that look on her;
I was afraid for her. *Dvergr* know this: Who is close to dying sees
the stars as suns. That day Lydi must have been long looking at
the terrible light of stars grown dangerously bright. My fear made
me clumsy, set my hands to shaking as I stroked her dark hair.
When she whispered my name, her voice sounded like faintest,
most distant memory, and it didn't cover the sound of quiet rustling from the shadows.

A dark form stirred on a pallet beneath the high west window;
a restless sleeper moaned softly. Long he was, as *mann-cynn* are,
and as broad in the shoulders as an ironsmith. I knew from the
sound of his breathing, from the depth of his sleeping, that my
Lydi had spent her strength in healing this man.

"Ah, my Lydi," I whispered, and my voice shook with fear.
"Tell me, my Lydi: Is it ever worth it?"

She didn't speak, only rested her head against my shoulder, covered my heart with a trembling hand. It was answer enough.

I spoke to her tenderly as I carried her away from the hearth.
I was not certain that she heard me, for she'd closed her eyes, and
her breathing, deep and even, sounded like a sleeper's. I walked
carefully, tried not to disturb her, for I knew that now my Lydi
sought healing for herself.

I didn't carry the witch to her bed. It seemed better to carry
her outside into the sun and the sweet enchantment of her gardens.

And so I did that, gave her into Dyfed's care. He took her gently from me, brought her to the warmest, brightest part of the garden. And strange it was to see them—Dyfed with his back to the stone-row, Lydi so small and seeming very frail in his arms. Only a winter ago I'd have sworn to anyone that I knew my friend Dyfed well. I'd learned about him in ale-houses and on battle-grounds, in the *cyning's* hall, and through years of wandering the border-lands. But the expression on his face now as he sat with Lydi, a look of great fondness, deep understanding, quiet respect, was not one I'd ever seen.

After a moment I understood that I was not seeing Dyfed at all, not looking at Ghost Foot. It was Cyfaill who sat with the witch in his arms, and suddenly lonely, I realized that I didn't know this Cyfaill at all. Quietly, careful not to disturb them, I went back into the cottage and stayed with the injured man who lay sleeping beneath the west window.

The Welshman's wounds had been bad ones, iron's bite, arrow's sting. Yet, a day after he'd surely thought to die, he was healing well and clean scars were forming where once his flesh had been torn. I knew, because I'd felt the power of the witch's magic, that in the healing sleep strength was returning to him.

I didn't have to study the man closely to know that he was not Vorgund. I had kept that one in my sight through all the battle of the day before, but always the Witch-Gatherer stayed one reach away from me, kept just out of my grasp. A day later nothing had changed. Vorgund had eluded me again, vanished into his wild-wood, safe and free. I guessed that he must be more than halfway to his northern army by now, a lord with more and better luck than the luckiest Dwarf or Man I'd ever known.

Weary now, very tired, I sat in the dark cottage with the wounded man, turning my cold disappointment over and over, examining its every aspect until at last I found a way to ease the emptiness of it.

This one was not Vorgund, but his bloodied shirt, his battle-wounds, argued that he was one of the Witch-Gatherer's men. Like it was, I thought coldly, he'd know as well as any where his lord was running to.

As I thought that, the man stirred again and woke. Dazed by the healing sleep, he asked me for water, trusted that I was a friend who would give it to him.

I was no friend of his; his lord was my bitterest enemy. But I was in Lydi's house now, and for her sake I drew water for him, held his head while he drank, settled him again when he was finished. He tried to stay awake long enough to thank me, tried hard to speak clearly. Only a few words did he manage, but they were enough to show me that this man was not wholly a stranger to me. I'd heard his voice before, and hoarse and sleep-heavy as it was, I recognized it now.

I answered him in his own language, spoke softly, but not gently. "The witch would tell you that you are welcome to it, Iwan, and so I suppose that you are."

He opened his grey eyes again, showed me startled fear as he tried to see who had answered him with the accent of a *blaidd Sais*. But he hadn't the strength for it; the healing sleep took hold of him again.

In the shadows the Saxon wolf smiled and thought that if he could not have Vorgund, this counselor of his was not a poor catch to bring back to Erich.

Lydi is wise in many kinds of lore. She knows the ways of magic, knows the ways of healing; understands how to make oils and ointments, poultices and distillations for the comfort of the sick. Lydi understands the prayer-language of the *Cristen* priests. She speaks the *Seaxe* language well, and if her accent makes it sing a little, the speech of our Northern fathers is not harmed by that. The lore and language she knows best, though, is the heart's own, and so it is difficult to hold a secret from her. Because I knew this, I didn't try to pretend that Dyfed and I had come to Gardd Seren for any reason but to take a wounded man from her care. There would have been no sense in it.

And so, because I didn't want to pretend, I left Lydi wholly to Dyfed's care, spent all my time with Iwan. When he woke, I gave him water; when he slept, I watched at his side. I didn't think of him as anything other than my prisoner, and I had an interest in his health. That night I didn't sleep in Lydi's bed, nor did I go to sleep by her hearth as Dyfed did. I sat with Iwan. My back to the west wall, I watched the bright light of Thunor's full moon pour through the south-facing windows above Lydi's bed.

When we don't call that moon Thunor's, we call him War Moon, for summer is the time for war. As I watched his light dress Lydi's dark hair with silver, watched it make her face pale as snow, leave a trail of shadow behind him as he crept out of her bed and into the cottage, I thought this was a good name for Thunor's Moon.

•   •   •

Early, before lark and sparrow, red jay and nuthatch, had finished their dawn-song, Lydi arose from her bed. I watched her as she dressed, watched her as she went to the hearth and spoke quietly with Dyfed. She called him by her own name for him and thanked him for caring for her, asked him if he would make up the fire and look after the wounded man now. I didn't hear his answer, didn't hear the other things he said to her, but when she turned to leave him, I saw him take her hand as though to keep her from something. She shook her head, smiled sadly, and slipped her hand from his. Lydi didn't stop to check Iwan, didn't stop to speak to me. She went out into the morning.

As I rose to follow her Dyfed stopped me. "Garroc, you still have time to change your mind. Don't do this, don't break her sanctuary."

"I'm taking the Welshman back with me, Ghost Foot." I looked at him closely, asked the hard question. "Are you with me, or will you be Cyfaill today and side with Lydi?"

He looked around the cottage, looked at the hearth, the shelves filled with little stone pots, drying herbs, boxes of powders. He looked at these things as one does who knows them well, as one familiar with the stone cottage and all that was in it. Sadness, like a shadow, crossed his face.

"Ay, Garroc," he said, "I'm Erich's man, as you are. If you want to do this foolish thing, do it. I won't leave you now."

I found Lydi in the gardens behind the cottage, sitting with her back to the stonerow I'd started to build in the spring. She sat looking up at the beautiful stars and didn't look away from them, didn't greet me.

It is a wonderful thing to see the stars shine in Gardd Seren. The sun's bright light has no power to hide them as it does in all other places, and often I feel that when I am in Gardd Seren I am visiting the country of dreams. I didn't feel that way now, didn't look up at the star-garden. The day before, I'd recognized Fate's pattern and so I knew what would happen in that bright morning. I didn't want my last memory of the enchanted stars to be filled with sorrow.

I sat beside the witch, put my own back to a stone I knew well, old Welfar the river-traveler, and said:

"My Lydi, we'll be leaving soon."

She reached to touch a leaf of angelica, a leaf half-opened to the new day. A golden bee alighted on the tip of her finger, hummed briefly, then flew away. In the sunlight her dark hair gleamed, the warming breeze played gently with it. I wanted to reach for her, wanted to smell the new day in her hair, but I didn't, held myself still for the same reason I didn't look at the blue, star-filled sky.

When Lydi looked at me, her eyes were dark as the shadows at the edge of the wildwood. She touched me lightly, put the tips of her fingers against my breast, then drew away quickly as though she'd been stung.

"You cannot take Iwan with you, Garroc."

"Yes," I said, choosing to misunderstand her words. "I can. I've sat with him the whole night. I've watched him carefully. Tired he is, as Aelfgar was that day when we left here. But he can ride. As Aelfgar was able to."

Lydi smiled sadly, shook her head over my folly. "*Prydydd*, please don't play word games with me. It isn't fair."

Warm the summer day's new sun, but I was cold as though winter had come. In me the shadow-wolf roused, growled dangerously, scenting its best food: sorrow and loss. I tried hard to calm the wolf, but I could not. I'd been living close to that grief-born shadow for too long now.

"Ay, then, I won't," I said harshly. "No games, my Lydi. Tell me: Who brought Iwan here to you?"

She flinched from my anger, but she didn't flinch from answering truthfully. Once before, she'd told me that there must be truth between us, for then there could be trust. Maybe she thought to remind me of that by using truth and trust now.

"Vorgund," she said. "And I promised him that his son could stay here in safety."

"His son!"

Ah, poor witch. She knew her trust misplaced at once, deeply regretted naming Iwan as Vorgund's son. I saw it in the lonely disappointment in her eyes, and my anger grew stronger, colder. When I spoke, I didn't choose my words carefully, could not stop the wolf from snarling.

"Then it's not a matter of sanctuary at all, Lydi, is it? It's a matter of doing your lord Vorgund's bidding."

Lydi took my hand, held it tightly. "Garroc, I gave Iwan sanctuary. You have had the same sanctuary from me; your friend has. Don't break my trust. Please don't—"

But I could do nothing else. "Tell me where Vorgund has gone."

"I will never tell you that, man dear. Why do you ask when you know that?"

Silence fell between us and a wood dove sighed, sighed as though she knew what I would say next.

"It's a hard place we've come to, my Lydi," I said, going bitterly down winter's way. "Maybe we should have considered this a long time ago. Maybe we should have thought that soon or late, one or both of us would have to make a choice between duty toward the ones who rule us and the love between us."

Lydi looked at me sadly, then let my hand go, and I knew how an unmoored and empty ship must feel when the wind and tide come to carry it far out to sea. Slowly, tiredly, she stood. In the sunlight her face was pale, drawn, as though she'd taken no healing at all from her night's sleep.

"Garroc, I made my choice a long time ago. And now you must make one." She looked over her shoulder, to the wildwood and the tall shining Cambrians, then looked away as though there were no answer for her there. "I am a witch, and I have the same strength that Vorgund's witches have. I can cast the same terrible enchantments they do. I can stop you from taking Iwan.

"But I will not. I will not. And so you must make your own choices, Garroc, as I have made mine. I will not try to force you to choose as I would wish." She smiled again, again sadly. "Man dear, each of us knows now that I have never been able to do that with any success."

A long silence grew between us again, deep and filled with her regret, my fear. At last she bent to kiss me, touched my face, rested her hand on my heart where it had so often rested before.

"Garroc, if you take Iwan from here, I will be sorry for him. He is no friend of your lord and I don't expect that your War Hawk will let him live. And I will be sorry for me. I have worked hard to build trust among the people of this valley. If Iwan is taken from me, that trust will be broken. But know this: I will not stop you. That is my choice, and it is kin to one I made a long time ago.

"Yet I will be sorriest for you, my love, because I don't think you want to hurt me, and I don't think you know how to end this cold journey you've started upon."

So saying, she left me to my empty victory. I watched her walk away and I thought that it was surely true that I would never see her again. If I'd had the courage to weep, I'd have wept then for the long lonely time stretching endlessly before me, maybe even for the choice I didn't know how to make.

·   ·   ·

Three rode away from Gardd Seren at noon—Iwan, Dyfed, and me. As it often does in late summer, the sky turned dark, filled with clouds the color of iron. As we rode through the wildwood, all creatures, furred and feathered, sought shelter, fell silent in the face of the oncoming storm.

Ah, but no. Not all. The wood doves, smoke-breasted, dark-eyed, didn't care that Thunor growled, didn't mind his bright spears of light, for that is the way with doves. They sing in storms, as they do all other times, sweetly, gently, not caring for gods' rages. They are very brave.

I never learned what Vorgund's son was thinking as he left the witch's sanctuary. He said nothing, spoke no word of blame to Lydi, no word to Dyfed or me at all. Welshmen have a full measure of warrior's iron in their souls. I considered it likely that Iwan was looking over his stock of courage to see how much of it he possessed.

Neither did I know what Dyfed was thinking, though I guessed from his icy silence that he considered me the worst kind of fool. I was partly right, and mostly wrong, but I didn't learn that until much later, when our old habit of holding tight to our secrets was broken.

Me, I was thinking of the winter past when Lydi and I had parted in anger, thinking of the spring past when we had forged a fragile truce. As I rode back through the stonelands and the wildwood to Aescwine and Cynnere and my half an army, I thought bitterly that the matter of my abandoned skald-craft which had come so often between Lydi and me had not finally been the thing to separate us.

I was wrong, but in a way I could not then understand. My abandonment of skald-craft had never truly been the matter between Lydi and me. What concerned her most, what I worked so hard to ignore or excuse, was the fact that I had formed the habit of reaching for bleak winter when I could as easily reach for bright summer. Denying myself the joy of song-crafting, history-keeping, was only one way of living cold in winter. Shattering Lydi's trust, violating her sanctuary, was another.

Maybe I would have seen that if I had not been too busy listening to the *sceadu-wulf* growling, if I had not so carefully told myself that I had no choice but to bring Iwan Vorgund's son to Erich.

When we returned to Aescwine and Cynnere, it was to find that a messenger had ridden hard to us from Erich. Joyful, that rider, and filled with good news of great victories. Some of the triumphs he told about were Erich's, some of his tales were filled with Penda King's great war-deeds.

Osric, the son-wealthy, land-impoverished *cyning*, no longer prowled Erich's southern borders, had learned well and fast the lessons the War Hawk set out to teach him. Our young *cyning*, it seemed, had shown a peculiar but successful skill for teaching, first illustrated his lessons with war and then made them easier to take by offering promises of peace.

"And now he wants you back in Rilling, Garroc. He told me that you should leave a good force here on the border, but not all the army must stay. He's had word from Penda King, and Wotan's Blade assures him that Vorgund is finished his warring for the summer." The messenger scratched his chin, thinking, then shrugged. "I don't know how the King knows it, but War Hawk is certain that he does. In any case, Erich sent me to bring you— and whatever of the army you won't leave behind—back to Rilling. He says that he is to ride with the King again and this time he wants you with him.

"Ay, Garroc," he went on, a gleam of envy in his eyes, "I think I'd give a lot to be riding with the King, but I'm told to stay here with your border-guard."

I cared nothing for his envy, had little thought for anything but his news, for if this messenger didn't understand how Penda could be certain that Vorgund was done warring for now, I was beginning to understand.

Two days before, Vorgund had spoken of Cadwalla and his tame Saxon wolf. Then I'd thought the Witch-Gatherer was speaking of some Northumbrian *cyning*. Now I didn't think so; now I remembered the treaty that Penda had ridden north to make in the spring. He'd taken many men with him, a strong army, as though he'd not been certain that he could trust the man he intended to ally himself with. So a wise man acts when he is forging a treaty with one he'd normally consider an enemy.

On the face of it, the King's was a bold move, for the folk of northern Wales are not fond of Eadwine of Northumbria and could make a common cause with Penda. But I wondered, as I made plans to shepherd Iwan Vorgund's son south to Erich, how well the King's bold thinking would be understood by his people. *Cyning* and soldier, *thegn* and farmer, the folk of the Marches had spent many years hating Welshmen, hating *Cristens*, and despising the incursions of their new young god. Maybe they wouldn't like this alliance with Cadwalla at all.

•   •   •

And so it might be thought, Sif, that I had a lot to consider as we rode south with Iwan Vorgund's son; maybe enough to let me forget for a time that in spring I'd come to the borderland looking for peace, that in summer I'd forsaken my search for peace and chosen vengeance instead. It might be thought that all the things I had to consider would claim my attention and drive out all else.

It might be thought, but it would not be rightly thought. Good as I had been until then at refusing to consider the things I deemed too painful or confusing to think about, that day it seemed I'd lost the skill.

WULFS-MONA
(Wolf's Moon)

🏵

IN the times I am telling you of, Sif, this little village of Rilling
did not look the way it does now. Even the high, stony hill over-
hanging the Rill was different. Ah, not in shape, but in name.
Maybe in its spirit. Then we called the hill *Rafenscylf*, Raven
Shelf; today you call it Godshill, for your *Cristen* priests like that
name better than Rafenscylf.

In times past I went often to that hill, that high place, and from
it I could look over the whole valley, see the river and the forest
and the small patches of farmland in the south. The *cynings-heall*
lay on the smooth, west side of the river a little north from here.
The trees have grown over now, but then it was a clear place. Safe
within high wooden walls, the hall was the largest building for
many miles around. I could see that, too, from Rafenscylf.

And early in the morning, when hearth-smoke was not yet rising from the *heall* and from the little thatch-roofed houses which
crowded round it, and forge smoke from the smithies, cooking
smoke from the ale-houses and bakehouses, I could see the Cambrians shining in the west.

In those times the Rill ran swift in spring, wandered slowly in
summer, just as it does now; and there was woodland to the east,
but it was much deeper and darker. A wildwood. And so, in that
time, when bold Penda was king and the lord's name was War
Hawk, people did not build their homes in the lee of Rafenscylf,
did not have gardens by the riverside. It was not safe to live outside
the embrace of the walls of the *cyning's* stockade, for wolves
prowled, outlaws roamed; sometimes *Wealas* came this far east.

193

If you go up to your Godshill tomorrow, Sif, when the air is filled with dawnlight and clear, you will see some of the things I could see then; more, for there is not as much forestland now. One thing you will not see, and that is the *cynings-heall.*

What remains of the hall, the fine strong hearth-stones who are called Earth Fast, High Standing, Tree's Bane, are part of your father's barrow now, part of the earth-hall where my old friend and young son sleeps. And that is right, Sif, for first I saw Hinthan, a small boy beside the Rill; last, I barrowed him there.

See the *heall,* Sif, when it was home to *cynings* and the soldiers who served them:

Long and wide, the hall. Well-built of squared timbers, planed wood. Rich tapestries, broidered with silken colors, decorated the walls. Some of those hangings were taken in war-raids, but two were the work of Halfdan's wife, for then—as now—no women are more skilled at this work than *Seaxe* women. Among the skilled, Halfdan's wife, Eadgyth Regenwald's daughter, was famed.

One of these tapestries showed men riding away from their women, sometimes to hunt, sometimes to fight. When the men went to war the women wept; when they went to hunt those women smiled joyfully. The other of these hangings was not finished, for Eadgyth had been working at it on the day she died. Bright the threads on the dark woven background, but no pattern had yet been formed on the day Eadgyth put her needle down for the last time. Some said it was meant to be one thing, some said another. Me, I think she meant to make a picture of a garden, for there were some flowers on it.

And yet the unfinished was hung beside the whole. The Hunter said it was there to remind him that beauty is no less a wonder because it is short-lived, and he was talking about his Eadgyth. A great one for remembering, Halfdan the Hunter.

The hall-crafters made high, broad windows in the walls, front and back, on both sides, and the sun liked to stream in through those windows, liked to fall in rich golden shafts, joyed to make Eadgyth's hangings glow. And when the sun shone through those windows, the gemmed *thegns* who sat at feast glittered; the iron buckle on the belt of the poorest servant gleamed like silver. The sun shone on the wings of the hawks as they soared through the high hall, glinted from their sharp beaks when they went to perch in the rafters. It made the rich thick coats of the well-fed hounds shine, and when Halfdan filled his large golden cup with wine, drank and passed it through the hall to his men, sun-gleam leaped all around that cup's rim, laughing; the light laughed no less in later days when Erich shared his wine.

There were pillars in that *heall,* two long straight lines on either side of the building, marching from the wide entry doors to the farthest wall where the *cynings,* first Halfdan and then his War Hawk son, sat before the deep stone-built hearth to take counsel with *thegns,* to share meat and mead with their loyal war-troop. Straight and strong, those pillars, dyed with the hearth-smoke and torch-smoke of many years. Blacker than winter's longest night, these pillars reached to hold the roof high, divided the hall into three parts. Along the narrow aisles, against the long walls beneath the tapestries, painted shields hung side by side with racked spears of strong ashwood.

In the wide center of the hall stood a long, broad trestle and many benches at mealtimes, but at night the table and benches were taken away. In Halfdan's time, and Erich's, no *cyning* slept there—and *thegns,* too, preferred their own houses and the beds of their wives. But we the *cyning's* soldiers, his war-troop, slept always in his hall, near his deep hearth. It might be thought that there we slept with iron, and sometimes this was true for the unlucky. But those who had better luck, stalked the ale houses for warmer bed-companions and brought them to the *heall.*

It was a good place to be, Sif, and most of us were content.

Still, not everyone was content there in that year of Halfdan's death. What Eadric told me of the berserkers in the summer, when I'd seen him last, was still so as summer aged to fall and fall died before winter.

This is true, Sif: All men know that the gods have bound Wolf-Fenris, Loki's deadly son, with strong chains made by Dwarfs and witches in the beginning of the world. All men also know that a time will come, a long and terrible winter, when Wolf-Fenris will break his chains and run howling after the sun and the moon. He will devour the sun, make dark her light. He will finally catch the moon and kill him. He is hard to sate, Wolf-Fenris. He will rage through all the worlds and bring about the great war we know will be called Ragnarok. This is the pattern the Norns have designed, the one they weave even now.

I'm thinking that Erich would have done well to remember this when he took his father's wolfish pack into his hall.

I

SIF, there are things you must know about the end of that summer
and the fall which followed; else my tale of winter will make little
sense to you. One of the things is this:

Penda King returned south on the winds of rumor. He didn't
stop to ask hospitality at Erich's hall, didn't even come very close
to Rilling. The *god-cynn* King wanted to return to his own *heall*
before he must come north again warring, for many of his men
were dead in the north, killed by Vorgund's witches and soldiers,
and he needed to find more. But he came close enough for folk
to hear talk of his strange northern alliance, forged in the spring
and used in the summer. Cadwalla's name sprang often to the lips
of displeased men, who muttered about a *Cristen,* a Welshman.
Some wondered openly if the King's famous boldness had turned
to madness. They said it was not a good thing for one descended
from Wotan to ally himself with a Christ-worshiper.

Another thing you must know, Sif, is that, though Lydi had
feared it, though all in Rilling wanted it, Iwan Vorgund's son,
wide-shouldered silent Welshman, didn't die at Erich's hands.
There were plenty, soldier and *thegn,* who'd gladly have done the
killing, taken vengeance for Halfdan's sake and the sakes of kin
and friends dead of war, but Erich didn't permit that.

The War Hawk's thinking was this: While Vorgund might have
lost a good deal of his army yet again, still he had witches, men
and women skilled in magic and dread. And so Erich guarded
Iwan Vorgund's son well and treated him fairly, as an honorable
man treats a hostage. He gave him good clothes to wear and a
small house to live in. And he set careful men to watch Iwan. The
Witch-Gatherer's son didn't go to use the midden trenches without company. The *cyning* sent word out to the western borders,
where Vorgund would hear, that Iwan was alive and would stay
that way for as long as Vorgund practiced the peace that Penda
King had forced upon him.

Dyfed was one of the men Erich sent riding away to the west,
and as I watched him leave Rilling, his red Werrehund loping beside, I wondered if news of Iwan's condition would reach Lydi.
I hoped that if it did she would think less harshly of me. But I
only hoped a little, for I didn't try to fool myself into thinking that

Iwan's chances for continued good health made up the full matter between Lydi and me.

As good as the idea of keeping Iwan hostage seemed to Erich, many didn't like it. They called Iwan *se Waelhwelp,* the Slaughter-whelp, and they thought that Iwan's young head would sit just as prettily on the pole of vengeance as his father's until such time as Vorgund's was available to us again. Among these was the father of Wulf and Waerstan, and on a hot summer's night, in a smoky ale-house not far from the hall, *thegn* Hnaef spent a good deal of silver and drank a good deal of ale while telling me of his disappointment.

"Ay," he said, wiping sweat from his face with one hand, ale from his red beard with the other, "it's truth, *dvergr:* When I saw you ride home with the Slaughter-whelp, I could hear my sons sighing for pleasure, could hear them saying that some vengeance would be taken at last. It burns my heart that Vorgund's son still lives."

I didn't doubt that his heart burned, but I did doubt that he'd heard his sons sighing. Hnaef didn't have the look of a man who heard ghosts in the night. He seemed too well-rested for that.

I told him that I thought Erich's reasons for keeping Iwan's head connected to his shoulders were good ones. Yet though I said it to Hnaef, this was not wholly true. Like many others, I'd have been glad to see Iwan's head hanging high, but I didn't talk about it much. In that summer, I didn't talk about anything much.

Such was not the case with *thegn* Hnaef.

"Ah, Garroc, these times are hard for me to understand. Half-dan goes unavenged, our friends and kin go unavenged. That's not the way it should be!" Hnaef's voice dropped low, he leaned forward across the oaken table. In the thick smoky air of the ale-house, his face seemed like a stranger's. "Some say that Erich's behavior is cowardly, *dvergr,* that the means of easy vengeance lives well-fed and well-treated an easy reach away. All know it: This is not how an honorable man treats the son of his father's killer."

I might have told him that it was how an honorable man treated a hostage, but Hnaef would not have heeded me and so I said nothing. Still, I listened closely now.

"Ay, Erich's behavior is strange," he muttered, "and it's not the only thing that's hard to understand. I've heard it—as you must have, Garroc—that Penda has made an alliance with a *Cristen,* a Welshman. Everyone knows that no man can trust a Welshman."

Hnaef became quiet and thoughtful for a time, studied me carefully in the way I'd lately seen others study me. Some thought that Erich liked to confide in me as his father had; some thought I knew the *cyning's* mind well, could shed some light on his puzzling way of thinking. It wasn't true, but I seldom paid for my ale all that summer. I didn't that night, either. Yet though Hnaef was open-handed with his silver, kept the ale flowing freely, only one of us came away from the ale-house satisfied, and that one was me.

Hnaef had gotten nothing more than my silence, but I'd gotten enough ale to help me sleep through most of the night without thinking too much about Lydi, almost enough to keep the voices of ghosts quiet.

Wulf's and Waerstan's, red Ecgwulf's and Ceowulf's, Haestan's and Godwig's . . . Ah, well, my Sif. There were a lot of them, and they made a mighty din.

That night I drank deep and drank well, for I needed sleep. In the morning I would ride north with Erich and his army. Penda hadn't yet become tired of war. Thunor's Moon, the War Moon, was only a thin sliver in the night sky now, but it filled the eyes of Erich War Hawk and Wotan's Blade. In the morning Erich would bring us to join Penda's new-swelled army. That night, as I made my wandering way back to the hall, I wondered if we would catch sight of Penda's new ally, and I wondered if we would have to fight beside Cadwalla the Welshman.

We didn't. Like it was Cadwalla had some business of his own to attend.

Another thing you should know, Sif, is that the *baresarks*, those we called the Hunter's pack, were not happy during that late summer and fall. You'd think they would have been, wouldn't you? As Thunor's Moon became Witch's, as Witch's became Harvest, Erich and Penda gave them rich war-fields to work, gave them plenty of killing to do. The berserkers cared nothing for the complaints of men like Hnaef, that Penda had made a foolish alliance. *Baresarks* fight where they are told to fight. Yet they were not happy, for though he kept them busy, Erich withheld the thing the *baresarks* most wanted: vengeance on Vorgund. In this, they considered the matter much as Hnaef did. They'd loved Halfdan, and so maybe old Aescwine was right after all: A *baresark's* regard is a dangerous thing.

This time it was not Eadric who told me of the berserker's discontent. This time Aelfgar told me.

This is how it happened.

It is natural that men stop fighting in the time of the harvest. Crops must be gathered, and no sensible king or lord would keep his men from that work lest the folk starve in winter. As did most *cynings* of that time, as many still do now, Erich kept no standing army. He kept a war-troop, a small group of men who shared his *heall* in winter. These were mostly Dwarfs, and some Men who would rather stay with their companions and the *cyning* than take their living from the fields. The rest of the *cyning's* army was made up of men who were hard soldiers in spring and summer, but in fall must go and be farmers again.

It was the same for Eadwine as it was for us, and so, with great reluctance, Faith-Breaker and Wotan's Blade left each other in peace when the Harvest moon was three nights from full, decided it would be best to let their *cynings* and *thegns* and soldiers go lay up defenses against winter's hunger.

One way of doing this was to harvest the fields, another was to harvest the forest—for though it is true that at the end of the fall farmers would bring the *cyning's* share of their rye and oats and corn and wheat to Rilling, still game must be caught and prepared for winter eating.

Hunting was what Erich's war-troop liked to do in fall, for we were not farmers and we were in the habit of killing. The moon we call *Huntincge,* Hunter's, is a good time for that, and *Wyrm's* Moon is, too, if the northern gales don't come. That year the winter storms came late, and so, early one grey cold morning, when the *Wyrm* was old, waning before winter, Aelfgar and I went into the wildwood east of the Rill to hunt.

Aelfgar and I didn't talk much on that day we hunted together; we made our way silently through the naked woods. During the summer and early fall we'd lost the habit of friendship. True it is that we'd both gone warring north with Erich, but scout-craft no longer interested Aelfgar and he had more inclination to spend time with new friends than old. Though I missed him, I thought it must be that he didn't want to be with old friends who would remind him of the time when his brother died, and so I didn't say much about it to him or to anyone else. It seemed to me that a man had a right to avoid the memory of pain if he could. And I, who now spent a good deal of time in ale-houses, hiding from ghost-voices, hiding from countless small memories of Lydi, didn't think I had cause to complain if Aelfgar chose his own way to try to lose painful memories.

Still, one old friend Aelfgar didn't forsake; often in the summer

I'd seen him with Blodrafen. In battle they fought like wolves, and
in fall when war was done they kept close in the *heall*.

Toward noon Aelfgar found a stream in a clear part of the forest, and near that, a good thick brake, one surrounded on all sides
by frost-blighted ferns and high reeds. We settled down to see what
our luck would bring us. Rain found us in the middle of the afternoon. Fitful at first, then quicker, it came on the wings of the cold
northwind. All the while, Aelfgar sat in silence, his back against
a grey beech's trunk, rain streaming silver down his face. He en-
dured the soaking patiently, seemed to have no care for the mud
seeping up from the ground where we sat. From time to time, he'd
lift his head, scent the wind the way a hound does when he's
searching for news of prey.

Toward late afternoon the wind dropped. The rain stopped suddenly. Mist gathered over the stream, wandered lazily up to the
sky. I watched the dreams of water become edged with rose and
gold as the sun won through ragged clouds. Behind us a jay
screamed. As though this were a signal, Aelfgar nodded, drew a
short soft breath. He slid an arrow from the quiver at his hip,
nocked it in shadow-silence. He drew himself up slowly until he
stood with his back to the beech, listened to what the breeze had
to say, then drew a long breath, let it go slowly, deliberately, as
though answering. At that moment a stag, high-stepping, broke
the cover of the brush downstream from us, walked to the water.

Sunlight, shafting down through the trees, shone on the stag's
horns, lay across his red shoulders, his gleaming white breast, like
a golden mantle. Tall proud king! I had seen his like before, but
only in dreams; heard speak of such kings, but only in songs.

The stag raised his head high, tested the breeze as Aelfgar had
only a moment ago. But the breeze, blowing from the north, didn't
speak to him, didn't warn of hunters. The mist floating along the
stream became more red than gold now as the sun angled down
the sky. Aelfgar raised his ready bow and I turned silently to watch
him.

Times like this, in the instant before his arrow flew, I'd seen respect and pity in him, and finally honest determination to do what
he must. As I looked up at him now, I saw no respect, no pity,
and my heart ached under the weight of sudden chill fear. Rapt
he was, his blue eyes gleaming with a hard and very cold light.
He smiled as at some enemy come unwary into his reach. Smiled,
ay, if that slow drawing of his lips across his teeth could rightly
be named a smile.

I shuddered, looked again at the stag and saw not what was,

but what would be: a crimson burst of blood pouring from the forest-king's mouth, staining the fine mantle that was the gift of the sun.

Still smiling his winter smile, Aelfgar sent his arrow to kill the stag.

The beast could not have felt a thing. Aelfgar's arrow caught him straight through the heart. Knees sagged, buckled, and the stag dropped. He fought hard, as a brave king will, kicking, arching his back against the arrow which had come to steal his life. A good fight he made, but a fatal one. In moments the stag lay forever still, blood pouring from his mouth into the water. Aelfgar howled high, a wolfish wail, and scrambled across the stream to claim his kill.

I should have gone to help him dress the stag, but I didn't. I was thinking about what I'd seen in Aelfgar's eyes as he loosed his arrow, sent honed flint into the stag's heart. I'd seen rapt joy, cold and sharp. He'd felt the kill before he'd made it, felt the power of knowing that the stag's sure death was his to deliver. And he'd liked the feeling.

On the way back to Rilling I asked Aelfgar where he'd learned to kill so joyously, and he told me that he'd learned it from Blodrafen, said darkly that he thought it was a good lesson.

Hard for me to ask the question, I who didn't speak much these days. But I asked it for the sake of the friendship which we'd shared. "Why is that, Aelfgar?"

Eyes hard as old ice, he said, "Because it feels good to kill. When I kill something, I feel like I am very strong."

"Ay, boy," I whispered, "you *are* very strong. The berserker is wrong: You don't need to kill to feel that way."

He didn't consider it, didn't turn the idea over in his mind, examining it from all sides as once he would have. He only looked at me as though he knew something I didn't, as though he pitied my ignorance.

"He's not wrong, Garroc. He told me that a star falling counts a death, and that night in the summer, when all the stars fell, I watched and remembered what he said. Gadd told me it wasn't so." Pain flickered in his eyes, softened them, then vanished, leaving behind ice and a man I no longer knew. "But Gadd is dead now, ay? One of those stars was his. And so Gadd was wrong, Blodrafen was right.

"Garroc, I wasn't strong enough to help Wulf when the raiders hurt him and I wasn't strong enough to help Haestan when you

told me to. I couldn't help—I couldn't help Gadd, either. I just
had to sit there and watch him die. He asked me to help him. He
said, 'Aelfgar, I hurt. Aelfgar, help me, I hurt.' But I couldn't help
him and he died. It was my fault, because I couldn't help him.
And maybe it was my fault because I looked at the stars and saw
his death—"

"No," I cried, suddenly afraid. "Aelfgar, it wasn't your fault!
A Welshman killed him, an enemy."

"Ay," he snarled, and that snarl made his handsome face un-
lovely. "A Welshman. Maybe even Vorgund or maybe Iwan
Slaughter-whelp."

I asked him how he thought this strength of his could help the
next person who needed him, but he only laughed, thumped a fist
hard against his chest.

"I don't care about that anymore, Garroc, because I'm strong
now and I don't have to. I'm strong enough now to take vengeance
for Gadd, and Blodrafen says that soon I will."

I didn't like the sound of that, and I thought hard about it as
I made my lonely way back to Rilling with a stranger who had
once been a friend. Dark-eyed and brooding, with the air of the
baresark about him, an air like the first hard scent of winter, he'd
told me something Erich had a great need to know.

I didn't have a chance to speak to the *cyning*, for when I returned to the *heall*, Dyfed told me that Cynewulf had sent word
to Erich that he was bringing his daughter, his Gled Golden-Hair,
to Rilling. Erich thought it would be a good and courteous thing
to go meet his bride and her father and keep them company on
their way. He'd left in the morning not long after Aelfgar and I
had gone into the woods.

That night I stayed late at the ale-house. When I came out into
the frost-glittering street I saw no moon in the sky. My wits were
dull, it took me a while to understand that the old *Wyrm* had gone,
left a shadow and an empty place where once his light had shone.
Tomorrow would see the rise of the moon we call Wolf's.

II

ERICH came riding back two days after he'd left, bright on a snowy winter morning, leading his betrothed to her wedding, her kin to the feasting. Swithgar, watching at the south wall, hailed the *cyning* home, and soon all of Rilling lined the long, broad street of the village to watch Erich War Hawk bring his Gled to the *heall*. The northwind blew strongly down a sky grey as iron, sent new-fallen snow dancing high. Soldier and hall-servant, smith and baker, brewer and tanner, we stood stamping feet for warmth. We wanted to have a look at Cynewulf's daughter, the young maid who was so famed for her beauty that all folk called her Gled Golden-Hair.

I stood with Dyfed that morning, hiding from the wind in the lee of the little house where Iwan Vorgund's son lived. We'd kept close to the Welshman these two days past, walked with him by day, slept on the floor before his door at night. It was ever the case that those on watch would try to trade their duty with others, and Dyfed and I had accepted the trade twice, for we thought that the news I'd had from Aelfgar didn't bode well for the Slaughter-whelp's safety, feared that some one of the guards would trade his watch to one who would rather that Iwan was dead.

This was not pleasant work for me. It required that I keep from the ale-houses, and that was not so easy to do as it had once been. Too, the sight of Iwan reminded me that I'd lost a lot when I brought him to Erich. And true it is that I often wished, as others did, that the *cyning* had taken swift vengeance and counted it for Halfdan's death. But Erich wanted a hostage, and so I thought it would have spoken but poorly of my honor—that honor for which I'd cast my Lydi's trust aside—to let others take Iwan's life when the *cyning* didn't wish it taken. So I was thinking, dark-minded and ill-humored, when I heard the first welcoming shouts rise from the south end of the street.

"Look at her, Garroc," Dyfed said, low-voiced as Erich and his Gled came into sight around the corner of the tallest grain-house. "Now there's a warm beauty, ay?"

She was that.

A young maid, Gled sat a little dappled mare, rode between the *cyning* and Cynewulf. Several women rode in train behind her, one her mother, the others kinswomen. These were not ill-favored, but among them Gled was the most beautiful. As she passed us, I thought that golden Gled had only recently become old enough to take a husband. She seemed still a little girl; traces of childish roundness yet graced her face and form.

Cynewulf had decked his daughter bravely. She shone with gold and silver; when the wind tossed her fine white cloak, all saw that it was warmly lined with marten's fur, saw jewels glittering against a gown of soft blue wool. Her richest treasures, though, were her golden hair, unbound as a maid's should be and hanging long to her waist, her great green eyes brighter than any jewel.

It was said that her father's *heall* didn't stand in a village but rose tall and lonely on dark moors. Well I could believe that, for Gled's summer-green eyes were wide with the wonder of all she saw about her—grain-houses, guest-houses, ale-shops and stables, cottars' homes, smith-shops and tanneries. Now and again she caught her breath; always she strove to see everything and everyone.

Ay, a child, for no proud woman would so innocently think that anything she saw was better to look at than she. And the *cyning* was enspelled. When once he leaned toward her, touched her shoulder, then pointed to the *heall*, I saw the kind of tenderness I'd never marked in him before. Young it was, only newly born. But in that moment I'd have wagered heavily that the War Hawk was not thinking about the convenience of this alliance at all. A man does not touch a treaty with the kind of gentleness Erich used when he touched golden Gled.

"Ah, Gled Golden-Hair," Dyfed sighed when they were past. "Well-named Gled."

I said nothing, only looked after them, thinking about the thing I'd seen in Erich's eyes. After a time I realized that I was not the only one to notice it. Soft behind me came the sound of a footstep. I turned to see Iwan Vorgund's son at the door.

Though he'd learned to speak our language in these months past, and spoke it handily with the same skipping, singing accent Lydi had, he always used the *Wealas* tongue when he spoke to Dyfed or me. So he did now. He jerked his chin toward the hall, smiled slyly.

"*Gwalch Rhyfel,* you call him. I think yon little girl will soon have your war hawk perched tamely on her wrist, yes?"

Dyfed laughed, a hard harsh sound. "You'd better hope not, Iwan. Just now it's his will alone that's keeping your head so comfortably close to your shoulders. The last thing you need is a little girl making his decisions for him. Most especially one who has no great fondness for your kind." He cocked his head, looked at me. "Ay, Garroc, didn't I hear it once that Cynewulf's two sons were killed by *Wealas* not many summers ago?"

I told him that I didn't know what he'd heard, but I'd heard something about it, heard also that Gled had wept long for her dear brothers.

Iwan said nothing, only withdrew into the house and closed the door firmly.

Erich meant to wed his golden Gled when the Wolf's moon was full, and Cynewulf, more agreeable than any had yet known him to be, said that the longest night of winter was best passed in feasting. And this worked well, for the moon would not rise full for ten more nights and it is a long doing when a *cyning* gets ready to bind himself to another kindred with a marriage.

Longer still, when both kindreds have not been friends. There is much feasting, and the great celebration lasts for days. Each side makes many speeches, loudly proclaiming that the wedding is the finest thing that all could look for. Soon they convince themselves that it is a greater thing than any had hoped for. Many gifts of land and goods are exchanged, husband to wife, husband to his wife's kin, the woman's kin to her husband. In all this, the woman come to wed gives nothing of land or goods. And this is right: She is giving herself. It is enough.

Ay, it's a long doing, and the preparations for Erich's marriage to Gled Cynewulf's daughter went on day and night until the Wolf's moon was nearly full. But Erich didn't forget about his hostage, and if there were some who didn't like it that Iwan still lived, there were many others who thought that the *cyning's* word was not to be questioned, only obeyed. These told Erich how things stood. And so, on the night of his return Erich gave word that four guards must stand always at the Welshman's door, that Iwan would not now have permission to walk abroad in the village as once he did. Dyfed and I were among those watch-keepers.

"Ay, well, Garroc," Dyfed said to me, on a night soon after the *cyning* gave his command. "It looks to be light duty at best. There are enough of us so that none will have to do it often. And it seems that things are quieter than they have been, ay?"

But I didn't think so. I thought that things only seemed that way, that it was difficult to hear the *baresarks* growling above the din of feasting, difficult to see them among so many others where they packed all close in the shadows and dark as the smoke-blackened rafters of the hall.

Difficult, but not impossible. In those days, as the Wolf's moon waxed fat, I watched the *baresarks* as closely as I did the Witch-Gatherer's son. And it gave me great sadness to see Aelfgar always among them, always close beside winter-eyed Blodrafen. He didn't look upon me with friendly eyes, and when we met in the hall or passed on the street, he didn't smile as once he would have. I hardly knew him at all, and this was a sad thing. Sadder yet was the feeling growing in me that when I saw Aelfgar, I saw a dangerous enemy.

III

ERICH gave a good house to Gled and her father and mother, two others for Gled's kinswomen and servants. Cynewulf's men, some twenty of them, he housed in the hall. With so many strangers around, men who but for this coming wedding would not be friends, some didn't find it easy to sleep. I was one of those, and when I was not keeping watch over Erich's hostage and must go to rest in the hall, my sleep was always thin. So it had been when I woke on the cold morning of the day Erich was to wed Cynewulf's daughter.

Thick the air around me, heavy with the smell of hearth-smoke, the stale odors of old ale and cold food. The feasting had been wild last night. I'd heard it from the ale-house not far away, and hadn't come back to the hall to sleep until all was finally quiet, and that was not long before. Now a great longing for the cold sharp air came over me, and I pulled on my boots and took up my mantle. Though I went quietly, for the sake of an ale-grown headache, I didn't get past Dyfed without waking him.

Ay, best to say I didn't get past his red dog, cast out of his place beside his master by a fair woman, and sleeping a small distance away from the two. Werrehund raised his head, made a small, questioning sound.

"Hush, dog," I whispered, and the red dog sighed deeply, went gladly back to sleeping.

But another woke. The young woman sleeping beside Dyfed raised up on one arm to see who walked by. She was a serving-woman in the *heall*, light-haired and pretty, plump and friendly. I liked her well, and Cyneleah was her name. Dyfed had made good use of his time away from battle-grounds. In the ale-houses he ever had Cyneleah on his knee; when he walked about the village she was often beside him.

Now, Cyneleah yawned and pushed her tangled hair away from her face. Her cheeks were pink and flushed with sleep, her grey eyes soft. "Ay, *dvergr*," she whispered, "has the snow stopped?"

I told her that I didn't know about that, bade her go back to sleep. She nodded, nestled against Dyfed again, tried not to wake him. But the damage to his sleep was done. When he saw me standing near, he said that he wouldn't mind a walk in the clean air just now.

I'd not had it in mind to take company with me; it always seemed best to walk alone and silently when my head was hurting after a night in the ale-house. And so I waited only impatiently while Dyfed dragged on his boots, rummaged about for his mantle. He spoke quietly to Cyneleah, but she, close and warm in the blankets, had fallen back to sleep already. We left the hall in silence, went out to the winter morning.

Eagle-winged Hraesvelgr gathered northwind, sent it racing southward that morning. We walked head-down, shoulders hunched, and I'd not gone far before my breath turned to stinging ice in my beard. The snow that had begun falling late in the afternoon before had stopped sometime in the night. Now the sky stretched high and brightest blue above a shining white world. My aching head didn't like all that leaping light. The smoky blue shadows of the buildings and the tall stockade were easier to see.

We made our way through the village, stopped at the bake-houses where women took new-made loaves from the round ovens. Though my head hurt I'd never been one to turn weak-bellied from a long night of drinking, and so the scent of that bread seemed sweet and good. I begged a loaf from a young dark-haired maid and shared my take with Dyfed. We ate as we walked past the ale-houses and the ironsmith's shop. When we came to the little house where Iwan Vorgund's son was kept, we greeted the guards posted there and shared out the rest of our bread with them.

Aescwine was one of these guards, and as he ate he told us that the Welshman had spent most of the night watching at the window, silent and brooding. "Filling his eyes with the moon and the mountains," he said.

I looked to the far western corner of the sky, saw the Wolf lingering late, hanging day-pale and ghostly; when I looked at the mountains I had to squint hard to keep my aching head calm. The new-risen sun gleamed like ruddy gold on the Cambrians' broad snowy flanks.

"Ay, Aescwine," I said. "Those mountains are home to the Welshman. Likely he'd rather fill his eyes with them than anything around here."

Aescwine supposed it was so, and said little else but that he was cold and tired with watching. His fellows agreed with him, and Dyfed told them to be patient, that relief would come soon.

"Like as not," he drawled, "that relief will be us. It's about time for our turn."

Quiet again, Dyfed and I walked to the river where the day's new sun had not yet melted the brittle dark ice gathered at the water's edge. After a time he looked over his shoulder at the *heall*, said that a day or so gone he'd heard Gled remark that the hall looked like a tall guardian rising above the flock of little houses.

"I thought that was a good saying, Garroc. It does look like that, ay?"

"Ay, it does."

Dyfed sighed, a deeply contented sound, and now he was not thinking about Gled. "It's a good thing to have a warm woman to sleep beside you in winter. I'm glad every night for Cyneleah."

Though it still hurt to see light shining, I watched the sun glint on the dark place in the Rill where the current had kept the water from freezing. Deeply blue, that water called to mind the color of Lydi's eyes.

Dyfed laid a hand on my shoulder. "Garroc, I've been thinking. Maybe—after this wedding, ay?—we can get leave of the *cyning* and ride west. We can find Lydi."

My eyes still on the river, I thought: Ay, that tune again.

He'd been whistling it since we'd been back in Rilling from the summer wars. Most times he whistled softly, gave only an amused look when I came late to the *heall* with one or another willing *dvergr* woman. As a good friend will, he always congratulated me that I would not have to spend my nights cold and alone. And ay, Sif, I didn't spend the nights cold, nor did I spend all of them alone. But still, I was lonely, and Dyfed, happy with his Cyneleah beside him, knew it.

"Ghost Foot," I said, "what was once between Lydi and me is broken now. It's beyond mending."

"Ah, Garroc. For all the time you've been with her, you don't know your Lydi very well, do you?" He tapped the empty, scarred place where his left eye used to be. "Swear to you, my friend, sometimes I think I see things more clearly with this than you do with both your fine far-sighted eyes."

"Could be." I pressed cold hands to the sides of my head, tried to quiet the restless ale-spawned pain.

Dyfed smiled without humor. "I don't often see you at the feasting, Garroc. Why is that? If it's drink you want, you don't have to pay good silver for it in the hall."

"I like the ale-house better." I looked at him meaningfully. "It's quieter."

"But those quiet nights of yours make hard mornings, don't they? What is it you're trying to drown in the ale, Garroc? Is it the plain good sense your heart would speak to you if you only let it?"

Ah, no, I thought. It's the great din of dead men's voices and the growling of the shadow-wolf who liked to feed on memories of a witch I thought never to see again.

Dyfed pressed hard now, eagerly. "Ride west with me, *freond min.* Or go there yourself if you don't want company. But go, ay? She's a rare treasure, your Lydi, and she's not lost to you yet."

"You know that, Dyfed, do you?"

"Yes," he said firmly. "I know it. It wasn't good what we did, Garroc. But—"

"There can be no 'but' about it. It wasn't good what we did."

"And you think there's no forgiving it, don't you?"

I looked out over the river again, watched a lone duck, dark-garbed for winter, paddle slowly, aimlessly, with the stream. He looked cold and sad.

Ah, Lydi. For all that I had not known what else to do, for all that I believed that pride and honor and even Fate made it so that I could not have done anything else, this still remained: I'd broken faith with my Lydi. I'd made her sanctuary useless, taken a man from her care. Well I knew that it had never been done in Seintwar before that day.

"Ghost Foot," I said, "I don't know how anyone could forgive that."

"I do."

I didn't bother to ask after this knowledge of his, for it seemed to me that he refused to look at the matter sensibly. And he pressed no harder.

"Ay, well, come on then, stubborn Garroc. Let's walk a while before we go back to the *heall.* Maybe it'll do you good to clear the ale-fumes out of your head."

We walked for a long time, sometimes quiet, sometimes talking of the small things friends talk about, but we didn't speak of Lydi again. When we came to the broad plank bridge across the Rill

we took it carefully, for it was coated in places with thick sheets
of ice. Once we'd crossed the river, Dyfed said that he thought
it would be a fine thing to climb up to Rafenscylf and see the white
world stretched out before us.

I told him that I saw no reason not to, for my headache had
gone. "Blown away with the ale-fumes, no doubt."

The easiest path wound along the east side of the hill, where
the sun had begun to melt the ice. Halfway to the top, where the
trees came close to the path, Dyfed saw something strange in the
softening snow and went to have a better look. I didn't follow, for
the wind was strong up there, pushed harder than it did below.
I'd no interest in having a bough-load of snow dumped on my
head.

Instead I wrapped my mantle tight around me and leaned my
back against a tall jutting stone. Sometimes in winter when I'd
roamed the silent snowy wildwood with my Lydi, we'd find high
places like this, and late at night, when all the stars shone, we'd
sit by a tall hot fire to watch the moon arc across the sky, watch
the stars wheeling. Then, late, we'd go back through the ice-
gleaming forest to Gardd Seren, back to the warm cottage and the
warmer bed. In the morning I'd wake, reach for her before ever
I opened my eyes. . . .

I stilled that thought, damped the memories as I'd have damped
a campfire's embers in driest summer. On these things the *sceadu-
wulf* fed, on these memories the grief-hound grew strong.

After a time I laid my hands against the cold stone, pressed my
palms tight to its rough sides, listened to it groan as ice melted
in the deep cracks.

It must be hard, old stone, to feel the ice break you.

But old stone would have none of my pity. In a deep voice, the
voice of the mother-earth heard in the bones of me, it whispered:

Never hard, *dvergr* my son, to feel the thing that must be felt.
Easy as hearing the thing that must be heard.

Simple words, Sif, and they roused things in me I didn't want
to consider, smoky images of the ale-house and the cold voices of
the ghosts which never left me in peace. Fast, as though I'd been
stung, I pushed away from the stone, walked away and didn't stop
until I stood close to the edge of the path. From there I greedily
filled my eyes with all that I could see—the white, white world,
the river and the snow-smoothed meadows stretching empty and
wide to the south.

Ay, but not so empty. Small and dark against the snow, something moved. I shaded my eyes and watched as the small dark

shape grew larger, spread across the white, became the forms of a mounted troop plunging hard through the snow, riding toward Rilling. Sun-glint leaped from something bright held high.

A spear tip, I thought.

I drew breath to call Dyfed, but he called to me first, dark-voiced. I went to where he stood, some way into the woods, and when I saw what he'd found, I had no liking for it.

Longer than his hand, wider than mine, the deep print made a dark blue hole in the snow. It was new, that track, made after the snow had stopped falling. But for the misplaced large toe and the marks of claws, it looked like the print of a man's naked foot.

"Bear," Dyfed whispered harshly.

I nodded, wordless. And I didn't think 'a bear.' I thought: The Bear.

Yes, some things we know without understanding how we know them: The bear was the same one who'd so badly injured Werre-hund, the one Aescwine had seen the night he'd sat on Cefn Arth mourning friends and his war-killed son. It was the bear I'd last seen in the wildwood beyond Cefn Arth, standing tall beside Rho-dri ap Iau's barrow.

And this is true, Sif: As I looked at the track I knew surely that the bear had come this great distance from his wildwood home with a purpose. I knew this because, standing there, I remembered the old tales of bears which Aescwine knew, and so I knew that bears are winter-sleepers and do not usually go about in snow.

In me, ale-stupored till now, the shadow-wolf roused and growled, spoke of the friends who had died on Cefn Arth. Token of ill-luck, that bear had been near when Ecgwulf and Godwig had died, when *thegn* Hnaef's sons were killed, when Haestan my battle-shadow had received mortal wounds. Though I'd never put words to the feeling before now, as I saw the tracks I realized that I'd come to think that the bear bore as much responsibility for my friends' deaths as the raiders who'd killed them.

Dyfed leaned his back against the tree, twisted a dark and deadly smile. He'd sworn vengeance on this bear. "An old friend, ay?"

"Ay, it looks that way. You found only this one print?"

"Only this." He scuffed at the track, covered it over with snow. In his eye I saw a scornful look, the look of a man who does not trouble himself overmuch about the enemy he's planning to fight. "But it's up here, Garroc, and I'm going to find it. I'm going to kill it."

It was not good to see the look in his eye, dangerous and reckless. Around me the wintry air grew even colder.

"Whatever you're going to do, Ghost Foot, you're not going to do it alone."

"Alone? No, I won't be alone. I'll have Werrehund with me, and whoever else wants to come and watch." He looked up at a small patch of bright blue sky showing through the trees. "I'm going to find a fine big spear and the best sword I can buy of the smith."

So saying, he pushed away from the tree, went out into the sunlight again. I followed, but slowly.

Dull I'd been through most of the fall and winter, ale-numbed and empty. But that morning, as I came out of the woods, I felt a change come on me. In all the months since I'd ridden away from the borderland and Cefn Arth, I'd tried hard to keep out of Fate's way, tried to keep ghostly voices silent, the shadow-wolf quiet in me, sad memories at bay. Now I felt the blood rise in me as it does before a battle—hot, and livening as the dangerous air when the Storm-god is about.

And I had a feeling that something was different about the day. Somewhere, far away where the Norns live, an intricate pattern was being woven. This was not a feeling I was unused to, and if it was not good, it was familiar.

As we went back down the snowy path to the river, I left Dyfed to his planning, watched the path when I had to, watched the oncoming riders when I could. Dyfed had no interest in them, but the feeling I'd had when I saw the bear's print, the feeling of Fate moving, grew stronger as the riders came closer.

When that feeling is on me, I cannot be truly surprised by anything that happens. And so, as Dyfed and I crossed the icy bridge and saw the approaching riders clearly, I was not surprised to see the *god-cynn* King riding out before the others. It seemed only right: Penda's bright thread had been part of Fate's pattern since the cold spring night when we'd lighted the pyre for Halfdan, sent the Hunter riding a fiery steed to Valholl.

Dyfed had no chance that day to enact his plans for bear-hunting. It was, as he'd said to Aescwine, our turn to guard Iwan, and we were about that most of the day. But we didn't keep the news of the bear's tracks to ourselves. Before I went to keep watch, I went to speak with Erich.

Busy he was, for the King had come unlooked for, and places must be found for his men, a house for Penda himself. But he took time for me, gave me the moment alone that I requested. When I told him my news, he remembered at once the stories that we'd brought back from the border . He thought for a time, then bade me keep the news to myself. He didn't want half the men in the *heall* galloping wildly up into the hills.

"Once they got scent of this bear of yours, Garroc, I'd likely not see them again till they caught it. No, keep it quiet, ay?"

He didn't believe the beast would pose danger to the walled village, and I didn't disagree. Even in the wildest of Aescwine's Daneland tales, no bear had ever attacked a strongly defended place. And no one, man or woman or child, ever wandered without Rilling's walls on winter nights.

My news given, I started to leave him, but Erich called me back, said that in the morning he'd give us all we needed of weapons and gear for bear-hunting, said that he'd gladly come with us, for he thought a bearskin would be a fair and wonderful morning-gift for his Gled.

Through all that cold day I kept watch over Iwan Vorgund's son with Dyfed and Cynnere and Swithgar. We talked about the wedding feast to come, talked about the King. Mindful of Erich's will, no mention was made of the bear, but I spent most of that day plying whetstone to iron, putting a keener edge on my dagger, a shining sharpness on my axe's blade.

Iwan Slaughter-whelp, who had spent most of the night before watching the mountains and filling his eyes with the moon, slept most of that day, still and quiet on his thick straw pallet, woolen blankets pulled high over his broad shoulders. But once he woke, leaned up on his elbow and smiled sourly as he watched me work. He said honing iron was a strange way to prepare for a wedding feast.

When I didn't answer him, he pulled the blankets high again and went back to sleep.

I only barely noticed. I was thinking of Erich and his hopes to bring back a bearskin for his new wife. And I was thinking about red Ecgwulf's boast that he'd clasp a bearskin mantle with fine Wyrms Mail. Ecgwulf was dead now, and Wyrms Mail was lost. The memory was as cold as Hraesvelgr's wind whistling down the sky, and I worked harder with the whetstone, gave all my attention to making my weapons fit.

IV

FIRELIGHT filled the *heall,* blazed from torches, from braziers and the wide, deep hearth. All that light gleamed bravely in golden arm-bands, leaped from silver buckles, danced as many colors in the jewels decorating the men and women come to see Halfdan's son wed Cynewulf's daughter.

We had no priests among us, as *Cristens* did then and do now. If sacrifice needed to be made to assure the gods of a man's friendship, he killed the bullock with his own blade, with his own two hands threw the god-gift of grain on the fires. None needed to speak for us when the gods could so easily be found, Thunor in the storm-sky, his Sif in spring-greening meadows. Heimdall Gate-Keeper sat always at the foot of the rainbow bridge and Wotan All-Father walked often on the earth, thirsting after knowledge and hidden secrets, making himself part of the lives of Dwarfs and Men—whether we liked that or not.

And so no priest was needed to bind Erich to his Gled and beg a boon of blessing. A *god-cynn* King did that. From my place at the board, not far below the gold-glittering *thegns* and their richly decked sons and daughters and wives—for Erich so valued his war band that he gave us good seats at his table—I saw and heard it all.

In the high seat at the head of the *heall,* the seat carved by Halfdan himself with the likenesses of gods and beasts and leafage, the seat that Gled would have shared with Erich had not the King come riding to Rilling that morning, Penda witnessed the marriage oaths. He placed Gled's hand in Erich's and commanded Halfdan's son to be a good husband to Gled, bade Cynewulf's daughter be a true and faithful wife to Erich. He spoke of dead Halfdan, said that in these months since the Hunter's death the son had shown himself to be as good a friend to his King, as good a *cyning* to his folk, as the father had been.

Then the King raised a great ale-horn, gold-wrapped and silver-based, the best Erich had to offer from his father's deep coffers. Handsome that King! Long-legged, thick-shouldered, golden-haired. His eyes were the color of storms. The get of gods, he looked like a god himself as he drank deeply, then passed the horn to Erich, called him friend. All the *heall* rose cheering.

Or so it seemed. Dark in the shadows at the back of the hall,

some didn't rise, didn't give voice to joy, and these were *baresarks.*
A gleam of gold I saw among them, Aelfgar's bright hair.

Again silence. Noise and quiet played through that night like
light and shadow. With grave formality, Erich gave the ale-horn
to his wife, and when she'd drunk he fastened the keys to his hall
and all the coffers that held food-store and treasure, onto the broad
jewel-studded girdle which Gled wore tight about her slender
waist.

Aescwine, seated beside me on the bench, elbowed me sharply,
nodded to Cynewulf. That *cyning's* face, sharp and thin, ruddy
with good wine, held an eager look.

"Like it is," old Aescwine whispered, "yon Cynewulf is already
counting up the lands and goods come to his daughter. I'm thinking that Erich had better do his work well in these cold nights.
The sooner that girl comes with child, the sooner she will be truly
his and not her father's."

I reached for the silver-mounted horn before me, still half-full
with better ale than I'd tasted in a long time. But I drank only
a little, for I was intent on thinking. I remembered Erich's mood
in the summer, when he first told me of his coming marriage; remembered the way he'd spoken of Gled. Then he'd considered this
marriage nothing more than a treaty between two *cynings,* the girl
no more than a player in the game, maybe as cunning and crafty
as her father. I had not disagreed with that thinking, for such is
often the way when great folk wed.

But now I didn't think this was the case. If Cynewulf had
schemes in mind, I'd have taken my oath that his girl didn't. There
was nothing cunning about little Gled, nothing crafty. When Erich
had fastened the heavy bunch of keys on her girdle, she'd reached
down, held them in both hands as though their weight was too
much for leather and gold and jewels to bear, looked up at Erich
with an expression so sweetly grateful for the faith those keys beto-
kened that it could well melt the hardest heart.

And the War Hawk's heart was not too hard that night.

Aescwine poured more ale for the both of us. He marked it as
a wonder that my horn was yet half-full, but I only heard him
dimly as I watched the *cyning* and his bride go about the hall to
speak with one person and another. Time and again folk rose from
the board to raise a pledge to the *cyning* and the child-woman who
was now his wife. Close upon each pledge a great shout of *Waes
Hael!* roared from the throats of the hundred and a half men and
women, *dvergr* and *mann-cynn,* gathered to celebrate.

And Wotan's Blade made his voice carry above all the rest as the well-wishing rolled like thunder through the hall.

Among us in those times it had lately become courteous for a man when he was in company to say that he wanted to breathe the air when, in fact, what he wanted to do was use the midden trenches. This amused old Aescwine greatly, for he thought it was at all times best for a man to say what he meant.

"You get into less trouble that way," he'd once told me. "Otherwise, what do you do when you need to empty yourself of too much ale—or worse, ay?—and someone who hasn't heard of this fine new courtesy of ours comes along with you to breathe the air? He's not going to be too happy, and you're going to feel like a fool for not saying what you meant in the first place. No, 'tis best for all concerned to speak plainly of what you intend."

And so, well on into the night Aescwine lurched up from the board, spoke plainly and none too quietly of what he intended. He leaned heavily on my shoulder, for the ale played foul with his balance, and I thought it would be best if I let him have that shoulder as he made his way through the hall. Great drinking inflames men in strange ways, makes them happy and boastful for a time, then calls up darker things, things that will change the hap of one man stumbling innocently against another to a deep and terrible offense. Aescwine, wavering on his feet now, looked like to offend half the Dwarfs and Men in the hall.

Now this is interesting to me, Sif, even all these long years since it happened: I'd spent a great deal of the winter drinking a lot. Times there were—and often—when I reached beyond a full plate of the best food for the ale and forgot wholly to eat. And it had not been easy to shun the ale-houses during the days when I stood watch over Iwan Vorgund's son. Yet this night, though the ale flowed like snow-melt, I did no more than swallow a little for courtesy when pledges were raised, and it may well have been that among all that great company I was soberest. True it was that I was clearer of head than most we passed on the way to the door.

Not long before, Gled Golden-Hair had left the hall in the company of her mother and many of the other women. As is done even still, they went to make the bride ready to receive her husband. The *heall* was filled now with the rough talk of men boasting of war-deeds. The thick air didn't muffle the King's laughter as he heard men—Cynewulf's and Erich's and his own—flinging drunken challenges that often didn't seem too friendly. And I thought, as I guided Aescwine along the length of the hall, that Penda's laughter didn't seem too sober.

I looked around for friends, saw Grimmbeald trap a serving-woman in his great arms, heard him say that he'd like something sweeter than her wine. Half the *heall* likely heard his bellow of laughter after she'd granted him what he wanted. Farther along the hall, Eadric stood near a rack of spears, talking with a Dwarf I didn't know. I watched the two as I shepherded Aescwine before me. Now and again they looked away from their conversation, and when I looked where they did, I saw a tight knot of men in a corner, bent close and talking. Among them I saw *thegn* Hnaef, and as I passed he looked up. The orange light of a cressetted torch fell across his face. The look he gave me was not friendly.

Now I looked sharper around the *heall,* and I saw that many had removed to the corners to talk, and most of these were *baresarks.* In the darkest corner, where braziers stood cold and torches guttered untended by servants who didn't like to interrupt berserkers' business, Blodrafen stood among his fellows. Close beside him Aelfgar hung upon the Blood Raven's words as though they were sweet mead and good meat. He looked as though he'd taken no other nourishment these weeks past. He was thinner than I'd ever known him to be, gaunt and white-faced like a man with a wasting sickness in him. I didn't like the feeling I had then, the feeling that darkness seemed to lie about Aelfgar now like a black cloak.

Aescwine saw it too, stopped in his tracks and leaned hard on my shoulder. "Too bad about that," he said. He shook his head. "Yon Aelfgar—Ay, *dvergr,* you should have kept him closer—should have kept him—" He shook his head again, harder, as though to shake loose the thought. Like it is he shook it clean away, for he lurched forward and would have fallen if I'd not caught him.

But he didn't need to finish the thought. I knew what he'd have said. And it came to me then that of all the things I'd hidden from in the ale-houses this winter, I'd hidden from this the best: I'd been no friend to Aelfgar, had let him go his way among *baresarks* who were no friends to anyone.

I laid both hands on Aescwine's shoulders and pushed him on. Cold it would be outside, but I didn't think it could be colder than the sudden feeling in me that something dark and dangerous was brewing in the hall's thick smoky air. I had not seen Dyfed for some time, and I thought I'd like to talk to him, hoped I'd find him among the crowd of Dwarfs and Men gathered near the tall doors.

Those doors were opened wide now, for the air in the hall had grown close with the mingled odors of food and drink and sweat. Some there were who truly wanted to breathe the air and these were cloaked and mantled against the cold. I didn't see Dyfed, but among them I found Cynnere and Swithgar, and these two laughed to see Aescwine staggering ahead of me.

"Ay, Garroc," Cynnere said, "I'll take him. He looks like he could . . . use some air." He drained a horn and gave it empty to Swithgar, wiped the back of his hand across his ale-foamed beard. "And I could, too, just now."

I didn't argue, nor did Aescwine mind being handed from one friend to another. When the two had gone, I asked Swithgar if he'd seen Dyfed. For answer he pointed into the night.

Snow had begun to fall, whirled high by wind, dancing wildly before it went to cover the ground, thin dust overlaying the hard crusty fall of the night before. High on the wooden wall, on the walk, Dyfed stood alone, looking out to the east, looking to Rafenscylf. Below, pacing anxiously in the snow, his red dog waited.

Swithgar tapped the empty ale-horn against the door, a restless rhythm. "He's been there a long time, Garroc. Watching, though it's not his duty tonight. Maybe he's had too much to drink, ay? Most everyone has." He grunted thoughtfully. "Maybe someone should go fetch him down from there. It's no place for an ale-addled man to be."

I didn't think Dyfed was drunk, but as the walk looked like a good place to have quiet words, I told Swithgar I'd see to him.

"As you say." He took his mantle from his shoulders and gave it to me. "Don't go cold though, *dvergr.*"

Werrehund greeted me with a faint wave of his red tail, sniffed at my hand and sounded a worried whimper. I patted him absently, looked up at the tall lean figure of my friend pacing along the watch-walk.

Snow swirled round him; behind him the sky was leaden and low. When he heard me climbing the ladder to the watch-walk, he reached down, took my arm as I topped the ladder, steadied me when I came onto the walk and would have lost my footing on the ice-slicked boards.

"Cold as Hel's deepest hall up here," Dyfed said.

"Ay, it's that cold." I put my back to the wall, looked at the *heall,* blazing with light. "It's a strange place to be when you could be with all the warm food and good ale in the hall."

He cocked his head, listened to the sounds of the feasting, muffled by distance and the falling snow. "It got too close in there. And . . ." He let the thought trail away, came to stand beside me.

Quiet, we watched the snow. It would not be a heavy fall. Though they covered the whole sky, the clouds were thin; behind them the Wolf's moon shone, a hazy smear of light. Dyfed pointed to the one building in the village that was dark and still. No light shone from the window of Iwan's house; hearth-smoke only wandered thinly from the stone chimney.

"Who watches?" I asked.

"Some men of Penda's. I don't know them, but like it is they're trusty."

"Ghost Foot," I said. "I don't think things are going well in the *heall.*"

"Ay, *baresarks* tight in their corners, Hnaef and his friends tight in theirs. I've seen it." He turned, looked again to the tall dark shadow that was Rafenscylf. "I've seen something else, too. Look there," he whispered, pointing.

I squinted into the night, thinking that he could not possibly have seen anything on high Raven Shelf. Yet, as I thought it, something darker than dark moved up there. From this distance it looked small, but I knew that for us to have seen it at all it must be very big.

Maybe big as the bear.

"How long has it been there?"

"As long as I've been up here. Probably longer. It comes down the slope sometimes, but always goes back to the top again. Ah, there. See?"

The dark thing dropped low, as a bear might drop to all fours; as a shadow might, it drifted down the hill. When it came to the place where I'd stood on the path that morning, it stopped, rose tall again.

"It's the bear, Garroc." Dyfed's voice was low and close in the darkness; it thrilled, put me in mind of Werrehund quivering with eagerness when he'd caught game-scent.

Ay, it was the bear.

Wind moaned coldly, plucked at my hair and beard with icy fingers. Sharp that wind, and fast. The snow had stopped while we were talking, and now I looked up, saw the clouds in grey tatters fleeing across the face of the Wolf's moon. I glanced over my shoulder at the hall, at Iwan's dark house. As I had in the summer on Cefn Arth, I shuddered with a deep feeling that bad luck stalked.

When I turned back to Rafenscylf, I saw that the bear had made some progress down the hill. It was not far from the eastern bank of the Rill now, and when it stopped, stood tall again, I saw it swaying slowly, as though searching for a scent on the icy air. I was surprised to see how far it had come, and how fast.

"It's got a long stride," Dyfed said, as though he knew my thought. "Aescwine says that they can cover a bit of ground when they want to. Looks like it wants to."

Close by the waterside, the bear raised one big paw high, brought it swiftly down. And I thought: That's a carefully considered gesture for a beast to make.

Faintly, I heard ice splinter. Because I was listening for it, I heard water rush. The ice would not hold the bear's great weight. Heavy with winter fat, disdaining the cold, the bear entered the river, swam strongly for the western bank.

"Garroc," Dyfed said softly, almost absently. "Can you lay your hands on your axe?"

"It's in the hall."

"Maybe you'd better go get it, ay?"

Warm, warm the blood in me, rising fast as it does before a battle. Still, eager though I was, I went carefully along the icy watchwalk, carefully down the ladder. I had no intention of hearing the tale of the bear-killing as I lay in some corner of the hall with a broken leg. I had every intention of being part of the tale.

Below, in the lee of the wall, Werrehund began to bark deadly challenge. Faintly from the hall came the barking of other hounds. Men shouted loudly.

Ay, surly with drink and wroth with the dogs, I thought as I gained the ground.

And then I didn't think more about it, for from without the walls came a great thundering roar and the gate shivered under a terrible blow.

V

THE bear was no bear, Sif.

Ay, it moaned like a bear outside the wall, hit the gate hard, made the wood shiver, as a beast who mindlessly fights a thing that bars its way. It smelled like a bear. The wind carried its thick musky scent. But the thing which raged outside the walls, howled and screamed above the wind, was no more a bear than my Lydi is a dove.

I knew it as I shoved my way through the crowd of Dwarfs and Men spilling out the doors of the hall, called out into the cold by the beast's thunderous bellowing. All along my skin I felt magic moving. It was like the feeling I had when my Lydi changed from dove to woman. And yet it was unlike, for though I was not comfortable with that charmed changing, I was never hurt by it. Now the sense of magic abroad raked me like claws.

I laid hands on my axe and saw fire's light glare on the dark walls of the small chamber where men left their weapons before they entered the *heall.* Flames leaped high outside, behind me where no such tall fire had been a moment ago. Someone screamed and I turned, thinking that the bear was upon us. As I did, I saw flames eating through the stockade wall as though the wood were rich fat. Witch-fire cloaked that wall, great long arms of it reaching out. As though the arms of flame had hands and fingers to grasp, they curled around a man—Ay, Grimmbeald!—who'd gone to see what beat at the wall.

The stench of burning hair and skin and bones filled the hall, carried there by the wind. Werrehund roared above the distant screams of women, the closer babble of men's voices, the fury of the other hounds. So the red dog sounded when he was fighting hard beside Dyfed. I struggled against the crowd of Dwarfs and Men who, drunk from the feasting, vied for sword and axe. I didn't get to the door before a hard hand grabbed my shoulder.

"Dvergr." The King's fingers bit hard into my shoulder, hard as though he'd splinter my bones. He was not very drunk, but he was not wholly sober. In the light of witch-fire his face showed pale with rage. *"Dvergr,* what's out there?"

"A witch, King, that thinks it's a bear." I strained to pull away, to run out into the fiery night. But Penda held tight, showed me the gleaming edge of his sword to convince me that I must stay a moment.

"Dvergr, are you sober or drunken?"

"Do you doubt me, King? Go out and look!"

He laughed then, a hard cold sound, and loosed me. "I don't doubt you. Answer me."

"Sober, King."

"Good," he said. "You'll fight at my back then."

I stared at him, not yet understanding. He explained it to me as though I were slow-witted.

"We're going to kill this witch that thinks it's a bear, *dvergr*—" He looked hard at me. "I know you, don't I?"

"Garroc," I said. "I am Garroc."

"Ah, the trusty mapper, the scout. Well, keep close to me, Garroc. They say a man's back is bare without a friend behind him. It's wolf-cold out there, too cold to fight naked, yes?"

Wolf-cold, ay it was that, and maybe I knew it better than the King did. From outside came a cry of pain, one I knew for Dyfed's, and in me, no longer stuporous from ale, the *sceadu-wulf* woke. It woke wild, with more strength than it had ever had before against the bonds I'd forged over so many years. As I followed the King out into the night, I was not sure whether those bonds would hold.

Skalds say that Wolf-Fenris will one day break his Dwarf-wrought chains and bring about the end of the world, will make a Sword Age. Loki's son will make an Axe Age when friend fights friend, brother kills brother. They say it will be a Wolf Age when Fenris runs free, and the earth will break apart in flames.

True it is, Sif: I thought that ending had come upon us when I left the hall with Penda King.

It seemed to me that all of Rilling was in flames. Grain-houses burned, great sheets of fire stretched high to the sky. The thick thatched roof of the ale-house where I'd spent most of winter was afire, would soon collapse. In the stables horses shrieked, wild with terror.

The first thing I heard clearly above the tumult of the hounds and the bear's bellow and men's drunken war-cries, was Swithgar's strong voice, shouting for true-hearted men to defend the *cyning.* The first thing I saw clearly was Erich, alone before a pack of ravening *baresark* wolves, sword high and gleaming in the red, red light of flames.

Close and quiet the berserkers had been in the *heall,* planning something. They couldn't have planned for this, though. Yet they were not slow in seizing the advantage. When all others had gone to see what roared at the wall, the berserkers had run on their own business. And now the embattled War Hawk fought hard, swung his sword like a scythe. I saw his face, just for a moment in the fiery light, and his courage shone bright.

I'd have left the King then, run to fight beside Erich, but Penda held hard to me. In the light of the witch-fire his face, twisted with battle-hunger, didn't put me in mind of fair *god-cynn.* I thought more of *helle-cynn.*

"I'm sworn to him, King!"

"Ay?" He turned me hard, pointed toward the burning stockade, to the great boiling of men and hounds where once the gate had been. Tall above them all rose the bear, a dark mountain of a beast. In the light of fire I saw blood on its claws, blood running from its long, terrible fangs. High above the din I heard a man scream, saw the bear's claws fouled with flesh.

"Then help me kill the bear, *dvergr*, because if Erich survives the wolves, he'll still have the witch to face."

The bear roared again and it seemed that the men surrounding him blew away, scattered as leaves before a gale. All but Dyfed, who stood alone before the witch-beast, raised a shining sword. Ah, but not wholly alone. The red dog, fangs dripping blood, fought beside him.

Behind me, Erich shouted, a cry of great-hearted defiance. A woman screamed in terror; Gled Golden-Hair, hunted from her bride-bed by wolves.

And I was caught between the need to get to the *cyning* and the need to run and fight beside my good friend. Penda took the decision from my hands, ran to join Dyfed's battle. I could not let him go friendless and naked to the fight, and so I went with him, heart-torn and grieving for the *cyning*, blown by cold winds to fight beside Dyfed.

Ragged and wounded, Dyfed raised his sword with trembling arms and the desperate look of a man who will soon use the last of his strength. The bear fell back a step, raised its head high and roared in pain and fury as Werrehund harried it from behind, snarling and tearing at its hind legs. Though Dyfed's blade had hurt the bear more than once, it was not near death. The witch-beast shook itself, flung Werrehund from it and swiped hard at Dyfed, tumbled him as a man might tumble a child. Sparks, like those flung up from burning wood, leaped from the beast's claws. This I saw as Penda and I broke through the crowd of Dwarfs and Men. And I saw another thing.

The bear didn't stand friendless. Iwan Vorgund's son fought beside it. I didn't wonder about this, and didn't learn the right of it until later. Then, as I shoved past Dwarfs and Men fallen back to watch the battle, I had no mind for thinking. None for planning, either. But I had good eyes, sharpened by fear and fury, and filled with the red glare leaping along Iwan Slaughter-whelp's sword as he dashed past the bear, leaped for Dyfed to finish the kill.

High his sword, shining above Dyfed, raised as an axe for hewing. Wild the light in his eyes, as though he felt already the blow of his strike, saw even now Dyfed's head rolling in the churned mud and snow.

The iron of his sword met the iron haft of my axe. The blow rang in the night, pealed loud before the full-throated roar of many voices smothered it. Iwan's face, wiped clean of triumph, shone naked in the moment before stunned surprise caught him. Dyfed rolled out from beneath our weapons, scrambled for his fallen sword as Iwan and I strove each to turn the other's iron. I shoved hard, the shadow-wolf in me raged, and Iwan's sword slipped, caught in the horn of my axe. I pressed again, sent him sprawling to the ground.

The terror in the eyes of Vorgund's son was mead and meat to the shadow-wolf. I raised my axe—light and swift as wind it seemed to me then—for the killing blow, brought it down with all my strength. Dyfed shouted warning; that warning was echoed by others. It came too late. The bear caught me hard with a broad and clawed paw, sent me crashing to the ground, weaponless, helpless.

Ay, big as a mountain, that bear! It loomed tall over me, blotted out the sky, and I could see blood on it, the blood of enemies, its own blood. It didn't look for me to leap up again, to charge it with no other weapon than my naked hands.

Penda shouted reckless challenge, bade the witch come fight a King who had no better use for Welshmen than for testing the sharpness of his sword.

Ah, but the bear had no interest in Penda yet. It hit me again, threw me to the ground. It was not so easy to rise again, and in the time it took, I saw that those who had been gathered to watch the fight were gone. From the direction of the *heall* I heard shouting as good men went to Erich's aid.

Now the beast turned to the King, deliberately, as a man will turn. Its small eyes glittered red with the reflection of witch-fire. Its lips, dark and loose, writhed, showed shining fangs long as a man's thumb. It raised its head, stretched its terrible arms wide. Flames danced on the tips of its claws like red daggers. A wave of terror swept hard through me.

I looked around for Dyfed and didn't see him. Late for it, I looked for Iwan Vorgund's son. I didn't see him either. But I saw my axe, and I scrambled for it.

Penda shouted loud. The witch-bear roared, reached for the King with fiery claws, snapped hard with bloody fangs. The King thrust his sword deep into the bear's belly and the beast tore it loose, flung the sword away as though it had never felt the iron. Breathing hard, the King fell back, no weapon now but the dagger in his hand, looking for a way to fight. He saw me, and the look that passed between us was all either of us needed. We knew what to do.

Hard I swung at that bear's leg, high it screamed when my axe's blade bit through muscle and bone. Hamstrung, it staggered. In that moment, Penda dashed in with his dagger's blade leveled, and when the bear reached out, clutched the King in a terrible embrace, its own strength drove the dagger home to its heart.

With that dire wound the witch lost some hold on its magic, lost some hold on its bear-shape. It howled and the howl was more than a beast's noise. It was filled with the shrill curses of an enraged witch. And those curses were carried on words so dark and loathsome that none who heard needed to know the Welsh speech to know he must tremble in terror.

But Penda King didn't tremble. Wotan's Blade didn't cry out for fear. The All-Father, the Raven-god, was his kin.

He snatched up his sword. Bright the war-light glaring from Penda's iron as he thrust and thrust again at the witch-bear. The bear toppled like a felled tree, and the King kept at it, hacking. Terrible the sound of the witch's death, a beast's hideous howling and a man's despairing shriek. And it was not a bear we saw lying there at the last. We saw a man, thin and old, his hands frozen in the semblance of claws grasping, his face ravaged by pain and terror and rage.

He wore fine clothes, that witch, and good strong boots, for when he was not a bear, he was a man and the cold could bite him. Over all he wore a cloak of rich thick wool dyed green, trimmed with the silver fur of a wildcat and held tight by a beautiful brooch. Dragons sported across that brooch, blue-enamel bodies twined so that the gold on which they lay showed as mail in the spaces between.

Red Ecgwulf called that brooch Wyrms Mail.

In the silence fallen, I heard fire snapping and the din of another battle, heard Erich's voice carried loud above the fighting, bright with triumph, ringing with it. And I heard Iwan Vorgund's son, breathing hard near me, panting oaths and curses. I turned, shaking with hurt, and when he saw me turn to him, the Witch-Gatherer's son laughed. His left arm hung crookedly, broken and useless. He didn't seem to feel the pain.

"Ay, the witch came for me, Garroc. Came to bring me back home. He wanted some vengeance, too, he did. He had a nephew, a stripling boy who died in a cattle raid . . ." His eyes were strangely bright and glittering. "Maybe you know the one. Maybe you killed him, brave border-guard, ay?"

Dry-mouthed, I remembered the last time I'd seen the bear. Then it had been summer and the beast had been standing in the shadow of a barrow. Rhodri ap Iau's barrow.

"Or maybe that one did." Iwan looked over his shoulder—and, cold, I looked where he did. Beyond us, in the shadows, Dyfed lay in the churned mud and snow. Blood fouled the ground beneath him, matted his hair, streamed down the side of his face. Whiter than the snow, his face. White as a dead man's.

As I looked at Dyfed, all the blood froze in me, useless to warm, and the shadow-wolf, held fast till now, roared, slavering and hungry, hungry.

The world became strangely quiet around me, colder than it had been only a moment ago, though then it had been winter-cold indeed. I didn't see the dead witch, no longer saw Dyfed lying bleeding in the snow. I saw nothing but the Witch-Gatherer's son.

With one mighty swing of my axe I cut Iwan Vorgund's son in two where he stood.

Iwan didn't cry out, made no sound, and so it was a time before the King looked around and saw what I'd done. He looked at me for a long moment, then at Dyfed, at Werrehund come to watch beside his master.

"Your friend, Garroc?"

I said nothing. My words were frozen within me.

"Good enough reason," he said softly. He looked around him, saw the burning buildings, listened to the din of battle, lessening now that true men had gone to help the *cyning.*

As from a great distance, I heard him say that it looked like Erich was winning his battle with the wolves.

"But I think he could use some help still, ay, Garroc?"

Numb and cold, I nodded wordlessly. I left Dyfed in the snow, Werrehund standing over him, and went to fight again beside the King. I didn't fight sane, fought in a way I'd never fought before. I fought as a *baresark,* fought with a heart numbed by grief, for I had no friend's warm hand to steady me.

VI

IT is hard to kill a *baresark*, Sif. I've seen some fight while the very heart-blood is pouring from them, and always on the face of a dead berserker is the same expression: deep and terrible surprise. I saw the surprise often that night. If any had managed to kill me, he'd have seen it on me.

The *baresarks* were not friendless, didn't go alone to kill their wolf-king's son. Among them were *thegn* Hnaef's men. Wulf and Waerstan's father could not forgive Erich for letting the Witch-Gatherer's son live while his own dear sons slept beneath barrow-stones. Cold his grief, hard his anger.

But the *cyning* had friends, too—trusty Dwarfs and Men of his war band who didn't abandon him, and hall-servants and men of the village who took up scythe and hammer and hoe. He had his father-in-law's men. Strange to see Cynewulf's warriors fighting beside Erich, strange to see Dwarfs and Men, who in wars past had tried hard to kill Halfdan's son, defend him from his own folk. But Cynewulf had made a good alliance, a powerful friend in this young War Hawk who stood high in the King's favor. Rich lands had come to his daughter through this marriage. He didn't want to lose these. And Erich had Wotan's Blade. The King fought back to back with Halfdan's son, kept all comers at bay, trusted that Erich would do the same.

I don't remember more than one thing clearly about the fighting, my Sif. That night passed in an icy, witless rage of killing. My memories of it are no clearer than dim shapes seen in a whirling winter storm. Now and here, as I sit warm by your fire, only this comes back to me:

I rose up from a killing, wiped the blade of my axe clean with my hands, and saw a woman cornered. She looked like Gled, and not like. In these past days I'd never seen little Gled as anything but a girl, petted and celebrated and pampered. That night, with the din of battle loud outside Erich's house, I saw that this was no child before me now, but a woman ringed round by war, one who had to face a kind of fear that the men about her didn't. I saw then that she didn't know me, didn't know if I'd come to help or to drag her like booty out of her husband's house.

Bedclothes, whitest linen, rich woolen blankets, lay around her

feet, strewn across the wooden floor. The bride-chamber had the
look of a plundered nest, Gled the look of a fledgling facing a pred-
ator's fangs. Hair like finest gold spilled all round her shoulders,
covered her thin nightdress, but not fully. The thin white linen
of her bride-night shift was torn. I saw the prints of bloody hands
on it.

I looked down at the man I'd killed, saw dumb surprise in his
open eyes, dimming now with death. In one hand he clutched a
red-smeared piece of Gled's nightdress. He was a *baresark* and
mann-cynn. Aelle was his name, and I'd cloven him nearly in two.

In the corner Gled drew a small careful breath, as if struggling
to keep from being sick.

The sounds of the fighting grew distant as Erich harried his enemies through the village. Gled, caught alone and without her husband near to help, held trembling hands out to me as though
begging me to be other than an enemy. Her terror melted some
of the ice in me and I tried to speak, tried to give her assurance
that I'd not come to do harm. But it was hard, hard to find words
strong enough to break past the storm-cold.

"Child," I said, halting and hoarse. "Where is my *cyning?*"

"Erich—"

She shook her head, then went suddenly tight and taut. Green
eyes widening again, she pointed behind me. I thought she meant
to tell me that Erich was without in the fighting.

But she didn't mean to tell me that. I knew it when I heard the
soft hiss of breathing behind me.

Blodrafen stood in the doorway and behind him loomed a thin
tall wraith. Aelfgar. Bloody-handed Aelfgar was, and he wiped
those red hands down the front of a torn shirt. The long weal of
a burn-mark showed purplish and glistening on the side of his face.
His beard, once gold-bright, was dirty and matted, burned half
away.

Bright in the light of all the fires burning without, tears traced
through the blood and dirt on his face. Absently, as though he
didn't know he was doing it, or had been doing it for so long it
didn't need thinking about, he dragged a sleeve across his face to
wipe away the tears, winced when he roughed the burn.

"Aelfgar," I said, my voice yet hoarse and difficult to use. "Boy,
boy . . ."

He said nothing, looked at me as though I were a stranger.

The *baresark* glanced at him, then turned back to me. His grey
old eyes glittered; a strange, triumphant smile thinned his lips.
Outside someone shouted—a high, frenzied war cry. The din of

battle, once distant, came closer, the sound beating at the walls of Erich's house like waves beating at a fragile shore.

"Ay, *dvergr*," he said, low. "The *sceadu-wulf* catches us all, sooner or later." He laughed, a terrible sound, wolfish and high. "There's winter in you now, and it hurts, like bitter cold hurts. You know it now, don't you?"

Ay, the *baresark* madness hurts, like bitter cold hurts, and it locks the heart tight in fetters of ice and rime. The sound I made for answer had no words, and behind me Gled moaned in terror. Well she might, poor child; she stood in a room full of madmen.

I turned to her, meant to urge her away from there, to fly to some safe place if she could find one. It was an ill-considered move.

The *baresark* hit me from behind, drove me to the floor. Hard his knees in my back, hard his hands, big and not fully fingered, as they fastened on my throat from behind. Blodrafen dug, his breath hissing like steam in my ear.

Gled screamed, but her cry didn't drown out the Blood Raven's high, cracked-voiced laughter.

I writhed under him, twisted and kicked out, managed to throw his balance off. I didn't wholly free myself from him, only flipped onto my back, but my hands were free now and I fastened them round his neck, pressed hard with both thumbs against his windpipe.

Sharp came Gled's cry behind me, and the Blood Raven laughed again, like winter gales howling. He drove his knee hard into my belly. In that moment, I saw Aelfgar, shadow-dark in the doorway, his face twisted by grief and fear, in his eyes stark and terrible confusion. Through the doorway beyond him, hanging bright over his shoulder, I saw stars shining. They might have been suns, so great their silver glare.

Hard to hear, then. Aelfgar's sudden cry sounded muffled and distant; I could not make out his words.

Then, sharp and clear, I heard the *baresark* scream high, saw his face twist with rage and shock. Ay, thin, Aelfgar was, and grief-wasted. But he had a strong arm still, and he drove his sword deep into the Blood Raven's back, so deep that the blade came full out through the *baresark's* chest and raked along my ribs.

Blodrafen shuddered hard as Aelfgar withdrew the blade. His wintry eyes, old and old, went wide with surprise and the kind of profound relief I'd never have understood before that night. When he moaned, he didn't moan against pain; more it was the sound a man makes when he comes in from winter-storm and feels the first ache of warmth from a hot high fire.

His death was the last thing I saw.

The warmth and strength of Aelfgar's arms as he lifted me, held me close, was the last thing I felt.

VII

I came to myself in a world gone silent. No barrow could be quieter. The first thing I saw clearly was Dyfed, lying not far away from me. The blood I'd seen on him was gone; someone had cleaned him well, combed his white, white hair, made him ready for the pyre. Last, they'd covered him with blankets that his mourners might not see his wounds.

Dead, I thought, they've laid me beside dead Ghost Foot, and so I must be dead.

Ay, I must be, for within me all things were still, silent as the world after a raging winter storm. The shadow-wolf in me didn't rouse. I listened for ghosts and heard none, not even Dyfed's.

Then, soft in the darkness, came a rustling, a whisper of sound as someone walked quietly. I held very still and waited for the touch of a Valkyrie's beckoning hand.

Sunlight, bright gold, thick amber, gave leaping life to tapestries, spilled across wooden walls, lay warm on my face.

I am in the *heall,* I thought, and so it hasn't burned; it's whole still.

I looked for Dyfed and I didn't see him lying covered, but saw him sitting with his back to the wall, his face lifted to the light that poured from the windows high above. A long dark bruise purpled the side of his face, a bruise shaped like a bear's paw, and along the sides of that bruise I saw burn blisters from the witch-beast's fiery claws. Bandages bound him tightly about the ribs, and they were white where they were not brown with old blood.

I looked for the joy I should have felt to see him living when I'd once been certain that he was dead, looked to feel the flooding warmth of relief. I felt none of that, felt nothing at all. As the ghosts and the shadow-wolf, all things of feeling within me—dark or bright—were still.

Maybe I stirred then, or made some sound, for Dyfed looked away from the sun; a smile tugged at the corners of his mouth. "Ah, Garroc," he whispered. "I *knew* you'd come back."

Hurt, he was yet a healer, and he cautioned me to lie still, told me that I was sword-cut and should not move lest I start the wounds bleeding again.

Ay, sword-cut, bitten by iron in shoulder and leg; iron had scraped my ribs. I wasn't about to move, was content to lie warm in the sunlight.

From out of the brightness a hand reached for me, brushed my hair away from my face. Soft, that hand, as a woman's is soft. There hung about it a scent I knew, a twining of comfrey and mountain mint, of meadowsweet and chamomile, the fragrance of healer-craft.

"Ah, my Lydi," I said, tight-throated and hoarse. I tried to feel something—surprise, wonder, joy. I felt nothing. It was as though the place where my heart used to be was empty.

The hand stroked gently. "No," a woman whispered.

No, of course not.

Dyfed moved then, leaned forward slowly, as a man who must be careful of hurts. He said something to the woman beside me. If she answered him, I didn't hear it, only barely felt Dyfed lift my hand and hold it. I left light again for sleep.

Erich, at his Gled's behest, had made a portion of his *heall*, the best place, closest to hearth and fire, into a place for those wounded in the fighting, for we who had defended him against the Hunter's pack, against treacherous Hnaef. He gave our care to Gled, gave her readily all that she asked of his stores, and she went among us day and night with a small army of women she had gathered from among the servants, and the wives and daughters of Erich's true and loyal *thegns*.

Many people were hurt in the fighting; many were killed during that Wolf Age. Because Dyfed didn't tend the injured, and I didn't count the dead, some time went by before I knew for certain who of our friends had survived that night. Among the lucky were Cynnere and old Aescwine, and Dyfed told me their tale with the air of one who hoped to win a smile or even a laugh.

And ay, most anyone would have laughed to hear the tale of those two, caught between Hnaef's unloyal men and the midden trenches when first the fighting broke out, and caught, choosing the trenches as the smaller of two evil fates until they could find their way back to the *heall* and weapons again. It seemed that no one would follow a man through the foul-smelling trenches to kill him, and so Aescwine and Cynnere got away, lived to find weapons, and to help Erich.

"Thing is though, they were never able to sneak up on anyone—

you could smell them coming before they were close enough to strike a good blow. They weren't too happy about it all, and Aescwine says he'd have killed a lot more if he could've had time to clean off a bit.''

I smiled, because he expected me to, and said that I supposed this was so. Then I went back to my silence.

Easier for me, that silence, for when I lay still and quiet, none came near me. This was important to me. I didn't want to let anyone so close that I'd see in his eyes the knowledge that I'd fought mad on the night of the *cyning's* marriage, that I'd fought as a *baresark*. I was bitterly ashamed of that.

I had a lot of time for thinking during those days, and one of the things I thought was this:

I had some hand in the events that brought the great fighting that swept through Rilling on the night the Wolf's moon ran full, bore some responsibility for it. If I'd left Iwan Vorgund's son with Lydi, left him safe in Gardd Seren as she'd begged me to, the witch-bear would not have come looking for him. And ay, soon or late the *baresarks* would have flared to battle, but maybe they'd have been easier to defeat if there had been no witch to fight.

I'd meddled in the affairs of my *cyning,* and I'd brought him back a hostage and a full share of trouble. Grimmbeald had died of the witch-bear's magic, and many others besides. As well, I thought, to lay their deaths at my feet as at the bear's.

On a day not long after the dark night of Erich's wedding, we who kept to the hall, still sick with our wounds, smelled pyre smoke. We didn't hear barrow-building, though, for the earth-hall was erected on Rafenscylf, too far away for even Dwarfs to hear its crafting. That day Dyfed said that he'd heard from his Cyneleah that Erich would kill the few of the *baresarks* and their friends who had survived the fighting.

I told him that I thought this was wise, but I didn't think too much about it until he said that one of the condemned was Aelfgar.

"And it seems hard to me, Garroc. He's no more than a child led astray by bad friends."

I thought he was right, but I didn't know what could be done about it.

"You could go to the *cyning,*" he said. "and speak for Aelfgar's life."

I shook my head. "No. I've meddled in the *cyning's* business one time too many. I won't do it again."

"Not even for Aelfgar?"

The sun was warm that day; snow dripped from the eaves of the hall. I listened to its patter, watched the tapestries shine. At last I said:

"Go do it yourself, Ghost Foot, if you think it will help."

"I'm not the one whose life he saved at the end, Garroc. Maybe you owe him that, ay?" He looked at me long, and the sorrow in him made him seem much older than he was, bent and bowed down with great care. "Maybe," he said, soft, "maybe you owe yourself that, too."

"I don't think I owe myself anything," I said coldly.

He spoke slowly, with a care and caution new to him who had always spoken freely with me before.

"Garroc, I heard about how you fought that night. *Freond min,*" he said gently, "will you never forgive yourself?"

I held still, listened to the snow melting, listened to the heavy, tired beat of my heart. Shame ached in me; I didn't speak as gently as he had, said bitterly:

"So there it is, Ghost Foot: You've a madman—a *baresark,* ay? —for a friend now."

He shook his head. "No. You're no berserker, Garroc. Hurt, maybe frightened, yes? But you're not mad. You went to that cold place." He gripped my hand in his own two—so hard, he was like to break the bones. "But you came back. *Baresarks* don't come back."

I freed my hand, turned away from him and the matter of Aelfgar.

The next day we heard joiners working, nailing board to board in gallows-building. Dyfed said nothing to me, only sat and listened to the building. It seemed to me that he winced a little each time hammer struck nail, as though the sound gave him pain.

After a time, he looked around, saw me watching, and said one word.

"Please."

In all the time I'd known him, good times and bad, I don't think Dyfed ever said 'please' in such a way as he did then.

Weary, weak, and afraid to leave this quiet place, afraid to go out among men building gallows, I got to my feet, made my way carefully along the hall to the great tall doors.

They'd a thirst for gallows-work in Rilling that cold, bright winter day. I saw it on the faces of all those I passed, Dwarfs and Men who had lost friends in the fighting. The witch-bear's fire had caused a good deal of damage at the southern end of the village;

many folk lost homes in the burning. These were glad to see the
gallows rising. I heard a hunger for vengeance in the darkness
lurking in Cynewulf's voice as he spoke to some of his men where
they stood watching the work. He had lost good men defending
his son-in-law.

As I passed by the scaffold, broad enough to hold many men,
I saw Penda King watching the building. He sat a tall horse, leaned
forward eagerly, listened to each hammer blow as though it were
sweet music. Maybe it was. He'd spent the day before smelling
pyre smoke and watching a barrow grow tall. When he saw me,
he greeted me fair, as he'd have greeted a good battle-friend.

"Ay, Garroc! *Dvergr*, it's good to see you again." He nodded
toward the hall. "They weren't giving out good news about your
health. I didn't think to see you up and about. Where are you
bound?"

"I'm looking for Erich, King."

"You'll find him in his house, just gone there a while ago. Ah,
dvergr, you're whiter than snow. Can't your errand wait?"

I told him it couldn't, thanked him for his care and went on
my way without waiting for dismissal.

I found Erich in the house near the *heall* where he'd brought
his wife the night of his wedding-feast. No sign did I see now of
the fighting which had gone on there; the bloodstains were sanded
from the floor, all was in order.

The *cyning* sat on a bench at the long board set in the middle
of the house. Back to the table, his long legs were stretched out
before him; he had a sword across his knee, a whetstone in his
hand. He looked like a wing-folded, brooding eagle—dark-eyed,
unlucky to cross. He didn't greet me, only flicked one flashing
glance my way and went back to honing his sword.

The song of stone on iron sounded like thin screaming.

None attended Erich but Gled, and she sat a little distance
away, near the hearth. I could not see that she was doing anything
more than staring into the flames. She looked around when I entered the house and came to greet me.

"*Dvergr*," she said softly, "I don't think you are wise to be going
about yet."

"Ay, Lady," I said. "Likely not. But I heard the hammers from
the hall."

She nodded wordlessly, as though she understood what brought
me out. She laid a hand in the crook of my arm, gently as though
she were asking escort and not offering assistance. No sign did I

see that she remembered that once, not long ago, she'd seen me with the berserker-madness on me. For that I was grateful.

"Will you come to the fire and be warm, Garroc?"

I thanked her, but said that I was come to speak with Erich. At the sound of his name, the *cyning* looked up, his blue eyes stormy. He said nothing, and Gled left us, but she didn't go far.

Erich watched me for a long moment, then put stone and iron aside. "You look two days dead, Garroc. What brings you out?"

Hard to find words; it was as though they were all locked up inside me. After a time I said, "*Cyning,* I've come to ask a grace."

"You've come to ask for Aelfgar's life."

I nodded.

"I won't give it to you, Garroc."

"*Cyning,* you know that Aelfgar isn't like other men. You know—"

He shook his head. "I know this: He's done man's work. When it was good work, all praised him. Should he go free now because suddenly I must remember that he's child-minded?" He clenched a fist, looked down at it as though studying something carefully. When he spoke again, his voice was very soft, but it was not gentle. "Ah, no, Garroc. I've learned my lesson, and a hard one it was to learn. When vengeance is due, it must be paid at once. Aelfgar has earned what his friends have earned."

Near the fire Gled stirred, raised her head and looked at her husband. Her face was pale, her hands shook a little when she rose and went to stand beside Erich. She kept silent for a moment, as though gathering her thoughts, then spoke quietly.

"Husband," she said, "I see that this thing troubles you. Hard it must be to condemn this man."

He said nothing, but his expression softened a little when she laid her small hand on his.

"I remember this Aelfgar," she said. "I remember, too, that Garroc defended me when I most needed him. I owe Garroc a debt of gratitude. Erich, it shames me that I haven't paid that debt. And, too, Garroc owes something to Aelfgar, who saved his life when a *baresark* would have choked it from him. It's right that he has come here to ask your help in paying his debt."

"Ay, hard it must be for you, Erich. But I think there may be a way through it."

"And what is that, little Gled? That I let an unloyal man, an oath-breaker, live?"

She nodded solemnly. "Yes. But you needn't let him live among us. He raised his hand against his *cyning.* You needn't forgive that.

But if, as you both say, this Aelfgar is child-minded, must he die for the crime of being ill-used by bad friends?"

She was silent again, and in the quiet I heard both the snap of fire in the hearth and the boom of the gallows-building without.

Gled lifted her head that she might look her War Hawk husband full in the eyes. "There is outlawry, Erich."

Ay, she was wise, that Gled!

And Erich knew it. He smiled sourly, looked from one to the other of us. "So this is the way of it, Garroc? You and my wife have leagued against me?"

I didn't think he was jesting, and so I kept quiet. Gled had the wisdom to do the same.

"Well then, that's how it will be." He took up Gled's hand, held it close. "I can't have my wife shamed, Garroc. Aelfgar will live, but not here."

I looked for a feeling of relief, of gratitude, to grow in me. Nothing stirred. But I knew the words to speak, knew how to give at least a semblance of the thing I could not feel.

Erich dismissed my thanks with a curt gesture. He was not wholly happy with what he'd granted. "Get him out of here before the day ends, Garroc. I don't want to see him."

I nodded.

"And get yourself back to your bed, *Faeders-freond*," he said with rough kindness. "You look better, but you don't look well."

There was something in what he said, but I didn't mean to go back to resting just yet. I had something to say to Aelfgar.

In those days, Sif, we called a gallows *wulfbeam,* the wolf-tree, and that day I walked past the scaffold with Aelfgar and thought that there could be no better name for that hanging place. The sun was bright and it warmed a little for all that the air was cold. Though I had but little strength, I spent some of it in seeing Aelfgar on his way, walked with him to the edge of the Rill. He was quiet, white-faced and thin. His months among the *baresarks* had done him no good.

As we walked, he said little, but I didn't think he had the look of one lost in thought. More he looked like a man who suddenly finds himself in a foreign place, a land filled with strangers. It came to me that he was not so much frightened as he was confused. He didn't understand how he'd come to this deadly place.

Ah, Aelfgar . . .

Erich had let him take his weapons with him, his bow and a quiver of arrows, a short-sword and a dagger. All else that he owned—and that was not much—he carried in a small leather scrip. Sometimes, as we walked, he juggled the scrip from hand to hand, as though weighing it. When we came to the river, we stood a while in silence. Then I said:

"Aelfgar, do you know that you can never come back?"

He nodded.

"You know that the *cyning* will send word of your outlawry all around the Marches?"

Again he nodded.

"Do you know what that means, Aelfgar?"

"Every man may kill me, whoever sees me, and he won't be held to blame. And—and I can never come home again."

"Ay, that. You have three days to get out of the Marches. Where will you go?"

"I don't know."

It was as I thought. "Do you remember the way to Lydi?"

His face brightened a little then. "Ay, I do. But maybe she wouldn't want me there when she knows why I've come. Maybe she won't want an outlaw near her."

"She's tolerated worse," I said softly. "Aelfgar, go to Lydi, ay?"

Brighter now, he asked, "Do you want me to tell her anything for you?"

"No. Just give her my greeting."

"Ay, well then." He shouldered his scrip, looked north along the river. Then he turned suddenly, sharply, and I saw tears in his eyes, a boy's tears, honest and heart-wrung. "Garroc, I'm sorry. I—I'm sorry for what I did. I'm sorry that I hurt you."

No sympathy, no pain for my friend who was cast out from his home and all that he knew, nothing like that did I feel. Not even anger that a *baresark* had so badly misused his friendship as to bring him to this pass, not even regret that I had not stopped it happening though I'd been warned that Blodrafen loved what he killed and killed what he loved.

When the *sceadu-wulf* left me, he had not taken only the ghosts with him.

I looked up at the sun, just now mounting the noon crest, told Aelfgar that he'd be wise not to waste more time. And so, without a word, with no farewell, Aelfgar started off, a lonely figure dark against the bright blue sky, the white, white snow. He didn't look back all the while I watched him, and I watched him until he was out of sight.

•   •   •

That day Erich had the heads of Iwan Vorgund's son and the old witch hewn from their bodies. He had them packed in ice and straw, wrapped in leather sacks. Then he told one of his swift riders to take those sacks as far into Welshlands as he dared, and to say to everyone he met along the way that Vorgund's son was dead.

Too, he was to say that witches might be terrible, but they were not immortal.

To the sack bearing the witch's head, the *cyning* attached Wyrms Mail. He'd known it for Ecgwulf's—few had not, so proud of his brooch had red Ecgwulf been—and he said that he thought the Sword Wolf would not mind, said that like it was Vorgund would hear the news of these deaths and have the leather sacks brought to him. Then Ecgwulf could laugh with the gods to know that his blue dragons had borne a witch's head home to Vorgund.

THUNORS-MONA
(Thunor's Moon)

DVERGR and *mann-cynn*, we are good ones for knowing the names
of our kin, Sif. We know that we are part of those who went before
us; who comes after will be a shining stave in a long song. Your
father was Hinthan, and his was Cenred, whose father was Saegar.
This Saegar was the first of your kin to lay aside the sword for
the plough. This he did after the Pendragon's son, the Bear King,
died. He judged it a good time to lay up land for his future sons.

Saegar's father was called Hinthan, and this first Hinthan had
a father who was born in Seaxeland and was named Godwulf Sea-
crafty. Godwulf's kin were soldiers. One of them was wed to a
king's sister, and her name was Ealfreda Guthulf's daughter.
These kinsmen of Godwulf's did not ride the longships to the Isle
in the time when great famine overtook the northern lands. Ealfreda's sons became *cynings* in Seaxeland and thought it best to re-
main in the place where they were born, keep their folk through
the hunger.

And so you have mighty kin across the cold grey sea, Sif. Should
you ever come to them, they will remember Godwulf *Saecraftig*,
the longship rider, and they will welcome you.

We *dvergr* have songs as long and longer. But now, in all lands,
in all places, that song will soon be ended.

The histories tell of no *cynings* among my kin, no heroes. Only
honorable folk, heavy-handed in war, word-fast in peace. I know
their names, and some of those names are bright.

Nyi heard the song of ice rending stone as the Frost giants

239

dragged their dead back to Jotunheim. He is the father of my kin. Fraeg Iron Hand, a killer of trolls, was Nyi's twice great-grandson.

Iron Hand's sons Regin and Jari helped in the raising up of a good king. Skurhild was their sister. Golden-haired, most like sun on glittering water was Skurhild. Though she loved that *dvergr* king, she refused to become his wife. Ah, Sif, that is a warm tale for a cold night!

Skurhild had a great-grandson who was called Onar, and this Onar was born in the same year that the White Christ walked out the door of his barrow to become a god.

Onar had a daughter called Gna and she was a witch, skilled in *wundorcraeft*, mighty in magic. Though Onar had no part in the emprise to steal the wondrous and fair golden apples from the goddess Idun's gardens, to snatch these fruits whose smallest virtue is the giving of long life, Gna did. Father and daughter, they heard Wotan's grim curse, knew the curse as a mortal wound to our race. Gna fled the northlands; they say she ran to the west. And so maybe my Lydi is some distant kin of mine, ay?

In after days, when his witch-daughter was gone from him, Onar called himself Nithi. In the old speech that name means Waning Moon.

Others there were after Onar Waning Moon, warriors all, *baresarks* some. I know their names. Grimwulf Aesc's son, Fierce Wolf, longship rider, was the last of my kin to father a child.

My father died in the spring, war-killed. I mourned then, dark winter-grieving while the earth grew and blossomed. Never had I known such cold sorrow, for as the bearing of children is deadly for many women, *dvergr* and *mann-cynn*, so it was for my own mother. I had never known her. And though most of my boyhood had been spent with Stane Saewulf's son, I loved my father, my only kin.

Grimwulf Aesc's son was a soldier. He went to many strange places, and when he came back to his old friend Stane, and to me, he brought a heartful of tales. Then he joyed to sit quiet and listen to the songs I made from them, and he was proud of his skald son, said that in me the histories lived. He hoped that I would find a way to send them onward, that when our race was dead *mann-cynn* would remember us.

Ay, I loved my father. Even in the later years, when the shadow-wolf found him. I grieved hard for his death, for his madness and for my own loss. This last of my kin was dead, and cold and alone, I made his barrow while the stones cried *baresark!*—I did not know if they welcomed my father or greeted me. Perhaps they did both. Grimwulf was not sane when he died. Young skald, or-phaned son, for a time neither was I.

That day, fleeing ghost-songs, fleeing grief, I buried the histo-ries, the undiscovered tales, in that dark earth-hall with Grimwulf Aesc's son. I told Stane that I thought my father's dreams of find-ing a way to carry the histories forward were none but a madman's fancy, told my old teacher that I knew then, more surely than I'd ever known it, that none would live after me to take the histories and find their future in them. But, saying this, I did not speak the truth.

The truth is that I could not look too closely at a soul where no hope lived, for I knew that no bright song, no brave tale, could be made in such a night-empty place. And so, after I gave my fa-ther and my songs into the keeping of barrow-stones, I took up grey cold iron and went looking for death on the battle-grounds, went searching for a way to Valholl and the only immortality Wotan had left me.

As I walked away from Grimwulf's barrow I heard the mourn-ing of every one of my ancient fathers. That was the first time I'd heard the cold thin wailing of the dead. It would not be the last, for I'd not only buried my father, I'd barrowed my own hope. And always, the empty place where hope used to be hurt. Sometimes it hurt more in spring than any other season.

I

WAR plans were made while the corpses of traitors hung heavy on the wolf-tree, while the people of Rilling nursed wounds, tried to think how they would rebuild their burned homes. Those plans were crafted by Erich War Hawk and Cynewulf, by Penda King. Dyfed and I witnessed the most of that making, for Penda liked to have scouts close at hand when he was working with maps, and of all Erich's scouts, Dyfed and I had ranged farthest. The King was careful of us—we were still weak from our wounds—but he kept us close and never used a map until one or the other of us told him it was good or told him how it must be changed. And so, as Wolf's Moon became Ice Moon, Penda and his *cynings* planned the assault on Eadwine's Northumbria, planned to seize rich lands from out the grasp of the king they called Faith-Breaker.

One name rang often through all the war-crafting, that of
Penda's Welsh ally. Few now complained of Penda's strange alliance with Cadwalla, for word had come to us of his large army,
his bold winter raids into Eadwine's lands beyond the River Humber. This winter-fighting was the craft of a man who wanted to
make the summer work easy. He didn't carry off cattle or slaves,
as Welshmen are known to do. He killed the cows and pigs and
sheep in the byres, the fowl in the yards; killed men and women
and little children. Last, when men and beasts were dead, he
burned grain-houses and tore down the cold-houses where winter
meat was stored, made sure that such as were left of Eadwine's
soldiers would go to him hungry in spring, would fight unfed and
disheartened in summer. All this Cadwalla did with very little re-
sistance from Eadwine. It was said that the king across the Humber spent his time with Christ-priests high and low, crying to the
god for mercy or hoping to win favor with great ceremony.

That winter, Cynewulf said that Eadwine would have done better to defend his folk with more than prayers, for Cadwalla prayed
to the same god and it seemed that when the White Christ was
choosing between the two, he found Cadwalla's prayers better.
And he said that once this war against Eadwine was won, Penda
would do well to look to his own back.

Cynewulf had heard it that the feud between Eadwine and Cadwalla had less to do with land-hunger than with broken trust. For,
so Cynewulf said, the two had been close as kin until Eadwine
Faith-Breaker went warring into Cadwalla's lands, forgot that
Cadwalla's father had fostered him when his own kin cast him out.
Because of his foster-brother's treachery, Cadwalla had no love
of the *Seaxe*, and an alliance with Penda would not change matters.

Ah, but when the *god-cynn* King heard that, his storm-eyes glittered; he laughed like thunder rolling, said that Cadwalla would
be well advised to keep on the good side of his young god and not
forget to look over his own shoulder when Wotan's Blade was
near. This was not an alliance of friends.

In all this plan-crafting none forgot about Vorgund Witch-
Gatherer. Penda said it and Cynewulf and Erich agreed: A strong
army must be left behind in the Marches. Vorgund must not be
allowed to gain a foothold here, for Cynewulf was not the only
cyning who would ride north to war. Everyone who owed Penda
loyalty would bring armies into Northumbria. To Erich, the Hun-

ter's War Hawk son, would fall the lot of keeping the Marches safe. If he failed, all gain in the north would be for nothing.

Too, the King said that he thought it best that Erich make certain to ride home with Vorgund's head on his spear. "You've fought the ill-contented once. Make certain, Erich, that you never have to do it again."

Dark-eyed, Erich told the King that he had no cause for concern. He'd learned a hard lesson this winter, he said. He'd learned that vengeance is best not put off.

The *cyning* was not the only one who had learned lessons in that bitter time. I, too, believed that I'd learned a good one, and it was this:

It was best always to keep tall walls around my heart, to add to the strength of those walls when I could.

Always and ever, since the day Grimwulf Aesc's son died a *baresark,* I'd gone in fear of the same fate, had done all that I could to prevent it from ever overtaking me. Ah, but not all that I could . . . Too close I'd gotten to friends, too near their bright fires. Now I thought that I'd been foolish to get used to warmth that could so easily be snatched away.

That winter, during the long terrible night when the Wolf's moon shone full on the fighting, I'd tasted what it was like to be mad, felt the rending pain a *baresark* feels. I never wanted to feel that pain again, and it seemed the best thing would be to never risk joy again for fear that were it taken from me, *baresark* madness would rush in to fill the empty place. As I saw it then, my own fate was a cold one, a long march through winter, with no spring to come. Best it was, I thought, to take no one on that march with me, for surely it would grow harder when they must leave me alone. And so, through the waxing and the waning of the Ice moon and the Snow moon, I worked hard to build high, thick walls around my heart.

I got what I wanted. Soon most of the Dwarfs and Men who'd named me friend in years past, Eadric and Swithgar, Cynnere, Aescwine and all the others, left me to myself.

All but one, and that one was my good Dyfed, quiet Ghost Foot, well-named Cyfaill. He sat patient and steadfast outside the wall, waiting.

As the world warmed to spring I was dream-reft, didn't lie down to the usual night-work of building Grimwulf's barrow, didn't dream any dream, good or ghost-haunted, of my own. And I didn't dream Lydi's dreams. I'd had no dream of hers since that hot summer night when the stars rained from the sky.

But, if the witch didn't dream of me, I could not help but think of her. Memories of Lydi are not easily banished.

And I thought about outlawed Aelfgar, kinless and friendless. I wondered if he'd found his way safely to Seintwar, if he lived in some kind of peace in Lydi's Gardd Seren. Yet, though I thought about him, I didn't talk about him ever, not even to Dyfed who talked about him often. Then came a time, when Penda King was gone back to his own hall, when Cynewulf had taken leave of his daughter and returned to his dark moors, that Dyfed and I had a chance to learn what fate Aelfgar had met in outlawry.

On a day when the air was filled with the sweet scents of the mother-earth quickening after winter-sleep, when the Rill was running fat and fast with snow-melt, and the forest beyond was noisy with the chatter of squirrels and the barking of foxes and the screaming of silver-coated wildcats, Erich sent Dyfed and me riding west to the borderland. Our War Hawk *cyning* had prowled restlessly through the winter, waited hungry for the time of war. Now, in the spring, as the Seer's moon rode full through the night, he told us he'd no wish to sit waiting longer. To Dyfed and me he gave the charge of searching out the Witch-Gatherer and finding the best way to him.

"This year," the *cyning* said. "This year I'll bring war to him."

And ay, it is true, Sif: Young Erich was as strange of mood as I was that year, but for a wholly different reason.

Gled Golden-Hair didn't go about Rilling with her usual light step. She walked more carefully, as though she carried some fragile treasure. She'd grown quick with child and now Erich Halfdan's son no longer spoke of the Marches as his father's lands. Those days, as the men who would make up his army began to return from the farms, crowd the streets of Rilling, fill his *heall* with hard-edged restlessness, I noticed that at all times Erich spoke of the Marches as his own.

Have you marked it, my Sif? Have you ever seen it in your own good husband? Nothing will anchor a man's heart more firmly to his land, be he *cyning* or crofter, than the warmth of a womb-filled wife in his arms.

And so, early in the morning on the first truly warm day of spring, Dyfed and I took good horses and our best weapons and rode west. I was not happy to be returning to the borderland, not happy to be going back to the place where I'd lost friends and lost my Lydi, but I was the *cyning's* man.

So it is with me. I always stand willingly where Fate put me.

II

I have known many springs since the one after the witch-bear and *baresarks* tore Rilling between them, but never have I known one brighter, more filled with beauty. The sun's warmth was sweeter than I'd ever known it to be, the air so filled with the wonderful scents of growing things that a man could taste them and long after linger over the tangy fragrance of flowers in the meadows, new leaves unfurling on oak and beech and ash, the full rich scent of good dark loam in the forests. Dyfed said that days like these made him feel strong and reckless, and as we followed the shining Rill north, then left it behind to turn west for the stony borderland, I saw that this was an apt saying.

Brave and bright he was. The marks of the witch-bear's paw were only small round scars where the fiery claws had burned him, but no other sign of the winter's wounds showed on him. Like his red dog, loping ahead of us, Dyfed had survived the bear. Like his Werrehund, he was hard to kill. He talked to me often during those spring days. Over the winter he'd become used to my silence, seemed to have decided that if there was distance between us, he wouldn't acknowledge it.

Sometimes he talked of Erich's plans for war, of golden Gled and the child to come. Most often he talked of his plump and pretty Cyneleah waiting for him in Rilling, and one night, when we'd made camp in a small dale not far from the mist-dragon's valley where Halfdan had fought his last battle, Dyfed said that he thought he might not be spending the next winter in the *heall*.

Though he talked often and at length during all the days we'd been gone from Rilling, he'd gotten none but short answers from me, polite nods mostly. But this surprised me, and I asked him where he thought he'd be staying if not in the hall.

Forewitol, the Seer's moon, was old that night, a slender shaving of light in the star fields. Shadowy and dark, Dyfed sat a little distance from the fire, skinning hares for our dinner. He didn't answer me right away, kept on with his work until the catch was clean and spitted. Then he brought the hares to the fire, set them for roasting. In the orange light of the flames I saw him smile when he said that there was a man in the village with a house to sell. He told me that he thought he might have enough silver to buy that house.

I looked at him long, watched him through the smoke of the fire. "You mean to wed Cyneleah, don't you?"

"Could be."

Long the silence between us while he waited for me to congratulate him. I was late with that, late in saying that I wished him well. I was thinking that something had changed in him. Restless Dyfed didn't seem so restless anymore. Always before he'd seemed to me as rootless as a leaf on the wind, blown here and there, and glad to be moving. That was no longer so, and I wondered when the change had come.

"Ah, Ghost Foot," I said at last. "Next you'll be telling me you're saving your silver to buy up a farm."

He laughed. "Maybe, *freond min.* Someday, maybe."

That night I lay awake for a long time after Dyfed went to sleep. The red dog had run off into the woods, hunting or doing some scouting of his own. I waited for him to come back, quiet-footed to steal the remains of our dinner. As I waited, I watched the thin old moon travel across the sky, spent the long night thinking.

I started out thinking about Dyfed and the strange idea of him turning farmer, but soon I found I was thinking about other things, about Lydi and what Gardd Seren looked like when it was greening in spring.

But only as you would think about a dream you'd had long, long ago in childhood, Sif, half-remembered, empty of the feelings that once gave it brief and potent life. It was the safest way.

We passed through the borderland valleys like shadows. Best, we thought, that none knew we were about, not even the villagers or farmers who would be friendly to the *cyning's* men. We wanted to enter the Welsh lands in stealth, and the wrong word from even one man could endanger us. And so, as the Seer's moon waned and Ghost Moon rose, we skirted the farms, rode wide of the few small villages. We avoided Cefn Arth, entered the Vorgund's lands from the low southern part of the border, only climbed north when we were well into the wildwood.

Dyfed and I knew this land well; none among Erich's men knew it better. We'd roamed here in winters past, hunted here, searched out its secret places. This time, in the warm spring, we didn't roam heedlessly. It was no lie Dyfed had given my *mearc-threat,* my border-troop, a year ago when we needed to tell them something other than that I'd brought Aelfgar, wounded and sick, to a Welsh witch. We did indeed have friends among the farmers who clung to the lands on the borders. Boundaries move, hauled north or dragged south, pushed east or pulled west by war, but Saxon farmers don't easily give up their lands. When the land was under Saxon sway, these stubborn farmers were happy. When Vorgund owned it, they hung on and were very careful.

We came to one of these farmers on the night when Ghost Moon was full. Godulf was his name, and he remembered us. Aelfreya his wife made us welcome, gave us good food and ale; his sons took our tired horses to the byre, fed them and brushed them and cared for our gear. Godulf's food was good, his ale better, but his news was bad indeed.

"Strange things're happening, *dvergr,* and that's saying something for this place where strange things happen often. Did you see the stars fall last summer?"

"Ay, I did, Godulf. I saw them."

"That wasn't good, I'm thinking; and things haven't been good since. Vorgund passed by here not long ago."

In the corner by the fire, Dyfed drew a long breath. I sat up straight, put aside the ale-horn. "Tell me," I said.

"I was out at the edge of the homefield not long ago, saw him and his ride by. They were headed south, all of them weaponed. Close I was, no farther than the width of the beck—and you know how thin yon beck is, even when it's spring-full. I could see their faces, Garroc; they caught me by surprise. Ay, they did, for not a sound did they make, *dvergr;* not a rattle of hoof on stone, not the smallest chime did I hear from their mail, though mail they were wearing—I saw it gleaming. I saw them talking, too, I did. But I heard not a word, not a breath, only saw their mouths moving." White-faced, he took up his wife's hand and held it in both his own. "They call their ghosts *ellyll* in the Welshlands, Garroc. I'm thinking Vorgund's two hundred—there were that many!— passed like *ellyll,* like ghosts."

"Did he see you?" Dyfed asked into the silence.

Godulf laughed. "See me? Young Dyfed, he could have counted the hairs on my head! Ay, he saw me. Gave me a polite smile and a nod, he did, and went on his way. He wasn't too worried about the like of me. I'd heard he was gathering witches all last year. It's true, isn't it?"

"It's true," Dyfed said. Firelight gleamed red on the burn marks of a witch-bear's claws as he bent over his red dog, stroked Werrehund's old war scars. He told Godulf about the witch-bear and about the death of Iwan Vorgund's son.

We talked long into the night, spoke in low voices as men do when they are afraid that someone may be hidden near who should

not hear what is said. Toward the end of the night, when dawn
was only an hour or two away, Dyfed asked the farmer if he'd seen
or heard word of a young man passing this way.

"Heading west and north," he said. "A friend of ours who set
out from Rilling in winter."

Godulf said he'd seen no one like that, said that he'd remember
it if he had. Then, yawning and tired, he bade us good night.

We left the farmer in the morning, thought it best to get ourselves back to Rilling.

Two other farms we visited as we made our way homeward.
Each stead-holder had some strange tale to tell, some story of dark
magic and the Welshman Vorgund. Godulf's nearest neighbor saw
the Witch-Gatherer riding; he talked about ghosts, too. He also
talked about fire in the sky, great eagles who rode between the stars
on sweeping wings of fire. He spoke of this shyly, as though he
expected us to scoff or call him mad. We did neither, only took
his news in silence as we ate his meat and drank his ale. We knew
about witches, Dyfed and I. At the end of the night Dyfed asked
his question again, asked for news of Aelfgar. This man answered
the same way Godulf had. He knew nothing of a tall bright-haired
young man making his way north and west.

The third farmer gave us news neither Dyfed nor I wanted to
hear, news we each deemed worse than tales of fire-winged eagles
or ghosts riding. He told us that the witch who lived in the star-
garden was gone from her valley.

"This fall past," he said, "I thought my boy was dying of the
sweating sickness. Times like that you'll ask help of anyone, even
a witch. She came to us, tended the boy, and so I went there again
to bring her the cow I'd promised her in the fall for making my
boy well. Winter was hard up here; I couldn't get the beast to her
any sooner. But I pay my debts. I went after the thaw.

"The valley was the valley; like it is the folk there won't trouble
themselves about wars and such. It's all too far away. But the
Gardd Seren was empty, filled with a strange misty fog, thick like
the fogs that come off the sea, but cold and biting as ice. No witch
there, no sign that she'd been there for some time."

He fell silent, thinking. After a time I tried to ask a question,
but I could not—my mouth was parched with fear, my words
would not come. Dyfed asked it for me, said quietly:

"Do you know what happened to the witch?"

The farmer shrugged. "Doubtless she's gone riding with the
others. Vorgund's gathered 'em all up, those witches. A troop of

them, he has. Or so I've heard. Ay, you tell me that Halfdan's son means to bring war to Vorgund Witch-Gatherer." He shook his head. "I tell you he needn't bother. Vorgund's already bringing it to him."

Werrehund came to lean against Dyfed, and Dyfed wrapped his arms round his red dog, held him close. "Was anyone there?"

"Ghost Foot, I told you: none."

His words sounded as final as barrow-stones falling into place.

It cannot be said that I rode home to the Marches with a heavy heart. In truth, there was not much heart in me, and what there was of it didn't count for much to weigh when I thought about what the farmer told us about Gardd Seren.

In the summer past, Lydi and I had talked of choices, talked of the love between us and the duty we each owed our lords. Then she'd said we had each made our choices long before. Hers had been for peace and healing, for making a safe place for the sick to get well, for the hurt to heal.

But I'd taken that safe place away from her, made a mock of her trusted sanctuary. Who would trust her now? Who would go to her and hope for haven? None. She'd let her Saxon wolf take Iwan Vorgund's son from her care. None could feel safe with her after that, none could ever trust her again. I'd made certain of that.

And so, I'd made certain that the safe place I'd sent Aelfgar to in the winter was no longer there. I didn't think that he could have found another haven. I didn't think that he'd long survived his sentence of outlawry.

If I'd left Iwan Vorgund's son with Lydi, as she'd asked me to do . . .

Still, though she was gone from Gardd Seren, I didn't believe that Lydi had chosen to join her lord and his witches. I could not think where she might be, but I could never believe that she'd gone to battle-grounds and war-fields with Vorgund Witch-Gatherer.

Neither could Dyfed; neither could her Cyfaill. But he didn't talk about it much, didn't talk about anything much as we rode homeward.

On the dark night when Ghost Moon fell at last before the shadow-wolf, we came to Cefn Arth, the border-ridge. We'd ridden far and hard and so we took the next day to rest our mounts. We slept well into the morning, then spent a long afternoon on Cefn Arth near to where the barrows stood, the tall one that

housed Ecgwulf and Godwig, Wulf and Waerstan, and the small
one where Haestan, my battle-shadow, lay.

Things were changed in me, and not the least change was that
I no longer heard the voices of the dead. They did not haunt my
waking days, they did not wander through my sleep at night. The
stillness within me was an eerie one, not a good one. I knew it even
then. It seemed strange to me to stay in that place and hear nothing
but silence.

That night it rained hard, and Dyfed and his red dog kept to
the wildwood with the horses, tried to stay dry beneath the trees.
But those trees were only newly fledged, didn't afford much protection. After a time Dyfed gave up trying to keep dry, came to
stand with me at the edge of the ridge.

We looked out over the Marches, at the rain falling in sweeping
grey curtains. Dyfed cocked his head, listened hard to the night.
We each heard the same thing: thunder growling far away in the
eastern sky. When I looked against the slant of the rain, I saw
clouds, deep and dark, running with the east wind. And I saw
something else.

Dyfed looked where I did. "What do you see, Garroc?"

I couldn't say for sure, and so I said nothing just then, only
walked north along the edge of the ridge. Dyfed followed.

"Garroc," he said uneasily, "what do you see?"

I pointed north. Something didn't seem right about the sky
there; almost it seemed that the darkest clouds ran up from the
ground, not along the paths of the sky as clouds should.

"Smoke," he said, low.

I nodded. Smoke. Red-edged as though there were a great burning going on in that valley, a blaze so strong that the rain could
not kill it. Dyfed shivered, and as he did, a long roll of thunder
tumbled down the sky.

As we walked back to our camp and the feeble, guttering campfire, I thought that Thunor was early come to the field of battle.

The next day we rode north along Cefn Arth and down into
the Marches. We saw what had been burning so hard in the night.
The village hadn't been a large one. Ay, it was hardly a village
at all, only a handful of buildings at a fording place in the little
river my *mearc-threat* and I had watched all the summer before.
From high Cefn Arth we'd never seen the buildings, though; we
hadn't known they were there.

Five small cottages and an ale-house grown up around a smith's
forge, two byres, maybe three—it was hard to tell—and a cold-
house that like was shared by all. The buildings were cold stinking

rubble when Dyfed and I saw them, and all fields around, the edges of the woods, were smoking ruins. We saw no cattle, no pigs or chickens; we saw no dogs or geese. Like it was they'd been run off into the forest, or kept to feed the ones who'd done this slaughter.

We saw some bodies though. Most were *mann-cynn*, old and young. One was a Dwarf, and he held a forge-hammer in his cold stiff hand. *Dvergr* and dead forever.

This was not the work of slavers, Dyfed said. He was sure it was Vorgund's work.

And later we learned that this was so. We learned that from Erich, for two days later, though we'd had no thought of finding him away from Rilling, we met the *cyning* and his army in the mist-dragon's vale.

Grim of face, he was, and he gave us hard news. The ruin that Dyfed and I had seen in the valley below Cefn Arth was the least of Vorgund's work. The war had come, and the Welshman rampaged through the Marches with an army of two hundred Dwarfs and Men, with seven deadly witches. He burned and killed, sowed terror like a farmer sowing seed, and he rejoiced in it.

III

THE Storm-god gathered many Dwarfs and Men during the time of Wanderer's Moon. My friend Eadric was one, and he died on the broad, sunny meadow which lay between the River Roden's slender arms. He died trying to kill a witch who had the fearsome form of a great eagle. Wings of flame and talons of iron had that witch-eagle. It swept down the hard blue sky, screaming deathsongs. Bold Eadric stood firm, and when the witch came close, fire streaming from its wings, Eadric Gunnar's son thrust his long ash spear deep into the *helle-cynn's* breast. He didn't kill it, and was rent to pieces by beak and talon, burned by the fiery wings. Yet Eadric was not dead before his friends finished his work for him.

I didn't hear his ghost, didn't feel his voice in my own heart and so I didn't know when the Valkyrie came for him. Still, I gave his name to Erich. *Eadric Gunnar's son.* Because of his courage, Vorgund had one less witch.

Many soldiers died that day, and the farmers who lived round the Roden sent others to take their places. We armed them with the weapons of the war-killed. Then we bound up the injured, burned and barrowed the dead, and went on, heartened by the witch's death.

Yet this victory was a small one, for though Erich's army was greater, Vorgund's witches worked their *wundorcraeft* so that the Welshman and his soldiers moved without sound, rode their horses as though riding shadows. The mother-earth didn't feel them moving, and so she didn't warn even the most attentive Dwarf when danger was near. Time and again Vorgund swept down on us, and we didn't know he was near until the first of us died on a Welsh sword.

That was hard for the Men among us who had grown used to having Dwarfs near to listen to the earth. Harder for *dvergr*, suddenly earth-deaf, and often I woke in the night with a bruised and bleeding fist, for in sleep I'd been striking the ground, hungry to hear the echo in my bones.

Anyone wagering would not have placed much silver on a certainty that Erich would win his war. Though he'd started the fighting with twice Vorgund's men, witches had thinned the War Hawk's ranks and now the odds were not good. But we fought hard nonetheless, maybe the harder because we didn't know how we could come alive through this war. Nothing puts the iron into a Saxon's soul faster than the suspicion that he has come up against an enemy he cannot beat. Then, *dvergr* or *mann-cynn*, he fights best, for then he is vying for the finest seat in the All-Father's hall.

And so through all the long spring, through all of Wanderer's Moon, the smoke of pyres turned the sky grey, meadow flowers drooped in the shadows of barrows. Vorgund and his witches pushed us far south, to the northernmost part of the Rill, forced Erich to retreat until the battles raged very close to Rilling.

Yet now we didn't count ourselves wholly lost, for it was true that every man Vorgund lost to death was replaced by none. Erich fought in his own lands. When there were no more strong young men to come out to take the places of the slain, boys and old men came, farmsteaders defending their lands. They took up the weapons of the dead and stood in their places.

As Stag Moon ran leaping through the summer nights, Erich split his army into two groups, one to harry the Welshman by day, one to force him to fight at night. And some advantage we gained from this, for now Vorgund's witches must always be ready, must never rest but spend their strength in magic day and night. They no longer used their *wundorcraeft* for stealth, saved it for battle-work.

Once again the mother-earth heard Vorgund's army riding; once again she warned of danger coming, and by the time Thunor's Moon rose, we'd gained some ground, pushed Vorgund west a little, and—brightest luck!—we'd killed three more of his witches. Now he had only three, and their magic was not so strong.

Dyfed came to me with news on a hot night, a thick night full of storm-promise. He walked slowly up the rocky slope of the hill where I stood keeping the watch. He'd been gone most of the day, afoot in the meadows and cool shady woods, searching for sign of Vorgund's army. A short time ago I'd heard the watch on the eastern side of the valley hail him. Soon after his return I saw the campfires go out and knew that Dyfed had brought Erich good news. Dwarfs and Men made ready for fighting.

My friend looked like a tall piece of the night walking, dark against the darkness. He came alone, didn't have his red dog with him. He dropped to a seat on the ground, leaned over drawn-up knees, groaning.

"Swear to you, Garroc, I've never been so tired."

I could believe it, for it was how he looked—white-faced, grimed with dirt and sweat. When he raised a hand to drag his white hair away from his face, that hand shook a little.

I asked him what he'd found out about Vorgund, but he didn't answer at once, only sat back against a boulder. In the silence thunder rolled. The Storm-god was coming close. At last Dyfed said that he'd found Vorgund camping deep in the woods north of the valley.

"He's got no two hundred now, Garroc. I counted eighty at most."

"Ay, but his three witches count for something."

He wiped sweat from his face, looked up at the grey sky. "Hot tonight, ay? If it's going to rain, I wish it would and soon. It'd feel good."

"It would." I went to sit beside him. "Ghost Foot, you don't look happy."

He laughed, but there was no humor in it. "Not happy? Ay, that's putting it neatly."

I waited for him to go on, waited while thunder grew louder and more frequent. Now when I looked up, I saw pale flashes of light throbbing in the deep-bellied clouds. From the north came the hissing wet wind makes in the forest.

"Ghost Foot, tell me."

He wiped his face again. "I didn't see three witches when I counted Vorgund's camp, Garroc. I saw four."

A silver spear tore open the dark sky—heatless light to show me Dyfed's wide and deep sorrow as he told me about the fourth witch, about Lydi.

"She kept apart from them all, soldiers and witches. I saw her among the wounded, going from one to another, helping and healing. . . ." He shook his head, ran his thumb absently along the white webbing of scars where his left eye used to be. "Ah, she looked lonely there."

I would not feel the weight of his news, hid myself close within the wall I'd built. "Ay, well, he is her lord." My voice sounded hollow to me, bloodless. "She had to make a choice soon or late."

Dyfed's head came up fast, his one good eye flashing like Thunor's own lightning. "*Dvergr,* you are a fool if you think that you or Vorgund have anything to do with Lydi's choice."

His anger sparked my own, and I laughed bitterly, said that he seemed to know the witch better than I did.

"Not better, Garroc. Differently."

Still surly, I said, "I wouldn't know about that, Ghost Foot. It's not a tale she chose to tell me. Not one you've ever spoken of."

He was quiet for a long time; the only sound I heard then was the thunder's low growl. At last he spoke, and when he did his voice was filled with wordless questions. So it was when he contemplated a wager, so it was when he reckoned odds. "It's a hard story, Garroc. And—I don't tell it easily."

In that moment I could have stopped the tale, told him that he needn't tell it. But I didn't, Sif, for I remembered the day in summer, a hot day on Cefn Arth, when Dyfed had looked toward the Marches and I'd known he'd not looked toward home. And even then, when all of skald-craft was still and dark in me, the curiosity remained.

"Ghost Foot," I said, and said it with more gentleness than I used toward anyone these long months past. "Tell me."

He did, slowly and with his eye on the gathering storm, as though it might be better to look at the dangerous sky than at me. He said that he was born in Wales. He told me quickly that his father was Saxon, told me slowly that his father had been a slave.

"I don't know what his name was, Garroc. Like it is my mother knew it, but . . . Ay, well. I do know that he was taken on some Welsh raid, brought back to work in the copper mines. He lived long enough to make a son. The woman was another Saxon slave. And then he died. Not of the lung-sickness, or a mine cave-in. He died of heart-sickness. My mother died soon after I learned to walk. I remember that, though I was very young. Maybe her heart was broken, too."

Wind hissed in the forest, Thunor prowled closer now, a god come to hear a tale. In the cold flash of lightning Dyfed's face showed pale.

The son of slaves, and so a slave himself, Dyfed worked the mines as his father did. And it's a thing about the mines in Wales: They weren't made by Men, but by *dvergr* in a far time. Welsh Men have the mines now, take the iron and tin, the silver and copper, from them. They have sunk new shafts, but never have done much to make the roofs of those old mines taller, the walls wider. And so, many slave-miners are younglings, children small enough to work in the shafts and tunnels ancient *dvergr* mine-makers had delved for themselves.

My friend told me he was born to the darkness, lived a brief and crippled childhood in the cold, cold blackness beneath the earth, and fled just as soon as he could. He was twelve then. Running north and east, hiding from those who hunted him, he made a brave flight.

The slave-hunters caught him at the edge of Seintwar.

Dyfed said it was probably true that they didn't mean to kill so valuable a prisoner. He also said it was truer than any truth I'd heard till now that he didn't mean to go back to the dark tunnels and the cold shafts where his only companions were rats, and children condemned to live out their brief lives in darkness. He'd rather have died in the sunlight. He fought, and his fury ignited the rage of those who would take him back to slavery. In the end no twelve-year-old boy could win against three strong men. A blow from a sword's bright edge took his left eye and gave him freedom.

Dead the boy Dyfed seemed, and so his hunters left him where he lay, rode back to their mines. They might have taken the body back with them as warning to the other slaves, but the season was high summer and Dyfed believed that the men didn't care to keep company with a corpse for two or three days in the blazing sun. And from there, he said, his luck got better. He came to himself at day's end.

"Was I surprised to find myself still living?" Dyfed crooked a wry grin. "Ay, I was. And I've never been surprised by anything again."

One-eyed, bloody, he walked the whole night, heading down to Seintwar.

Sif, I have made that walk in the time it takes the sun to show itself after the sky first turns light. It took Dyfed from day's end till dawn to drag himself the distance. He found a byre, a small stone-built barn, and crawled into the hay to sleep or die. The farmer who found him thought he was dead, but when he lifted the boy out of his clean sweet nest, he knew it was otherwise. That farmer did what folk in Seintwar always do when someone is sick or hurt and there is no *Cristen* priest around to see: He sent for the witch.

"Lydi could do nothing to heal an eye that was no longer there," Dyfed said, "but she healed my other hurts. No, I don't wear a slave's mark now. But I did then, the *beag-run,* the collar-mark, ay? Lydi had the collar struck, and healed the sores. Then she told me that from that day on I must only work when I wished to.

"I worked often. I liked tending her gardens; I liked the healer's work, mixing the oils and salves and powders. And I liked the way it made me feel to look up to the sky and see all the stars. Stars by day, riding side by side with the sun. It's the only true home I ever knew, and I stayed there for some years, learning healer-craft and learning about Lydi.

"Often and often, Garroc, I saw her live by her choice, saw her help all who came to her, plague none with questions or judgment. Once she even worked up a salve for the *Cristen* priest. Ay, she did. Poor wight came walking up from the valley, leading a little grey ass. Nervous he was; he'd take no seat when Lydi offered one and looked always over his shoulder as though he feared someone might see that he'd come to a witch. He told her a tale of how his ass was troubled with saddle-galls." Dyfed twitched a smile. "The beast looked well enough to me. . . . Ay, well, maybe I'm not remembering the whole story. It was a time ago.

"I liked it there in Gardd Seren. I think the people of the valley came to believe that I'd stay there as the witch's adept."

He laughed when he saw my startled look. "No, no, not in magic, Garroc. We soon proved that I've no skill at that! But in healing, ay? I'm not too bad at that. Maybe—for a while—I thought I'd stay, too. But came a time when I needed to see the lands where my father had been born. Lydi let me make that choice."

And then Dyfed told me that he never really knew what he was: Welsh because he was born in Wales, or Saxon because both his parents were. And he never knew his true name. He thought that perhaps he hadn't been given one. "Boy" his masters had called him when they weren't calling him worse; if his mother had a name for him, he couldn't remember it. He let Lydi call him Cyfaill and liked that name well enough, and later he took a name for himself. It is a mark of my friend's sense of humor that he named himself after the land where the Welsh god of the underworld had been born. And later still, when he and I first began to roam the western borderlands, holding tight to our secrets, I began to call him Ghost Foot. All these names he'd answer to as easily as though any was his true name.

"So, yes," he told me, "I know Lydi well, Garroc. I've known her since childhood, grew up in her star-garden. And this I know best: Lydi will heal whoever needs it and she does not see it as choosing for one against another. Lydi chooses, always, for her arts, for her magic and her healing. She can't do anything else and still be whole."

I tried hard not to be moved by Dyfed's tale, tried not to feel it. Instead, I looked out over the dark valley, listened to the thunder and the faint sounds of restless horses. After a time I said:

"Lydi makes her choices and insists that she be allowed to live by them. You make yours, and she gives you no argument. Tell me, Ghost Foot," I said bitterly, "why won't she let me live in peace with mine?"

Dyfed cocked his head, squinted his one eye, as he did when he wanted to see something closely. He spoke awkwardly, tried to find words to talk about a thing I'd never invited him to discuss.

"You're talking about your skald-craft, ay? You think you've made a choice, Garroc? You think a person can choose to leave an art like that by the roadside as though it were nothing more than a worn-out boot? Ah, *freond min*," he said softly. "You can't choose to leave that art, any more than you can choose to be born with it. You don't choose it, Garroc. It chooses you, and when you starve the art, my friend, you starve yourself. Lydi knows that."

He sat silent for a while, ran his hand along the rough flanks of the stone at his back. Soft that caress, tender, and when he looked at me again, his one blue eye gleamed brightly, shone with both anger and sorrow.

"Garroc, my friend, old Wotan has stolen something from *mann-cynn* with his terrible curse. He's stolen the companions of our youth, ay? The folk we knew from our first days. It will be a great grief to us when there are no more Dwarfs. It will be a mourning-day for Men when we finally understand that ours are the only voices we hear in the world. No Man alive now will see that mourning-day, but that doesn't mean we don't know that some grandchild of ours will be poorer when it comes. I pity those far children. With none to help them learn the right of it, after a time they'll not remember.

"Like me and the priest's ass, ay?"

Then, with no other word, he got up and left me.

Me, I stayed where I was, watching the lightning leap in the sky. In me, though I had not wanted it, something loosened, something changed. The tall wall I'd built no longer seemed so tall, no longer seemed so strong. A part of that strong Dwarf-built wall—a part of me—had been touched by Dyfed's tale, and by his own sorrow over the fate of Dwarfs. That part shivered a little and broke somewhat, as stone does when the mother-earth trembles in deep and secret places.

Most of the fighting now took place in the wildwood west of the Rill. That was hard fighting, Sif, for Vorgund and for Erich. War in the wildwood is not a matter of ground captured; it is a matter of men killed. Sometimes the fighting would roll out of the wildwood like thunder rolling out of the sky, and then others died besides soldiers. Now the folk who lived on the little farmsteads in the river valleys suffered as greatly as soldiers did. Their young men, their half-grown boys and old men, had all been spent in the war. They had none to defend them now, for Vorgund was never careful of the steads, and Erich had become more careless. Those two, they each had one goal, the death of the other, and each went after that goal with narrowed sights.

Hard to tell, in that terrible summer, who would carry the other's head from the battle-ground. Vorgund's witches were weak, but still they made a difference. If a man knows that the huge iron-taloned, fire-winged eagle in the sky is a witch who is not so strong as he used to be, still the man's horse doesn't know it. It seemed that as many men died of the trampling of a panicked horse as of witch-fire and Welshmen's swords and arrows. I no longer heard the voices of the dead, had not heard the ghosts of the war-killed since winter. But I had eyes to see, and when battles were over, won or lost, I looked out over the killing-ground and saw many dead. Most of them were Erich's men.

Sometimes, late at night, Dyfed and I would watch a small blue light drift from one quarter of the battle-grounds to another, slow and patient, shining like an amethyst held high to the moon's light. Others saw that light, too, and whispered fearfully. of ghosts or worse—walking dead. Dyfed and I knew better, knew what that light was. A healer-witch went among the dead and dying, and sometimes it was that in the morning a friend would come back to us—a friend we'd thought was dead would stumble off the grounds where the war-killed lay, praising his luck that he'd only been a little hurt.

Ay, Lydi. My Lydi.

She didn't withhold her help from any, went to deadly war-grounds to give it. It was her choice. And each night I went out to keep watch, searched the killing-grounds with the cold hand of fear clutching at my heart, afraid that should Lydi become caught between her choice and the choices of Erich and Vorgund, she'd die of all of them.

In me, things were no longer as still as they had been.

On a night when Thunor's Moon was full, a small band of *baresarks* came to join in the fighting. They said they'd been in the north with Cadwalla and Penda King, said that the King's war went well, that Eadwine had fled to the mountains. Quiet it was in Northumbria now, the stillness before the storm. In that quiet these berserkers decided that they'd do better for themselves to come south, for they'd all heard in the north that Erich had been fighting hard and long. Happier the *cyning* would have been to have a troop of mounted men to welcome, but Erich, too, had eyes to count the dead. And so, though *baresarks* had been no friends to him in winter, now in summer he welcomed these. War had come too close to Rilling, to his golden Gled and the child who would be born soon. Erich was not of a mood to turn any help aside.

Baresarks. Though Erich did, I didn't welcome them, Sif. I didn't like having to be near them again.

WICCES-MONA
(Witch's Moon)

AH riddles, Sif, nets of wonder woven from words!

Here is one Dyfed told me as we walked watch on a hot night during the summer-war, a long dark night when Thunor's Moon was only a slim red sickle, thin and old in the sky:

> Here is a wonder:
> Take this from one hoard,
> Place it in another;
> The first trove is no poorer,
> Yet the second is richer.

That night was the last we'd see of the Storm-god's moon; the next night would be moon-reft as the sky awaited the slender new Witch's moon. Too, magic and enchantment were near to every man's mind that summer, for many had died of it. And so I gave answers that had to do with enspelled things. Each of my answers was wrong.

"Only a gift," Dyfed said, "a simple gift. The friendship you give to another enriches you as well, yes?"

I told him that I supposed it was so.

Dyfed told other riddles that night, and some of them led me to believe that he had his Cyneleah much on his mind, for these were lusty riddles indeed. The last one he told me, he gave with a sly grin; said he'd wager anything I liked that I would not know the answer to it.

I wagered some silver, bade him say on. These were his words:

Where is the dark, the high-arched hall,
Hung with jeweled tapestries
Woven of dreams and rain-hope,
Stitched with the threads of song?
A haunted king rules there.
As he flees the wolf's shadow
In swift splendor,
He turns and looks—
Beyond, he sees a thing most fair.

I knew the answer to that one: The dark hall is the night, for
the haunted king who rules there is the moon. And if that king
turned in his swift fight to look, he would see the fair mother-earth
from high in his hall. But as I took my friend's silver, I thought
that there might well be another answer, and it as good. There
was that about Dyfed, a shading of his voice, a look in his one
blue eye, that made me think that the answer might as easily be
'the heart of Garroc Silent Skald.'

When I considered that, I wished my friend would leave the
weaving of riddles to others, but later, when I saw clearly what
fate the Norns had been weaving for me all this year past, I
wondered if Dyfed had seer's powers.

He didn't, of course. He was only Dyfed, only Ghost Foot, only
Cyfaill—a man made of flesh and bone and blood. And so, later
when I was wondering, I came to decide that Dyfed's riddle had
somewhat to do with faith in me, trust in the haunted heart of
Garroc Silent Skald.

And faith is a good gift for one friend to give another.

I

THE boy limped into Erich's battlefield encampment at the end
of the longest, hottest day of summer. His thin face white beneath
a griming of sweat and soot, his grey eyes wide and wounded, he
could not have seen more than nine winters, and even for that
number he was small. Erich and Vorgund had fought hard that
day. Fierce war hawk, Halfdan's son had driven Vorgund's army
steadily north. Some farmsteads had lain in the way of that battle-
path. They didn't now. The dread fire-eagles had flown low over
the little steads at noon. This boy had the look of one who'd been

under war's hard fist, and the smell of smoke followed him like a ghost.

Kin-reft and wandering, I thought—some farmer's orphaned son. I'd seen so many like him that summer. Weary and hurt, their homes in ruin, they staggered wherever their legs carried them. As he passed me, the boy stumbled a little over nothing but his own exhaustion. I caught his arm and steadied him.

Small and thin, his arm felt fragile in my hand. He flinched at my touch, then stood still, as a rabbit stands when it's hoping that the wolf will lope past, leave it in peace. His grey eyes were brimful of ghosts as he waited to see if I would hinder or harm.

Bone-tired, I was, Sif, with the roar of battle still bellowing in my skull, screaming in my axe-weary arms. In my heart I heard only the hollow echoes of the day's fighting, a distant din of thunder. I wanted a fire and food. We'd found a tun of wine in the storehouse of one farm earlier that day. I wanted some. But I'd get none of that yet. I had watch to walk.

Tired, tired, I didn't have it in me to treat with a heart-ruined refugee. I let go his arm, turned away from the boy with the ghost-grey eyes.

The slender curve of the Witch's moon rose in the east, wore sunset light, gleamed like a scythe's thin-edged blade. In the west the red, red sun floated in a smoky purple sky, sagged wearily toward the distant Cambrians. Strange light, sharp-edged and golden against the blue shadows of the dimming, spilled across the battle-field, across the meadow where the dead lay. Cool wind off the Rill hissed through tall grass. Ravens quarreled over the bodies of the war-killed, dark drunken feasters.

I heard no ghosts as I paced the watch at the meadow's edge, saw no Valkyries riding the wind. For me the battle's aftermath was a quiet time now, and I was not yet wholly used to that. Sometimes I would turn my hearing inward, listening for the voices of the dead; sometimes I would be surprised by the silence in me, as a man is surprised by the absence of the longtime aching he'd lived with most of his life. That day, fey-minded and enspelled by the moody sunset, I had the sudden feeling that this silence of ghosts was not different than the stillness before a storm.

A linnet, its black-edged wings whirring, its red cap bright in the dimming's light, arrowed past me. I watched it stitch the sky, fly east toward the Rill and the green shady forest rising dark beyond. These were not pine woods; in these lowlands the forests were leaf woods. The east wind came from there, ruffled the smooth surface of the river, tossed the trees' manes. I wondered how far into the forest Vorgund and his army had limped.

They'd not been strong when Erich had hounded them across the water, and the witches were weary; the three, the iron-taloned *helle-cynn*, shimmered as dream-figures shimmer when they are not sure what shape they will use. When they were fire-eagles, they yet flew; when exhaustion took them, and the eye was not sure that these things were eagles at all, they dropped low, staggered on the wind.

Glad those witches must have been to follow their lord's retreat into the woods where their fire was not wanted, their wings not needed. I didn't think that Vorgund had more than thirty men with him now, less than a quarter of his army. His witches and soldiers were exhausted.

As were Erich's men. Though he'd not been pleased to see Vorgund vanish into the forest, the War-Hawk *cyning* held tight to patience, let his army rest. But only for a time. The new-come *baresarks* made Erich's army strong, and I didn't think he'd change his pattern of night-fighting now.

I leaned on my grounded axe, watched thin wispy clouds play around the red horn of the Witch moon. Wind hissed, ravens quarreled. Though I could not hear them, ghosts sang. And, soft behind me, from across the river, from the edge of the forest, came one low, sweet note.

A wood dove's sigh.

Night crept out from beneath the forest's eaves; shadows covered the marshy ground between the wildwood and the darkening water. The wind pushed stronger now, cool on my face, tugging at my hair and beard.

Wings clapped, grey wings bright in the last light. A dove flew, caught the quick breeze over the Rill, let it help her across the water. Close to me she came, close enough for me to see the soft feathers dressing her breast, feathers the color of smoke. Her eyes shone jewel-bright, blue as no dove's are, and my heart hammered against my ribs.

Lydi!

I let my axe fall. Light was in me, ay, light like a sudden wide shaft of sun leaping from behind dark clouds. I held up my hands, as I'd done before; held them high. I forgot in that moment to be afraid of the magic.

And she, small dove, trimmed her wings, folded them back as she does to alight—then shot quickly away, flew low for the river. I heard the reeds whisper as she passed over them.

Too, I heard a slow and weary tread behind me.

I turned sharply, axe high, then grounded it again when Aescwine lifted his hand in silent greeting, came to stand beside me. No sign did I mark that he'd seen me reach for the dove, but it was hard these days to tell what Aescwine was thinking. The summer-war had changed his face.

He'd gotten a few more war-scars, had Aescwine, and one—a long knife trail twisting from his upper lip to just below his right eye—gave him the look of always sneering. He joked about it, said he got into more fights now because people didn't like the way he smiled. I thought this was too bad, for none was moved less often to sneer than peaceable Aescwine.

"Young skald," he said, "I've come to relieve your watch."

Ay, young skald. Always he called me that, and nothing I could say would stop him. He'd kept his distance from me in the winter, didn't seek me out in spring, but now in summer, when we were thrown together in war-camps, he'd resumed his easy friendly way with me. He was old, Aescwine, but he had some patience with foolish youth.

"You've come early, Aescwine."

He looked over his shoulder at the dancing lights of campfires, the long thin trails of smoke rising slowly to the sky. "I was feeling too restless back there. Used to be I could come off the war-ground and be asleep the next moment." He shook his head. "These days, with the world all full of witches and *helle-cynn*, I can't. If you can, youngster, you might as well."

Weary I was, and the whole weight of the day, once for a moment lifted, had fallen back upon my heart. I thought it would be good to stretch out near a fire with a full belly and maybe some of that wine, and so I thanked Aescwine and left him to watching.

Ay, Erich had *baresarks* with him that summer. I didn't know more than the names of a few of them. I didn't like to come too close to them, huddled and dark as ravens, for fear that I'd remember what it was like to hear the winter winds, the shadow-wolf's howl. But one *baresark* I did know. Black-haired and barrel-chested, he was *mann-cynn*, and his name was Ordulf.

Things had not been good between Ordulf Baeldaeg's son and me that summer. Ordulf was a bully, and in those days I didn't have a crowd of friends around me, and likely I seemed easy game to him. All war-scarred he was, like most of us, and one of those scars, the long one between two of his ribs, he'd gotten from me. Once I had to show him that my axe could defend me. But it's hard to kill a *baresark*; Ordulf healed up well and I was sorry to see it.

That night, as I came into camp from the watch, I saw Ordulf stalking the smoky dimming. When our paths crossed, he snarled; his small black eyes smoldered with hatred. But he passed me peacefully enough. Maybe he didn't like the thin moon's light shining on the honed edge of my axe's blade. Still, I kept him in sight as I walked through the camp to the fire I shared with Dyfed, and that was not hard to do. We'd been late choosing a place to make our fire, Dyfed and I, and so we'd had to take a place close to where the *baresarks* camped, near to Ordulf's fire. Because this was so, I learned that the little refugee, the kin-reft boy with the ghost-grey eyes, was still with us.

Werrehund, sleeping before the fire, opened an eye, thumped his tail once in greeting. Dyfed gave me some food, told me that the waterskin was filled not with water but with our portion of wine. I ate silently, tired from the day's fighting, strangely disheartened now, wishing I'd not come so close to Lydi only to see her fly away from me. I wanted to say something about this to Dyfed, tell him that I'd been so near to talking with the healer-witch. But I didn't.

Ah, a little shaken, that wall in me, not so strong as it once was, but it had not fallen yet. For something to do, for something to keep my thoughts away from Lydi, I watched the boy at Ordulf's campfire.

Thin, that little boy, thinner in darkness than he'd at first seemed in the light. He sat close to the fire, his back to me, alone and watching the embers. He didn't look up until Ordulf's shadow, dark and broad, cut across him. When he turned to the *baresark*, I saw that his grey eyes had regained some life—though they were not yet bright as a boy's eyes should be. He caught up a waterskin from the ground, handed it to Ordulf. The berserker snatched the waterskin and struck the boy hard in the side of the head with almost the same motion.

The boy made no cry, only got his legs under him and scrambled to his feet. Rubbing the side of his head with a grubby hand, he edged back into the light of Ordulf's fire.

Dyfed cursed low under his breath, moved restlessly.

I caught his arm, shook my head. "Leave it be, Ghost Foot."

"The boy—"

"He's managed to keep himself near the strongest man in camp. Like it is he wants it that way."

Dyfed took a long pull at the wine, wiped the back of his hand across his mouth. "Why would he do that?"

"Why not? He wouldn't be here if he had a better place to go. Like it is he's an orphan now, ay? Well, none stands more alone than the kinless. He's not dull-witted; he knows that when you run with the biggest wolf, the lesser wolves will leave you alone."

Dyfed laughed sourly. "But he still has to fear the biggest wolf."

The light of Ordulf's fire shimmered like bright tears in the little refugee's eyes, gilded the edges of the darkening bruise staining his face. From a deep place in me, bitterness welled. This was not the first time I'd noticed that *mann-cynn* is foolishly wasteful of children. Small claims they are on immortality, but they are claims that the gods will honor nonetheless.

With no word, Dyfed passed the wine to me and I took it, drank deeply.

None stands more alone than the kinless. . . .

For all my careful indifference, my words found an empty place in me to echo, and those echoes were cold and dark and hurtful. I didn't want to think about the fatherless. From there it was only a small step to thinking about the sonless. Again I drank, and didn't pass the wine back until Dyfed asked for it. Then I stretched before the fire, hoping for sleep.

Yet, for all the warm wine in me, it was a long time before I slept, and when I did, the pain-stirred echoes in me took on a shape, became familiar sounds. In all the long winter past, through the spring and the summer of battle, I'd had no dream. That night I dreamed a voice, deep and almost familiar for all that it was roughened from howling battle-cries. My voice.

> Of our treasures we are reft,
> King and crofter alike.
> We are god-cursed.
> We are beggared.
>
> Vacant the hall of our hearts.
> Cold and cold our arms!
> They hold no fair child.
>
> Fading the light of our souls.
> Empty and empty our eyes!
> They see no youngling's smile.
>
> As prayers to heedless gods:

Our proud histories are echoes,
Tales told to no one,
Songs sung to empty cradles.

Like a ghost, the words of my last song, my father's barrow-
song, wandered through my sleeping. I was not unhappy when
Aescwine, coming back from his watch, woke me with word that
the *cyning* wanted to speak with me.

Night had only just fallen, for full dark is a long time coming
in the summer months. The Witch moon, not so red now, had not
climbed to his highest seat in night's star-hung hall when I left
the fire and went to answer Erich's summons.

Brazier light burnished Erich's hair to gold, made his face seem
sculpted of black shadows. Weary, he looked, thin-faced, and pale
where the shadows didn't touch him. He'd been fighting hard all
summer, riding out before us in battle, using all he had of heart-
strength to drive the invader from his Marches. A price had to
be paid for that, and Erich paid it as he sat watching and planning.
He was a young man, had seen only twenty-one winters, but he
looked older that night than Halfdan had looked on the day he
died.

Erich wasted no time on greeting, only called me *Faeders-freond*
and told me that he had some night-work for me to do.

Ay, Father's friend . . . I didn't think there'd be much chance
to sleep again tonight.

My feeling was true. This night Erich had no map stretched out
before him. What need? These were his own lands, and he'd seen
Vorgund flee to the forest. Erich wanted scouts to find Vorgund's
woodland camp; quick and quiet scouts, he said. He didn't want
to wait for Vorgund to come out of the woods, worse to slip away
in stealth.

"His witches are tired, now, Garroc," he said, "and I don't
mean to give them time to rest. Vorgund can't have gone far into
the woods. By now he's likely thinking that I won't follow him
until day's light." The Hunter's son smiled with fell humor, ran
a finger along the flat of the sword hanging from his belt. "I'd like
to greet him and his weary witches sometime before dawn. I want
you to find him, Garroc, and I want you to come back to me before
moonset with the best map of the paths to where he's hiding. You
know what I need."

I did: the clearest path to the enemy, then the most direct path
of attack, and then the least likely. Erich was like his father in

making war plans; when he could, he liked to know the battle-ground well before his men set their feet on it.

He had no more orders, I no questions. I left him then, thinking that I'd take Dyfed with me, quick and silent Ghost Foot. I didn't think I'd need any other companion.

Ay, Sif, *I* didn't think so, but Dyfed did. I found him and his red dog keeping watch, pacing the edge of the battle-field. The Witch moon didn't give much light, stars crowded the sky thickly, and as I walked away from camp I saw Dyfed turn his face to them as though breathing their light. When I called to him he greeted me gladly, and when I told him what Erich needed, he walked quietly back to the camp with me, the dog trotting between us. But we'd not gone far when Dyfed said:

"Garroc, have you thought about Lydi? If we lead Erich to Vorgund's hiding place, we're like to find her there."

I'd thought about that. Time and again through this summer-war she'd been in the way of danger. After each terrible battle, I'd seen her blue witch-light, today I'd seen the dove, and so I knew that, time and again, she'd come unhurt through the fighting.

Ah, but it would be hard fighting tonight, I knew that, too.

"Ghost Foot," I said, "she has friends in us, ay? If Erich has his way, there'll be fighting tonight. Best, I think, that we make it our business to find Lydi first when that fighting starts."

He agreed at once, said that I could depend on him. Then, "I've been thinking about that youngster Ordulf keeps with him, Garroc."

I said nothing, not considering that this had to do with our night-work. My silence didn't stop him.

"That boy was raised on one of the steads near here. I'm thinking he'd know the woods better than you or I could."

"Maybe."

"Why don't we take him with us?" He laughed then, and I knew that the misgiving I felt showed clearly in my face. "Ah, Garroc. How long since you've been a boy?"

"Longer than you've been alive, *freond min*."

Werrehund stretched high on his hind legs, put his front paws on Dyfed's shoulders. Grinning, the dog licked at his master's face and Dyfed snorted, pushed the dog's head away. But he didn't push the dog himself away, instead he hugged the beast hard, let him fall back to ground in his own time.

"Ay, well," he said when Werrehund was again on all four feet.

"Maybe it has been that long. But try to remember how boys are. Wager this one's done some hunting in these woods, been all over them. Vorgund couldn't have gone too far, only to the closest protected place, a *denn* or a hollow or some such place. Wager that boy knows where all the good secret places are."

It might be so, and if it were, a good deal of searching could be saved. And if it weren't, we'd lose nothing in the trying. Still, I didn't like the idea of taking a boy into the night-forest.

Ah, no Sif, that wasn't so, and I knew it. I didn't like the idea of taking *that* boy into the forest, of taking him anywhere, for I didn't think of him now without hearing the faint echoes of my father's barrow-song.

And so, having admitted that, to myself though not to Dyfed, I gave way. "Go find him," I said, "and meet me at the river." Then I bethought myself, called him back. "You'd best leave the dog behind, ay? We'll need to be quiet tonight."

He agreed, though Werrehund, who could understand more than some would think, didn't. He laid his ears back flat against his head, stretched long and low against the ground as he did when he wanted to play. As I walked toward the river, I heard my friend tell his dog that we wouldn't be gone long, just long enough to find some war-work. Better, he said, for noisy dogs to stay in camp and see what food they could find.

Like it was the red dog agreed to that, for when I turned I saw him running ahead of Dyfed, reminded that he was hungry.

II

WE were not three who met beyond the light of the army's camp-fires; we were four. Ordulf stood at the water's edge with Dyfed and the little refugee. I was not pleased to see him.

"*Baresark,*" I said coolly, "we're not fighting tonight, we're at scout-work."

He spat. "It doesn't matter to me what you're about. I go where the boy goes." A baleful, greedy light gleamed in his small black eyes. "He's mine, *dvergr.*"

I heard the hiss of Dyfed's sharply drawn breath. Cold in me, like a fist clenching, I knew what my friend thought, and I knew, too, as Dyfed did, that should Ordulf someday come close enough to the western border, he'd have little trouble finding a Welshman who'd pay good silver for a young slave. That kind of trade had passed across borders before now.

I glanced quickly at the boy and knew that he hadn't even the shadow of the thought Dyfed did. What that one had was a heart full of memories of better days than this one, and those wouldn't last long. Ordulf had already begun to turn those memories to ghosts and the boy was learning that he'd have to suffer it. He was yet too young to know differently, or maybe too hurt and frightened to fight it.

It's no small thing to see your home burned, Sif, not easy to see kin killed. Those sorrows are heavy ones; often strong men cannot bear them. It was not a thing for surprise that this little boy could not.

Ordulf bared his teeth, a smile like ice. He took a fistful of the boy's dark hair, yanked his head back so that they were eye to eye. "Tell him, boy. Where you go, I go."

The boy's lips moved soundlessly; he tried to nod.

"*Bearn*," I said as though the berserker had not spoken. "Child, Ghost Foot thinks you know this wood well. Is he right?"

He nodded, and his eyes told me that he didn't lie.

"What do they call you, *bearn?*"

He said nothing.

I glanced up at Ordulf, and the sullen, hard look of him told me that he didn't know the boy's name either. Ordulf might be this boy's proof against lesser wolves, and for that protection he'd pay the price of bruises and a *baresark's* rages, take what risks he must. But he knew this, the boy: When all else is stolen, a man's name is still his own to give or hold.

Ay, Ordulf, *baresark* and bullying coward. He liked best to force others to do as he wished, but he hadn't forced the boy's name from him. Somehow that thought gave a small joy. But only a small one. I didn't like it that Ordulf had managed to force his will on me. And he'd done that, had his way because I didn't like to think what payment the helpless little boy would make in bruises and beatings if I turned the berserker away now, humiliated.

"*Bearn,* tell me where Vorgund would be most likely to camp."

He dropped to his knees, smoothed the hard dirt. I went down on my heels beside him, watched as he traced the earth with his small finger. The map he sketched showed Erich's encampment, the Rill racing swiftly before us, and a broad hollow well beyond and to the north. He studied his map, then extended the line of the river until it curved around the hollow. He stabbed his dusty finger at the hollow and looked at me.

"How far, *bearn?*"

The boy didn't speak to me, but to Ordulf, hulking and dark over his shoulder, a shadow-hearted giant. "You could get there before the moon's highest," he whispered.

If he was right, we'd have plenty of time to do quiet scout-work. I studied the sketch again, and when I looked up, it was to see the boy studying me as closely.

Then a strange thing happened: I saw my image reflected in the child's grey eyes as clearly as though I were looking into a still pool. Ah, haunted Dwarf, cold as bleak winter and lonely with it . . .

Like wind moaning around a barrow came, unbidden, the song that had so recently haunted my sleep.

> Vacant the hall of our hearts.
> Cold and cold our arms!
> They hold no fair child.
> Fading the light of our souls.
> Empty and empty our eyes!
> They see no youngling's smile.

It seemed to me that the grey-eyed boy knew something of that winter-sorrow, and what moved in me then frightened me. Bad enough to live with an old and unhealing wound; seeing it freshly bleeding in this boy caught me hard between fear and aching pity. I wanted to get away from him.

And that is not so strange, Sif, is it? I'd been hiding from grief most of my life. But the other feeling, the pity—that was strange, as was the sudden feeling that I wanted to hold that sad little boy, to soothe away his sorrow.

I scowled, said roughly, "What, boy?"

He looked away as though he had not heard me, and as he did, Ordulf's huge hand caught him hard on the back of the head, knocked him flat. "Answer when you're spoken to," the *baresark* snarled. He moved to follow his blow with a kick.

Dyfed blocked Ordulf's kick and stiff-armed him away from the boy. Deadly anger gleamed in his one blue eye, like moonlight on ice. "Leave off, *baresark*," he snarled.

"Both of you leave off," I snapped.

Ordulf, his big fists balled, turned on me. Dyfed reached for his short-sword. He need not have. My axe came to hand before I could think.

"I'll take you off at the knees, Ordulf."

I didn't warn; I promised. And the *baresark* knew it. The pace he stepped back was distance enough for me, admission that he wanted no quarrel with my iron.

I pulled the boy to his feet. "Back to your map now, *bearn*."

He dropped again to his knees on the path. Dyfed stood over him, close; Ordulf didn't move. As I leaned on my grounded axe, a cloud slipped in front of the slim moon. The night deepened and was growing quickly older. I questioned the boy about the hollow; he only spoke when a gesture would not do. Still, he satisfied me that he knew the forest. According to him, there was no other place but the hollow where Vorgund could rest his soldiers and witches.

"Well enough," I said at last. I had formed a simple plan. "Ghost Foot, after we cross the river, you angle north and east." I barely paused before I went on, but in that moment I took a long step toward the strange fate the Norns were weaving for me. "Take Ordulf. The boy and I will go north and west along the river. No matter what you find in the hollow, Ghost Foot: Wait for me, ay? We'll scout it together."

Dyfed nodded, but I could tell by the hard set of his jaw that he was not happy to have to go in company with a *baresark*. Once before I'd asked him to keep peace between himself and a berserker. I didn't this time. This one was not the Blood Raven. I had no need of him and, if it were possible, less liking for him. Maybe he saw that, my friend Dyfed. He smiled grimly, but said nothing more than that he wished me luck.

And I, as I always did, told him that he'd better not be so free-handed with something he might need for himself.

Ordulf was no happier with my order than Dyfed. He scowled darkly at me, growled something under his breath that I didn't hear. But the boy heard it, for I saw him pale as he watched the *baresark* and Dyfed cross the river and slip silently beneath the forest's dark eaves.

When they'd gone, the boy looked suddenly lost, abandoned. Indeed, had I released him, he would have loped after Ordulf like a pup after his master. And I, amazed, wondered how it was that he could count it any but a grace that he could walk for a while without Ordulf's hard fist holding storm-promise over his head.

Ah, but he was alone with one of the lesser wolves, and I saw by his skittish movements that he didn't know what this wolf might do. With a gentleness that surprised me no less than it must have him, I took the boy's shoulder, said it was time to cross the water.

We did that easily enough, for the Rill was sluggish that summer, and low; in some places the water didn't spread wide enough to reach the banks. Once the boy slipped on moss-slicked stones and I reached out to catch him. He said nothing, only freed himself from my hand—carefully, ay, for he didn't dare risk offending me—and went on. When we set foot on the bank, he moved wordlessly ahead of me, didn't look back to see whether I followed.

Cool it was in that forest; the wind moved strongly. We went quietly along the river path, and when we left that and slipped into the forest, any doubt I'd had that the boy knew the forest vanished. Though I could not see it for the screening brush and trees, I heard the Rill running on my left, heard the stones beneath their fine cloaks of green moss exchanging gossip as the water sighed past. Crickets and tree-frogs filled the darkness with bright song. None could have heard the boy's footfalls over the sound of the water's passage, the shrill of the night-singers. Someone had taught this one his woodcraft well.

The boy found thin deer trails, skirted the marshy ground near the unseen river's banks whenever he could. I set in memory all his turns and the look of each wispy game trail we followed. From time to time he stopped, lifted his head as a hound will when scenting the way. During one of those pauses, the moon's faint light fell across his face. Ordulf's bruises stained his pale skin like dark shadows, and in that moment I thought of Aelfgar. Not as he'd once looked, bright and full of a boy's innocent joys, but as he'd looked in winter, heart-hungry, confused and hurt.

Ah, Aelfgar! He'd not worn a *baresark's* bruises openly, as this boy did, but he'd had them just the same. And kin-reft Aelfgar had been in the end, as this one was now. Friendless in the winter, outlawed and fated to wander in a foreign place searching for the home of a friend.

Far behind, at the river's edge, a fox barked. Crickets and frogs fell silent. I shivered with sudden cold.

None in the borderland had seen sign or heard word of Aelfgar that winter, and if his luck had brought him to Gardd Seren, then his luck had been bad. He'd come friendless to an empty place, for Lydi had left it for this land of war. He'd not have stayed alive long in Welsh lands after that.

Some sound I must have made, for the boy looked at me, his

grey eyes narrowed as though gauging me. It was how a starveling pup, alone and masterless, looks at all those he passes, wondering if he'll be dealt a blow or a kick, hoping that he'll get by unseen, be ignored altogether.

How easily this little one touched the heart of me! How easily he stirred to restless life memories I judged better left undisturbed, memories I'd tried hard to keep walled within me. I turned away from him, pretended not to notice his look, told him gruffly that we'd best be going if he'd not lost his way.

He hadn't, and I followed him again. Soon the trees began to thin; one of the game trails made an abrupt turn to the east. We took it for a short while, then all unlooked-for, we came into in a narrow clearing. Only several strides wide, the clear ground ran in a large circle to the north and south, and was bordered by tall, thick-boled oaks. Rock oaks, *dvergr* call these giants, for moonlight on their uneven grey bark gives them the seeming of being hewn from stone. Now Witch Moon slanted his thin light directly across their rough trunks, made a high rock wall of the ancient oaks.

The boy pointed silently.

No guard did I see, no soldier posted to ward his lord's resting place, but I knew that Vorgund and his witches were there. I'd seen witches' hollows before now, I'd seen Gardd Seren and I'd seen the bluebell wood where last I'd loved my Lydi. I knew as well as any man—ay, better than some—what the sharp tingling of magic feels like as it creeps along the skin.

Working hard to put down the instinctive dread that magic calls up in me, I cursed softly, swore bitterly. The boy, standing near, held deer-still waiting for my anger to fall on him—a blow or a kick. He was certain that he'd angered me, sure that I would make him pay for that anger in the coin Ordulf liked best.

I reached for his shoulder, more roughly than I'd meant to, and said, "Stand easy, *bearn*. Stand easy."

But he was not easy. He strained back from me, eyes narrow, face as stiff as a dead man's, waiting for the blow or the kick, friendless in the forest with a wolf.

And I saw this, too, Sif: It had not always been so for the boy. Beneath the fear was another thing, a yearning for a time not so long ago when he'd known softer things than fear and beatings, warmer feelings than sorrow and reaving.

Once more my heart stirred; again I wanted to hold that little child, to shelter him from his sorrow and fear. But I was long out of the practice of inviting others close, and so I didn't reach to comfort the boy. Instead, I turned aside yet again from a pain that too closely mirrored my own.

The harsh *chak! chak!* of a golden brown wheatear chopped through the night's stillness: Dyfed's signal. I returned the sign, and a lean dark shadow, white hair gleaming in the clear moonlight, slipped soundlessly from behind a broad oak to the west. Ordulf, dark-eyed towering *baresark,* followed. He gestured sharply for the boy to join him, and though he was a long moment about it, the child left me.

Dyfed slipped soundlessly across the moonlit clearing, and when he came close I saw that his face was pale, his hand shook a little where it lay on the hilt of his short-sword.

"Garroc," he whispered. He glanced over his shoulder at the ringed oaks. "Have you been close to there?"

Before I could answer, Ordulf said:

"A little dark and your brave friend wanted to run for the light." He sneered. "No need to worry about him going into the hollow without you, *dvergr.* You couldn't drag him in there with promises of gold."

Ay, then Dyfed's face was not so pale! Then it flamed red with anger, maybe with shame. He clenched the hilt of his sword, would have drawn it hissing from the sheath if I'd not stopped him.

I ignored Ordulf, asked Dyfed what it was he'd seen in the hollow.

"Nothing, but—"

Ordulf snorted. "Nothing but darkness."

Quietly I unstrapped my axe, grounded it where the *baresark* could see the moonlight running along the iron's edge. The whites of his eyes showed livid, his face grew dark and flushed. But he said nothing, only yanked hard at the boy's arm, drew him away, left Dyfed and me alone to talk.

"Ghost Foot," I said, "tell me."

"The *baresark* is right. Nothing, only darkness. But there's something wrong with it. Ay, something . . .

"Show me."

He led me to a place where the tall oaks didn't grow so close. Sharp the scrabbling claws of magic on my skin as we came near the break in the trees' ring, and I knew that Dyfed spoke truly when he said something was wrong about the darkness. It was thicker than any darkness I'd ever known. From below came the wandering smoke of campfires, the rich scents of cooked game and fish, but I didn't see even the smallest ember of a light in that place.

Behind me I heard the shrill singing of crickets, from the hollow only the soft lap and sigh of water moving, a small stream by the sound. Behind me the clear space in the forest lay white, the colors of earth and trees and grass bleached by the moon's thin light; in the hollow not even the smallest shimmer of moonlight glanced from stone or leaf, from the slow-moving water.

Dyfed took a deep breath, let it out slowly. "Witch-crafted, Garroc, ay?" He turned his back on the blackness, leaned against a tree, his face to the moonlight. Maybe the dark in the hollow didn't look too unlike the dark in deep mines to Dyfed.

Soft behind us came a sound, the hiss of drawn breath. I turned to see Ordulf and the boy. The *baresark* glared from beneath lowering brows; the boy edged a little toward me.

His small hand touched mine on my axe's helve, and his fingers were cold as though he'd been holding ice. Still, he leaned a little forward until he was very close to the darkness. He took a half-step forward, and I caught him back. This time he didn't shy from my touch; this time he kept close to me.

"So, Ghost Foot," Ordulf sneered. "Is the dark still dark?"

Dyfed reached again for his sword, then let his hand fall away. "Maybe you'd like to go see for yourself, ay?"

I didn't like the sound of that, didn't like the idea of any one of us going into that hollow where darkness seemed to breathe with a life of its own.

"No one goes," I said. "Ordulf, witches guard this place—"

He snorted. "Ay, witches. They don't have the strength they once had, Garroc. Maybe," he said, his voice low and dangerous, "maybe the *cyning* would do well by the man who goes into the dark to count his enemies for him, ay?" The berserker's small eyes narrowed, and he looked at me with great scorn. "I'll be that man," he said, "since you and quivering Ghost Foot don't have the belly for it."

With no other word, he stepped beyond the sentinel oaks.

Behind us the night flared blue; cool radiance flooded the little clearing, sent shadows skittering along the ground, up the wall of darkness ahead. The boy cried out in fear, Dyfed with sudden bright joy. I turned to see a dove gliding, a winged shadow in her own flaring light. Blinding that light, and I had looked straight into the dazzling heart of it.

A long moment after the others did, I saw Lydi, dark-haired, amethyst-eyed *dvergr* witch, coming toward me.

III

LYDI'S hand shook as she reached for me, trembled as she fell short of touching my own hand. It was as though she could not bring herself to come even that close to the darkness behind me.

"Come away from the hollow," she begged, her voice low with dread.

I whispered urgently, "Is Vorgund there?"

Dark-eyed with fear, she nodded slowly. "And you needn't worry about anyone hearing you, Garroc. The hollow is no part of this world. What you see is a shadow of where they truly are. Hel's Hall, you call it. Annwn, the Underworld, we say. This is where Vorgund's witches brought him to rest. Ay, for a night, they said." She shuddered deeply. "But I . . . I could not go there with them, not even for the sake of the injured who are dying without my help.

"Garroc, the witches will bring Vorgund and his army out safely"—she drew a breath and it trembled like a sob—"but for those who die there. And they've laid a warding-spell on the place. Who enters without their protection will never come out, must stay with the dead. Please, take the child and come away!" She turned to Dyfed, said urgently, "Cyfaill, come away."

Leaves rustled behind me. The boy turned sharply, let go my hand, but Dyfed reached for the child, held hard, kept him from going into the hollow. The rustling came again; close on that sound I heard the *baresark's* voice, strained and rough.

"Ay, *dvergr*," Ordulf said, "tell Ghost Foot there's nothing to fear in this place." He laughed, an empty sound. "Not even the dark."

Blue light flared again; again shadows leaped against the darkness. Behind me I heard Lydi say, "No, Cyfaill, no. Stay here. Garroc," she pleaded, "come away—"

But I didn't, for now I saw Ordulf, a giant's shadow beyond the oaks. The boy saw him, too, and reached out a small hand. By the brightness of Lydi's witch-light I saw fear struggle with great relief in his wide grey eyes, saw Ordulf, shadow-dark, reach for him.

They were no fleshed fingers which came out of that darkness, but the death-pared bones of a skeleton.

Blue witch-light gleamed on those bones and Lydi cried, "Cy-faill! No!"

But she either warned too late, or Dyfed was not of a mind to heed. He put himself between the boy and the darkness. The hand that would have touched the boy grabbed for Dyfed now, fell upon him like some great unclean spider. The bone-hand gripped hard; another flashed out from the darkness, gripped a dagger shining blue and white in the witch-lighted night.

Strong my arm and strong my axe's blade. I struck hard at that bony wrist, a harder blow than I'd ever struck before. My blade turned on it as though the bones were made of iron. I struck again, and my axe rang loudly, fell from nerveless hands. The thing that had been *baresark* Ordulf drove the dagger deep into Dyfed's side. So close was I that I heard iron scrape bone.

"No!" I roared.

Blood-covered, Dyfed fell back, fell away from the boy and the thing that had been Ordulf. I heard the boy cry out again, heard the sob torn from deep in Lydi's heart. Then all sound faded, paled before a coldness I'd kept caged for many months. The shadow-wolf howled in me, winter-wind wailed as the *scin-hond*, the phantom-hand, the raven's-talon, clutched at the boy again and held him.

The child went rigid with terror, incapable of either scream or whimper. I grabbed his hands in my own two and hauled. I might as well have pitted myself against Hel's own grip. Ordulf's strength was not mortal.

Wide and wide, the boy's grey eyes, filled with ghosts and dread.

Cold rage swept me, and the shadow-wolf lent strength—as it had done once before in winter. Torn I was then, wanting its strength—needing it—and dreading the terrible berserker-rage that must follow.

The light behind me flared like a great blue sun. I was blind from it, could see nothing. In me the wolf raged, and the magic flowing from the hollow became stronger, like claws raking my arms and face. In the blinding blue glare, I saw nothing, not the boy, not Dyfed who lay dagger-struck on the ground.

Then the light calmed; then my Lydi stood beside me.

Ay, Lydi, and not Lydi.

It was the shape of her, slender and small, but sheathed in blue light as though it were clothing, she didn't have a solid seeming. Her dark, dark hair billowed about her as though in a gale. Her eyes shone with the pale color of amethysts.

When her eyes are like that, Sif, she can see into the deepest places of a man. And so I knew that she saw the *sceadu-wulf* in me, felt the madness howling in my heart.

She didn't flinch, who should have run from the terrible thing that I was. Nor did she work magic for healing, though she might have. She only laid her hand on my shoulder, gently, tenderly, and there in the warmth of her acceptance, of her love for me, mad or sane, broken or whole, I understood a thing I'd never understood before.

It was no harder to still the shadow-wolf than it was to heed it. It was only a matter of choosing, and either choice would be hard-bought.

And so I chose, and the grief-hound fell quiet.

In the eerie silence which followed the stilling of the wolf, before the songs of crickets and the soughing of wind returned, Lydi spoke. Her voice seemed thin, dreamed.

"Man dear, help me—lend me your strength, keep hold of the child, Garroc."

And I saw that I yet gripped the boy's hands, felt it in the ache of muscle and bone.

Lydi took a step toward the hollow. Her hand slid down my arm, her fingers closed tight round my wrist as though the feel of me were her lifeline back to the light. She slipped into the darkness. Behind me I heard Dyfed groan, a thick sound, as though blood were in his throat. Then he was silent. Then the whole forest grew still.

Small my Lydi—and so very faint the light surrounding her! She stood beside the dark and terrible shadow, the thing that had been *baresark* Ordulf.

"Free the child," she said. "*Ellyll*, fiend, let him go! Ay, you are dead, you have walked into the darkness. He is living, and he didn't choose to walk here. So the warding-spell went, so it works:

> Who chooses dark, finds dark;
> Who looks for death, finds death;
> Who crosses here, does not cross back.

"*Ellyll*, let him go!"

Her blue light flared; by its glow I saw the shadow-fiend become white bones and skull. Dark empty sockets it had for eyes, and when it opened its jaw to speak, nothing but cold mourning wind came from that gaping place where a tongue should have been.

The healer-witch raised both arms high, and as she did my heart leaped in me, swelled to bursting. All the blue light of her gathered itself, grew bright, bright, and the darkness fled before it.

Ay, but the shadow-fiend still held tight to the boy; the cold wailing wind of its voice held fear in it now, terror. The dead man roared, as wind roars down a winter sky, as a shadow-wolf once roared in me.

Come with me!

In my grip the boy's hands grew strengthless. Now I held them so hard, I feared I was grinding the bones.

Lydi took the choice from the boy.

Came a high hawk's cry, the sound a falcon makes in rage. The blue light swirled, spread wide, then gleamed sharply on beak and deadly talons, ran like lightning along dark wings as the witch flew at the shadow-fiend, scattered bones in high disdain.

Rattling, wailing like the wind in desolate places, the thing that had been *baresark* Ordulf collapsed; bone fell from bone. The empty-eyed skull rolled down the slope of the hollow, and the healer-witch, the blue light-hawk, fled the darkness.

The boy sobbed once, let go my hands, and I turned from him, shaken and wordless. Lydi stood beside me again, leaned heavily against me, and in that moment I had no thought for the boy.

I gathered Lydi close, held her tightly. She shook as though she were standing naked in a winter storm; clung to me trembling, weary and gasping for breath. She had been in Hel's Hall, and she was cold with it.

"Lydi, my Lydi . . ."

I tried to warm her, ran my hands along her arms, her back. Still she shivered as though she could never be warm again. She turned in my arms, looked down at Dyfed where he lay on the ground. I knew that her fear was no longer for herself. Blood gleamed in the faint moonlight; blood seeped from the dagger wound in his side.

I went to my knees beside him, took his hand in my own two. Cold, his hand; his skin felt lifeless and waxy. But he knew me, and he smiled a little, crookedly.

"I knew you'd come back," he whispered thickly.

So weak his voice, so frail. Blood stained his lips. I wiped it away with my fingers. "Ghost Foot," I whispered, "Dyfed, my friend, be still now."

"Soon enough . . ." He moved then, just a little, turned his head to look at something beyond me. "Ah, that boy of yours, Garroc . . . he's making . . . his choice now. . . ."

What choice, I wondered. But I had no need to ask him, for

Lydi clutched at my shoulder; her fingers dug hard, and I turned, saw her white-faced in the moonlight, saw her take a step toward the dark place. She reached for the grey-eyed boy still standing there.

"No," she whispered. "Child, no . . ."

He didn't heed the witch, turned from her and walked toward the hollow and the darkness.

IV

THE boy stood near the lip of the hollow, half in the darkness, half in the moonlight. On the doorstep of Hel's Hall, he stood, and a long ache of fear filled me.

He's making his choice, Dyfed had said.

I knew it was true, knew that he'd had no chance to choose before, only waited for darkness or light to claim him.

And I was frightened, for if once he crossed into the shadows, he would not return. I got to my feet, went to him slowly.

"Garroc," Lydi cried. "No! Don't follow him!"

The boy turned when he heard her cry. Lost he looked; tears the color of spider's webs traced glittering paths along his cheeks.

"This isn't a choice he knows how to make, my Lydi. He needs help, ay? Please. Help him if you can."

She looked at me, surprise flashing in her amethyst eyes, for I'd never asked for her magic before. She nodded slowly, said:

"But you must help me, man dear, for I am not strong now."

I gave her my hand, and at once I felt easier, believed that the boy would come safely away from the dark, for this would be about magic; my Lydi's gentle *wundorcraeft* would help him.

Again blue light gathered round the witch, but faintly.

"Child," she said, "you don't belong in darkness. There are better places for you. See!"

And, touching the boy, touching me, she made a bridge between his heart and mine; all the things she gave the boy to see, I saw.

The sun, warm and bright, lay across golden fields; the moon graced the Rill with a silver net of light. A boy—ay, this boy!— ran across the sunlit meadow to chase the wind; in a hunter's camp beside the river he slept in moonlight, held close in the arms of a tall, grey-eyed man. Tenderly that man stroked the boy's face, brushed his dark hair from his cheek. This was his father.

"Come away from the dark, child," Lydi whispered.

It could not be that the boy didn't hear her. Still, he didn't come away, only shook his head. And I knew, because magic bound us, that it was the heartsore gesture of one who makes ready to abandon a field of battle.

As I, so did my Lydi understand the boy's heart. But the light around her failed, flickered, guttered like a candle burned low. She looked up at me, tears shimmering in her eyes. "Garroc, I have no more strength. Man dear, call him, call him."

I call him? Ah, Sif, how could I call him?

Never had I called anyone to me. Most of my life I'd spent turning away from any who tried to come near. And this boy—I'd turned away from him often during this long night, and the last time only a moment ago.

This was supposed to be about witch-magic, about enchantments and power. What word of Garroc Silent Skald's could move this boy?

But this was not about magic, unless the *wundorcraeft* of the Norns weaving, spinning together the threads of two fates. This was about truths I'd never faced, truths I'd once chosen berserker-madness rather than face. I knew it when, in the moonlight, I saw Ordulf's bruises, purple and black along the boy's thin arms, on his white face. He'd paid in pain for a *baresark's* false protection, as in winter I'd paid in madness for the lie of the *sceadu-wulf's* strength.

The night darkened; a long line of clouds, come slowly from the east, shrouded the Witch moon. The shadows of the sentinel oaks became part of the night, and from those shadows the boy watched me. The pain in him was a reflection of the ache in me, and it harried me, shivering and bereaved, into dark places filled with lightless hearths and broken circles.

> Of our treasures we are reft,
> King and crofter alike.
> We are god-cursed.
> We are beggared.

Ay, that song, that barrow-song, whispered in me, ghostly.

Lydi's hand tightened on my wrist; she gasped a little. She'd not heard that song before, Sif. I'd not meant for her to hear it ever.

"Oh, Garroc," she whispered, "please call the boy. Call him!"

Thinking that I was trying, I said hoarsely, "Boy, come away."

My words gave him nothing; I saw it in the way he looked into the shade of the Underworld, as though it was enough that someone, even Hel, wanted him.

"Boy!" I cried. No echo of my voice did I hear; the night and shadows muffled my cry, gave it a bloodless sound. "Wait, *bearn*, wait, child!"

He lifted his head, looked back to the darkness again, to the shadow-hung hall where Hel rules. He smiled a little. He was choosing.

Oh, youngling, I thought, what would be better? Death and ending, or the whole long life you have ahead? Ah, youngling, lonely child, how can you find the courage to choose for life?

The wind quickened, freed the Witch moon of shadows, sent light to us in the forest. In that wind I heard whispers from my own empty aching places, the ghosts of never-born sons and never-born songs, the wind weeping round my own father's barrow.

In that wind I heard the boy's memory of war's din, distant now, like flames fluttering. I heard his heart breaking, heard him weeping a day gone over his tall, grey-eyed father, killed when iron-shod war ran trampling through a once-peaceful valley.

"Ah, *bearn*," I said, shivering in the icy wind of our bereavement, "don't look at that again."

But seeing it, the boy could not turn away.

"Let it go, *bearn*!" I dropped my next words like bitter barrow-stones into the boy's silence. "Our fathers are dead . . . it's not for us to follow them yet."

The boy turned, shrugged off Lydi's hand. Our bridge was broken. Still, I didn't need the witch's touch to feel the ache in the boy, the sharp-fanged gnawing pain of his loneliness.

Ah, kin-reft, I thought, and who should know better about that reaving than one whose kindred, dimming now and failing, will not increase?

The boy took another step toward the darkness in the hollow, toward the death *baresark* Ordulf had found.

"Youngling!" My cry sounded as desolate as dead Ordulf's last wail. And I don't know yet for whom I pleaded—the boy or myself.

The boy stiffened, looked up at me slowly. In his ghost-grey eyes a light came, a spark, an ember. A hunger for hope.

I took Lydi's hand gently from mine. Alone, I went down on my knees. Shaken to my heart, I who had turned away from everything of life and love, who had held tight to nothing but war and killing, held my hands out to the boy, my arms wide and empty as any prospect I had of siring a son.

"Youngling, come to me."

He hung there for a long moment, between darkness and light, life and death. I offered him no answer, nothing but the chance to live, to take loss with gain, joy with sorrow. It was not much to choose for, my slim promise of hope, and it is all we ever get.

"Youngling," I whispered.

He turned his grey eyes to me, and no ghosts did I see there, only a light like a beacon. When he spoke, his voice was filled with yearning for warmth. "Garroc."

He'd never used my name before now. I trembled to hear it echoing in the empty hall of my heart.

"Ah, youngling, come to me now."

He staggered a little, reached for me the way a blind man reaches for a wall. His hands clutched my arms and he sobbed once.

Softly, Lydi touched the side of my face, then quietly she left me. Ay, she goes back to Ghost Foot, I thought. Ghost Foot . . . was he still living?

Almost I turned away to look. Almost. But I didn't. I gathered the boy close to me, stayed with him. I spoke softly, tender words of comfort, ay, quiet words of welcome I'd never known till then.

So small he was, thin and hungry. Little child, he shook hard, shuddered with fear and sorrow. I stroked his back, tried to gentle his fear, and soon he flung his arms around my neck and wept, a mighty storm whose violence could have shaken his soul from his body. But it didn't, for I held him close, gave him a safe warm place to weep over his sorrow.

After a time, I held him a little away from me, wiped his face clean of tears, asked him his name.

He smiled a little, for he remembered that once before I'd asked for his name.

"Hinthan Cenred's son," he said, and he lifted his chin proudly. "Hinthan. My father says—my father said it means Hunter in the old speech, the Seaxeland tongue. And he said it's a good name, so good the old *cyning* used it."

"Your father spoke true, young Hinthan. Halfdan liked it best when we called him Hunter."

I matched his smile with my own, and the warmth in me felt better than the first good warmth of spring. And I remembered something—Dyfed's small riddle.

Here is a wonder: Take this from one hoard, place it in another. The first trove is no poorer, yet the second is richer.

Only a gift, he'd said, a simple gift. The friendship you give to another enriches you as well.

It is so with friendship, and now I'd learned that when the gifts are courage and hope, that riddle's answer holds as true. For in me that night my heart was stronger than it had ever been.

And well that this was so.

Now, by the moon's pale light I looked for Lydi and saw her, the healer-witch bent over her Cyfaill where he lay on the ground. She bowed her head, lifted his hand to her lips, kissed it tenderly.

Dyfed, one-eyed Ghost Foot, was dead.

Good Cyfaill, who knew that I'd come back from the cold places, who knew that I'd see something fair if I but looked behind the wolf's shadow, was gone from me.

And I knew that I could grieve for him, I who had grieved for no one, father, *cyning*, or friend in all the long seventeen years past, for I felt small thin arms, Hinthan's arms, steal round my neck. He laid his head on my shoulder, silently offered the gift I had given him. A safe and warm place to sorrow, and hope when the weeping is done.

V

Not much time had passed between the first moment I'd seen the witch-hollow, felt magic creeping along my skin, and the moment when, my first grieving for Dyfed eased, I knew that I must get back to Erich. Ah, Sif, it seemed like—and in many ways was—the length of a lifetime, but the moon hadn't moved far down the sky when I told Lydi that I must return to Erich's camp.

I looked to the dark-filled hollow, to Hinthan curled sleeping and exhausted beside me. "My Lydi, some things have changed, ay?"

Bright her eyes when she lifted them to me, shining. She said nothing, only nodded. I stroked her pale cheek gently. Weary, she was. Her night's work had been hard.

The cool east wind rustled leaves, tumbled Dyfed's white hair. I laid a hand on his still breast and a wave of sorrow surged in me, sorrow for my friend gone, for those who did not yet know that he was dead. One was Cyneleah, plump and pretty hall-servant, waiting in Rilling for her Ghost Foot to come home.

Close behind the sorrow came the memory of the night Dyfed

and I had sat listening to the Storm-god prowling the sky and talked of choices.

"And some things haven't changed," I said. "There is still Vorgund. There is still Erich."

She had some courage herself, my Lydi. "I have not been in Vorgund's camp since yesterday, Garroc. I cannot tell you how it is with him, or what he plans. And even if I could, I—"

"If you could, I wouldn't ask you to. I've learned some things, my Lydi, though it took me a good deal of time, ay? But I owe my *cyning* a true report. Only tell me this, if you will: Do you know for certain that the witches will bring Vorgund out to the world again in the morning?"

She thought for a moment, then got up, walked toward the hollow. She didn't go very close to it, and she walked quietly. But some sound must have disturbed Hinthan's sleep. He woke, slipped his hand into my own when he saw Lydi walking toward the darkness. His fingers were cold with fear.

I spoke a soothing word, told him that all was well, but he didn't lie down again until Lydi came back to us. She sat close to me, stroked the boy's hair when he laid his head on her knee.

"They've worked hard, those three witches. Black spells and foul magic. I have no love for them, Garroc. They made a bargain with the folk of the Underworld, a bargain that will let them rest undisturbed tonight. When day comes, Vorgund will find himself back in the world again."

She shuddered, her face paler than before. Almost I asked what bargain the witches had made for their lord, but in the end I didn't want to know. When *helle-cynn* make contracts with Hel herself, it's best not to ask too closely after the details.

The night around us grew still, the wind dropped, the silver songs of crickets seemed far away. Hard it was to think about leaving Lydi then, hard to go back to the places of war.

"Lydi, what of Dyfed? It hurts me to leave him here."

She touched the side of his cold face. Unafraid of the dead, she brushed his white hair away from his forehead. "I will look after him, man dear. He won't lie here." She glanced at Hinthan. He stirred a little, then stilled. Lydi framed her question carefully. "Do you mean to bring the child with you?"

'That boy of yours,' Dyfed had said, and said truly. This boy of mine . . . A bond had been forged between us that night, and what magic there was in it was not a witch's enchantment. It had to do with truth, and it had to do with love.

Yet that is magic of a kind.

But this still remained: What had I to do with children? What more did I have besides a fledgling love for this little one who'd exchanged fair gifts of hope and courage with me? No place but a *cyning's* war camp in summer, his *heall* in winter, did I have to call home. It seemed to me then that a child needed more than that.

As though she knew my thought—and maybe she did, who knows me well—Lydi placed her hand on my breast, took the measure of my heart. "He can come with me for now, Garroc. This day past I have been staying in the woods with . . . a friend. Your Hinthan will be welcome."

It didn't escape me that she had almost named her friend, but had suddenly chosen not to. And as I wondered who that friend could be, a sharp pang of jealousy cut my heart. A year it had been since last I'd seen her, and then we'd parted in sorrow. Would it be so strange, then, if my Lydi had found some fine young Dwarf of the *Wealas* kin to love her, one who didn't grudge her the choices she made, the magic arts she loved?

Ah, not so strange . . . and maybe that was why she hesitated to name her friend to me. 'Man dear,' she still called me, but maybe that was habit and nothing more.

My voice was thick when I answered her, but I tried to answer her fair, tried hard to remember what I'd learned about choices and the right to make them.

"I would be grateful, Lydi, if you would keep him safe for me. But for a time only. When the fighting is done, I'll come for him."

I said it as though I knew that I would come alive from the warfield, said it certain that I would not be killed in the fighting. And yet I didn't know that, Sif. How can a man know a thing like that?

What I did know is this: Hinthan and I had not exchanged our gifts for nothing, not planted our seeds of courage and hope simply to let winter wither them. Hinthan and I, we were done with winter. We'd made that choice together this night. That I knew in the deepest part of me; and heart's-knowledge, soul's-wisdom, is not to be questioned.

I stroked the boy's tumbled dark hair, leaned over him to whisper a farewell that he would not hear, promised him that I would come back to him. With no other word, too thick in the throat to speak, I kissed the witch, took up my axe and left.

VI

VORGUND Witch-Gatherer had struck a deal with Hel, made a bargain with Loki's dark daughter. Maybe he gave the ruler of the Underworld a different name, called her by the *Cristen* word 'Devil,' or by the name of the old *Wealas* god, grey-skinned Arawn, the terrible King of Annwn. The name did not matter. He'd bargained with Death, went to sleep in the Country of the Shades, counted a night of safety worth any price.

How hard do you think grey Arawn laughed on that morning, Sif? How wildly did the Devil howl when the dawn fogs rose from the dark hollow, shimmering like blood-mist in the rosy light? Do you think that Loki's daughter considered it a good joke when Erich War Hawk followed me back to the wildwood, stealthy and silent, surrounded the hollow with his army, waited on her doorstep for Vorgund to wake?

Ay, she bargains hard, does Hel, does the sister of Wolf-Fenris.

Like it is Vorgund did not bid his weary witches to pay for his safe night's sleep with the life of their lord. Still, that's the payment he made, and I saw that he knew it, saw it in his dark eyes when he stood alone, reft of his witches who were too weak now to help him, separated from his warriors, who were too hard pressed to defend themselves from Saxon iron to defend him. He fought hard, with great courage and no little skill. But he'd bargained with Hel in the night, and in the day she let Erich Halfdan's son collect the due.

He liked to oblige the gods when he could, did Halfdan's son. Vorgund Witch-Gatherer died on Erich's sword, and when his heart's blood spilled out on the ground his tattered army did not stay to mourn him, but fled into the forest. By noon they were all dead, witches and soldiers. Erich did not let even one of them escape.

And when the War Hawk left the forest, called his army back to the Rill and the wide sunny meadows, he rode with Vorgund's head raised high on his sword.

VII

I went into the wildwood beyond the meadow, west of the Rill.
Erich didn't want much of me; he had other things to do than
gather the dead-call. Wild he was that day, like a sharp-taloned
eagle sailing the blue fields of the sky. Bright shining war hawk,
he'd driven the *Wealas* from his Marches; at last he'd taken vengeance for the Hunter's death.

Some talk there'd been of riding back to Rilling, of taking time
to bring the injured to the care of the women there, for we'd not
fought this last battle far from home. But that talk died fast. We
were not long back in the meadow camp before a horseman came,
riding as though storm-driven. It only needed to be seen that he
rode down from the north to know that he was a messenger from
Penda King. He shouted for Erich, was off his lathered horse and
running for the *cyning* before anyone could ask his news.

Still, we didn't wonder long. His news went swiftly abroad, and
it was this:

It seemed that the White Christ could not make up his mind
which of his supporters he liked best. In winter he'd been Cadwalla's friend; through spring and early summer the young god had
stood by the Welshman's side. Now, in late summer, the god had
chosen for Eadwine. Penda and Cadwalla had been driven back
into the northern part of the Marches, and Wotan's Blade had sent
this rider south, called for the War Hawk.

I knew I'd not be staying long in this place, and so when the
day had grown old, the shadows long, I left the meadow camp,
went into the forest to find the healer-witch. I hadn't forgotten
that Lydi was not alone, that she had a friend with her; still I could
not leave her without a word of farewell. Whoever her friend was,
surely he'd not grudge me that.

And there was the matter of Hinthan to settle.

I didn't go alone. Werrehund came with me. Aescwine had told
me that the dog had been strange and quiet all the time Dyfed and
I had been away in the forest, said the red dog had sat alone by
the water's edge, watching and waiting. Then, in the darkest part
of night, Werrehund quietly left his watch-post by the Rill and
went to sleep near our campfire, his head on the old scrip that held
the tools of Dyfed's healer-craft.

"He knew," Aescwine said. "He knew that Ghost Foot was dead before ever you came back with the ill word."

And when we'd gone to fight the red dog didn't come with us, stayed behind in the meadow as though he'd decided that he was done with the things of war. When we came back, he didn't greet us, didn't move all during the day, not even to eat or to drink. And so I was surprised that he went with me into the wildwood. But I was not unhappy, for I'd heard tales of dogs who'd followed their masters, heartbroken, to death. Because I'd feared that red Werrehund would be like these, I thought it was a good sign that he wanted to come with me.

The red dog found the barrow, found it hidden in the shade of an overgrown apple garth. Late sunlight slanted golden across the stones, made the shadows between seem soft. All around stood apple trees, heavy with fruit. These had been planted by the Roman men in the time before the longship-riders, in a time before even the Bear King. The Roman farms were long abandoned; still the trees stood, and the scent of ripening fruit sweetened the air, memory and promise both.

There is this about a Dwarf-built thing: It looks as though it is part of the earth, a feature of the mother that has stood since before ever *dvergr* and *mann-cynn* began to measure time. This is not because a Dwarf compels a stone to stand where he wants it to stand, but because the stone is content to be in that place. So it was with Dyfed's barrow.

Ay, Sif, I knew it was his; I knew that my friend slept in this earth-hall. I knew it because his red dog went at once to lie in the shade of the stones, rested his head on the footstone as he'd rested against Dyfed's scrip all the night before, all the day gone. I touched the stones, and when they spoke I didn't see the barrow clearly, but through a dazzle of tears. These stones, these old, old kin, had heard someone mourning and offered me the echo of that sorrow.

I sat beside the red dog, put my back to the barrow, gently smoothed Werrehund's rough fur. Soft the breeze that day, smelling of sunlight and sweet apples and the deeper, untamed scents of the wildwood. It touched me like a comforting hand, like Dyfed's own hand when he offered assurance to the sick or injured, companionship to the heart-stricken.

The stones were warm against my back; their voices echoed deep in my bones.

It will be a great grief to us when there are no more Dwarfs,

said the barrow-stones. It will be a mourning-day when we finally
understand that ours are the only voices we hear in the world.

I knew those words, Sif; I had heard them before. But when
I'd first heard them, the mother-earth had not spoken them; they'd
come from deep in the heart of a friend who was *mann-cynn.*

Werrehund stirred beside me, lifted his head, scented the quickening breeze. I stroked his shoulders, soothed him, and the breeze
fell still, made way for another voice, thin as a whisper. This was
not the voice of the mother-earth. This voice didn't echo in my
bones. I had known it well for many years, and the echo of it was
in my heart.

*Garroc, no Man alive now will see that mourning-day. But that
doesn't mean we don't know that some grandchild of ours will be
poorer when it comes. I pity those far children. With none to help
them learn the right of it, after a time they'll not remember.*

Like me and the priest's ass, ay?

And this was the voice of a ghost, Sif, faint and far and real.

Always before I had cowered before the songs of the dead as
though they were the voices of madness. I didn't now, and because
I held firm, because I'd learned a little about truth and how to
face it, I listened to the way my heart beat to hear my friend's
voice, found a gift in the way it stirred and warmed.

And so it was that I heard another voice, the voice of Grimwulf
Aesc's son.

He spoke no reprimand to his Garroc Silent Skald, gave no ac-
cusing word to his son who had abandoned the light and lived in
shadow for so long. *Baresark* when he died, he didn't speak with
the voice of madness now. Nor did he speak gently. He was all
his life a soldier; he was not a gentle man. He said:

Never forget!

This is true, Sif, the ache of your heart as it opens is much like
the ache of your heart when it breaks. When I swore to my father
that I would not again try to forget all those of our race who had
gone before me, those who walked with me now, I swore to him
on barrow-stones only dimly seen through tears.

And Grimwulf said:

Garroc, my skald, find a way to help Men remember us.

I gave him my oath on the barrow-stones that covered a friend,
swore as I had not had the courage to do before, that I would find
a way to keep the memories alive.

His voice fell silent on a lingering sigh.

Yet all was not still in me. There in the ancient apple garth, in that place of memory, I heard once again the voices of all the ghosts who had once spoken to me.

In the years past I'd had no skill at telling one ghostly voice from another; in the winter past, fear and the great din of them had driven me to ale-houses. Yet now in summer, when the ghosts returned to me after their long silence, I knew each voice well.

I knew red Ecgwulf's voice from Godwig's, Haestan's from Ceowulf's, Wulf's from Waerstan's—ay, Halfdan's from Dunnere's—one from another among all those who had died, whose names I'd given to Halfdan, whose names I'd given to Erich, his son.

Thin those voices; yet they didn't wail coldly as they once had. They didn't moan, or rush upon me like winter gales. Now they sounded like the warm wave of noise I'd hear when I walked a watch on the wall at Rilling, when below and behind me the *heall* was filled with light and laughter, the boasts and challenges of Dwarfs and Men. Then, alone with the night, standing beneath a glittering sweep of stars and watching the moon lay ribbons of light on the Rill's dark water, I would hear snatches of songs from the hall, threads of a wild and wonderful tale of someone's luck at war, another's love-gained glory.

So it was at the end of that summer day as I sat with Dyfed's red dog in the shade of a barrow. The ghosts whispered softly in my heart, a hundred tales and more, told in the voices of the Dwarfs and Men who had lived them. And for the first time in many years I yearned for the *skald leygr*, hungered for the storyteller's light I'd turned away from on the day I made the barrow for Grimwulf Aesc's son, on the cold day in spring when my father died.

That was how the dead helped me to settle a matter of the soul, but there still remained some matters of the heart to be settled. The living helped me to do that.

I had left Erich's war-camp looking for the witch, had stopped in the ancient apple garth to find my soul. It is a joyful thing to find light, and a wearying thing as well. I sat long beside Dyfed's barrow, sat long with the red dog, listened to ghosts. I don't remember when it was I gave over listening for sleeping, but I do remember that the long dimming of the day lay upon the earth when I woke. I had not slept alone; friends had come to watch beside me.

One was Lydi, and she sat very close to me. I felt her hand in mine when I woke.

Another was Hinthan. He was not so close, kept himself a little distance away from the barrow. Ah, but his face lighted when he saw me wake.

There was a third, the friend who had stayed in the wildwood with Lydi when she could not go with Vorgund into Hel's Hall. He stood in the deeper shadows, his arms around the red dog as Werrehund stretched high on hind legs to lick his face. When he saw me watching, he spoke a quieting word and the dog dropped again to four feet, listened and obeyed as most beasts did when they heard his soothing voice.

Aelfgar stepped out of the wildwood's shadows, walked into the old light of the dimming. When last I'd seen him he had been thin, wasted by grief, hurt and battle-sick. Then his golden beard had been burned half away by witch-fire; then he'd looked lost and lorn as he'd set out upon the exile's lonely road.

Not so now. Now he was again bright and strong. He was again Aelfgar.

He greeted me with no words, but greeted me fair nonetheless. It seemed to me that all my bones must crack from the strength of him when he embraced me, and it seemed to me that I'd never felt a better thing in all my days.

Aelfgar and Hinthan had become friends. Boy and child-minded man, they'd forged their friendship swiftly, as children do. That night they went to a stream that ran swift in the wildwood, caught fat fishes for our supper. We cooked their catch in a little glade, not far from Dyfed's barrow, ate as well as any king does who has good food at his board and dear friends to share it with him. And later, in the light of the fire, while Hinthan repaired the fishing nets with sure steady hands, I sat with my Lydi near and heard the tale of Aelfgar's winter.

He told me that he'd wandered long in the Welsh lands. Once or twice he'd run afoul of hunters, had to fight, and then he must make his way far south to avoid villages and farms. When he was well-lost, hungry and friendless, sure that he'd die alone in foreign lands, he'd decided that the only thing to do was to present his case to every dove he saw.

"Because I figured that soon or late, one of them might be Lydi, ay?" Aelfgar grinned broadly. "And I was right—but I was very hoarse by the time I finally found the right one."

At that Lydi smiled, took up her strand of the tale.

"He stayed with me all through the winter, Garroc. And when

I left the garden in the spring to follow Vorgund to the places of war, Aelfgar came with me."

"Ay, I did," Aelfgar said quietly. "And we stayed in Vorgund's camp. And he wasn't too happy to have me, but Lydi said that she needed me by her. It was strange, Garroc. I didn't fight against Erich, never picked up a weapon all summer. Still . . . still it felt wrong. And it made me sad to know that I can never go back." He looked up, blue eyes quick with sudden hope. "Is that still so?"

Hard to tell him that it was still so. Hard to tell him that it would be best if he didn't stay in the Marches long, best if Erich never learned that he'd been here.

He thought about that for a time, and while he did he ran his hands slowly along the red dog's sides, found Werrehund's old bear-gotten scars. At last he said:

"It's all right, Garroc. I think I'm done with war. I think I'm finished being a soldier and a scout. I don't know what else I can be. Gadd only taught me how to hunt and fight. I know that I can't be a healer. I can't—I don't—" He took a long breath, let it out slowly. "In my mind I won't ever be old enough for that, ay? But I know I can tend gardens. I know the difference between herbs and weeds." He smiled shyly. "Or I will when Branwen is done teaching me."

Ay, Branwen, the honey-haired girl. I glanced at Lydi and she lowered her eyes, smiled in such a way as to let me know that Branwen would be a while at her teaching, and would enjoy it though it last a lifetime. And so I knew that my friend Aelfgar had found a good home in the land of exile.

Quiet the night; no wind stirred, and it seemed that the silver songs of crickets, the barking of foxes, the rustling of night creatures, didn't come into this little glade. In the silence I looked at Hinthan, still bent over the fishing nets, and thought that there was yet another matter to be decided, another home to be found.

Hinthan had spoken no word all through the night. His habit of silence was still on him. Yet he was never far from me, and at times when I would look up, I'd see him watching me, waiting patiently for a time when we two could talk. In such a way did he watch me now, and I was not alone seeing it.

Lydi rose, kissed me softly, and said to Aelfgar that she would like to walk in the woods, said that she would be pleased if he and the red dog would keep her company.

When they were gone, Hinthan left his nets, came into the fire's light. Ordulf's bruises still showed as shadows on his pale face, still stained his thin arms. I touched his face gently, asked him if he knew that the witch could make those bruises well.

He nodded. "Aelfgar told me. But—they're mine."

"And you want to hold to them?"

Hard the light in his eyes, a harder light than I'd ever seen in a child's eyes. He'd surrendered a lot of his pride since the day that he'd limped into Erich's camp; a lot he'd let Ordulf take from him. He didn't want to forget that yet.

All things are not made well in the space of a night. All wounds are not healed at once.

Times there are when words are treasures; times there are when words are only poor things. I knew the difference between those times, and so I said nothing, only held out my hand to him, hoped that he still remembered what it was like to reach for it.

He'd not forgotten, that boy of mine. He took my hand, held tight to it.

"Hinthan, tell me."

Long the silence between us, long as ages, long as waiting for hopes to grow. When he spoke at last, he spoke boldly.

"I want to go with you, Garroc."

Ah, Hinthan. *Mann-cynn* and no kin of mine. He was a farmer's son, used to watching the seasons come and go in growth and harvest, used to drifting into sleep to the cow's gentle lowing in the byre.

Yet we shared some things, and he'd walked away from darkness in the same moment I did. We'd reached for light and found it each holding tight to the other's hand.

But I didn't know what right I had to take this child with me, didn't think I had any right at all to bring him into the north, into the heart of Penda King's war. Children need better places to sleep than cold camps where no fires can be lighted for fear that an enemy will see and sweep down in the night to kill. Children need better food than the lean fare of war, better folk to cling to than soldiers who listen always for the Valkyries, the sound of the Night-Maidens riding.

I tried to tell him some of this, tried to tell him that he must go with Lydi and Aelfgar, must wait in Seintwar until fall when I would come back.

He drew himself up straight and tall, did Hinthan. My Sif, that little boy who was to be your father firmed his jaw, lifted his head proudly. "Aelfgar said you taught him scout-craft."

"He said that, did he? Ay, well, I did, but—"

"And he said that he was only a little bigger than me when his brother taught him hunting. My father taught me to hunt." His grey eyes flashed, a triumphant look I would come to know well. "And you let me lead you last night, Garroc. You trusted me."

"Ah, youngling, it's not a matter of trust. It's a matter of—"

"I am a day older now than I was yesterday." He smiled a little, a crooked lifting of the corner of his mouth. "So it can't be that I'm too young."

He was too young, Sif, only a child, and he was not then as old as your youngest son is tonight. Too young for soldier's work, too young for scout-craft. It was in my mind to tell him that he must go with Lydi and Aelfgar, wait for me in Seintwar until fall. The words were on my lips, ready for speaking, when he reached for my hand again, grasped it firmly.

Cold his hand! As cold as it had been the night before, and it trembled. All the proud defiance was gone from his grey eyes. I thought I saw ghosts there again when he said:

"Garroc. Please don't leave me again."

"Youngling," I whispered, "I'm going back to war."

He knew it. It didn't matter. Last night he had learned how to choose, and he wasn't going to let anyone take choice from him now. I knew, with sure understanding, that if I left him now he would find a way to follow. We had already begun to make places in our hearts for each other.

This I had learned, if no more: The Norns weave choices into their patterns, leave them for Dwarfs and Men to find and ponder. What would have become of Hinthan if I had left him with Lydi and Aelfgar?

I didn't believe that he'd have stayed with them, knew that he'd try to follow me. But I didn't know that he would find me again, and so I made my own choice that night. I chose to take him with me. This choice I made partly for his sake, mostly for my own.

My fledgling love for the boy who had taught me how to reach for light and hope, who had found his courage to live in the very moment I'd found my own, was growing fast.

VIII

MOONLIGHT gave silver to the stones of Dyfed's barrow, made the shadows between seem sharp-edged. Lydi ran her fingers along them as though greeting old friends.

"Cyfaill," she whispered, and I heard great sorrow and loss in her voice.

I put my arms around her and she turned away from the barrow, buried her face in my shoulder, held me close. The night breeze stirred, rich with the smell of ripening apples, of dew on the grasses, and sharp-scented stone.

The night was old; soon day would come. I could not stay longer, but we two had this moment alone, granted us by Aelfgar, who had lingered behind in the glade with Hinthan.

The witch sighed, a trembling breath. "Cyfaill and Dyfed and Ghost Foot. I didn't know his true name."

"He didn't know either, my Lydi. Me, I think Cyfaill was his true name. He was a good friend. None will forget him."

Lydi looked up at me then, her blue eyes still bright with tears. "Who will remember him but you and me?"

I took her hand, placed it on my heart. Over her shoulder I saw the light of the young Witch moon shining. Bright light, silvery sheen, it looked much like the light a skald sees in dreams.

"My Lydi, all who hear his song will remember him."

Hope quickened in her then; I felt it stirring. Breathlessly, as though she were afraid to put words to that hope, she said, "Man dear, have you made your choice at last?"

"Yes." I held her tighter, felt her heart beating in rhythm with mine. "I want what I can have. I want you, with no more truces between us, only truth and whatever that truth gives us to face." Harder to say the next thing, but not so hard as it had once been. "And if my sons are never-born, my Lydi, still my songs will live. I want these things."

"And you will have them," she said, and said it as though hers was the power to fill those wants.

Faint from the forest came Aelfgar's voice. He would come no closer to the barrow, for he was an outlaw in the land where he'd once lived; it was not wise for him to go nearer to Erich's camp. Hinthan must come alone now, and I didn't think he'd be long about it. I lifted Lydi's hands to my lips, then held her close.

"I'll be back in the fall, my Lydi."

Ah, choices! She didn't like this one I'd made, didn't like it that I was going north to fight in the King's great war. But she accepted it, for she knew that some things could change, some could not. I was Erich's man, as I'd been his father's. So it was with me.

Lydi held tight to me and said that she would look for me in the fall, would welcome me when I came back to Gardd Seren.

"And Hinthan," she said, "for I think he'll be long with you.

And I think he will always be a friend of mine. He's taught you
something I could never help you learn, man dear."

Lydi placed her hand again on my heart. How warm that hand,
how warm my heart!

"He's taught you that this is no place to keep shadows. And
now that the shadows are gone, there is room for him. And room
for me."

I didn't try to tell her that there had always been room for her,
as once I might have. I was not so young as I'd once been. I'd
never made room for her before. Too crowded with fear and shadows my heart had been. Now I was only grateful that this was no
longer so, thankful that she knew it.

Quietly, Hinthan broke the cover of the forest, waited at the
edge of the clearing. He didn't come forward until I held out my
hand to him. Ay, alone he was, with not even the red dog to walk
beside him.

"The dog didn't want to come," he said. "Aelfgar tried to make
him go with me, but he wouldn't. He's Aelfgar's dog now, isn't
he?"

"Ay, he is, and that's well. They're old friends. We'll see Werrehund again, Hinthan, in the fall when we come back."

Hinthan nodded slowly, then reached his hand to Lydi, spoke
a fair thanks and farewell, asked shyly if we would see her again
in fall as well.

The witch smiled, stroked his dark hair. "You will always be
welcome in the star-garden, child."

Hinthan's grey eyes grew wide; he drew a long breath as the
idea of a garden of stars stirred wonder in him. But there was no
time for questions or the answers to them.

"You must ask Garroc about it," Lydi said. "He's been there—
many times." She looked at the sky, saw the darkness fading as
dawn approached. "But now you two must leave, yes?"

Ah, hard it was to leave my witch then, hard—as it always is.
One word of love my Lydi whispered, and I gave it softly back
to her.

Then Hinthan slipped his hand in mine and walked into the
wildwood with me, kept close beside me when the covering of the
trees seemed to make the night suddenly darker. When we came
to the edge of the forest he stopped, looked up at the sky where
the last stars of night had grown pale, out to the lights of Erich's
war-camp gleaming in the wide meadow.

"Is that what a star-garden looks like, Garroc?"

"Ah, youngling," I said, "Gardd Seren looks nothing like that."

"Will you tell me what it looks like?"

I smiled, took his hand again, and led him out to the meadow, to the fires of friends. As we walked I spoke softly, told him about the star-garden, the witch-woven wonder in the land of the *Wealas*, made by Dwarfs of the Welsh kin, Dwarfs who might well have been some distant kin of mine. And I told him the tale of a white-haired boy who had lived there for a time, learned healer-work before he came out into his father's homeland to learn the skills of war.

I didn't stop to think or to search for the words I needed. In the borderland between night and day, as soft rosy dawn came to fill the sky, another light touched me.

Shining and silver, the *skald leygr* showed me the words that would let Hinthan's heart see what his eyes had never seen, a witch's magic garden; words that would help him know a man he'd only known briefly in life, one-eyed Dyfed, the healer, the riddle-crafter who was sometimes called Ghost Foot, who was always Cyfaill.

SIF

Ellisif sat still, listened to her heart beat; listened to the hearth-fire's soft breathing, the wind's sigh quickening outside the cottage. She was in a borderland, a place where the tale was not, where the shadows rippling along the hearth-stones seemed like something dreamed. As someone who dreams, she saw the cottage around her, the babe in her arms. She thought that some time ago her daughter must have waked, cried for her milk. She must have tended to that and rocked the infant gently back to sleep. But she had no memory of having done these things.

Garroc sat with his back to the hearth wall. The fire's light gleamed in his golden beard, gilded the war-scars on his hands. His blue eyes were filled with his secret smile as he touched her cheek, stroked it softly.

"My Sif," he said, his voice low. "Come back now, ay?"

Ellisif shivered, cold in this place where the tale was not, aching and empty and so very sad, for Garroc's touch woke her fully to the understanding that now the tale had become the dream.

The gods were gone; the golden kings, the fiery enchantments, the bright courage of lords and simple soldiers, shone only in memory now. The boy who would be her father was gone, and the world was again centered here in the little cottage, a world whose bounds were not much wider than the Rill running spring-fat beyond the apple garth in the east, the village on the western bank.

"We've gone far this night, Sif, ay? A long way back for this small part of the debt." Garroc leaned his head against the hearth-stones, drew a slow breath, let it out in a deep sigh. He had the look of one who'd done a long day's work and was satisfied with it.

"Eldfather," she said softly, "I never knew this thing about my father. I never knew how it was with him when he was a boy."

And suddenly she understood that there was so much about Hinthan that she'd never known. Like Garroc, he'd been a soldier the most of his life. Like Garroc, he'd followed the soldier's pattern of wintering at home and fighting far away in the warm months. It was not a thing Ellisif had ever thought to question. It was simply the way things were, and she'd known all her life that her lot was no different than that of many another soldier's child.

And yet now . . . now she'd had a glimpse of the part of Hinthan's life that had always been separate from her own and she hungered for more. Now it seemed that her memories of her father were pitifully few.

And in the years since Hinthan's death even these had become tarnished by her fear of the nightwind and the voice she heard woven into the wind's sigh.

"Eldfather, why did he never share this part of him with me?"

"He wasn't much for weaving tales, that boy of mine. He did other things well, but this he always left for me. And me . . . well, it took some time to know that I couldn't give you this beginning of Hinthan's tale without first giving you my own." Garroc smiled, and Ellisif knew that he smiled as one who has lately learned to forgive his own fears. "Or maybe it's right to say that it took me some time to find the courage to give you my own, so that I could give you his. I feared the ghosts for a long time, my Sif. The fear is gone, but it isn't so easy to go back to the time when it was strong."

Now the babe stirred, roused by the sound of her mother's voice. Garroc sat away from the hearth wall, took the infant, held her easily against his shoulder. He let the sleepy child nuzzle his neck, tangle her tiny fingers in his hair and beard.

Ellisif remembered that he'd held her sons this way. And seeing her daughter in his arms, held close against his heart, it was as though she could remember what it had been like to be so small and kept so safe, to know that in such a strong place none could touch her who was not minded to be gentle. Ah, Garroc used to hold her like that.

So, too, had her father held her, that long time ago when she was so small.

They sat that way, silent for a while, he with his arms filled with the infant, she with her heart empty of all but the echoes of his tale. Again the sadness of ending settled on her, and she sighed.

"Sif, are you thinking that the tale is done?"

She nodded, and she felt the warm trace of tears on her cheeks, the sudden surprise of knowing only now that she wept.

"Ah, no, Sif. It's not done. Child, it's like a river, ay? It moves, sometimes swiftly, sometimes not. Sometimes rising, sometimes low. And it has eddies that turn us full around, bring us back to a place we'd long thought we would not see again."

Garroc bent over the babe in his arms, kissed the top of her head, the fine dark hair, and gave her back to her mother. Outside the wind spoke, whispered in the roof thatching, murmured round the eaves of the cottage.

Ellisif closed her eyes tightly. She knew the wind's voice. How could she not know her father's voice? And yet she still feared it.

"My Sif," Garroc said softly, "it's not everyone who can hear the ghosts. Only the lucky ones."

Spirit-kin! Was there ever a time when he didn't know what she thought, what her heart felt?

"Your father is not lost to you, Sif. Not as long as you have the heart-strength to listen to the memory."

Garroc rose from his place by the fire, slowly and a little stiffly, for his muscles were not so supple as they'd once been. He crossed the cottage, opened the door to see the time, let in the night and the low-voiced east wind. Like a man who hears the voice of an old friend, he cocked his head as though considering something his friend is saying.

In that moment Ellisif made a choice.

She took the child quietly to her own bed. When she came back into the hearth-room, she paused, gathered her courage tight to her heart. After a moment, she held out her hand as she used to do when, as a child, she wanted her eldfather's company for a walk along the river, a far ramble to a place where she'd not been before.

The moon had long gone behind the tall, distant Cambrians; only the late stars remained to light the last of night's darkness. Garroc smiled and Ellisif felt fear fall away, as shadows flee the sun's warm light.

She went with him into the night, into the cool air sweet with the fragrance of her new garden, light with the scent of apple blossoms from the garth at the edge of the Rill. Eagerly she went with Garroc to hear again her father's voice, so long loved and so long missed.

Joyfully, she went with her eldfather to find all the memories that she'd mistaken for ghosts.